T0129173

CHRONICLES OF RHYDIN

CHRONICLES OF RHYDIN

LEGEND OF THE RED DRAGON

AARON GOODING JR.

CHRONICLES OF RHYDIN
LEGEND OF THE RED DRAGON

Copyright © 2017 Aaron Gooding Jr.

All rights reserved. No part of this book may be used or reproduced by any means, graphic, electronic, or mechanical, including photocopying, recording, taping or by any information storage retrieval system without the written permission of the author except in the case of brief quotations embodied in critical articles and reviews.

iUniverse books may be ordered through booksellers or by contacting:

iUniverse
1663 Liberty Drive
Bloomington, IN 47403
www.iuniverse.com
1-800-Authors (1-800-288-4677)

Because of the dynamic nature of the Internet, any web addresses or links contained in this book may have changed since publication and may no longer be valid. The views expressed in this work are solely those of the author and do not necessarily reflect the views of the publisher, and the publisher hereby disclaims any responsibility for them.

This is a work of fiction. All of the characters, names, incidents, organizations, and dialogue in this novel are either the products of the author's imagination or are used fictitiously.

Any people depicted in stock imagery provided by Thinkstock are models, and such images are being used for illustrative purposes only. Certain stock imagery © Thinkstock.

ISBN: 978-1-5320-2935-6 (sc)
ISBN: 978-1-5320-2936-3 (hc)
ISBN: 978-1-5320-2934-9 (e)

Library of Congress Control Number: 2017912997

Print information available on the last page.

iUniverse rev. date: 08/22/2017

BEGINNINGS

It was a calm night. The moon was full and the stars were bright. There was a cool crisp wisp of wind blowing about. A tall, dark figure emerged from the forest of redwood trees. The figure wore a dark long coat and a hood over his head to hide his face. The figure made his way toward an inn that was established in the middle of a small clearing. The figure was curious as to whom or what inhabited the establishment. As he walked toward the inn, he noticed a sign right outside the wooden doors. The words, 'Welcome to the Red Dragon Inn' were carved into a slab of wood that sat several feet in front of the doors. He walked to the wooden doors and pulled on the door handles which resembled that of a dragon's head forged from iron. The wooden doors creaked as the cloaked figure opened the doors. The heavy smell of ale, wine, and whiskey filled his nostrils. In the inn, humans and dwarves, along with several other hooded figures, lounging and drinking to their heart's content. The inn seemed to be an establishment for any and all to visit. There was a bar where various drinks were being served to his right. Across from the bar was a fireplace and a lounge area where many were talking and resting. The cloaked figure slowly walked towards the fireplace to warm himself after coming in from the cool night. As he walked toward the fireplace, a few of the inhabitants in the inn stopped what they were talking about to look at the cloaked stranger and whispered amongst themselves.

"Who is that?" a man turned to one of his friends.

"A lot of hooded visitors tonight," a dwarf man whispered to another.

The cloaked man stood in front of the fireplace hearing what it was being said about him. After being warmed he slowly made his way towards the bar for a drink. He sat at the end of the bar counter and waited for the barkeeper.

"What can I get you, m' lord?" the barmaid was very young. Perhaps around the age of twenty. She had thick, curly red hair; her eyes were a hypnotizing emerald green. Her skin was ever so lightly tanned which brought out the vibrant color of her eyes. When she spoke to him, her voice was sweet and soothing. For some strange reason, he felt like he knew this young woman, but he could not think of where he would know her from.

"A glass of scotch please, Miss," the cloaked stranger requested in a low, calm voice. The young barmaid poured the drink into a glass and gave it to the stranger. The cloaked stranger took the glass and sipped it.

"Thank you, Miss," was all that he said.

"You're welcome," she responded with a smile. She started to walk back towards another patron sitting at the bar, but stopped.

"You want to ask me something, correct?" he turned his eyes to her as she stopped. She turned towards him.

"A-Aye, sir," her voice cracked with her response, but with a deep breath she collected herself. "Um, you are not from around here, are you? I mean, if ya haven't noticed, many of the patrons here have been talkin' and askin' about you since you set foot in this Inn," she attempted to make eye contact with the stranger, but his eyes were hidden under the hood. The stranger's grin was hidden by the hood. He took another sip of scotch before answering her question.

"No Miss, I am not from around here. I am from Earth. I was born and raised there," he raised his head and eyes from the bar counter to look deeply into her green eyes. He sensed innocence and curiosity in her but had a feeling that there was more beneath the surface. He thought that she would be of great help to him.

"If I am not pryin' into your business m' lord, may I ask what you are doin' here on Rhydin?" she asked.

"I am looking for someone," his tone suggested that he wanted no more questions on the matter.

"Alright then. I'll let you be," she turned to attend to someone else but stopped once more, "May I ask something else m' lord?" she could not help but to ask.

"You may," he took another sip.

"What is your name?" she fiddled with the strings of her apron as she approached him.

"My name is Fid, Miss," he said to her as he pulled back the hood to reveal the features that were hidden. His skin was the color of mahogany. His deep brown hair was in thin locks that hung to be just below his shoulders. The eyes of this man were only slightly darker than the complexion of his skin. There was a calm intensity within them. What was most noticeable were his ears. They came to point and extended beyond his locked hair.

"Y-you're an Elf?" her eyes widened as he revealed his face and race.

"That I am. You seem surprised to see one," he responded to her.

"N-no, it is not t-that at all, m' lord," she attempted to control the stammer in her voice with controlled breathing. She leaned closer toward him and whispered, "there have been Bounty Hunters comin' in here lookin' for Elves".

"Bounty Hunters you say?" his ears perked up to listen intently.

"Yes, m' lord. There is a Dark Warlord, who dwells in the southeast at the foot of the Western Mountains, that hired these Mercenaries to hunt Elves. It was foretold by the Guardian Spirit that if the Dark Tyrant does not stop his plot to rule over these lands with an iron fist, then there would be an Elf who bears the Essence of the Red Dragon who will come and vanquish him," she told him.

"I see, the...Essence of the Red Dragon," he thought about what she told him. "I thank you for the warning, Miss," he nodded his head to her. A moment later his ears twitched. A dagger was thrown at him from across the room but he managed to catch it by the hilt. The point of the blade was within inches of his head. Fid followed the path of the dagger to see who threw it. There were two Bounty Hunters at the bar counter and another two in the lounge area. All four stood with weapons drawn and poised to strike. Fid gulped the rest of his scotch and then calmly placed two silver pieces on the counter for the tender.

"Thank you for the drink and the valuable information," he looked to her before turning his full attention to the Bounty Hunters.

"You're welcome….Fid," she took the silver pieces and crouched behind the counter knowing a fight was going to ensue. The other inhabitants of the Inn sensed a fight as well and took cover behind chairs, pillars, and tables. His attention turned towards the four Hunters facing him. The Bounty Hunters wore dark clothing and dark masks only revealing their dark, sinister eyes. Strapped to their hips and backs were swords, daggers, and iron shackles. Fid's eyes were fixed upon these Hunters as they approached him but then sensed the gathering of potent energy from behind him. The two Hunters attacking from the lounge area were suddenly hit by two orbs of energy. Fid looked behind him and saw there were two other cloaked figures sitting at the bar counter. They were the ones who released those intense orbs of energy. Fid then drew his blade and charged at the two remaining Bounty Hunters. One Hunter slashed with his sword, but Fid quickly maneuvered to one side and slashed the Hunter from navel to chest, killing him. Without stopping his momentum, he leapt towards the bar counter and, with one foot, launched himself at the other Bounty Hunter giving a forceful kick to his head causing the Hunter to spin and land on his neck. Fid sheathed his blade as the two cloaked figures ran up on either side of him grabbing him by his arms and rushed out of the inn.

"What are you two doing?" Fid asked.

"We are taking you to a safer place. There are bound to be more of them," the male looked all around to see if there were in fact more lurking about in the shadows of the woods.

"We all have to watch out for each other," the female spoke in a hushed tone. Fid thought to himself that these two cloaked strangers might be Elves as well.

They hurried towards the edge of the clearing in the forest and saw four horses resting there, most likely belonging to Bounty Hunters from the inn. The three of them mounted the horses and rode deeper into the forest. They rode for miles upon miles until they reached the eastern border of the forest.

The trio rode through the night, putting the eastern border of the woods miles behind them. The horses they took rode through the lush grasslands and over gentle hills of what was called the Eastern Province of this land. Fid periodically looked behind them to see if they were being followed, but saw no one. Ahead of them, Fid could see what appeared to be a palace. With his Elf eyes, he could see three tall spires within the confines of a stone wall. It seemed these two were leading Fid to this palace. Did they call this palace home?

Not two hundred yards away from the palace wall, they heard the hoof beats of horses approaching from the north. There were more of the Bounty Hunters dressed in dark clothing seeking to intercept them before they reached the gate of the palace wall. It seemed that they were comrades of those they encountered and disposed of in the Red Dragon Inn. The Bounty Hunters threw what seemed to be fist sized orbs, but once these orbs hit the ground they exploded with intense flares of flame leaving small craters in the ground and throwing up bits of earth and rock. The three rode through, avoiding the explosions. One hit in front of them throwing them off their horses. They quickly got up to their feet and drew their weapons. The male drew a broad sword, the female drew two short swords and Fid drew his blade. The male gazed at Fid's blade as if he had seen it before, for it was like no other. The blade's hilt and guard were made of a shimmering silver; the blade itself was tempered steel and on the double edged blade itself was the image of a Red Dragon breathing fire towards the tip. The male regained his focus as a Bounty Hunter was charging at him with two hatchets. The male quickly dodged his attack and slashed at the Bounty Hunter's side. The female's movements and attacks were swift and fluid. She used the momentum and weight of her attackers against them, throwing them off balance. The male's movements were strong and dynamic. With one to two moves, the male incapacitated his attackers. Fid took on three to four opponents at a time. His attacks and counter attacks were wild, swift, and intense. The Bounty Hunters were blindsided by his attacks and it seemed like they could not even lay a hand on him. As a Bounty Hunter was about to take a stab at the male with his dagger, an arrow was fired though the Bounty Hunter's throat. On the wall of the palace, there were Elf soldiers firing a barrage of arrows at the Hunters, providing an escape for the three. The three ran towards the gates while the Bounty Hunters were taking arrow fire from the palace walls. With the gates opened, they safely made it inside the palace walls.

Fid and the cloaked strangers were greeted inside of the walls by armed Elf soldiers who wore lightweight armor and were ready to escort them in to the palace. The three began to walk with the soldiers, two soldiers on their right and left sides, one in front and one behind them. Fid looked upon the palace as they walked through the courtyard. The courtyard was lush with small trees, exotic flowers from every corner of Rhydin. A fountain made of marble with a Dragon with ruby jewels for eyes was the center piece. Fid marveled at this courtyard as they approached the main doors. On either side of the main door were twenty foot stone statues of what looked like Elf Kings of the past.

"Cretus and Tidus, both were Great Kings of the Elf Kingdom nearly one thousand years ago. Cretus ruled the Eastern Province and Tidus ruled the Western Province. Both led the Elven Army against the Dark Lord Sekmet, alongside Giltia, the Dragon-Lord. Giltia and the Elf Kings were strong allies during that time," the male said to Fid.

"And what kind of times were they?" Fid asked. He had learned of no such battle on Rhydin before and was intrigued by what he was being told. With the mention of Giltia and Sekmet, Fid's mind felt as though there was a maelstrom swirling about within. Dizziness overtook him so much though he reached for a table to brace himself upon. The images of the Palace hall slowly shifted to that of a great battle. Was this a hallucination?

He saw the bodies of Orcs, Ogres, Winged Demons, Elves, Men, and Dragons. Much carnage littered the battlefield with blood soaked the earth. These images lasted but a few moments and then Fid regained his focus. The female noticed that he was not focused but did not say anything, she only looked at him.

"These lands were plagued by the evil powers of Sekmet. Orcs overran these lands and pillaged every village. Ogres, in violent rages, killed anything and everything in sight. They occasionally killed each other if they were angry, or hungry, enough," the male looked to Fid from over his shoulder. "The Elf Empire was not what it is".

"And how do you know all of this?" Fid asked.

"Because, my friend, I am Aero, the Elf Ruler of the Eastern Province," he turned and removed his hood, revealing that he was indeed an Elf. He had shoulder length dark brown hair; his eyes were as dark as the blackest night. His skin was of a fair complexion. Aero appeared to be of a young age, for Elves. Aero had a calm and collective aura surrounding him.

"And I am Paige, Aero's younger sister. I rule the Woodland Realm of the Elves," Aero removing his hood prompted her to remove hers. Paige was an Elf who had dirty blonde hair and piercing dark eyes, much like Aero. Her youth showed in her face but she was far from innocent. There was also a sense of fire in her spirits.

"And what is your name, my friend?" Aero asked him. Fid's attention turned to Aero.

"My name is Fid," he responded.

"Fid?" a name that Aero has not heard of on Rhydin. "We have a few questions of our own for you," Aero said as they entered the palace gates and walked in to the foyer of the palace. The escort of Elf guards left them to return to their posts.

"Go on," Fid responded after he gazed upon the shimmering, elaborately tiled flooring and the tall marble columns that led to a high ceiling where a large golden chandelier hung.

"First, where are you from?" Paige's tone was stern, near demanding.

"I was born and raised on Earth," Fid seemed unfazed by her aggression. The three started to walk down a long hallway. In this hall, there was a red carpet running down the middle. The walls were built of stone and were decorated with various portraits of family members and ancestors.

"An Elf born and raised on Earth. That is quite interesting," Aero stated.

"I am only half Elf. My father was human and my mother, whom I have never met, was of Elf descent," Fid told Aero.

"Only half Elf?" this bit of information piqued Aero's interest. "That is quite a rarity my friend," with every moment, it showed that Aero was growing more and more intrigued by Fid. "I sense a great concentration of power and ability residing within you. Who trained you?" he knew that with the skills Fid possessed that someone cultivated all that he demonstrated.

"I was trained by Master Chen Shun. I trained under him for five years on Earth," he answered.

"Only five years?" Paige raised an eyebrow at him.

"I learn quickly," Fid responded.

"I am sure," Paige's skepticism was heard in her voice.

"Your speed and movements are none like I have ever seen before. This Master Chen Shun, what methods does he use to teach his pupils?" Aero asked.

"Master Chen Shun has studied many forms of combat on Earth. He has learned to channel and manipulate his own energy from Masters who came before him. He has even spent time here on Rhydin learning to better his skills as a combat artist," Fid responded. "He passes on that same knowledge of being in tune with one's body and inner energy as well as manipulating and outwardly projecting our energy," he added. The three came to the end of the hallway. There was a wooden door with what seemed to be a Coat of Arms above the doorway. They entered the room and Fid found they were in, what seemed to be, the Palace Armory. It was not like any other armory for any common army. There were rare weapons that seemed to be specially forged. There were weapons of every type from swords and daggers to various types of shuriken.

"This is not the Palace Armory," Aero said to Fid. Fid looked into Aero's eyes as if he read his mind. "I know that is what you were thinking. But no my friend this is my personal collection," there was a sense of pride on Aero's face.

"My dear brother has a fascination with the rare and one of a kind," Paige stated.

"I see, and where have you...acquire these weapons?" Fid knew little of blacksmithing, but he knew these weapons were not like the weapons Aero, Paige, and their soldiers wielded.

"Mostly from the enemies that I, or my, sister has defeated in battle" Aero replied.

"Much like a trophy" Fid stated.

"Yes, you may say that. And I want to ask you something else," Aero said.

"Go on," Fid replied.

"How did you come to acquire that sword of yours? I noticed the craftsmanship of the Blade while we were fighting the Bounty Hunters. I know it was not forged in any type of blacksmith's shop or mines on Earth," Aero's eyes dropped to the sword that was sheathed on Fid's waist. Fid then looked at the blade and then to Paige and Aero.

"It was a gift from my father on my fourteenth birthday. He said that my mother had given it to him as a gift. My father was the leader of our village's army and he valiantly fought for our village. He gave it to me and said that it will give me strength while in a battle for my life," his eyes held a great deal of sorrow in them as he recalled the memory of his father.

"And what of your father? What happened to him?" Paige sensed his sorrow.

"Our village in the Mountains was attacked by a horde of vampires. They burned everything and killed many. I obviously was one of the survivors. I saw the carnage with my own two eyes. Houses were burned to the ground; bodies were dismembered, and were drained of their blood. I was fifteen at the time. I have not seen my father since," tears began to well in his eyes. Paige sensed Fid's pain and placed her hand upon his shoulder to comfort him. Fid sat in a chair and a tear ran down his cheek. "I hunted that pack of vampires ever since I turned the age of eighteen. I have not found them yet. But I swore, on my father's name, that I would find them and avenge my village and my father." his determination was seen in his eyes despite the tears rolling down his cheeks.

"How will you find this pack?" Aero asked.

"I searched every Vampire realm on Earth and my search has led me here to Rhydin. Their leader, whose name is Brakus, has an unmistakable mark on his cheek. He received that mark during the attack of my village. It is a scar that runs from his cheek through his left eye. I slashed at him as he was attempting to attack a young, red haired girl," replied Fid. "This is the reason why I am here on Rhydin. The information that I received from the Vampires I came across led me here." Aero and Paige felt there was a sense of anger and loathing towards the Vampire horde emitting from him.

"I am truly sorry to hear about your tragic loss my friend," Aero expressed.

"I can have my troops patrol the woods for this Vampire horde, Fid," Paige offered.

"I thank you both, but I feel as though I need to do this on my own," Fid responded.

"I understand that you wish to avenge your father and village, but are you confident that you can accomplish this task on your own?" Aero looked to Fid with a questioning eye. Fid said nothing but looked into Aero's eyes. Aero knew that Fid could not accomplish the task and not come out alive. He may kill over half of the horde but sooner or later, during the battle, Fid will succumb to fatigue or will be caught off guard and soon share the same fate as his kin.

"I want to make an offer to you, my friend," Aero said.

"And what would that be?" Fid asked.

"I am offering to make you a General in my army," Aero stated. Fid's eyes widened at this offer. Paige's head snapped to face Aero and glared at him with a defiant gaze.

"I-I thank you for the honor my friend, but I know nothing about leading an army," Fid was use to being on his own. He knew nothing of having the responsibility of having an Army behind him.

"That is quite alright my friend. I sense that you are a natural leader and when the time comes you will lead a great army into the most profound war this world has ever seen. I also offer this to you," Aero turned to open a case and in it was a blade identical to that of Fid's.

"The blade that was bestowed upon you is the other half of a set. They are known as the Twin Dragon Blades. They were forged specially for the Dragon-Lord, Giltia, many generations ago. I observed your mastery with the one blade and now I offer the other to you," Aero held out the blade for him to take. Fid looked at the blade and then into Aero's eyes. He then hesitantly took the blade and held it in front of him.

"It is identical to that of my own in every way, even the weight is identical. I thank you for this gift Aero. I-I do not know what to say," Fid was at a loss for words. Paige glared at her brother for giving the blade their father had given him to a stranger.

"Say nothing my friend. But do think about my offer. Sleep on it tonight. There are plenty of rooms for you to stay," Aero sensed Paige's malcontent. "Paige will show you to your room" his eyes with from Fid to Paige.

"Follow me," Paige motioned for Fid to follow her. As Fid past her in the doorway she gave a sharp look at Aero. He sensed she would return with a few harsh words for him on the matter. Paige led Fid down the hall towards the staircase. On the walls of the hall were paintings of what seemed to be Elf Kings of the past.

"Paige who are these men?" Fid asked pointing to the paintings.

"You were correct in thinking they are Kings of the past. This hallway is known to the Elf Kingdom as the Hall of Kings," Paige's eyes were unwavering. Fid was startled that she had read what he was thinking.

"How did you know what I was thinking?" Fid raised an inquisitive eyebrow.

"Few of us Elves on Rhydin developed the ability to read the minds of others as well as communicate using the power of our minds. We have developed this skill so that we may speak with one another so that the enemy does not know our plans," she looked over her shoulder to him.

"I see," Fid nodded his head. He looked at one of the paintings and, once more, his vision slowly blurred and images, or memories, were playing before his eyes. This time, the King in the painting was beside another. He was shaking hands with who seemed to be a Knight. This Knight bore the emblem of the Dragon Knights on his breastplate. The emblem was a Red Dragon with the Egyptian symbol of Ra over it. Behind the Dragon Knight was an army of other Dragon Knights and Dragons of all shapes and sizes. Behind the Elf Kings was their army of Elves armed and prepared to march to battle. Fid then regained his focus and his attention turned back to Paige.

"Fid, are you alright?" Paige again noticed his focus was unclear.

"Yes Paige, I am….fine," Fid held his head in his hand attempting to relieve the whirl of images in his mind. He was confused and puzzled as to why his mind would have flashes of images and memories that were not his own. He did not understand why he was having these flashbacks and why it was happening to him now. Paige noticed his feelings but could not pinpoint why he was like this. To her, his mind was clouded and cluttered with racing emotions and thoughts.

"That painting is King Cretus. Aero told you he was the Ruler of the Eastern Province and that he and his brother King Tidus had fought alongside with The Dragon Lord, Giltia," she pointed to the portrait.

"Yes, I remember," his eyes looked back at the portrait.

"Come on. Let me show you to your room. You need your rest," Paige sensed Fid attempting to gain a grasp of something he could not reach.

"Yes…. Yes let us go," Fid was still distracted from the sudden flashbacks that swirled about in his mind. As the two continued to walk down the Hallway of Kings, Fid had the feeling that the souls of the past Kings were watching him through those paintings.

They climbed a staircase and walked down another red carpeted hallway toward the room at the end. Paige opened the wooden doors to the room Fid would be staying. Unlike the halls of the Palace, the bedroom was fully carpeted. This was so the room can retain heat during the winter months. Fid entered the room and headed towards the large, arched window at the opposite end of the room. He found there was a large bed with a thick quilt to his right. Next to the bed was a wooden desk with quill, inkwell, and a tall, thick candle sitting on top. There was also a polished, wooden wardrobe opposite of the bed. He looked out the window to the hills outside of the Palace walls. Paige was standing inside of the doorway looking at Fid attempting to figure him out, but she could not pinpoint what else motivates him. All that was within his heart and mind was vengeance.

"If you are in need of anything, the palace maids are on call," Paige finally spoke after allowing Fid to explore his room.

"Thank you," Fid smiled and looking back at Paige.

"Get your rest, Fid. You will need it," she urged.

"I plan to," once more, he smiled. He then turned his attention back to the hills outside of his window towards the west. Fid began to think about Aero's proposal about being a General in his army. He thought about the possibility that he could use a handful of soldiers to hunt down the vampire horde that attacked his village six years ago.

Paige turned to leave closing the door behind her. She then headed back down towards the armory where she and Fid left Aero. Aero was still standing there, seemingly waiting for her.

"You want to say something to me I am sensing," he sat and crossed his arms in front of his chest.

"Well Brother, you are sensing correctly. Why are you giving our father's sword to a stranger that no one on Rhydin has heard of?" her voice was raised and full of anger and frustration.

"Because I believe he has the ability to wield the power of the Twin Dragon Blades and unlock their true power," he looked in to her eyes.

"That is absurd, Aero! Only the one bearing the Essence of the Red Dragon will able to wield their true power. All the rest have relinquished nearly all of their life force to that blade," Paige still angered by her brother's decision. "You know I am displeased with your decision, Brother. If Fid does not have the power to properly wield those blades, his life force will be lost to those Blades and it will be on your hands," her eyes flashed a bright white as she left the armory and headed to her room. Aero was left sitting in the armory with his hands folded seemingly thinking about his decision in giving the other Dragon Blade to Fid.

"Another spat with your sister?" a young elf woman approached the armory interrupting his thoughts. Her voice was melodious to his ears. He looked to the doorway to find the raven haired Elf smiling brightly. Her smile lightened his heart from the disagreement he and Paige had.

"I suppose you heard it all, Melina," he rose from the chair to gaze in to her azure eyes.

"Do you truly believe this new Elf will be able to wield those Blades?" she returned his deep gaze.

"I do," Aero nodded.

"Very well. I trust your judgment," she gave a light kiss to his lips.

The next morning, Fid was awoken by a palace maid setting down a silver platter of breakfast on the table for him. Fid sat up to look at the maid.

"I-I am sorry m' lord. Did I wake you?" the maid bowed apologetically.

"Yes, but that is alright. I needed to be woken up. I would have slept the whole day. Thank you," Fid rubbed his eyes from the sleep and looked more closely at the woman. "You're the woman from the Red Dragon Inn," it took a few moments, but he noticed who it was.

"That I am," the maid gave a smile.

"By day one life, by night another," a grin grew on his face.

"It would seem so, m' lord," she a light giggle.

"What is your name?" he looked to her as she finished setting the place for him to eat.

"My name is Rosey, m' lord," she turned to face him. "Will there be anything else?"

"No, thank you....Rosey" he gave a shake of his head. She then turned to walk out.

"Thank you for the information. You were right. The three of us were attacked outside of the palace," he called to her before she could leave.

"Yes, I know. That is what I'm good at. Findin' out information and passin' it along," there was a smile across her face.

"I see. Quite interesting. Thank you again, Rosey," he bowed his head in gratitude.

"You are welcome, m' lord," she said as she was leaving the room. He thought to himself, as she left, that she still looked familiar to him but he could not place her anywhere in his life or travels that he may have met her. He shrugged the thought off and rose from the bed to find a bowl with warm water in it. He used the cloth that was laid out on the silver platter to wash his face. He then sat to eat the food that was placed on the table.

After finishing his meal, Fid got dressed and headed downstairs to look for Aero. Throughout the halls, Fid saw there were many Elf guards patrolling, and standing guard. As he wandered about the Palace, he still thought of picking several Elf soldiers to lead them in a hunt for Brakus. Fid eventually found Aero standing on a balcony looking down onto the hills outside of the palace walls. Fid walked to be beside him and looked out to the green hills of that Province.

"It is a pleasure to have your company," Aero continued to gaze outwards with his hands patiently folded behind his back.

"It is a beautiful day, Aero," Fid looked to the cloudless, azure sky. A slight breeze caressed his face that put him at ease.

"That it is my friend," Aero nodded in agreement. There were a few moments of silence between them, then Aero decided to break the silence, "Have you thought about my proposal?".

"That I have," Fid turned his body to fully face Aero. "I would be honored to serve in your army under your leadership… King Aero," he placed his right fist on his chest and bowed his head in respect to him.

"You need not bow, my friend," he gave a shake of his head to the formality. "We are equals in the fight against the evil that seeks to overtake these lands," Aero looked back to the land of his Province as if reminding himself of what he was fighting for. Fid lifted his head to make direct eye contact with him. "I want you to be certain you are doing this for the right reasons, my friend," Fid felt as though Aero was reading his mind once more. It was as if Aero sensed his intention of using the soldiers to hunt down the vampire horde.

"Where is Paige?" Fid thought he would have seen her while he wandered about the Palace.

"She left to return to the Woodland Realm early this morning. She received word there was a vampire horde crossing her lands. The leader has a scar across his face," Aero watched for a reaction from Fid.

"Where did you say there were?" with that news, Fid's eyes flared with a faint ember. The muscles in his body tensed and flexed.

"They were last seen crossing the Woodland Realm, but you are not going alone my friend. I am coming, along with soldiers," despite the change in Fid's demeanor, Aero remained calm with his hands still folded behind his back.

"Very well, but I must warn you to stay out of my way. And to leave Brakus to me," his eyes still burned with rage.

"You must control your rage my friend. Anger and rage lead to careless actions and fatal mistakes. You must calm yourself," Aero spoke in the calmest of voice. Never had he seen such anger and rage within an Elf. Perhaps it was due to Fid being half Elf.

"You are correct. I am sorry, my friend. I am filled with bitterness and rage that I have let them control my actions thus far," Fid closed his eyes and breathed several deep breaths to calm his body and mind. "When can your soldiers be ready to leave?".

"Your soldiers can be ready within moments. All you need to do is pull that rope on that wall," Aero pointed to the rope that dangled from the ceiling. Fid walked to the wall and pulled on the rope. A bellowing horn sounded throughout the halls of the Palace. Within a few moments, Elf soldiers rushed into the room forming five, single file lines. Fid looked into the soldier's eyes and was thoroughly impressed. He sensed focus and intensity in their souls.

"I am impressed, Aero. Who trained them?" Fid walked down each file, continuing to inspect the soldiers.

"I thought you would be impressed. And to answer your question I trained them myself," Aero folded his arms in front of his chest with a slight grin on his face.

"How efficient are they in battle?" Fid turned to see the pride on Aero's face.

"They have not lost a battle while I have been Ruler," Aero continued to grin with pride.

"Allow for me fetch my swords and we shall be off. The more time spent here talking the more time the vampire clan has to distance themselves," Fid began to head towards the staircase but Aero placed his hand on Fid's shoulder to stop him. "Why do you stop me?" Fid whipped his head around to face Aero with a questioning expression.

"You need not go upstairs my friend," Aero gave a shake of his head.

"My swords are in my Chambers," Fid's body once more tensed. He did not want to delay the hunt any longer. Aero then pointed to a soldier standing at attention holding Fid's blades in front of him. Fid walked over to the soldier who seemed to be a Lieutenant according to the number of bars on his shoulder pad. Fid took the sheathed blades and strapped them to his waist. He then looked at the soldier.

"Thank you, Soldier," he nodded in gratitude.

"You are welcome sir," the soldier's eyes were forward and not making eye contact with Fid.

"What is your name and rank, Soldier?" Fid asked sternly.

"Lieutenant Demus, Sir," his voice was stern.

"Have you ever battled with vampires before Lieutenant?" Fid circled the soldier with intense eyes gauging the Demus's strength and will.

"No sir," Demus still was unwavering.

"The best way to kill a vampire is to cleave their heads from their bodies," Fid began to remember the men of his Village defending against the monsters. There were only a few of the vampires that were slain.

"Yes sir. Thank you, Sir," Demus acknowledged Fid's counsel. Satisfied with the Lieutenant, Fid turned his attention to the rest of the troops.

"While battling the Vampire Horde you must show no mercy for you shall receive none. Their weakness is decapitation. Remove their heads and the monsters shall be defeated. And defeat them we shall. We will chase these beasts to the ends of this world. We will not rest until each and every member of this rabble is dead. This is the day the Elf army with conquer this Vampire Horde!" with these words, Fid roused the spirits and courage of the troops. The troops drove the butts of their spears into the floor all in unison, gradually getting faster.

"Troops...move out!!" Fid sounded the battle cry. He, Aero, and the troops rushed out of the Palace doors and gates to mount their horses that were readied and waiting for them. They rode through the day, crossing the land beyond the palace walls and then in to the woods. The Elf soldiers spread themselves out, covering more ground while riding through the tall redwood. With each moment they drew closer to the vampire horde.

The Elf army had been riding for a majority of the day in pursuit of the Vampire Horde. With each stride of their steeds, they drew closer and closer to them. They halted their pursuit for a few moments to rest and feed their horses. The soldiers took out pouches of water and food from their satchels.

"Eat and drink. Keep up your strength. You will need it when we fight the Vampire Horde," Fid announced. Fid took his pouch and took a few swigs of water. When the troops halted their pursuit, Aero had climbed to the higher branches of a redwood tree. Aero looked to see how far ahead the Vampire Horde was.

"Aero, what do your eyes see?!" Fid called up to him.

"The Horde turns south. They are less than a day's pursuit away. We shall overtake them by night fall if we leave now!" Aero yelled down to Fid.

"Troops.....we head south!!" Fid announced. The Elf troops picked up their food, water, and weapons. They mounted their horses with great haste and continued their pursuit.

Dusk began to fall upon the land and the Elf troops drew closer and closer to the Horde. During their pursuit, Aero heard Paige's voice within his mind, *"Aero, my troops will intercept the horde at Eagle-Eye Lake".*

"Very well Paige, we will meet you there," replied Aero. Aero and Fid's troops continued their pursuit of the horde and made their way to Eagle-Eye Lake.

"Fid, Paige's troops are intercepting the Horde at Eagle-Eye Lake" Aero turned his head to Fid.

"How do you know this?" Fid furrowed his eyebrows.

"We spoke to each other using our minds. We are able speak to each other's mind no matter how far away we are in this world. Though we cannot talk to each other if we are on different worlds," Aero told him.

"Paige has told me that you and her have that type of connection. But I was unaware you both can have a long range connection," Fid said.

"Many cannot. It is an anomaly amongst the Elves to have such extensive communication with our minds. Paige and I trained together to hone our various abilities and techniques and as a result developed a connection that is indestructible," Aero said.

"I see. I suppose that explains that you two possess high concentrations of energy and the soldiers do not have the same type of abilities," Fid concluded.

"You are an intelligent one," Aero grinned at Fid's deduction.

It was nearly nightfall when Fid, Aero, and the troops came to a clearing in the forest. They dismounted their horses and then began to climb a hill. When they arrived at the top, they saw Paige's troops had already engaged the horde. Paige's troops were outnumbered and were struggling to keep them at bay. The Elf troops were fighting for their lives. Fid and Aero saw this and both drew their weapons.

"Draw weapons!" Aero announced to the troops. The troops drew their swords without hesitation.

"Archers ready your arrows. Give them cover fire. They are weak at the heart!" Fid raised one of his blades for the archers to see. The archers drew arrows from their quivers and took aim. "Archers... fire!!" Fid gave a downward slash of his blade. The archers released a barrage of arrows down towards the horde. The impeccable accuracy of the Elf Archers severely wounded several of them when the arrows pierced their hearts. Paige looked up to the top of the hill seeing Fid, Aero, and their troops.

"It is about time," she muttered to herself.

"Fid, lead the charge. I will follow with a second wave of troops," Aero turned his head to Fid. He knew that Fid would want an opportunity to face Brakus.

"Yes, Aero," he gave a nod of his head. "Troops, prepare to charge!" Fid announced. Half of the troops had their swords and spears ready. Fid tightly clenched the hilts of both Dragon Blades. The blades began to glow a deep crimson. Fid sensed an immense amount of energy emitting from them. His eyes began to glow like the embers of a fire in reaction to the blades' energy. He ordered Lieutenant Demus to sound the charge. Lieutenant Demus blew into a conical horn, seemingly made from the horn of an ox, to sound the charge. The troops charged down the hill towards the horde. The barrage of arrows continued to rain down from the top of the hill over the troops' shoulders and heads. The horde's attention turned towards the charging troops. The two forces collided with bone shattering blows. Swords clashed, shields were split, and spears splintered. Fid fought his way to where Paige was.

"Paige, are you alright?" although he was concerned, his focus was on cutting down a vampire who attacked with a jagged dagger.

"You are late. It appeared as if the two of you were never going to arrive," her tone was sarcastic in light of dodging a dagger swipe and then slashing the vampire's throat. She then noticed that the Dragon Blades were glowing and emitting intense energy. She found Fid was not overwhelmed by the power. 'How is that possible? How could he not be overwhelmed by the power of those blades?' she thought to herself. Fid was dodging and countering every blow and slash that was thrown at him. It appeared he was more powerful than when they faced the Bounty Hunters.

While the fight was waging down below, Aero was watching from the top of the hill. He spoke to Paige's mind, "*Much energy is building within him, but it is not just the blades emitting the energy*".

"*You sense it too, dear brother,*" she responded sarcastically. "*Why not join us?*"

"*I just might,*" he drew his broad sword and ordered for the remaining troops to charge down the hill. They charged down sweeping through the remaining members of the horde like a whirlwind blowing though a village of straw and twig huts. From the corner of his eye, Fid spotted the leader of the clan. That same scar ran down his left cheek. Fid's eyes glowed red with rage and the energy of the two blades dramatically increased. The leader of the clan fled and Fid gave chase deeper into the forest. He saw the clan leader had leapt to the trees, so he continued to track him while still on the ground. Brakus made great leaps from branch to branch of the redwood trees, but Fid did not lose sight of him. They made their way to another clearing in the forest of redwood. This clearing was smaller than the last clearing where the two forces first clashed. Brakus jumped down into the clearing and turned to face Fid. He drew his jagged edged blade and released a banshee-like shriek at Fid. The shriek was shrill and wretched. It had pierced in to the ears of Fid and knocked him off balance. Fid fell to the ground and rolled down the short hill leading to the small clearing. Brakus saw the opportunity to strike. Fid quickly dodged his attack and got to his feet drawing his Dragon Blades.

"Tell me, Elf. Why do you pursue me so? What have I done to incur your wrath?" Brakus hissed at Fid.

"Your reign of terror has come to an end, Brakus. No more will you prey upon the innocent. And no more will you lust for blood. Never again! This night will be your last," anger was building within Fid and it showed in his eyes as they flared red.

"And who are you to threaten me, Boy?!" Brakus hissed again at him.

"You attacked a village in the Mountains back on Earth. You slaughtered many innocents," Fid stared in the abyss-like eyes of Brakus.

"There were so many villages. My memory is not what it used to be," he laughed.

"I am the young boy who gave you that scar on your face," Fid pointed his blade at him. Brakus then ran his fingers against his cheek. Rage began to build within and his eyes glowed red.

"You! No one has ever left a mark on me. You will pay with your blood for what you did," Brakus hissed at Fid.

"And you will pay with your life for what you did to my village!" Fid shifted his feet in to an aggressive stance and held the Dragon Blades out and ready to attack his enemy. Brakus reached down to his belt for small daggers and threw them at Fid. Fid easily deflected the daggers with his blades. They both charged at each other with weapons in hand. Sparks flew as their blades clashed. Each were attacking and countering each other. Fid's moves were quick but were countered by Brakus' powerful blocks and counter attacks.

As the fight went on, neither showed any signs of fatigue. Fid threw a kick towards Brakus' head but Brakus blocked the kick and slashed Fid's leg. Fid let out a shout of pain. He clutched the wound leaving him open to all of Brakus' attacks. Brakus threw punches and kicks to his ribs and head. Fid was unable to deflect all of the attacks and showed that he was physically fatigued and weary. Fid was bleeding from his mouth and nose. There were cuts beneath his eyes and on his arms from Brakus' sharp claws. Brakus kicked Fid in the ribs sending him backwards into a redwood tree. Fid laid there with blood trickling from his nose and possibly had a few bruised and broken ribs. Brakus walked toward Fid with a malicious grin on his face.

"You thought you could kill me. No one has been able to defeat me or lay a hand on me, until you left this scar on my face. You will pay with your blood, Boy" Brakus raised his blade preparing to give the final strike. Fid closed his eyes and focused his energy.

"Tri-Form" Fid split into three entities. Two were formed from pure energy and one was the true Fid. Brakus slashed at the wrong one.

"So Brakus, can you guess which one is the true me," all three surrounded Brakus. Brakus looked with anger and frustration. "You have gone too long without paying for the chaos and destruction that you have caused across Earth and Rhydin," all three entities said in unison. Brakus slashed at one entity but it was a fake. "This night you pay for all of the sins you have committed against the weak and innocent," Fid said as all three entities charged towards Brakus and attacked him. One entity slashed but missed, the second caught Brakus off guard and gave a forceful kick to his ribs and the third slashing Brakus from navel to chest. Brakus was thrown into a boulder creating an impression in it. The three entities walked toward Brakus and then combined to the true Fid. Fid stopped several feet away from Brakus and glared at him. Once again, his eyes began to flare red.

"I will avenge my village and my father. This is the night for vengeance," Fid raised both of the Dragon Blades to the sky. The wind began to blow and howl violently as it gathered around Fid. Dark clouds quickly moved in covering the night sky. A faint aura of fire surrounded Fid and the Dragon Blades. The true power of the Twin Dragon Blades seemed to be awakening.

Meanwhile, Aero, Paige, and the other troops finished their fight with the rest of the horde when they noticed the drastic change in the night sky.

"Could it be?" Paige planted her feet, trying not to let the wind knock her down.

"Yes. It is him. The era in which evil will be vanquished has begun," Aero looked off into the distance to where the highest concentration of energy was.

Fid's eyes grew even more intense as they glowed a scorching red as the fire of his Essence was burning from deep within his heart. Its raw power was coursing through his body and the steel of his Blades. He was focusing the fiery fury of his Essence to scorch the soul of the enemy that stood before him. With each breath that Fid took, the aura of fire grew and intensified around his body and the Dragon Blades. Glowing embers were flying from the steel of the Dragon Blades and an aura of fire rose from Fid's feet and slowly traveled up his body through his arms and to the tips of the Dragon Blades. Brakus struggled to his feet to make a final, desperate lunge with his blade towards Fid.

"Wrong move you bastard!" Fid's eyes flashed with flame. "Inferno…. Rage!" his voice echoed as he slashed the air between him and Brakus. An immense cyclone of flames had been building within the Dragon Blades themselves and was unleashed upon the charging Brakus. Brakus was caught in the cyclone's fiery fury. His skin was charring as he let out agonizing screams of horror and pain. After a few moments within the cyclone of the raging wildfire, Brakus finally burst into a cloud of ash.

A deep trench and scorched trees were the result of the immense power of the Dragon Blades. The fire faded from Fid's body and the Dragon Blades. He was left breathing heavily. With a wince of pain and a sharp intake of air, Fid clutched his injured ribs. After a few moments, his vision began to blur and then his eyes rolled in to the back of his head. His body was weak. The strength in his muscles faded. His knees buckled from under him. He collapsed onto his side, dropping the Dragon Blades next to him. He laid there for a few moments and heard several others approach. He saw Aero kneeling down to him and then saw Paige next to him before he succumbed to unconsciousness.

"It is going to be alright my friend. You will make it," Aero said to him but Fid's eyes had already gone black.

Two mornings had passed before Fid slowly opened his eyes to find himself in his room in the palace. His ribs were bandaged and his cuts and gashes had been stitched. He turned his head to Rosey sitting by the side of his bed keeping a close eye on him.

"Thank the Heavens you are alright, m' lord. I was gettin' worried you wouldn't wake up," relief was in her eyes.

"It is…good to see you as well….Rosey," he groaned while holding his ribs. "How many were broken?" he looked in to her eyes for a truthful answer.

"I counted about three broken and two more bruised, m' lord," her tone shifted from being relived to that of being solemn. Fid let out a deep sigh and looked up to the ceiling. Rosey rose from the chair and headed towards the door.

"If you need me for anythin' m' lord you can just pull that rope beside your bed," she said to him as he looked out of the window towards the west. She sighed and walked out closing the door behind her with Fid continuing to look out to the green hills outside.

SHADOWS OF THE PAST

THREE MONTHS PASSED SINCE FID avenged his village and father by killing the vampire clan leader, Brakus. Since then, Fid became acquainted with the palace. His ribs had healed sometime ago. His ability to heal his body was much more rapid than that of others. For any normal being it would take two months for their body to completely heal but Fid's ribs healed within a month's time. The cuts that marred his face and arms were completely healed as if he were not touched at all.

Rosey entered his room carrying a silver platter with Fid's meal. She placed it on the table while Fid was at the window looking out towards the hills as if he is in a meditative state. He wore a crimson colored robe with golden trim and a dragon embroidered on the back. She tried to be quiet while setting the table.

"Good morning, Rosey," he said to her without turning to face her.

"Oh, um… g'mornin', m' lord. And how are you this mornin'?" his greeting startled her causing her to fumble with the utensils. "I hope that I didn't disturb you?" she looked up from the platter and utensils to him.

"I am doing well this morning, and no, you did not," he turned to face her. She grinned at him and made her way towards the door.

"Oh, Lord Aero wanted you to go down to the War Room after you have finished your meal," she told him.

"Did he mention what he wanted?" he raised a questioning eyebrow.

"He did not m' lord. Will there be anythin' else?" she folded her hands patiently standing before him.

"No. No thank you Rosey. Everything is fine," he gave a slight shake of his head. She left his room and headed downstairs to continue her duties. Fid sat to eat his meal and wondered why Aero would want him to come down.

After finishing his meal, Fid headed downstairs to meet Aero in the War Room. He walked down the carpeted hallway and approached the door. Above the door was another family crest much like the one above the armory. This time, he noticed there was a crystal attached to the middle of the crest. It looked like the crystal that hung around his neck. It was in the shape of a diamond and held a fiery red hue. It was a ruby in fact. He held the crystal that hung around his neck. It was as if holding the crystal caused his mind to conjure images. The images he saw were of the same crystal but it is around the neck of King Cretus and King Tidus. The scene lasted only a few moments. He wondered if Aero was the direct descendent of Kind Cretus or King Tidus. Why was his crystal identical to that of the crest above the doorway? He blinked his eyes several times to regain his focus. After composing himself, he walked through the doorway to see Aero standing at the bay window in the room looking out to the horizon.

"I am glad you can join me this morning, my friend," Aero turned to face him when he heard Fid walk in to the room.

"Good morning, Aero," he responded. "I was told that you wished to see to me?" he stopped at the center of the room.

"Yes, I do. Please, follow me," he pulled a lever on the wall and a doorway opened on the far wall. They both walked through and Fid found himself in a dojo style room. It appeared to be where Aero and Paige trained. There were staffs, practice swords carved from wood, shuriken, and cork targets mounted on the far wall. There were training dummies hanging from the ceiling.

"I am assuming this is where you train," Fid looked all around.

"You are correct in assuming so," Aero walked towards the wall that held the shuriken. He took a few into his hand and looked at them.

"Why did you want to see me this morning?" Fid turned his attention to Aero. Aero looked from the shuriken to him.

"Defend yourself!" with a flick of his wrist, Aero threw the shuriken at Fid. His eyes widened just before he flipped out of the way.

"What are you doing Aero?! What has gotten into you?!" Fid landed in to a crouching position then shifted in to a defensive stance.

"How strong are you, my friend?" Aero gave a grin as he took a practice sword from the wall. Fid threw off his robe and took a fighting stance. He was unarmed but that did not matter to him. Aero and Fid circled the room facing each other, both in fighting stances ready for what the other may do. They slowly drew closer to each other as they continued to circle the room. Aero swung the wooden sword towards Fid's head, but Fid bent himself backwards to dodge the blow. Fid then rolled forward and Aero flipped over him. Both were on their feet and began to throw punches and kicks at each other. Aero was swinging and thrusting the practice sword to make contact with Fid, but each attack was evaded. Both were attacking and counter-attacking one another. Fid jumped over Aero to the wall with staffs and he took one. Fid swung the staff at Aero's knee, but he flipped over Fid and in midair swung the wooden sword making contact with Fid's back with a dull crack causing him to fall forward. Aero had a grin on his face.

"Come now, you can do much better than that….General," Aero's tone was to stir Fid's fighting spirit, the very same he demonstrated in his fight against Brakus. Fid kipped up to his feet to return to his fighting stance. After a few moments of staring at one another in silence, Aero decided to break it, "Master Chen Shun would be disappointed in his pupil. For he has not even landed a blow on his opponent," he grinned, still hoping to rouse Fid's inner energy. With a clench of his teeth, Fid gathered and focused his energy. His fists were tightly balled and the muscles in his arms tensed. Aero sensed the rising energy and grinned even more for this is what he wanted. He wanted to know what Fid's true limits were.

Lieutenant Demus was searching the hallways of the Palace for Fid. There was a parchment in his hand that bore his name. He came to the War Room and found the door to the dojo was open. He peered his head in and found Aero and Fid sparring with one another. His eyes widened with excitement and hurriedly made his way down the hall and told every soldier that he came upon what was happening. Along with a handful of Elf troops, Demus was searching for Paige and Melina in every room of the palace. They found them sitting at a table in the study. Paige was reading through some documents while Melina was reading a book by the window.

"Lady Paige, Lady Melina!" he approached out of breath. "Lord Aero is sparring with General Fid right now in the dojo".

"How interesting," Melina gave a smile of interest when she looked up from her book. It was when Fid fully recovered from his wounds, that she and Fid were formally introduced to one another. She heard stories of his abilities, but never saw them with her own eyes. She would take this opportunity to observe for herself.

"Take me there," Paige immediately put the documents she was reading down on the table and followed the soldiers down to the dojo.

They saw the two were in fighting stances and were poised to strike. They watched from the balcony that overlooked the dojo. They were completely silent and not a breath was heard from anyone who gathered.

"You will see what Master's Shun's student is capable of right now!" Fid lunged at Aero with his staff. Fid's attacks were quicker and stronger. Aero blocked and dodged each attack. As Fid spun and swung his staff, Aero tried to block it but the practice sword shattered from Fid's attack. The force of the blow sent Aero backwards against the wall. Aero grinned and gathered energy. His eyes glowed just as he threw a barrage of energy orbs at Fid. Fid charged at Aero with great quickness. With that same quickness, he dodged the energy orbs and deflected several with the staff. He leapt and attempted an overhead strike. Aero rolled to the side making Fid miss. The force of the strike put the staff through the padded floor. Aero quickly rose to his feet and noticed the hole in the floor.

"Pity, this floor was refurbished not long ago," a hint of disappointment was in his voice as he leapt to the wall with staffs, grabbing one. They both threw attacks at each other and both were countering each other. Their movements were so quick that if one were to blink they would miss several. The sound of redwood staffs echoed through the nearby halls.

Paige and Melina sensed the steady increase in Fid's energy levels and were thoroughly impressed and shocked at the same time.

"Fid is most impressive," Melina observed his technique and energy level closely.

"Indeed, he is. Even more so than three months ago," Paige gave a nod of her head. She then began to speak to Aero's mind with her own, "*Aero, do you sense the strength of his energy? They are equal to mine and to yours.*"

"*Yes, I know that, dear Sister. I am the one who is fighting him. I am quite aware his energy, but I do not think he is aware of how powerful he is. The strength of the energy he is demonstrating is miniscule compared to what he displayed three months ago,*" he countered Fid's blows.

They both swung their staffs at each other's head making contact with the other's staff. Each threw a kick to each other's abdomen sending the other backwards to the ground. Both immediately kipped up to their feet. Aero lunged at Fid with his staff but his attack was countered and his staff broken with one swing of Fid's staff. Fid spun and thrust the butt end of the staff at Aero's throat stopping a few inches away. Immense heat was seeping from the butt of the staff and a few red embers faintly glowed. Both were breathing heavily and looking directly in to each other's eyes. Both were very intense and focused. Aero grinned at the intensity shown in his eyes. Melina, Paige, Demus, and the other Elf Soldiers clapped from the balcony above them both. Fid looked up to see who had gathered to watch and then back to Aero who still had a big smile across his face.

"Well done, my friend. You have shown me quite a bit during this sparring session," Aero relaxed his body and folded his hands behind his back.

"Like what?" Fid asked him as he lowered his staff from Aero's throat.

"You have shown me that you are more than capable of leading this army. You have also shown me just how powerful you are, but I am sensing that this is just the beginning of your abilities," Aero saw the faint fire of Fid's spirit in his eyes. It was like the light of a fire in the distance.

"What are you saying?" Fid raised a questioning eyebrow.

"I am saying that you are much stronger than you think. There is a slumbering power within you, my friend. You displayed that power three months ago and I believe that even then you were just demonstrating a small amount of your power," Aero's voice grew with excitement.

"So what are you saying? That I can be the most powerful being on Rhydin?" skepticism and disbelief were in Fid's voice.

"On Rhydin and on Earth," Aero's excitement shone in his eyes.

"That's impossible," Fid tossed the staff aside and began to walk out of the room but Aero stopped him by placing his hand on Fid's shoulder.

"You fear your abilities. You are of afraid of how powerful you can be. You shun them instead of embracing them," Aero tried to look in to Fid's eyes and speak to his heart. Fid shrugged his hand away. It was with that shrug that Aero noticed the crystal around his neck. He knew that it was the family crystal for he, his sister, and Melina wear the very same around their necks. He was puzzled as to why Fid wore that crystal around his neck. He never noticed it before. Possible because it was always underneath the tunics he wore. How did he get it? Who gave it to him? Many other questions and thoughts ran through his mind.

"You know nothing about me," Fid snapped at Aero and stormed out of the dojo.

He came to the Hallway of Kings and stopped in front of the portrait of King Tidus, the past Ruler of the Western Province. He looked to the portrait and it seemed as though the portrait was staring straight into his soul with his piercing eyes. Fid looked deeper into the portrait and then he heard a voice speak to him.

"*Fid….,*" the voice called out to him. The voice was clear and resonant. Fid's eyes widened and took a few steps away from the portrait as he saw the image of Tidus emerge from the portrait. Fid noticed the crystal around his neck. It was identical to the one that hung around the necks of Aero, Paige, and Melina and was the same crystal in the middle of the family crest. Tidus seemed to examine Fid from toe to head while pacing in front of him. His eyes then fell upon the crystal around Fid's neck and grinned.

"*So, you are the wielder of the Twin Dragon Blades. You do not appear to be capable of wielding some weapons,*" a smirk grew on his face.

"Could you wield the power of the Blades?" Fid retorted. Tidus grinned once more.

"*You have a quick tongue, boy. I wager you are quick with your Blades as well,*" Tidus placed his hands on the buckle of his belt.

"I have been told that I am," Fid replied.

"*Tell me something, where did you come into possessing that trinket hanging from your neck?*" Tidus referred to the crystal.

"I have had it since I was a child. Why do you ask?" Fid held the crystal between his thumb and forefinger.

"*That crystal is the symbol of the alliance the Elf Rulers and the Dragon Knights made a millennium ago. The Dragon Knights wear jade crystals and the Elf Rulers wear the ruby crystals,*" Tidus's fingers found his own crystal.

"So what are you saying? That I am a descendent of an Elf Ruler?" there was skepticism in Fid's voice.

"*You do wear a ruby crystal, Fid,*" Tidus retorted

"That is impossible. I was born and raised on Earth. And who's descendent would I be?" Fid felt confused and shocked all at the same time. Tidus grinned and looked past Fid to the portrait of Cretus across the hallway. Fid's attention fell upon the portrait. His eyes widened and he backed away from the portrait.

"No, it cannot be," Fid shook his head and turned back to face Tidus. Tidus was fading back into the portrait. "Tell me. How could this be?" Fid implored for Tidus to reveal the secret. Tidus looked down the hallway and grinned. He then faded back into the portrait.

"Fid, are you here?" Aero called to him as he came down the hallway. Aero saw him looking at the portrait of Tidus. Aero sensed Fid was in a state of shock and confusion. He walked up beside him and placed his hand on his shoulder. He then looked to the portrait of Tidus.

"That portrait of Tidus always seems to look into your soul and speak to you," Aero said. Fid looked at Aero as if he knew what happened in the hallway. Did Fid imagine Tidus emerging from the portrait? Or did the actual soul of Tidus speak to him.

"Tidus was a great ruler of the Western Province. He was very wise and had of way of telling you something without directly saying it," Aero looked from the portrait to Fid.

"You are the Ruler of this Kingdom, Aero. Who is your ancestor?" he looked to Aero. Aero looked into Fid's eyes then turned to face the portrait of Cretus. Fid's heart began to race, his breathing became slightly heavier and his eyes widened. At that moment, Demus rushed down the hallway with the same parchment in his hand.

"General Fid, General Fid! I have important news sir," he stopped in front of him and held out the parchment he intended to give Fid before he found them sparring. Fid took it and read it. A long sigh escaped his lips. His eyes seemed to dull in color as if the life had been drained from them. He looked to Aero with tears welling in his eyes.

"What is it my friend?" Aero's concern for Fid showed on his face and in his eyes. He sensed great pain starting to dwell within his heart.

"My aunt is dying," Fid could not hold back the tears. They flowed freely down his cheeks as the thoughts of his aunt played within his mind. "She helped my father raise me. She is the only mother that I truly knew," tears streamed down his cheeks. He knelt down to one knee and murmured a prayer in what did not sound like the Elf language. Not even a language that was spoken on Rhydin. It sounded like a language that was native to Earth. Aero had only heard it once before from a native of Earth. A shaman if his recalled correctly. Aero began to feel Fid's pain. He then placed a hand on his shoulder.

"Go to her, my friend. She needs you," Aero's voice was calm. Fid opened his eyes and tears continued to roll down his cheeks. He took a deep breath to gather himself.

"I will go back to Earth and spend time with her," his eyes were looking to the floor. "But I would like for you to travel with me," he looked from the carpeted floor into Aero's eyes. Aero looked back at him.

"Are you certain you want me there? I do not want to intrude upon family affairs," he wished to be there, but wanted to make sure that is truly what Fid wanted. It was at that moment that Melina and Paige approached them. There was a sense of urgency in Paige's eyes as she approached Aero and placed her hand on his shoulder. She began to speak to his mind, *"Aero, I have just received word that Orcs are making their way north from the southeast through the Western Province".*

"Intercept them with great haste. Take Lieutenant Demus with you," Aero responded. *"Melina is more than capable of defending this Palace,"* he added, looking to her. Melina nodded her head. She was able to hear his thoughts, but was not capable of speaking to either his or Paige's minds.

"You should have Demus take troops through the Southern half of the Woodland Realm coming from behind and Paige should cut through the Northern half meeting them head on," Fid interrupted. Both Aero and Paige looked at Fid in awe. Fid rose to his feet and headed towards the stairwell leading upstairs. They then looked to each other and then their eyes followed Fid to the stairwell. Both were still in amazement that Fid heard their thoughts

"How was he able to read our thoughts?!" exclaimed Paige, "We are the only ones who are able to read the thoughts of others and talk to each other's mind."

"Or so we thought," Melina said with a grin.

"His abilities have grown steadily over the course of these three months ever since he killed Brakus. I have been keeping a watchful eye on his energy levels and they have climbed tremendously. I will go with him to Earth. I have a feeling there is something, or someone, waiting for him other than his Aunt," Aero stated.

"I understand, Brother. I will take the troops north and Demus will go through the south as Fid suggested," Paige said. Demus nodded his head acknowledging his orders.

"Hunt them and eradicate them," Aero told her.

"As always, Brother," she gave grin. She and Demus turned and headed down the hall to gather the Elf troops to carry out their plan of attack.

"Be careful travelling to Earth," Melina said as she drew within inches of him.

"Be vigilant watching over our home," Aero said.

"Nothing shall pass these walls so long as I am here," Melina said with a smile.

After gathering what belongings he needed, Aero made his way to Fid's room. Aero stood in the doorway and watched Fid gather his water pouch, his hooded long coat, gloves, and the Twin Dragon Blades. He slipped into his long coat and pulled the hood over his head.

"I am ready to go. We need to make our way to the Ruins of Keshnar that lay in the northeast of the Woodland Realm so that we may use the Gate of Caelum to travel to Earth," he rose and turned to face Aero. Aero nodded and turned to go down the staircase. They both walked to the stables to get themselves horses to make the travel to Keshnar. They took the reins of the horses and walked them to the main gate of the palace. Fid's horse had a very thick black coat. It was soft to the touch and he could tell that the horse was very strong. Its eyes were dark as if looking into an abyss, much like his own.

"You have chosen one of the best horses in my stable, Fid. His name is Sundancer." Aero said to him.

"No. I think he chose me. He looked right into my eyes and I got pulled into them. Much like others are with me," he stroked Sundancer's coarse mane. He smiled as well as he and Aero mounted their horses and made their way into the woods.

The Sun's rays were shining down through the canopy of the redwood forest. They rode through thick brush and shallow streams. For miles upon miles they rode deep into the forest. Fid's mind was solely on the failing health of his aunt. This was the woman who took over as a mother figure in his life when his own mother died. He wanted nothing more than to see her once more before she was called to Heaven.

Dusk began to fall over the forest as Aero and Fid came upon the ruins of Keshnar. They both dismounted and left their horses on the outskirts of the Ruins. They knew not how long they would be away. It was best to allow for the horses to roam freely and graze until their return. Aero assured Fid that they would not wander too far. With that reassurance, they then made their way into what was the City of Keshnar. The ruins reminded Fid of one of his visits to ruins of the southern continent back on Earth. He recalled they were the ruins of a people known as the Aztecs. They ventured further into the ruins of Keshnar. The ruins were overrun with vines and over-brush. Walls were crumbling and were so frail that if one were to lean on one of these walls, it would collapse. Small animals and birds had made their homes in the holes, cracks and crevices of the decrepit structures. They walked through the rubble and fallen brick, towards the structure that stood at the center of the ancient city.

"The structure in the middle of these ruins is the City's temple. The people who inhabited this ancient city worshipped the Sun god, much like the Aztecs back on Earth. That is where the Gate Caelum stands," Fid pointed to the temple for Aero to see. Aero nodded and they moved on. They made their way up the stairs towards the entrance of the temple. They reached the top and gazed upon the entranceway into the temple. Carved at the top of the doorway was the Eye of Ra. To them, it seemed like the Eye followed them as they entered the hallowed temple. The hallway that lead deeper into the temple was pitch black.

"This is a darkness that not even my eyes can pierce. Light would be much appreciated," Aero's voice echoed off of the hall's walls.

"An issue easily remedied," Fid slightly bowed his head and folded his hands in front of his face. A small ball of flame materialized above Fid's folded hands. Fid threw the fireball down the hallway lighting the torches. Aero was surprised, yet impressed, that Fid summoned an orb of fire. Was he able to conjure flame all along? They continued on their way to the Gate of Caelum through the narrow halls of the Keshnar Temple. As the two were walking down a flight of stairs, Aero sensed Fid's distress, "Fid, everything will work out for the best. Situations such as these tend do to so".

"Yes, I know. It is just that this would be my third parent that I have lost. My birth mother died when I was but a toddler. My father was lost to me in the attack on my village so many years ago. And now my aunt who took on the role of being my mother," he said as tears began to well in the corners of his eyes, but he wiped them away before they could roll down his cheeks. Fid then inhaled a deep breath, "Let us keep moving," he urged for them to resume their way down the stairs. Aero nodded and followed behind him.

They reached the chamber in which the Gate stood. The Gate stood at the center of the chamber. The Gate was built from very dense stone with ancient glyphs carved around the stone edge of the Gate. The Gate was formed from four rings of various glyphs. It seemed each glyph and each ring meant something to the traveler's destination.

"I have never used the Gate of Caelum before. How does it work and what are those glyphs carved on the edge of the Gate?" Aero looked to them with curious eyes as he pointed to them.

"Those glyphs were used by the Kesharians to indicate the vast number of worlds. The Kesharian people were very adept to studying the stars. From these studies they studied various ways to travel from world to world. There have also been rumors of documents being found of studies undergoing of travel from universe to universe. From their study of the stars, planets, and mysticism, the Keshnarians built the Gates of Caelum," he told Aero as he pointed to a console several feet in front of the Gate. The two drew closer to the console and they saw four rings of glyphs that were identical to the glyphs on the Gate. The outer most ring however looked as if it is not complete.

"Fid, why is it the outermost ring does not look complete and the inner most are?" Aero traced his finger along the edge of the ring. Fid thought for a moment before giving his thought, "All I know is the inner most ring represents which gate on the planet. The second ring represents the planet. The third ring represents the galaxy. And now that you have noticed there are in fact glyphs seemingly missing. Perhaps there were studies conducted by the Keshnarians in traveling between universes," Fid's ears perked up at the thought of this discovery. "There have been whispers and rumors of there being universes that parallel our own, but I thought of them only as stories. Nothing more," Fid's eyes widened at the prospect.

"How is one to know which planet is which by these symbols?" Aero asked.

"With this," Fid took a parchment out of his pouch. The parchment had the symbols and which planet they represented and which galaxy each planet was in. Fid walked over to the console and touched the symbols. As he touched the symbols, the corresponding symbols on the Gate glowed and the Gate opened as Fid touched the last symbol. As the Gate opened, a bright white light emitted from the opening. Aero and Fid covered their eyes as the light hit them and flooded the room. They lowered their hands away from their faces and gazed upon the phenomenon that had transpired in front of them.

"This is one of the most amazing sites I have ever seen. And I have been around this world many times my friend," Aero's eyes were fixed upon the Gate with awe in them.

"Let us go through Aero. We cannot waste much more time awing at this site," Fid's eyes were focused on the Gate's opening. His body tensed not knowing what awaited him.

"You are correct, my friend. Your Aunt needs you," Aero nodded and placed his hand on Fid's shoulder. They both walked towards the bright light emitting from the Gate.

"What does it feel like when you pass through the Gate?" Aero asked as they approach the gate.

"You will not have time to think about it or feel anything, my friend," he responded with a grin and a glance to Aero.

"I see," Aero took a deep breath as they passed through the Gate.

Before Aero could think about the feeling while passing through the Gate, they found themselves in the lush forests of the Mountains. With gazing eyes, Aero marveled at the site of the tall white pine trees, the Sun beams pierced through the forest canopy and the birds were singing from high atop the pine trees.

"This is truly an amazing place, my friend. It is so peaceful and the air is so refreshing," Aero looked out to the Sun setting behind the mountain range.

"Looks can be deceiving, my friend. Like Rhydin, there are many battles being waged across this world. There are battles for power over these lands," Fid shook his head at the arrogance and the greed of those who wished for war. "Rhydin and Earth were always known as the Twin Planets. Whatever evil or good occurs on one planet, it finds a way of appearing on the other," he added.

"Two Planets, One Fate," Aero remembered learning of the Planets' shared fate as a child.

"Indeed, but we must move on to the village. I will show you much more later," Fid nodded in the direction of his Village.

"I agree, my friend," they both began to walk deeper into the forest of pine trees.

Along the way to the village, Fid began to lose himself in his thoughts. He thought back to the times that he spent with his Aunt. The thought that he lingered upon was back when he was a very young child. The memory was from when he was around the age of seven, if he recalled correctly. He had just returned from a mathematics lesson and tears were streaming down his cheeks. He had sat on the side of his cabin while holding his knees up to his chest. His Aunt Addie was hanging garments on the clothesline and heard Fid crying. She put what she was doing aside and walked over to her upset nephew. She knelt down beside him, "Fid, what's bothering you, Honey?" she pulled him close to her to hold him. The young Fid wiped the tears away from his cheeks.

"Nothing, Aunt Addie," he replied while trying not to hyperventilate. Before he could react, she grabbed his pointed ear and pulled on it. His eyes widened and he knew that if he tried to pull away it would only get worst.

"Ouch, ouch, ouch, Aunt Addie!" exclaimed Fid as her fingers were latched onto his ear.

"Now you know Aunt Addie knows when something is wrong with her nephew. Now are you going to tell me or are you going to be stubborn about it?" her voice was stern as she continued to pull on his ear.

"Ok, Ok. I will tell you," he responded without hesitation. She let go of his ear. Fid rubbed at its tenderness.

"Now what's bothering you, Child?" she asked as if it were the first time asking him.

"Well…at the mathematics group lesson…the other kids started to make fun of me," he tried to hold back a tear as he remembered the hurtful incident.

"What were they saying child?" her tone returned to that of being stern, but Fid was not the target.

"They called me a 'pointy-earred freak' because of my ears," he replied as he twitched them.

"Oh child, there is not a thing wrong with you. You are just different which just makes you special and unique," she ran her fingers through his short dreadlocks.

"Thanks, Aunt Addie," he said as he buried his head into his knees. There was a moment of silence and then she asked him, "Do you know what I see when I look at you, child?"

"What's that?" his face was still buried in his knees.

"I see a King who will lead a great nation. I see a kind hearted person who will go out of his way to help someone else. I see a guardian who will put his life second to someone he cares most about," she stated trying to reassure him while looking into his piercing dark eyes. Fid looked back into her eyes and tears began to well in the corners of his eyes. He firmly hugged her and cried more.

"Thank you, Aunt Addie," he said in between sniffles.

"You're welcome, Child," she smiled and held him.

Fid regained his focus as they reached the outskirts of the village. Fid looked upon the village and was thoroughly shocked. The village that he left several months ago was lush with green grass, birds were singing, children were playing, and the smell of the villagers cooking in their cabins and huts filled the air. But now, the village was barren; there were no children playing as if it were an abandoned village and the smell of fire and ash filled their nostrils. Fid's heart felt heavy at the site of his village. The two walked around the village looking for any sign of life within the village.

"What happened here?" Fid dropped to his knees at the site of the seemingly abandoned village.

"By the looks of it, this village has had some frequent visits from Lycans," Aero knelt to the ground looking at a footprint.

"Lycans?" Fid raised an eyebrow at the term he had never heard before.

"Werewolves," Aero responded. Fid nodded his head. "I see no remains of any of the Villagers. But, I do see blood. Perhaps there are wounded," Aero rose to his feet and dusted his hands and knees off.

"Why would Lycans only wound the villagers and not kill them?" Fid thought aloud.

"Perhaps they are keeping them alive. For what, I do not know," Aero gave a shake of his head to the reasoning of the Lycans' actions.

"How many of them are there? Can you tell?" Fid looked to the tracks in the ground around them.

"There seems to be fifteen to twenty from the appearance of these tracks. There could be more," Aero looked towards the ground as well, counting the sets of prints in the ground.

"We had better search for the Villagers," Fid did not want to linger on the threat from the Lycans. There will be a time for that.

"I agree. And to also ask them about what exactly is going on in this village," Aero's focus narrowed as well when he sensed Fid's. Fid nodded and the two walked further into the barren village. As they were exploring the village they did in fact find signs of people still living in the cabins and huts. They found wet clothes hanging to dry outside of the cabins, the smell of cooking food became more prevalent as they drew closer to the center of the village. As they drew closer to the center of the village they saw a cabin with smoke billowing from the chimney.

"That cabin is where the village meetings are held. There seems to be one in progress," Fid pointed to it. Aero nodded and they made their way towards the door of the cabin. Fid stopped in front of the door with his hand on the door handle. He took a deep breath before entering the cabin. Aero placed his hand on Fid's shoulder for reassurance. Fid looked to Aero then to the door. He turned the door handle and pushed the door open. He stood in the doorway and looked upon the villagers who were having a lively debate about their plight.

"We cannot stand for this any longer. They have taken over our village and our lives. We must be rid of these beasts!" an older man was addressing the Villagers from the front of the crowded room.

"But how? Every time we try to fight them we lose. These beasts are too strong for us. We cannot win against them," another man rose to his feet.

"I can," Fid took a few steps from the doorway. The attention of the villagers turned to him and began to chatter amongst themselves. He and Aero walked further in the crowded cabin.

"Fid, is that you Son?" asked the older man who was addressing the villagers.

"Yes, it is Kamaan," Fid walked towards him with open arms to embrace the old man.

"How long has it been since you left us, my boy?" Kamaan asked with his hands on Fid's shoulders.

"Too long," Fid gave a faint smile. Kamaan looked over Fid's shoulder to Aero.

"You must introduce us to your friend," he beckoned Aero to join everyone else. The eyes of the villagers fell upon Aero as he walked down the aisle. The villagers whispered amongst themselves, wondering who the Elf was.

"Villagers, I present to you, Lord Aero, Ruler of the Eastern Province of Rhydin," Fid announced loud enough for all to hear. The villagers were in awe as they beheld an Elf Ruler of Rhydin. They all bowed their heads in respect to Aero.

"I thank you for this most generous welcome, but please do not bow", Aero pleaded, "I do not come here for praise, but to support my friend".

"You two could not have come at a better time," Kamaan looked into Fid's eyes. Fid sensed his dismay.

"What is wrong, Old Friend? What exactly has been going on? All I know is that my Aunt Addie has fallen deathly ill," his eyebrows furrowed at the thought of the Lycan threat.

"Yes, your aunt is deathly ill. The illness has spread throughout her body. The medicine man from the Cherokee has told me she does not have much time. She has held on for a very long time, Fid. She wants to see you, Son," he said.

"Take me to her, please," a tear rolled down Fid's cheek.

"She has been strong for you her entire life my friend. Stay strong for her," Aero said in a lowered tone for only Fid to hear. Fid nodded and followed Kamaan outside and towards the hut where his aunt rested. Fid and Kamaan stopped short of the doorway to the hut. Kamaan looked into Fid's eyes, "She waits for you". Fid nodded and took a deep breath before entering the hut. As he entered the hut, his eyes fell upon his aunt. She laid in a bed on the other side of the hut bundled under a bear skin blanket with a cold rag over her forehead to bring down her fever. Fid's heart ached from the sight of his aunt in this state. He remembered his aunt being strong and independent, but now she laid on her death bed, helpless and dependent upon others for her needs. Tears welled up in his eyes as he walked closer to bedside. He knelt by her side and bowed his head. He began to say a prayer in the language native to the mountains. Aunt Addie's eyes opened slightly as she turned her head slowly to face him.

"Fid? Is that you child?" her voice was weak and raspy. Fid raised his head to meet her eyes. The once bright and vivid eyes of his A\ aunt were now dull and drained of all the life that was once there.

"Yes Aunt Addie. I am here," he took her hand in to his.

"It is good to see you, Child. You've grown so much. What have you been eating?" there was a slight grin on her face, despite the pain that was ravaging her body. Fid smiled as well as a tear rolled down his cheek. "Why do you cry child? There is no reason for it," she reached up to wipe the tear from his cheek.

"So much has happened since I have been away from the village. You became sick and the village has lost its life. What has happened here, Aunt Addie?" he held her hand to his cheek. The warmth he remembered was gone.

"Lycans. Werewolves have made frequent visits. They threaten us if we don't give them what they want. They take our food. They hurt our young men," speaking of their misfortune only upset her, causing her to cough.

"You should not upset yourself Aunt Addie," he tried to calm her down. She nodded her head slightly and began to slow her breathing down.

"There is a small box on top of that table, Child. Will you bring that over to me?" she pointed to the table a few feet away from bedside. Fid rose to his feet and reached to take the box and hand it to his aunt. She took the box and undid the golden clasp. She then opened the box and uncovered the item that laid within. It was a golden bracelet with the Eye of Ra engraved in to it. Fid's eyes widened at the sight of the bracelet.

"I-It cannot be. The Bracelet of Ra....here? In this village?" his shock was heard in his voice. His eyes gazed upon the Bracelet and it seemed to glow with intense energy. He then looked to his aunt.

"This is one of the Ancient Relics. The Bracelet of Ra is the key to finding the others. Why are you giving this to me now?" Fid was still in awe of the Bracelet even being in his aunt's possession.

"It is your destiny child," she coughed, then continued. "when you were born, your heart was not healthy. The village shaman told your father and mother that you would not live long. Your parents were naturally upset. They asked for help from the surrounding villages but no one came. Then one day, a Red Dragon from the Western Mountains of Rhydin answered your parents' cry for help. The Red Dragon breathed a portion of his Essence in to your body. It was like the breath of life. This Essence settled in your heart and repaired it. From that day until the day you die, that Essence will live within you. It was a miracle the Red Dragon heard your parents' plea for help," she said.

"So you are saying that I have a portion of the Red Dragon's Essence beating in my chest?" there was skepticism in his voice.

"Believe it, Child. In that chest of yours the Essence of the Red Dragon thrives and grows," her tone was to ease the doubt in Fid's mind.

"What was the Dragon's name, Aunt Addie?" he tilted his head to the side. She coughed then answered, "Well let me remember. His name was..... Tufar".

"Tufar?" he knew that name, but he could not remember where he had heard it.

"Tufar also gave the Bracelet of Ra to your parents to give to you when you were ready," she coughed more. She handed Fid the box with the Bracelet.

"Put it on child. It's your destiny," she urged. Fid took the Bracelet from the box and fastened it on his right wrist. When he fastened the gold clasp, the Bracelet glowed a vibrant gold. Fid felt the raw energy flow throughout his body. His eyes glowed white and a golden aura surrounded his body. Aunt Addie turned away from the bright light emitting from Fid's body. The glow flooded the cabin and could have been seen from the surrounding cabins and huts.

The energy the Bracelet of Ra emitted was so palpable that Aero felt it in the air around him. The Villagers even felt that something was different in the air, but could not place its origin. Aero was astonished at this tremendous climb in power. Aero knew this came from Fid and now knew for sure that Fid was more powerful than he and Paige combined. Aero wondered what the cause was in the sudden climb in Fid's power.

The aura seeped in to Fid's body. He was breathing heavily from the energy surge that coursed through his body. He then looked to his aunt with wide, wild eyes.

"You are well on your way to fulfilling your destiny," she took a few deep breaths. Fid walked back over to her bedside.

"What do you know about my destiny, Aunt Addie?" he raised an inquisitive eyebrow.

"All will be revealed with time, my child," she forced a grin. Fid dropped his head in disappointment, "but I do know that *my* destiny is fulfilled," she added.

"What was your destiny, Aunt Addie?" he raised his head. She turned to face Fid and gently placed her hand on his cheek.

"It was to set you on your path", her smile trembled. She did not want to show tears to her nephew.

"Thank you, Aunt Addie. You have done so much for me throughout my life. You have been that beacon of light when I was in the shadows," he leaned close to kiss her forehead.

"Now that your path has been set Child, you must now free this village from the Lycan menace," her voice shifted to be stern.

"I,and Aero, will get rid of the Lycan pack," the conviction in his voice matched her tone.

"Aero? Who is Aero, child?" she was unaware Fid came with anyone.

"Aero is the Elf Ruler of the Eastern Province of Rhydin. He and his sister helped me track down Brakus," he knew that Aunt Addie would be proud of the company he kept.

"So you did find the vampire who attacked our village," there was relief in her voice. She was concerned of the pat of vengeance he took. Her fear was of him being consumed by it.

"Yes Aunt Addie. I found him and avenged our village," he gave a nod of his head.

"That's good, Child," her voice began to fade with each word.

"Get your rest, Aunt Addie. Keep your strength up. I and Aero will return," he rose to his feet and then kissed her forehead. She smiled at him as he turned to leave the cabin. As he walked out, Aunt Addie faced the ceiling of the hut. She inhaled and then exhaled a deep breath.

Fid found Aero outside the cabin looking up at the moon. He walked to be at his side.

"The moon is beautiful tonight," his eyes didn't leave the stars and moon.

"Yes. Yes it is," Fid's mind was on the thought of his aunt and what she gave him. He looked down to the Bracelet of Ra. The moonlight gleamed off of it. Aero noticed the Bracelet on his wrist but did not ask about it because he was certain he will find out about it later. At the moment, they wanted to focus on dealing with the Lycan menace.

"Are you ready to track the Lycan pack down, my friend?" Aero looked from the Bracelet to him. Fid turned to Aero with building intensity in his eyes.

"I am," his eyes flared. Kamaan approached them, "My friends, you will be able to find the Lycans in a camp two miles east of here," he looked to them both.

"Thank you, Old Friend. This village will be free of this menace shortly," Kamaan always trusted Fid's words

"Bless you two. This village is very grateful for what you are about to do," he placed his hands on both of their shoulders. Relief was in his eyes. He was not sure how much longer they'd last with the Lycan Pack frequently terrorizing them.

"We better be on our way, Fid. We shall move under the cover of night," Aero pat Fid on the shoulder. Fid nodded as they pulled the hoods of their long coats over their heads and ran into the forest.

With the moonlight being the only light that lit their way, they made their way through the dark, dense forest to the Lycan camp. They sensed they were getting closer and closer to the camp. Using their uncanny sense of hearing, they heard the voices of the Lycan pack a half a mile away.

They crouched in the bushes as they came within thirty yards of the camp. Fid and Aero watched the Lycan camp for a while. Aero signaled Fid to let him know how many Lycans there were in the camp. Fid nodded and motioned for Aero to jump to the trees and make his way towards the camp. Aero nodded then jumped up to the branches of the pine that surrounded them. Fid rose to his feet and made his way to the path that took him to the main entrance of the Lycan camp. There were two Lycans, in human form, guarding the entrance of the camp. Their attention turned towards the hooded Fid.

"Please, pardon me gentleman. I seem to have lost my way. I was wondering if you two can help me," Fid's head was lowered and his hands were folding within the sleeves of his long coat. The two guards slowly walked to him with their fists clenched and showing signs they may transform in to their beast form. At that moment, Aero jumped from the trees with sword drawn cutting the guards down. Both Fid and Aero dragged the bodies into the bushes and made their way into the camp. They both took cover between tents and barrels. Fid drew his blades and cut down a Lycan that wa passing by. As they went to drag the body into the bushes another passing Lycan spotted the two Elves and sounded an alarm for the rest of the pack.

"It appears we are about to have unwanted company," Aero's eyes became more alert with the alarm being sounded.

"It would seem so," Fid clenched his teeth in preparation for a fight. They threw their long coats aside and readied their swords. The pack began to empty out of their tents and soon surrounded the two intruding Elves.

"There is an unfair advantage, my friend. Thirty Lycans against two Elves," Aero observed the surrounding Lycans in their human forms.

"Yes, there is an unfair advantage....... for them," an confident grin grew on Fid's face. Lycans from different ends of the camp began to charge at the two Elves. Aero and Fid blocked and countered the attacks of the Lycans. They were not necessarily killing them, but were crippling them. Fid and Aero spun around each other slashing at the legs and arms of the attacking Lycans. They used their agility and nimbleness against the brute strength of the Lycans.

"That is enough!" a voice ordered the rest of the Lycan pack to cease their attack on the Elves. Fid and Aero were out of breath. They looked towards the one who seemed to be the Alpha of the pack. The Alpha looked upon the two intruders with malice in his eyes. He then motioned for the Lycans to lower their weapons. Fid and Aero remained on their guard. The Alpha slowly walked towards Fid and Aero with his eyes unwavering from them. The man stood taller than six feet, towering over the two Elves. His hair was short and dark. His face looked like it was chiseled from granite. His arms and fists were massive. There was an evil grin on his face. Fid locked eyes with this man and looked deep into them.

"Who are you? Why have you oppressed my village?!" Fid's eyes flared. The leader let out an evil laugh causing the remaining Lycans to laugh as well.

"Why do you laugh?" Aero stepped closer to the Alpha.

"You will have to forgive me. I am Craven and I am the one who is to bring your heart to the one who hired us," he pointed at Fid. Fid's heart dropped wondering why this man wanted to kill him.

"You see we are mercenaries. Our services go to the one with the most gold. Our orders are to bring your heart to him. Brakus failed to accomplish this task, twice. He failed to kill you when his horde attacked your village all those years ago and he failed to kill you on Rhydin," Craven was looking directly at Fid when Brakus' purpose was explained. Fid's eyes widened at the reason why his village was attacked. They attacked the village to get at him. Guilt began to run through his mind and heart.

"The one who hired us, is Sekmet," he revealed to Fid. Fid's and Aero's bodies tensed when they heard the name of Sekmet.

"It cannot be," Aero uttered with disbelief in his voice.

"I thought Sekmet was destroyed a thousand years ago," Fid looked to Aero.

"Indeed, he was," Aero nodded with widened eyes.

"But, there was a Witch from beyond the Western Mountains of Rhydin who resurrected Sekmet's soul and placed it back in to his body. To him, she gave an army of Orc warriors who were infused with her dark influence. Sekmet owes his life to this Witch. He vowed his allegiance to her and vowed to take over the lands east of the mountains for her. When the Elf Kingdom, and all of the others, fell to Sekmet's iron fist, the Witch then planned to take over the rest of Rhydin, and then Earth. The only reason why we agreed to bring your beating heart to him was so we would have immunity from his army once they have swept over Earth and Rhydin," Craven gave an uncaring shrug of his shoulders.

"You disgust me," Aero spat.

"There are those like us whose first instinct is to survive," growled Craven. Aero walked towards Craven as if to attack but Fid held him back.

"I will make a deal with you, Craven," Fid stepped towards Craven.

"You have perked my interest," Craven responded with a grin on his face.

"I will fight you, one on one. No weapons and no interference from either Aero, nor the rest of your pack. If I win, you and your pack will leave my village alone, never to return," Fid's tone was demanding.

"And if I win?" Craven raised an eyebrow.

"You will have my life," Fid let out a sigh. The rest of the pack shouted out to Craven, "Take the deal! Easy pickings Craven!" Aero gave a sharp look to Fid as if he had gone mad. Craven looked from his men to Fid and grinned, "Deal". The rest of the pack cheered at the decision. Aero turned Fid to face him, "What do you think you are doing? Do you know what you are dealing with? These men have obviously been sent here to specifically kill you. They have trained for this moment".

"Do not worry, my friend. I brought down a vampire three months ago and I can bring down a Lycan," confidence was in Fid's eyes.

"They are two totally different creatures," Aero groaned. Fid handed his Dragon Blades to Aero.

"You speak truth, but the same strategy can be used," Fid gave an unconcerned grin.

"I hope you know what you are doing. If not, you are dead," Aero gave an audible sigh.

"I will be fine, my friend," Fid replied as he put his hand on Aero's shoulder. Fid closed his eyes and focused his energy. He let out a deep breath and opened his eyes. The pack formed a circle around Craven and Fid. Fid walked closer to the center of the circle. Craven had an evil grin on his face as he threw off his animal skin vest. He then looked up towards the full moon and slowly began to transform. The hair on his body grew longer, his nails grew rapidly and soon took on the form of razor sharp claws, and he even grew a few feet in height. His head began to take on the form of a wolf. Fid's eyes widened as he watched this transformation.

"Oh my goodness. What did I get myself in to?" he muttered to himself. At that moment, the transformed Craven let out a bellowing howl and charged straight for Fid to throw his shoulder in to Fid's chest sending him backwards on to the ground. Craven then picked

Fid up from the ground over his head and threw him in to a tree, cracking it. Aero winched as Fid's ribs smashed against the tree. Fid rose to his feet slowly, holding his ribs. He then saw the nearly eight foot monster stalking him. Fid took a fighting stance preparing himself to deflect whatever attack was thrown at him. The pack cheered Craven on as he unleashed an onslaught of attacks upon Fid. Fid attempted to block his blows but they were so forceful that they broke through Fid's defenses. Each blow made contact with Fid's ribs and jaw. Fid began to bruise and bleed from his nose, mouth, and under his eye. Craven threw an uppercut to Fid's jaw sending him several feet backwards. He laid there for a few moments. As he laid there, Craven howled at the moon in celebration. Aero watched in disbelief. He had to fight the urge to go to Fid's aid. This was difficult for him to watch. He winced and sucked in sharp breaths with each blow dealt to Fid's body.

"How could Fid fall so easily? He cannot. It should not be possible a mere Lycan can defeat him," he muttered to himself. At that moment, Craven slowly made his way towards the fallen Elf. Fid heard the footsteps of Craven and could do nothing but helplessly lay there. His body felt broken and would not respond to his will to move. He turned his head to the side giving up all hope in rallying in this fight. He furrowed his eyebrows when he thought he saw a faint gathering light near a tree. He rapidly blinked his eyes thinking it was a figment of his mind, but then this light spoke, *"Don't you give up child,"* It was the voice of his Aunt Addie that he heard." *Look within yourself and you will find the strength. Get up, and fight.... Get up, and fight,"* the light of his aunt faded to nothing, but continued to echo, 'Get up and fight'. These words resonate in Fid's mind. He began to mutter the words to himself desperately trying to will himself to find the power within his spirit to get up and defeat this foe. His eyes looked to the Bracelet of Ra on his wrist. Looking to the Bracelet of Ra triggered another flash of a memory that seemed to not be his own. It was a brief glimpse of what appeared to be him looking down to his wrist to see the Bracelet of Ra. It was not his arm that he gazed upon though. The arm he looked to was fully covered in armor that he had never seen before with the Bracelet of Ra fitting with it. After Fid regained his focus, it began to glow a vibrant gold and an aura slowly surrounded his body. Craven stopped in his approach. His ears perked up as he saw the aura slowly engulf Fid's body. Fid kipped up to his feet with his wounds rapidly healing. He slowly raised his head and opened his eyes. His eyes were flushed white with energy emitting from them. Anger fumed from Craven seeing that his opponent was not defeated. Craven charged at Fid with his claws ready to slash at his throat.

"Wrong move you bastard," Fid's voice resonated throughout the forest as he released an intense concentration of energy from the Bracelet of Ra at Craven. This powerful beam of energy threw Craven back in to a white pine tree, cracking it. The blast from Fid singed Craven's skin. Smoke even rose from the scorch mark. While Craven was in a daze, Fid dashed towards him and began to viciously attack Craven's ribs with thunderous punches and quick kicks. Fid threw a kick to Craven's jaw sending him face first into the ground. Craven slowly transformed back in to his human form. Blood trickled from his mouth as he looked up at Fid. Fid grabbed Craven by the neck, lifting him up against a tree. Craven growled at Fid as blood trickled from his nose and mouth.

"I can easily end you here and now. Leave my village alone and never return," Fid forcefully said through his clenched teeth.

"I am a man of my word. We will leave, but I am to warn you Sekmet will keep hunting you until he has your heart," Fid released Craven from his grip, letting him down to his feet.

The glow from Fid's eyes and the aura that surrounded his body faded. He fell to his knees breathing heavily. Aero walked over to help Fid to his feet. There was a wide grin on his face seeing the power Fid demonstrated. The rest of the pack gathered around the two combatants with a few of them helping Craven walk. Aero and Fid turned to walk out of the Lycan camp to return to the village.

"Fid!" Craven called out. Both Aero and Fid turned to face Craven and his pack, "you're a great fighter".

"And you are an honorable man, Craven," Fid gave a respectful bow of his head with Craven doing the same as they parted ways.

As they made their way back to the village, Aero periodically looked down at the Bracelet on Fid's wrist.

"Why not ask me what the bracelet is instead of wondering?" Fid gave a grin to Aero. Aero gave a chuckle realizing he was making it obvious that he was curious of the Bracelet, "Alright. What is that Bracelet on your wrist?'

"This is the Bracelet of Ra. My aunt gave it to me right before we set out to hunt down the Lycan pack," Aero's eyes widened as Fid told him that the Bracelet of Ra was in his possession.

"You mean to tell me that you wield the power of the Bracelet of Ra. The key to finding the other Ancient Relics?!" there was clear excitement in Aero's voice.

"Yes, Aero. This is the legendary Bracelet of Ra," Fid nodded while giving a glance to it.

"But, how is it that the bracelet came to your village? How long has it been there? Who gave it….," Fid stopped Aero in mid-thought. Aero's mind was racing with so many questions.

"I know that you have questions as to how the bracelet came to my village. My aunt told me that I was suppose to die because I was born with a very bad heart. My parents searched across the land for someone to help with my condition. No one could. I was on the threshold of death when the Red Dragon, Tufar, came to the village and breathed a portion of his essence in to me to repair my heart. He also gave the Bracelet of Ra to my parents and aunt to give to me when I was ready," to him, the story seemed unlikely yet it was true.

"T-Tufar? Tufar gave you a portion of his Essence and the Bracelet of Ra to you?!" Aero's eyes slowly widened as Fid described what seemed to be a curse but turned out to be a blessing.

"It would seem so," he winced and clutched his ribs as he was starting to feel the aftermath of the fight.

"You have no inkling as to who Tufar, is do you?" his voice was more accusing than inquisitive.

"Should I?" Fid shook his head.

"Tufar is the oldest and the most powerful Dragon on Rhydin and Earth. He is over one thousand years old. He was in the war against Sekmet one thousand years ago. His Dragon Knight was Giltia, the Dragon-Lord," Aero still could not believe Fid did not know, but then Fid only recently arrived to Rhydin.

"You are saying that I have a portion of the essence of the greatest Dragon that Rhydin and Earth has ever seen?" disbelief was in Fid's voice.

"Yes. And some say he is still alive with other Dragons and Dragon Knights waiting to be called upon," Aero nodded.

"And who would be the one to summon them?" Fid raised his eyebrow.

"They would only answer to the Dragon Lord," he responded.

"Hopefully he can help us in the war against Sekmet," Fid thought it would be advantageous to find this Dragon-Lord.

"Yes. Hopefully," Aero agreed.

Fid and Aero sensed a grim cloud had fallen over the village. As they walked towards the center of the village, they saw people gathered around the hut that Aunt Addie was resting. The villagers turned to notice that Aero and Fid returned. Fid and Aero looked upon the grim expressions in the people's eyes. They had been crying and were grieving over some misfortune. Kamaan emerged from the crowd and greeted them.

"It's good to see that you two have returned. I assume you were successful," he had been crying as well. Fid could hear it in his voice.

"Yes, we were successful. You will be bothered by the Lycan pack no more," Aero proudly said, placing his hand on Kamaan's shoulder. Fid noticed that Kamaan had not looked at him as if he was avoiding eye contact.

"Kamaan, what has happened here?" Fid leaned toward him. Kamaan said nothing but looked at him briefly, then looked toward the ground. "Kamaan, what is wrong? Tell me," Fid implored. Kamaan hesitated to answer. Tears began to well in his eyes as he looked in to Fid's eyes.

"Your aunt... Your aunt has passed on, Fid. She passed not long after you left," tears rolled down his cheeks. Fid fell to his knees with tears beginning to stream down his cheeks. "I am so sorry my friend," Kamaan knelt down with Fid and held him. Aero placed his hand on Fid's shoulder to comfort him.

They buried Aunt Addie's wooden casket on a hilltop overlooking Wolf Lake. Aunt Addie always took Fid to the hilltop every evening to watch the sunset over the lake. The villagers laid down flowers at the head stone. Some prayed and sung spirituals in celebration of her life. Fid, with tears welling in his eyes, walked up to the head stone and recited a prayer in the language of the Cherokee,

> *"I give this one thought to keep.*
> *I am with you still- I do not sleep.*
> *I am a thousand winds that blow.*
> *I am the diamond glints of snow.*
> *I am the sunlight on the ripened grain.*
> *I am the gentle Autumn rain.*
> *When you awaken in the morning's hush.*
> *I am the swift uplifting rush*
> *Of quiet birds in the circling flight.*
> *I am the soft stars that shine at night.*
> *Do not think of me as gone*
> *I am with you still- in each new dawn."*

Aero also paid his respects saying a prayer in the Elf language. Fid then turned to the sunset over Wolf Lake, with Aero joining him.

Fid was silent on their return journey to the Gate of Caelum. His mind dwelt on the thoughts of his now passed aunt. She was not only his aunt, but a mother, a mentor and most of all, his guardian. Aero would catch glimpses of Fid looking down at the Bracelet of Ra.

That was the last thing that his aunt gave to him. Aero sensed that the bracelet is all that Fid had of her.

"I want to offer a word to you my friend, and then I will leave you to grieve. That bracelet is not the only thing that you have of your aunt. You have her memories, her teachings, and her spirit is with you. In a way, she is alive within you. Hey legacy lives through you. Please, keep that within your mind," Fid may not have seemed to have been listening to what Aero had to say but he indeed did and took his words to heart.

Upon reaching the Gate of Caelum, Fid pressed the tiles for the Gate to open to Rhydin. Aero stepped through the Gate first while Fid lingered for a few moments looking back to the forest. This was the land in which he was raised. He looked upon it and remembered the memories he created here and then muttered to himself, "Thank you Aunt Addie. You will always stay in my heart and my spirit. Your memory will thrive. I will return, I promise".

The Hero Within

T HEY SOON FOUND THEMSELVES BACK in the Keshnarian Ruins
on Rhydin. They made their way to their horses on the outskirts
of the ruins and mounted them to make the journey back to the
Eastern Palace. Fid hesitated to ride on as Aero had already gone
ahead several yards. Aero noticed Fid was not by his side. He looked
back and rode to his side. He looked in to Fid's eyes and saw his pain.

"You do not have to come back to the palace with me just yet. I
suggest you go somewhere to cleanse your mind and spirit. Preferably
this forest," Aero looked to the forest canopy. Fid looked up from the
ground to Aero, "I may take your advice my friend. I may just find a
place in this redwood forest to clear my head. Thank you".

"I will bid you farewell for now, my friend. Take care of yourself,"
Aero said as he turned his horse to ride back to his palace.

"Thank you, Aero," Fid forced a smile and nodded.

"You are welcome," he smiled then turned and rode back to the
palace.

Fid looked down to Sundancer and stroked his mane while
looking to his surroundings. The redwood forest was so quiet and
peaceful. He admired the scenery of the sunlight shining through the
redwood canopy. He took a deep breath inhaling the fresh air before
galloping deeper in to the forest.

He rode south, past Eagle Eye Lake, until he arrived at a clearing
in the forest. He slowed Sundancer to a halt and dismounted. This
clearing was familiar to him. He remembered this was the clearing he
had defeated Brakus. He remembered the power that surged through

his body that night. Was that the power that Aero has talked to him about or was the power he demonstrated against Craven his true power? He could not help but think that maybe this is only the beginning of his hidden strength. How was he supposed to tap into this inner strength? So many questions about himself raced through his mind that his thoughts had become clouded and unfocused as of late. He decided that going into a meditative state will help him sort his thoughts and feelings. He tied Sundancer's reins to a bush and walked over to a most familiar rock. This was the rock that Brakus was thrown into. He sat on top of the rock, crossing his legs. After a moment, he closed his eyes and took several deep breaths. Fid began to feel the slightest change in the wind, he heard the crawling of insects up and down the surrounding redwood. He was more in tune with his body so much so that he felt the blood flow through his veins. He even heard his own heartbeat. His body began to ease and relax the further he slipped in to this meditative state. A faint, flame-like aura surrounded his body as he delved in to a deep meditation. Day turned to night and night slowly turned to day. Fid remained in his meditative state for three days.

During those three days, Fid's heart, mind, body, and soul aligned to become one. There was no more discord. His mind was not clouded. He was starting to understand the power that laid dormant within his body. The aura that surrounded his body for three days dissipated. He opened his eyes as he took a deep breath and exhaled as if letting out the troubles that burdened his life. Fid saw that Sundancer was still patiently waiting for him by the tree where he had left him. Fid jumped down from the rock in which he was perched and walked towards Sundancer with a smile on his face.

"You are a very patient horse, Sundancer," he reached in to the saddle satchel and pulled out an apple to feed Sundancer. His ears then twitched. Within a few moments Fid heard a twig snap. He drew his blade as he turned toward the sound. In the bushes, he found a pair of bright amber eyes watching him. He then drew his other blade ready to fend off whatever enemy it may be. Then out of the bushes walked a black panther. Fid was puzzled at the fact that he had not seen a panther as long as he has been on Rhydin. What was even more puzzling to Fid was the fact that the panther wore a green collar. Was it someone's pet that wandered away? He sheathed his blades sensing there would be no trouble coming from the panther. Fid turned to mount Sundancer and then heard the panther take a few steps towards him. He turned to face it and found the panther had its head cocked to one side as if it were curious. Fid took a step towards the panther, but it took a step away from Fid as if it were afraid of him. Fid's eyes met with the panther's and held out his hand.

"It is alright. I do not want to harm you. You are too beautiful a creature to harm," he said to the panther with a slight smile. Again the panther cocked its head to one side and began to walk towards Fid. His eyes widened as a glow began to emit from the panther. Slowly the panther transformed into a young woman. Her amber colored eyes met Fid's as she sauntered towards him. In her human form, she kept a few of her panther traits. Her panther ears stuck out from underneath her long, thick black hair. Her tail swayed from side to side as she strolled towards him. Fid was taken aback by the sight of the panther turning into a radiant young woman whose tanned skin seemed to glow as the Sun caressed it. His eyes wandered from hers down her curvaceous body to her long toned legs. She stopped a few feet away from Fid giving him a slight grin. Her beauty shown through even though she wore a tattered and torn rag of a dress that reached down to be just above her knees.

"Thank you. That's very kind of you to say," she gave a bright smile as she looked him up and down. Fid took a few steps back. She stepped forward along with him maintaining eye contact. A grin was still on her face. "You've never seen a were-cat before, have you?" she folded her hands behind her back while curiously tilting her head to the side. Fid shook his head 'no'. His eyes still locked with hers. He could not help but to stare into her hypnotizing eyes. She giggled at Fid's speechlessness. She bit her lower lip exposing her cat-like teeth and took a few steps closer to him, "My name is Maia. What is yours?" Fid forced himself to regain his composure and focused on Maia.

"Fid. My name is Fid," he responded stiffly.

"Fid huh? Well, Fid. You are the first person I have ever seen set on fire and not burn," she smiled referring to Fid's aura while he was in his meditative state.

"I was just merely meditating. It was nothing extraordinary," he gave a shrug of his shoulders.

"Not from what I saw surrounding you," she gave a shake of her head.

"What happened?" he asked with a raised eyebrow.

"For three days, I watched bushes bend, clouds of dirt whirl, and I thought I saw a faint dragon encircle you. Even the most fearsome beasts of the woods cowered. I've never seen anything like it," her eyes brightened and her voice rose higher in pitch as she was growing excited all over again talking about what she witnessed.

"I was in that meditative state for three days?" he was in disbelief that it was even possible. It did not feel as though he were in that state for that period of time. Maia nodded her head. Fid looked down to his hands now feeling the newly arisen energy flowing throughout his body. He felt more in tune with his body and, furthermore, his senses seemed heightened.

"What are you? No other being that I know of has that type of power," she leaned in to him as if examining his face.

"I know what I am now. But it is what I am turning into that I do not know," he closed his fists tightly.

"Well nonetheless, you have something very special," that was when her collar started to glow. Her eyes shot wide and her breathing became rapid and heavy. Fid saw that she was backing away from him and toward the forest.

"What is wrong? Where are you going?" he took a step toward her and reached out his hand to her.

"Um, I really have to get back," her tone was apologetic, yet there was fear in it.

"Get back where?" it seemed to Fid there were dire consequences for her if she did not return at that moment.

"I'm sorry. I have to go. I will meet you another time," she stepped toward him and gave him a light kiss on the cheek, then ran into the forest. Fid watched her leave with the lingering thought of her. He then mounted Sundancer and rode off towards Aero's palace.

Night fell upon Rhydin as Fid reached the stables of the Eastern Palace. He led Sundancer to his pen and bid him goodnight. As he walked towards the palace doors he could not help but to think about Maia. He had never seen a creature quite like her. He thought about her sweet voice and the way she looked at him with those hypnotizing amber eyes. Her long flowing dark hair was like the darkest of nights. The softness and tone of her skin as it was kissed by the Sun. Even her lilac scent lingered with him.

He walked up to his room to find Aero staring out of the window onto the green hills. Fid stopped at the doorway wondering why he was standing there. Aero turned to face Fid with their eyes meeting.

"You have finally returned," a grin on his face.

"Yes, I have," Fid took a few steps into the room. Aero looked him up and down, then gave a wider smile. Fid grew puzzled as to why Aero was smiling, "What are you thinking?". Aero laughed walking to him and placed both hands on his shoulders.

"You have met someone special while you were out in the forest?" a grin was on his face. Fid could only smile in response to Aero's statement.

"I have," he affirmed the statement while pulling a few strands of his dreadlocks from his face.

"Who is she?" Aero asked.

"Her name is Maia. She is what you may call a were-cat. She shifts from being a panther to that of half cat, half human form. She has long, flowing black hair; a very curvaceous body; long toned legs and these hypnotizing amber eyes. I cannot get the image of her eyes off of my mind. When I first laid my eyes upon her, I was entranced as if I were under some sort of spell," he was pacing around his room. Aero chuckled at Fid's infatuation with this woman he spoke of. It reminded him of the first time he met Melina. Aero's smile slowly faded within moments. Fid noticed this and had a confused expression on his face, "There is something else on your mind," Fid observed. Aero nodded his head. "What is it?".

"There is no easy way to tell you this, my friend. These past few days Melina, Paige, and I have been doing much thinking about you. Gathering clues as to where you came from," he folded his hands behind his back attempting to remain calm, but his fingers fidgeted with one another.

"What clues?" Fid asked even more confused.

"That you had one of the Twin Dragon Blades in your possession when you first arrived on Rhydin. That you are half Elf being raised on Earth and that you wear our family crystal around your neck," Aero told him.

"What are you saying?" Fid's body tensed and his breathing gradually grew heavier.

"Let me ask you, do you recall your mother at all? Even if it is the faintest of memories," he asked Fid.

"Only from what my father and my aunt told me," he smiled and continued, "I can just imagine what she was like. She was radiant with beauty; her hair was dark and flowing. Her eyes were crystal blue and if you looked into them, it was as if she were looking deep into your soul," he was smiling as the image of his mother was etched into his mind. Aero watched the expression on Fid's face as it brightened while he thought of what his mother may be like. Aero then walked back toward the window with his head bowed slightly. Fid regained his focus and saw that Aero has gone back to the window.

"What is wrong?" Fid took a few steps toward him.

"Nothing is wrong, my friend. The description of your mother reminds me of my own mother," he turned to face Fid.

"Is that so?" his heart began to quicken in pace.

"Allow me to tell you what happened to my mother. From what I and Paige remember, our father and mother did not have a very happy marriage. They argued quite frequently and most of it was petty. There were times when she would leave the palace and not return for quite some time. This became more frequent until the time she did not come back. I was around the age of seven when my mother had mysteriously left that day. Along with her disappearance one of the Twin Dragon Blades had gone missing, as well as a family crystal. Now, twenty years later you show up wearing the family crystal around your neck, you wield one of the Twin Dragon Blades with great skill and you are an Earth born Elf," his eyes brightened as he told Fid.

"What are you telling me?" Fid could not help his heavy breaths nor the trembling in his muscles.

"This may come as a shock to you my friend and very hard to believe. Paige and I strongly believe that you are our half brother. This would make you an Elf Ruler of Rhydin," he looked into Fid's eyes to show that he truly believed in this. Fid's eyes widened and his jaw dropped.

"I-I do not know what to say. My mind is telling me that this cannot be, but my heart is telling me quite the opposite," Fid walked to his bed and sat on the edge. Aero sat beside him in the chair.

"I know that this is a heavy weight to place upon your shoulders on top of everything else that has transpired in the past few months. But Paige, Melina, and I believed that this would help you piece together your past and to better understand who you are and what you are destined to become," Fid's heart was racing and was breathing heavily almost to the point of losing his breathing. Aero placed a hand on his shoulder, "Would you like time alone to allow this to seep into your mind?" Fid nodded while trying to get his breaths under control. Aero lightly pat him on the shoulder and walked out of the door. Paige was leaning against the opposite wall while Melina was standing next to her with her hands folded, awaiting Aero.

"How did he take the news?" Paige asked in a hushed tone.

"He is in shock as was expected, but we shall see tomorrow," Aero told her.

"We should not expect anything else. When he first arrived, he did not know he has the blood of Cretus flowing through his veins.

He believed himself to be a Half Elf born in a simple village on Earth," Melina said.

"Agreed. He will need time to allow for this to seep in to his mind, heart, and soul," Aero said. Paige nodded her head and they all walked down the hallway leaving Fid sitting on the side of his bed.

In her panther form, Maia ran towards a villa a mile to the northwest of the Woodland Realm. The villa was surrounded by a tall brick wall. There were men who stood on the wall keeping a watchful eye for intruders. One of the men saw Maia and the glowing collar around her neck. One of the guards signaled for the drawbridge to be lowered. Maia ran through the gate and slowly shifted to her human form. A shiver of fear ran up her spine as she saw a tall man standing in the shadows.

"Where have you been?" the man asked in a grim voice.

"I was in the woods, M-Master," Maia responded in a meek voice as her ears flattened against her head.

"You are late," his voice became more stern. The man stepped out of the shadows and toward Maia, who stood in fear of this man. He was not a heavily built man, but he seemed to be massive compared to Maia. His hair and beard were dark. His dark eyes only showed hate and malice.

"I-I know, Master. I lost track of the time and did not see…," Maia's ramble was cut off when she was struck across the face from the man's hand. A tear began to roll down her cheek as she looked back to him.

"I give you a chance to get out of the villa and how do you repay me?! By being late and neglecting your duties!" Maia bent at the knees, cowering from this man. He raised his right hand at her. Each finger on his right hand had a ring on it. There was an oval shaped ring that was larger than the others. The ring glowed brightly and it sent a shock of pain throughout Maia's body. She dropped to her knees, clenching her teeth and ripped at the collar. "Do not ever disobey me again," the man said through his clenched teeth. He lowered his hand and walked away. The pain in Maia's body subsided. She was breathing heavily and began to cry curled up on the stone ground.

A Hero is Needed

Aero and Paige re-visited Fid's room the next day to check on how he fared processing the news that was told to him the previous night. Aero gently knocked on the door. They waited a few moments, but there was no answer. Aero knocked once more only a little harder. Again there was no answer.

"Fid? Are you in there? Paige and I wish to speak with you," Aero drew close to the door. There was no answer, nor was there any sound heard from the room from what Paige and Aero could determine. They looked to one another with puzzled expressions on their faces. Paige tried to turn the doorknob, but it is locked. She took a few steps back and then kicked the door open. They found that Fid was not there. They both gave a heavy sigh.

"We must have scared him off. He is not going to come back," she gave a shake of her head.

"No. He will come back. He needs time to meditate on it," Aero responded.

"And how do you know this, dear Brother?" Paige asked while folding her arms in front of her chest and raising an eyebrow.

"He is not one to run away from a difficult issue. He takes time to come to grips with it. He also left his favorite long coat on the bedpost. He goes nowhere without it. He did not go far Paige, I assure you," he pointed to the bedpost with a smile.

Miles away Fid was meditating once again in the same clearing in the forest he was in before. He was sitting on top of the boulder at the center of the clearing. There was a gentle breeze blowing about the forest. The sun shone upon him and there was a warm aura surrounding him as if he were drawing energy from the Sun. The breeze blew a little harder with pebbles, twigs, and leaves blowing all around him. He was at peace. He cleared his mind so that he may think about what was said to him by Aero. Could it be true that Aero and Paige were his half brother and sister? He never met his mother. He only knew her from what his father told him. He was half elf. His father did give him one half of the Twin Dragon Blades and he did wear the Ruby Crystal around his neck this Elf Family wore. Were these things given to him so they may find each other one day? He took a deep breath and opened his eyes with the warm glow of an aura fading from his body.

"I think I know what I need to do," he thought aloud as he jumped down to the ground below, then strapped the Dragon Blades to his waist. His ears twitched as he heard a rustle in the bushes behind him. He smiled when he recognized the footsteps. "You may come out," he said without looking back. Maia, in panther form, made her way out of the bushes and gradually shifted to her human form. She sauntered to his side. She wrapped her arms around his waist and placed her head on his shoulder. She purred slightly as she rested comfortably against him.

"What is troubling you?" from his somewhat tensed body, she sensed that there was a burden on his mind.

"A big weight has been placed upon my shoulders," he glanced over his shoulder at her.

"Will you tell me what it is?" she looked up at him and saw the heavy weight in his eyes.

"I have just come to find out that I may be a part of a long family line of royalty," he exhaled a deep breath.

"Why so troubled then? That's a very good thing," her eyes brightened and her voice raised with excitement.

"Being in a line such as this is a heavy responsibility. Especially during these times," his voice did not carry the same excitement that hers did.

"But it should not be any trouble for you. You have such great power and, from what I hear, you have skill in leading an army. And with these ears I hear a lot," she pointed to her panther ears. Fid gave a slight chuckle, with Maia sharing in the laugh. "Do I see a smile on that face of yours?" she gently placed her hand on his cheek. They looked into each other's eyes being drawn to one another.

"Come, I have something to show you," he gently took her hand in to his. She took his hand and smiled at him. Fid led her north through the forest. Her collar began to glow, but she did not notice as her attention was solely on Fid.

After walking for a little while, they came to another clearing. At the center of the clearing was a lake. Maia's eyes brightened as she looked upon it. The air around the lake seemed cooler than the rest of the forest. The water of the lake was so clear that one can see to the bottom.

"Let us get to higher ground. I want to show you something," he jumped up to take a hold of the trunk of a redwood and climbed his way towards the top. Maia grinned and shifted to her panther form. She began to climb the redwood clawing her way to the top. They both reached the higher branches and looked out to the vast lake. Fid looked up to the Sun as it approached high noon. Maia shifted back to human form and looked to Fid.

"Why are we up here? What are we looking for?" her ears perked up with intrigue.

"Do you know why this is called Eagle-Eye Lake?" he looked down to her.

"No. Why is it called Eagle-Eye Lake," now her interest was piqued.

"When the Sun hits exactly mid-day every seven days, the water of the lake turns to that of an Eagle's Eye. There is a stone at the exact center of the lake that gives the appearance of the eye's pupil. And the eye looks towards the Northern Mountains," he pointed his finger from the lake to the north, tracing Eagle Eye Lake's sight. Maia's eyes lit up as the Sun hit mid-day. The color of the lake turned yellow and at the center was that stone. The Lake itself was in the shape of an Eagle eye.

"This is so beautiful, Fid. Thank you so much for showing this to me," a bright smile grew on her face and her ears perked up.

"You are welcome. This is the first time I am seeing this sight myself," he turned his head to face her. He then noticed that her collar was glowing brightly.

"Your collar is glowing," his eyebrow furrowed at the troubling glow. She looked down and began to panic. Her breathing became heavy, her eyes widened, and her body tensed and trembled. Fid placed both hands on her shoulders trying to calm her down. He looked into her eyes and asked, "What is wrong? Why are you in such a panic?"

"I-I have to g-get back," even her voice shook as if in fear. She was trembling as she began to descend from the high branches of the redwood. They both reached the ground and Maia tried to run off, but Fid grabbed her by the arm to turn her around to face him. He placed both hands on her shoulders once more to hold her firmly and look into her eyes. She whimpered as she tried to free herself from his grip, "Let me go, let me go. I have to go. I am in big trouble," tears welled in her tightly shut eyes.

"Why are you so afraid?" Fid continued to restrain her. She looked back into his eyes. Panic and distress were in them, her breathing was still heavy but she stopped struggling. She began to calm down with deep breaths.

"This collar tells me that I have to go back," she averted his gaze by looking to the ground.

"You must tell me more, Maia," he did not allow for her to look anywhere else other than his eyes.

"This collar belongs to Duke Thaius," her eyes still averted his as if in shame. Confusion was in his eyes.

"I am a slave to him, Fid!" she finally admitted. "He sends me out for some time and calls me back. That is why I have this damn collar around my neck! And if I don't get back to him soon I will be in a lot of trouble!" she ripped at the collar trying to take it off. She fell to her knees with tears streaming down her face. Fid knelt down to held her close to him. She buried her face in his chest and cried. He gave a comforting kiss on her forehead. "All I need is a champion to save me from this," she said in between sobs. He felt her pain. She was lost in a cruel world. All she knew was pain and suffering. All he could do at that moment was hold her close to him. At least for that moment, she was safe. That was when his ears twitched as an arrow flew toward his head. He caught the arrow by its shaft. His eyes looked up to see six men mounted on horses riding toward the two of them. Both Fid and Maia quickly rose to their feet. Maia hid slightly behind him. The men surrounded Fid and Maia. Five of the men drew and aimed arrows at them both. One of the men wore all black with a dark velvet cape. There was a ring on every finger of his right hand. One in particular stood out to Fid. It was larger than the others. He wore it on his left middle finger. It was a smooth, oval shaped ring and it glowed a deep emerald. He had a broad sword strapped to his left hip. Fid could tell that this man was tall, maybe even taller than himself. Fid took a few steps toward the man with Maia holding a tight grip on his arm.

"Duke Thaius, I presume?" Fid addressed the man. The man dismounted his horse and took a few steps toward Fid.

"You presume correctly," he responded in an arrogant tone. He then looked to Maia who still gripped Fid's arm and hid behind him.

"Maia, it's time for you to return to your duties," he reached out his hand to her. Maia pulled back and looked up at Fid. Fid looked back at her and sensed her fear.

"It appears that she does not wish to return with you," Fid looked from the frightened Maia to Duke Thaius. Thaius glared at Maia and then to Fid.

"Oh, she will come back with me," he growled. He pointed his ring towards the collar. The ring glowed brighter as a course of pain surged through her body. She writhed in pain on the ground as the pain increasingly grew worse. Fid immediately dropped to his knees beside her and tried to remove the collar by force, but with no success.

"Stop, you are hurting her!" Fid demanded.

"I will only stop if she agrees to come back with me," no remorse was on Duke Thaius's face as he continued to inflict pain on Maia. He looked back to Maia who is still in excruciating pain.

"Stop!" Fid pleaded. Thaius stopped the hold he had on the collar. Fid helped Maia up to her feet. She hugged him tightly and Fid held her firmly. "He will hurt me Fid. He will beat me for not going back to him when I was supposed to. He is a tyrant. Please, help me." she whispered her plea to him. One of Thaius' men grabbed her from Fid and placed restraints on her wrists. The man then hoisted her up to Thaius' horse. Fid watched Maia as there was a look of fear on her face. Thaius glared at Fid and motioned for his men to ride back to his villa. As Thaius and his men rode off, from thirty yards away Maia yelled to Fid, "Help me!"

Fid ran as fast as he could to give chase to them. He whistled for his horse, Sundancer. Moments later, Sundancer raced out of the bushes as he caught up to Fid. Fid grabbed hold of the saddle and swung himself onto Sundancer's back. They rode off in chase of Thaius and his men.

Maia continued to look back to see if Fid was in pursuit after them, but did not see him. Thaius looked back at Maia out of the corner of his eye and gave an evil snicker.

"You think he is coming after you, don't you?" he mocked. She did not answer but continued to look back. "Why would he come after a ragged tabby cat like yourself?" he sneered. She lowered her head and sobbed.

"My lord!" one of Thaius' men yelled for him.

"What is it now?!" his patience had grown thin since he had to travel outside of the walls of his villa in search of his property.

"That Elf is chasing us," he looked back. Thaius looked back as well to see Fid chasing them.

"Take care of him," he ordered. His henchmen slowed up and turned around to charge toward Fid. Fid's anger swelled within him. He took aim with the Bracelet of Ra. As the men drew within twenty yards of him Fid threw unleashed the bracelet's power at them, killing three of the five. Fid drew both the Twin Dragon Blades and as he rode passed the men he slashed at their necks, decapitating them. He then sheathed his blades and continued his pursuit.

As Thaius and Maia rode northeast, toward the edge of the forest, they could see the wall surrounding his villa. He looked back and saw that Fid was still alive. Maia looked back as well. Her eyes brightened and a smile came across her face. Thaius growled and signaled for the men that guarded the edge of the forest to be on guard. There were watch posts built among the lower branches of the redwood trees. These watch posts were where men who worked for Duke Thaius watched the comings and goings of those venturing through the woods.

Fid saw there were men in the trees so he leapt from Sundancer to the trees. He jumped from branch to branch with his blades drawn. The men were ready to ambush Fid, but saw only Sundancer ride by. They looked to one another in confusion, unaware that Fid was in the trees as well. One by one the men were cut down by Fid's violent slashes. Fid jumped from the trees and landed back on Sundancer and rode out of the forest toward the wall surrounding the villa. He could see that he was catching up to Thaius and Maia.

Thaius looked back once more, as did Maia, to see that Fid was still alive and was gaining ground on them. Maia squealed in excitement and Thaius growled once more and signaled for the guard at the gate to fire a volley of arrows at the intruder. The draw bridge of the wall lowered as Thaius approached. Fid saw the volley of arrows and, as best he could, encouraged Sundancer to ride faster.

"Come on Sundancer. I believe you can make it," Sundancer rode as hard as he could but began to slow down as he was visibly growing fatigued. Fid continued to plead with Sundancer. Fid closed his eyes and took a deep breath. He focused his energy as a red aura surrounded him. The energy flowing through Fid began to course through Sundancer. Sundancer reared up to his hind legs and took off faster and harder than before.

The men on the top of the wall aimed their arrows as they saw Fid and his horse approaching. A red glow emitted from the hooves of Sundancer as a flame ignited. The men on the wall released their arrows towards Fid. Fid held his breath and braced himself as the arrows drew closer. Sundancer eyes flared a fiery red as his body was engulfed in flames with a sudden burst.

"Sundancer?" Fid knew not how Sundancer came to be engulfed in flames. It seemed he was of a rare, mystical breed. The arrows turned to cinders as they drew close to Sundancer and Fid. As they drew within thirty yards of the wall the bridge began to close. Fid stood on Sundancer's back and told him to ride harder and to wait for his order. They came within fifteen yards and Fid told Sundancer to jump as far as he could into the air. Sundancer leapt into the air and, like a boulder being launched from a catapult, Fid launched himself in to the air at the peak of Sundancer's jump. While in the air, Fid conjured a ball of flame in the palm of his hand and threw it at the men at the wall killing them in an eruption of fire. With a few feet to spare, he made it inside of the walls of Thaius's villa. Fid slid down the drawbridge. Seeing Thaius's men with arrows aimed and ready to fire, Fid launched himself from the drawbridge to flip over the men. While in the air, he twisted himself to throw fireballs at their backs to scorch their armor and flesh. Fid landed on his feet, then ran in search of Thaius and Maia.

Fid ran along the cobblestone pathways that weaved through the villa's yard of lush, green grass and small gardens of a multitude of fragrant flowers. Fid drew close to the three story villa when he was beginning to sense Thaius was near. Fid drew both blades to prepare to guard himself. As he entered the villa, he saw no sign of Maia or Thaius. Fid left the foyer and entered one of the hallways. He searched each of the rooms that he came upon in that long hallway. His ears then twitched warning him of impeding danger. As he turned to his right, a spear was flying straight for his chest. Fid pivoted to one side to avoid the spear. Thaius, with sword in hand, charged straight for Fid. He saw Thaius lunging at him and did the same with both Dragon Blades ready. Fid and Thaius clashed. The sound of swords was heard throughout the halls. Sparks rose from the swords as they made contact. Thaius blocked each of Fid's attacks. He grinned because Fid had not landed a strike on him. Thaius threw a kick to his chest throwing him onto his back. Thaius laughed mocking Fid, "This is pathetic. Aren't you the same Elf who killed Brakus? From the way you are fighting it wouldn't seem so". Fid's rage within him grew, his eyes flared, and he gripped his blades tighter, kipping up to his feet. He took a fighting stance and focused his energy to his swords. They glowed brightly red and then burst into flame. Thaius' eyes widened and a scowl formed on his face. Frustration built within Thaius as he saw Fid growing stronger and more focused. Fid lunged towards Thaius with one blade which Thaius blocked, but then attacked with the other slashing his arm. Thaius jumped backwards holding the wound and then glared at Fid. His skin was charred from the intense heat of the blade's flame. Thaius growled and rushed to pull a rope that hung from the ceiling of the hallway to sound the villa alarm. Soldiers rushed in and formed a wall between Thaius and Fid. Thaius fled while the soldiers stood on guard with their spears, swords, and battle axes pointing at Fid. Fid's eyes continued to glow brightly as he sheathed the blades. Fid walked toward the soldiers. His fist glowed red and slowly began to be engulfed in flames. The soldiers charged towards him. As they came within ten yards of Fid, he threw his flame engulfed fist into the floor. A wave of flames rushed towards the soldiers engulfing them. The soldiers scattered screaming as they were set ablaze. Fid drew his blade as he was walking toward the scattering soldiers and cut them down as he walked passed them.

Fid walked further into the villa in search of Thaius and Maia. He drew his other blade knowing that Thaius was lurking about. Slowly walking further into the villa, Fid neither heard or sensed Thaius' presence. Fid became weary and anxious. He knew not where he would attack from. He entered the dining hall of the villa. At the center was a long, polished wooden table with at least a dozen wooden armchairs with high backs set around the table. Several tall candles were set along the table in line with one another. There was an elaborate floral arrangement that was set as the centerpiece. As he investigated further in to the dining hall, his ears twitched sensing an arrow flying toward him but it was too late. The arrow pierced his right shoulder. He immediately took it out and suddenly the room around him began to spin. He felt dizzy and his vision became distorted. Fid violently slashed at the air around him hoping to hit something since he could not see clearly. Thaius rushed to Fid's blind side and kicked him in the jaw. Fid fell to the ground and Thaius gave several crushing kicks to his ribs. At this point, Fid dropped his blades, and was unable to defend himself. Thaius picked Fid up to his feet and repeatedly punched him in the ribs and jaw. Fid was then thrown into a wall leaving an impression in it. Thaius slowly walked towards Fid with his sword drawn.

He gave an evil laugh as he triumphantly stood over Fid, "You really thought you could defeat me, didn't you?" Fid lifted his eyes to look at Thaius raising his blade to give the final blow. As Thaius' blade was about to strike, an arrow was shot through his wrist. Thaius screamed in agonizing pain. He then looked to where the arrow was shot from. Maia, with bow in hand and a short sword and quiver of arrows strapped to her hip, stood there glaring at Thaius.

"You?!" his eyes widened out of anger at her betrayal. Maia drew and aimed another arrow. Thaius started to walk toward her.

"I would not take another step if I were you," a growl was deep in her throat. Thaius gave an evil grin and aimed his ring at the collar around Maia's neck. She fired another arrow, this time through his right wrist not allowing him to use the power of the ring. He yelled in pain once more. He pulled both arrows out of his wrists and took several more steps toward her with a hand out to reach her. Maia fired another arrow, this time through his knee. Although he was limping he continued to endure the pain and stalked her. She released several more arrows at his shoulders, thighs, and stomach. His strength was failing from the massive amount of blood he was losing. He could not find the will power to pull the numerous arrows out of his body. As he staggered toward her, she lowered her bow. "I am warning you for the last time Thaius, Do not come any closer," she said sternly. He came within a few feet of her and tried to grab her neck. "Wrong move you bastard," she backed up from his hand and spun. While spinning she drew the short sword and slashed at Thaius' neck cutting his head from his shoulders.

Sheathing the blade, she rushed to Fid and looked over his wounds. Blood trickled from his nose and mouth. There were gashes under his eyes. Fid was barely conscious. Maia knelt by his side.

"Oh my gosh! Fid, are you ok?! Please, say something!" in her panic, she did not know what to do for Fid. Maia got up to her feet and frantically looked around to see what to do.

The only thing Maia could do at the moment was to turn to her panther form and to carry Fid and the Dragon Blades on her back through the Villa, then outside to the draw bridge and get Sundancer to carry him the rest of the way. She transformed into her panther form and maneuvered Fid onto her back along with the Dragon Blades and carried him. It was a labor for her to carry Fid's dead weight on her back, especially since Fid was a bit larger than she was. Once she reached the bridge she placed Fid against the wall and transformed to her human form. She found the lever that let the bridge down and pulled it. At the entrance of the villa, Sundancer awaited them. Sundancer knelt down as Maia dragged Fid over to him and lifted him onto his back. Maia leapt onto Sundancer's back and they rode through the forest on their way to the Eastern Palace.

Unlikely Alliance

Fid finally woke from his unconscious state several days after invading Duke Thaius's villa to rescue Maia. As he opened his eyes and became more aware of where he was, he heard the light breathing of someone at the foot of the bed. He slightly raised up to see Maia lying there, curled up in a little ball sleeping with her tail happily swaying from side to side. Fid gave a little groan as he sat up more in the bed. Maia's ears perked up when she heard Fid's movements. She immediately woke up and her eyes brightened when she saw that he was well. She pounced on him and gave a firm hug. He returned the embrace and they laid there in each other's arms.

Maia left Fid's room after a few hours so that he could rest from the wounds he suffered from Thaius. She made her way downstairs towards the kitchen to get something for him to eat. On her way down the hall, she found Paige sitting on one of the Palace balconies reading some documents. Paige looked up from her readings at Maia. Maia had been at the foot of Fid's bed while he was recovering. Seeing her out of his room seemingly meant that he was awake. She stood up with anxious eyes, "How is he?".

"He has healed completely. He just needs to rest," relief was in Maia's eyes and her smile.

"I am glad. I was worried," Paige breathed a sigh of relief.

"I was worried as well. It's strange though," Maia tilted her head curiously.

"What is?" Paige knew that Fid was ever growing stronger. She wondered what Maia witnessed.

"The poison that Thaius used on Fid should have killed him within minutes," Maia was still grasping that Fid survived the poison's effects.

"What kind of poison was it?" Paige furrowed her eyebrows at the mention of poison.

"The poison comes from the pasai," Maia shuddered at the mention of the snake.

"Are you saying the poison came from one of the rarest and most poisonous snakes on either Earth and Rhydin?" disbelief was in Paige's eyes.

"Yes," Maia nodded. Paige sat down and placed her face in her hands. Maia's ears flattened against her head as she took a few steps toward her.

"How is this possible? Not that I am ungrateful that he's alive, but he should not be moving let alone breathing," Paige sat and rested her head in her hands while attempting to figure out what was happening with Fid.

"There must be something special about him," the answer was simple to Maia.

"You are not too far from the truth," Paige looked up to her.

"What are you saying?" Maia curiously tilted her head to the side. Paige gave a sigh, "There have been events occurring that lead me, my brother Aero, and his wife Melina to believe that the next Dragon Lord is in fact Fid". Maia's ears perked up and her eyes widened. She placed her hand over her mouth in shock, "So you are saying that Fid can potentially be the one to lead a Legion of Dragons and their Knights?"

"Indeed," Paige nodded.

"Well this is good. We need him especially during these times on Rhydin," Maia's voice brightened with excitement.

"We know. But we do not know if he is mentally prepared for the task that lies ahead for him. There are many trials he must face in order to reach his full potential. Thus far, he has overcome minute challenges. There are far more perilous journeys and obstacles that he must endure," Paige's voice became more grim knowing what Fid could face.

"When would he be ready?" Maia asked. Paige looked up at Maia and paused for a few moments, "We do not know," she sighed. Maia dropped her head with her ears flattening.

Fid was sitting on the side of his bed with his head in his hands. There had been so much that transpired since his arrival on Rhydin. Was it too much for him to handle? What else lied in front of him? Would he be ready for it? His thoughts were interrupted by someone knocking on the door. Fid rose from the bed and opened the door. He found Aero standing there with his hands folded behind his back. Fid let him in.

"How are you feeling my friend?" he asked.

"Aero, I prefer that you call me Brother, not friend," Aero's eyes brightened and a wide smile grew on his face knowing that Fid accepted his lineage. In his excitement, Aero gave a warm embrace to Fid.

"So you have come to realize the truth," Aero could not help but to continue to smile.

"I have. Everything that has led me here to Rhydin happened for a reason. I not only think that it was to meet you, Paige, and Melina, but I believe that I have a much larger role to play here," Fid looked over his shoulder to the window looking out to the reset of the land.

"That you do my brother, that you do," Aero nodded with a smile. At that moment, Maia and Paige joined them. Maia walked to Fid's side. She locked her arm with his and placed her head on his shoulder. Aero saw the way Maia behaved around Fid and gave a grin, glancing to Paige. She noticed the same thing and returned the glance to Aero.

"Dear Sister, I believe Fid has something to tell you," Aero looked to her Paige.

"What is it Fid?" Paige looked to him anticipating his news.

"Tell her what you just told me," Aero encourages. Fid turned to face Paige and took a few steps toward her.

"Paige, I have come to the realization that I am in fact your half-brother," a big smile appeared on her face and she gave a warm, welcoming embrace to him. Aero then joined and embraced them both. Maia's tail happily swayed from side to side seeing the love shown.

Hours later, Fid and Maia met Aero, Melina, and Paige in the study. Maia took a seat on a couch that was on the opposite side of the room. She motioned for Fid to sit next to her. When he sat, she moved to be right next to him and curled up to him. Lieutenant Demus walked into the room a few minutes later and leaned against the wall.

"I have called this meeting to put in to action our next move in this war," Aero declared.

"What do we intend to do, Brother?" Paige had leaned forward in her seat.

"We cannot face the powers of Sekmet on our own. We need help from other races to aid us," Aero looked to those that gathered.

"And who do you intend on calling upon?" Aero looked to Fid and sighed.

"I intend on first calling upon Lord Zell. He is the ruler of the Vampire Coven in the Southeast Province," Fid leaned forward in the couch with clenched teeth and a growing anger within him.

"You would call upon Vampires to help us Aero?" his voice was stern as he stood from the couch.

"Fid, you must put your personal feelings aside. Lord Zell rules a large Coven on Rhydin. He would be a great asset to our cause," Aero met Fid's aggressive glare with a calm spirit that shone through his eyes.

"Fid, not all Vampires are corrupt like Brakus. It is rare for Lord Zell to deal with outsiders, but it has been said that he is a fair Ruler," Melina saw the fire in his eyes. It would seem Fid had not put the incident with the vampires in the past.

"Murderous creatures," Fid mumbled under his breath as he sat back down next to Maia who held a concerned expression on her face.

"Maia, Fid, and myself will go to negotiate an alliance with Lord Zell and his Coven. Meanwhile Lieutenant Demus and Paige will go to Earth and find the clan of Rangers that live in the Mountains. Melina will stay here at the Palace to protect its walls," Aero looked to each person as he revealed his plan.

"Understood sir," Demus nodded and gave his salute.

"Once we accomplish our missions, we will return here," all voice their understanding to Aero's plan.

"If Demus and I are successful in finding the Rangers on Earth, where will they lodge?" Aero paused at Paige's question.

"The town of Belnar has built huts and houses for allied soldiers," he remembered a pact the Elf Kingdom made with the humans of the Mainland. In this pact, it stated that each kingdom would provide lodging for soldiers and citizens if it were needed. "The town is just over the northern hill".

"Alright then," Paige rose from her seat, as did Zidane and Maia.

"May the Heavens be with us on our journeys," Aero said as everyone left the room to prepare themselves for this mission. Fid was in his bed chamber strapping on his armor as Maia walked in to the room. She was holding a hand carved bow in one hand. On one hip she wore a quiver of arrows and on the other hip a short sword was strapped. Her thick black hair was pulled and tied into a pony tail. Fid smiled as he strapped on his blades to his waist, then walked over to her. He gently placed his hands on her shoulders sensing that she was nervous. Her finger was repeatedly tapping her outer thigh.

"Are you nervous?" his voice was calm as he looked in to her amber eyes.

"Yes," she continued to tap her outer thigh with her finger.

"Do not be. There is nothing to fear. I and Aero will be there with you. We will protect you if it is needed. I owe you my life for saving me back at the Villa," he reassured her. She smiled and embraced him.

"You do owe me," she giggled then gave a light kiss on his cheek.

The five departed from the palace on horseback. Paige and Lieutenant Demus rode northwest to the Keshnarian ruins while

Aero, Fid, and Maia headed south to form an alliance with the Vampire Coven. Melina stood at the Eastern Palace gate to bid them good luck in their journeys. The Coven was less than a two day's ride. Day turned to night and night turned to day as the trio rode on toward the Vampire Coven. As the Sun set behind the Western Mountains, the three drew closer to the Mansion. As they drew closer, Fid's mind began to wander to various thoughts and it eventually slipped in to what seemed to be another memory. What he saw was of the Great War a millennium ago. He saw the silhouettes of three figures on a hill overlooking the carnage that went on below them. He could make out that there was a figure that wore armor and carried a lance and on its wrist was the Bracelet of Ra; another figure wore a cloak and carried a Scepter and there was a female figure who wore a gold Necklace. The Scepter and the Necklace were reminiscent of the Bracelet of Ra. It was as if they were forged by the same craftsman. Despite clearly seeing the objects, he could not make out the faces of the figures who wield those items. Fid soon regained his focus and found they fifty yards from the mansion.

Night fell upon Rhydin as a thick fog rolled in to hover over the ground. There was an dark, eerie feeling that hung in the air that sent shivers up and down Maia's back. The spires of the mansion were tall and menacing. There were stone statues of gargoyles around the roof of the mansion. Aero, Fid, and Maia rode to the arched wooden door and dismounted their horses. Aero walked to the door and used the iron knocker that was in the shape of a horned demon's head. A few moments passed before the door opened. It was answered by a young woman. Her skin was dark, her eyes were ice cold blue and her hair was straight and dark. She wore a corset with a long, form fitting skirt. Her cold eyes glanced over Aero and Maia. When they fell upon Fid, she gave a devilish grin revealing her sharp fangs as she licked them.

"What is your business here?" her voice was dark, yet soothing as if attempting to entice Fid.

"We wish to speak with Lord Zell," Aero folded his hands behind his back.

"Is he expecting you?" her voice was stern when she addressed Aero.

"No, he is not," Aero responded with a slight shake of his head.

"I cannot help you then. Lord Zell does not like unexpected visitors," she was closing the door until Fid took a forceful grip on the door.

"It is urgent that we speak with him," Fid said forcefully, looking deeply into her eyes. Her cold gaze was weakened by the fire in Fid's eyes. Her grin returned to her face as she licked her fangs.

"Very well, follow me," she turned to lead them in to the mansion. The trio followed this female vampire further into the mansion. They walked down a hallway that was lined with portraits of other vampires. She led them through a series of corridors which finally led to what seemed to be the throne room. On the opposite side of the room there was a man sitting atop the throne. His skin was darker than Fid's. He had long black hair that pulled back in to a ponytail. He wore dark clothing with a dark cape and held a scepter. His dark, cold eyes fell upon the three that entered the room.

"Sonia, who are these three and what business do they have in my Mansion?" he asked coldly. Sonia did nothing but bowed her head in reverence to him. Aero stepped forward and answered, "I am Aero, Elf Ruler of the Eastern Province. This is my brother Fid and our friend, Maia. We come with urgent business Lord Zell".

"And what business would that be?" he sat forward in the throne.

"We wish to form an alliance with you. During these times of war, our people should be united to confront our common foes. By ourselves we cannot ward off these forces, but together we can put an end to this war," it was clear that Aero's reasoning was conjured to convince the vampire lord.

"Why should the Vampire Nation provide aid to the likes of the Elves? The Elf Empire did nothing when the mongrel scum known as the lycans rose against us. No one came to answer our calls for aid as they overran our Province and killed many. Where was the Elf Empire when those beasts rebelled against us? There was no Alliance then, why should there be one now?" venom was in his words. Although the battle between the vampires and lycans happened years ago, it seemed that Zell did not forgive the Elf Empire.

"If we do not band together, Sekmet will surely destroy each of us to take over all of Rhydin. As a single nation, we are weak against his forces, but together we are stronger," Aero stepped towards Zell showing that he would not easily be turned away.

"You will need more than our two armies combined to fight the forces of Sekmet. Take our forces combined and multiply it by ten. That is how strong Sekmet's forces are. We would have no chance in stopping him," Zell's stubbornness was clear.

"We do have a fighting chance. We have the wielder of the Twin Dragon Blades, the Bearer of the Red Dragon Essence," Aero presented Fid to the vampire lord. Zell stood from the throne and stepped down toward them. Zell's cold eyes looked Fid over. He then grinned and laughed. Aero, Fid, and Maia looked at each other in confusion.

"Why do you laugh?" Fid was not pleased of Zell's amusement. Zell then made eye contact with him and stepped closer to him.

"You really think you are ready to take on the responsibility and the power the Bearer of the Dragon Essence possesses? Are you ready to face the perils and trials that you are to face once you have reached your full and true powers? Are you ready to lead an army of ten thousand into battle against the one who is so evil that hell itself rejected him?" Zell was circling Fid like a vulture stalking a carcass. Fid paused for a moment before answering, he looked and met Zell's eyes, "When the time comes, I will". Zell chuckled at his response, then turned to walk back to his throne and sat.

"You have a great spirit Fid and you are brave. Perhaps too brave," Zell leaned back in to the throne. "Nonetheless, these virtues will not help you in the fight against him".

"Will you help us?" Aero stepped toward Zell. Zell took a deep breath, "I am afraid I cannot provide you with the army of vampires that you seek".

"Why not?" Maia burst out. Zell looked at Maia, "Vampires cannot walk during the day. Our skin will burn if the sun's rays touch our skin," he leaned forward in the throne.

"Oh. Right," her ears flattened against her head sheepishly and took a few steps backwards so that she stood behind Fid.

"But there is one I can send with you. He is the only Day Walker among us. He has led a myriad of battles against Sekmet's Trolls that dwell in the southern caves. He will be an essential asset to your cause," Zell told them.

"Where can we find him?" Aero asked.

"Sonia will take you to him," he motioned for Sonia to take them.

"Thank you, Lord Zell," Fid respectfully bowed his head to him. Zell slightly bowed his head in response. The three then followed Sonia out of the room.

"They will need all of the help they can muster," Zell muttered to himself.

Sonia led the trio down a different set of corridors. There were suits of ancient armor, various types of swords, and numerous other weapons in glass casings and others were mounted on the walls. As they passed by, Fid was fascinated with the various types and designs of the weapons.

"Lord Zell collected these weapons from the enemies that he conquered," Sonia gave a graceful sweep of her hand and arm to present Lord Zell's trophies.

"It appears that you and Lord Zell would get along, Brother," Fid looked to Aero with a grin. Aero responded with a small laugh. As Sonia led the three through the corridors of the Mansion, they passed several Vampires who lingered in the halls talking to one another. As the unfamiliar trio passed by with Sonia leading them, they stopped in their conversations and gazed upon them, but mostly at Fid. The four then came to an arched wooden door with an iron door handle.

Sonia opened the door and led the trio in. There were aisles upon aisles of bookshelves fully stocked with varying books. The walls were even shelved with books and various documents. They evidently were led into the library of the Mansion. They followed Sonia down several aisles to an area where desks and chairs were set. At a desk next to the bay window sat a young man. His skin was dark just like that of Zell's and Sonia's. Their skin was not of typical vampires who normally had pale skin due to the lack of sun caressing their skin. His hair was short, dark, and slicked back. The most noticeable features were his cold, piercing gray eyes. He was studying some documents that were laid out in front of him. Sonia motioned for the three to stay where they were as she approached the young man. She spoke into his ear and he looked up from his parchments and studied the trio who stood before him. His eyes then fell upon the Bracelet of Ra that Fid wore. He rose from his chair and walked over to Fid with his eyes fixated upon the bracelet. Taking Fid's wrist, he examined the bracelet closely. The young man then looked to Fid and then back to the Bracelet, "Is this the Bracelet of Ra?".

"It is," Fid responded with a raised eyebrow. Fid found the behavior of this young vampire a bit odd. The young man stood in awe that his assumption was confirmed. His eyes were widened in disbelief, yet there was a growing excitement in them.

"The bearer of the Bracelet of Ra stands before me. This is a once in a lifetime honor," his excitement was even heard in his voice. Aero, Fid, and Maia did nothing but looked at one another and then to the young vampire. "Please, excuse me. The excitement has overwhelmed me. Allow me to introduce myself. My name is Kulla," he finally composed himself enough to bow his head. Aero the stepped forward and bowed his as well.

"I am Aero, the Elf Ruler of the Eastern Province of Rhydin. This is Maia and my brother, Fid," both Maia and Fid stepped forward and bowed their head as Aero introduced them.

"Am I correct in saying that you are here in need of help?" Kulla folded his arms in front of his chest.

"Yes," Aero nodded his head. "We need assistance in the war against Sekmet. Our forces are not strong enough".

"I am afraid Lord Zell's forces cannot help you. For you see, vampires do not fare well in sunlight," Kulla gestured toward his kin that were scattered throughout the library.

"Yes, he informed us of this, but he said that you can help us," Fid stepped toward Kulla. "Lord Zell also said that you are a Day Walker," Fid's eyes met his cold, gray eyes.

"Lord Zell is correct in saying that I am the only Day Walker. And possibly the only one in this mansion who can best help you," Kulla's gaze never left Fid's.

"Will you help us?" Maia asked.

"I will under one condition," Kull's eyes departed from Fid's to look at the young, were-cat woman with a grin.

"And what would that be?" there was contempt in Fid's voice.

"That when we search for the other Ancient Relics, that I obtain the Scepter of Osiris," Kulla's gaze grew colder at Fid's tone.

"*When* we search for the Ancient Relics? Why is it a need that we search for them?!" Fid objected with furrowed eyebrows and angered voice.

"These Relics are the most powerful weapons on Rhydin and Earth. You wearing the Bracelet of Ra set the chain reaction of the Relics reappearing. If these weapons fall into the wrong hands, like Sekmet's, both worlds are in grave danger," Kulla was calm in his response despite Fid's aggression.

"Did you know of this Aero," Fid turned his eyes to Aero.

"I did not," Aero gave a shake of his head. Fid sighed and looked back to Kulla. "How do we find the other Relics?".

"It is said the Necklace of Isis appears every high noon at the bottom of Eagle Eye Lake every seven days once the chain reaction has been put into motion. And then after the Necklace has been found, the Bracelet of Ra will glow and show the way to the Scepter of Osiris," it was as if Kulla was reciting a prophecy.

"Seven days you said?" Maia's panther ears perked up at the mention of the Necklace of Isis.

"Yes," Kulla nodded to her.

"Fid and I were at the Lake five days ago and it glowed," she recalled when Fid took her in to the trees to look down upon the lake.

"That means that the Necklace of Isis will reappear at high noon in two days," there urgency in Kulla's voice.

"We must leave at once," Aero said as he felt Paige attempting to make her presence known within his mind. He placed his forefinger to his temple to focus on her voice.

"*We have run in to a bit of trouble, dear Brother,*" Paige's voice resonated in his mind.

"*What is it?*" concern grew in Aero's mind when Paige spoke of trouble.

"*A contingent of Orcs are crossing the Woodland Realm and is heading toward the Eastern Palace. We will hold them off as long as we can, but I do not know for how long,*" anxiety was in her voice.

"*I will meet you at the edge of the woods,*" he replied.

"What is wrong?" Fid saw Aero with his fingers to his temple and was focusing on something.

"Paige and Demus have run in to a contingent of Orcs marching toward the Eastern Palace. I will meet them and give aid," he turned to face Fid and Maia.

"We will help," Fid heard stories of the Orcs. They were brutes known for their size and strength. It was said they rivaled the Lycans in their stature and strength. They wore thick armor and wielded heavy weaponry.

"No. You must find the Ancient Relics. We will meet you in the palace of the Western Province" Aero turned to leave the library, but then turned his head to add, "Your palace".

"My palace?" Fid asked as if he did not understand.

"Yes, your palace. But you must not linger here. You three do not have much time before the Necklace of Isis reappears," Aero urged. Kulla began to gather some documents in a pouch and strapped his broad sword to his hip. He threw on his long dark coat that was draped over the chair. Before leaving the room Kulla turned to give Sonia an embrace. Zell was waiting for them at the main entrance of the Mansion. Kulla placed his fist to his heart and bowed his head.

"This is a mission of much urgency Kulla. You are to help these people save this world and Earth from the spread of Sekmet's tyranny. This Coven is counting on you, Kulla. You must not fail," Zell placed his hands upon Kulla's shoulders.

"I will not fail, Father," Kulla's confidence showed in his eyes and was heard in his voice.

"I know you will not," Zell gave a proud smile, "Your horse is waiting outside for you".

"We thank you for your assistance, Lord Zell," Aero's thankfulness was heard in his voice. Although they did not get an army, they did forge an alliance through Kulla. Zell nodded and opened the door for the four to leave. Aero, Kulla, Fid and Maia mounted their horses and rode off. Aero rode north toward the east edge of the Forest as Fid, Maia, and Kulla rode toward Eagle Eye Lake in search of the Necklace of Isis.

The Search Begins

It was in the far southwest, in the recesses of the Western Mountains, where a shroud of darkness hovered and a giant wall had been erected. It stood between the rest of Rhydin and a dark Fortress that stood three hundred yards from the iron wall. It stood tall with a menacing spire. On the dark, barren land between the Fortress and the wall were rows upon rows of ragged tents where Orcs slept, snarled, and fought one another. A brutish breed they were. An Orc who stood less than six feet off of the ground was considered to be a runt. Their bodies were muscular and seemed to have been carved from granite. They were known for their strength as well as their uncanny sense of smell, making them ideal trackers. Their ability to hear and see great distances paralleled that of the Elves. Their ears came to points like the Elves. Their green skin made them excellent for forest ambushes. Several of these fully armored and heavily armed Orcs patrolled the top of the iron wall to warn those within the walls of any impending attacks. Their dark eyes did not waver from the land beyond the wall. The Orcs were not the only race of creature keeping a watchful eye. Above the Orcs flew winged demons. An unnatural breed they were and were believed to be the result of dark summoning. Their eyes were yellow and lidless. Horns grew from the sides of their heads. Their hands and arms were mangled and claws grew from their gnarled fingers. They grew tails three feet long and spikes grew at the ends. Their skin was scaly and rough.

At the center of this dark Fortress laid the throne room where the Dark Tyrant dictated his orders to his underlings. Very little light was let in to this chamber. It was dark and unwelcoming. Coats of demonic armor and weapons were displayed on the walls. The heads of various Dragons lined the opposite wall. These Dragon heads were trophies of his Dragon Hunts. In the middle of the chamber, there was a throne crafted from marble. In front of the throne, there were four silhouettes kneeling with their heads lowered. These four seemed to be the Generals of the Orc army. One silhouette belonged to a tall, slender, short haired woman. Her eyes were to the stone floor. The three others were male. One was fully armored with twin sickled blades strapped to his waist. His crimson eyes were to the floor as well. There was another heavily armored male who wielded twin maces. His head was lowered in reverence. The other male was the largest of the three that knelt before the throne. He wore no armor and carried a large war hammer. Before them was the dark, silhouette of the heavily armor tyrant. He sat upon the throne with malice in his eyes. A thick, dark aura fumed from his very being.

"The Elves have been a thorn in my side for far too long," discontent was in his dark voice. "I want the Ancient Relics to be in my possession so that I can destroy them all in one fell swoop," he growled. "You are to take a platoon of Orc to go to Eagle Eye Lake and retrieve the Necklace of Isis," he ordered the woman. She nodded her head at what she was to do. "I have no doubt the Elves will attempt to get their hands on it as well. That means they will have the Bracelet of Ra in their possession as well. Kill them and take the Bracelet," the woman once more nodded. "Your eyes will see where the Bracelet of Ra will show the location of the Scepter of Osiris. Go there immediately," the Tyrant ordered the red eyed male. He nodded at this orders from his master. "And you two...," the Tyrant spoke to the other fully armored male and the largest of them. "You both will lead attacks on the Eastern and Western Palaces. Weaken their forces. Take the Palaces from them. Drive them out!" the Tyrant slammed his fist on the arm of his throne. Both of them nodded their heads. "Eradicate the Elves," the Tyrant growled.

"Yes, Lord Sekmet," the four said in unison.

Without stopping, the trio rode through the night and a better part of the next day without resting. Fid, Maia, and Kulla drew closer to Eagle Eye Lake where, at the bottom, they hoped to find the Necklace of Isis. A fog rolled in along the floor of the forest. The air was cool and crisp. The morning sun shone through the forest canopy. They had yet to reach the lake. The trio had a ways to go before they reached their goal.

The sun slowly climbed the sky as the morning faded away and noon approached. Fid, Maia, and Kulla reached the lake and dismounted their horses. Kulla looked up to the sun to see where it was exactly in the sky.

"We have a few moments, my friends," Fid and Maia nodded acknowledging Kulla. Fid walked to the edge of the lake with Maia by his side, arm in arm with him, looking out to the lake. Kulla walked to be beside Fid. "Why do you despise my kind, Fid?".

"When I was fourteen, a horde of vampires attacked my village. They killed nearly everyone. I have not seen my father since then. He is believed to have been killed by that horde," Fid's pain was heard in his voice.

"I am truly sorry to hear of that tragedy, but not all of us are that way, Fid. There are those, like my coven, who are devoted to this world and would do anything to protect it," Kulla said.

"I am sure," skepticism in Fid's voice. At that moment, Fid's ears twitched. He drew his Dragon Blade to deflect several small, metallic blades that cut through the air toward them. He then drew his other blade as Kulla drew his broad sword and Maia took aim with her bow. In front of them was a platoon of Orcs. With them was a tall, slender woman with silver hair that had streaks of scattered black hair. She wore iron plated armor on her forearms, shoulders, and shins. She wore dark leather pants and leather top. On her dark leather top was the emblem of a dragon. Fid wondered why she wore a dragon emblem. Her eyes were an ice cold blue. There was an evil grin across her face as she faced her foes. Fid, Kulla and Maia stood ready.

"And to whom do we owe this surprise?" Kulla pointed his sword at the woman.

"My name is Ivy. I am one of Lord Sekmet's Generals and your exterminator," she responded with a crack and swing of her whip to take Fid's leg out from under him. She then ordered the Orcs to attack them. Kulla leapt at the Orcs, slashing violently at them. Maia fired arrow after arrow at the Orcs hitting at the shoulder and head. Fid kipped up to his feet and joined Kulla. Maia continued to fire arrows at the Orcs. Ivy stood back and watched them with her arms folded, especially Fid. He was the one with the Bracelet of Ra on his wrist. Fid was her target.

"He is impressive, but not strong enough to defeat Lord Sekmet," she muttered to herself. Her attention turned to Maia who was taking down her Orc soldiers with her arrows. "She is most troublesome though," she cracked her whip to throw small metallic blades toward Maia. She did not notice them at first. At the last minute, she saw them and flipped backwards to avoid the small blades. She saw that Ivy had thrown the blades at her and was ready to attack her. The sun reached its highest point in the sky. Ivy noticed this and jumped to the air toward the lake. She was met in the air by Fid. He kicked her to the ground, stopping her short of the lake.

"Maia, go retrieve the Necklace!" Fid looked back to her. She immediately dropped her bow and quiver of arrows just as she was diving in to the lake. Fid then faced Ivy with both blades held in front of him. She gave an malicious grin and charged toward him. Fid took a fighting stance. Ivy reached for her hip and threw small daggers at him. As Fid blocked the daggers, Ivy slid to a halt in her charge cracking her whip across Fid's stomach. He fell backwards a few feet. He bled steadily from the wound. He kipped up to his feet and lunged at her. Fid slashed at her, but she was quick and maneuvered out of the way. She continued to dodge every attack of his. She ducked one of his attacks and pulled a knife to stab Fid in the leg. He fell to one knee as she kicked him in the face. Fid dropped his blades and looked up to find Ivy standing over him with the knife in hand. She raised the knife ready to stab him in the throat when Kulla grabbed her by the wrist to stop her. He threw her back several feet in to a tree. With a scowl on her face at the vampire's interference she recovered and approached them with deadly intention in her eyes. She wrapped her whip around her waist and extended her arms outward. She clapped her hands creating a shockwave that surged toward Kulla. This power sent him backwards into a redwood. Fid avoided the first shockwave and rose to his feet to lunge at Ivy but was sent backwards by another powerful shockwave of Ivy's. The remaining Orcs surrounded Kulla and Fid with Ivy approaching them.

The water of the lake began to bubble and swirl. The attention of Ivy and the Orcs turned toward the lake as Maia began to rise from the lake. A pink aura surrounded her body as she rose from the water. Her arms were outstretched to her sides; her head was bowed slightly and her eyes glowed white. Fid, Kulla, and Ivy saw the golden Necklace around Maia's neck. It was a solid gold band that scooped just above her chest. The symbol of Isis was engraved at the center. She lowered herself to Fid and Kulla's side. Fid laid on the ground bleeding from his stomach and leg and Kulla braced himself against the tree holding his ribs. Ivy gave an evil smirk to Maia and ordered for Orcs to attack her. Two charged at her with one swinging its axe at her head. She dodged the attack drawing her short blade and slashed the Orc from navel to chest and spun to slash the neck of the other. Maia then turned to face Ivy, who had a look of frustration. Ivy then clapped her hands sending a shockwave toward her. Maia extended her hands and placed an transparent barrier of energy in front of her, Fid, and Kulla to negate the power of the shockwave. Using what seemed to be telekinetic energy, Maia summoned her bow and quiver of arrows from the ground. She drew and took aim with one arrow. Energy began to gather throughout the arrow emanating from the Necklace. It swirled along the shaft of the arrow and gathered at the arrow's head.

"Arrow of Isis!" her voice echoed throughout the forest as she released the arrow. The arrow roared and surged towards Ivy and her platoon of Orcs. Ivy jumped to the trees as the arrow turned everything in its wake to ash, leaving a deep trench in the ground. The aura that was around her body faded away as she went to help Fid to his feet and tend to his wounds.

"It would seem the Necklace of Isis enhances the mental abilities of its bearer," Kulla said as he walked to their side.

"It would seem so," she looked up to Kulla as she bandaged Fid's wounds.

"You handled the powers with skill," Fid winced and sharply sucked in some air trying to bear the pain of his wounds.

"It was almost as if the Necklace took over and worked with me. I was conscious of what I was doing. I thought about what I wanted to do and the Necklace aided me," her fingers reached up and traced the necklace's symbol.

"Very useful abilities," Kulla nodded.

"Indeed," as he said this, the Bracelet began to glow and pull him toward the Lake. It stopped at the edge and had him face the Northern Mountains. The Bracelet began to glow and a beam of light shot out from the Bracelet up in to the Northern Mountains. Fid scanned where the beam of light pointed.

"I believe I see where it is," Fid squinted his eyes to focus his vision.

"How can you see?" Kulla asked.

"He is an Elf," Kulla gave a sharp look to Maia and she returned the same glare.

"The Scepter lies on an altar of stone near the top of that range," Fid pointed to it.

"We have to climb up there?" Maia asked complainingly.

"In order to retrieve the Scepter of Osiris, yes we do. Unless you are going to use your new found powers to will it here," Kulla mocked her. Maia shot a sharp look at Kulla and he returned it.

"Will you two cease this petty arguing?! We have a mission to accomplish and two worlds to save," Fid scolded them. Both Maia and Kulla scowled at each other then turned back to Fid. "Let us make our way to that mountain peak," he said. Fid whistled for Sundancer and Kulla called for his horse. Fid hoisted Maia onto Sundancer and then lifted himself onto his back. Kulla mounted his horse and the trio rode toward the Northern Mountains to retrieve the Scepter of Osiris. Ivy was still in the trees when the Bracelet of Ra revealed the location of the Scepter of Osiris. She whistled and a raven swooped in from a nearby tree branch. There was a tube attached to its back. Ivy took a small parchment and wrote a note on it. She tightly rolled the note and slipped it in to the tube. She then whistled for the raven to take flight.

Dusk began to fall upon Rhydin as Fid, Maia, and Kulla drew close to the foot of the mountain. The air grew cooler and crisp with gentle breezes blowing about. A fog rolled over the ground as they climbed higher along the mountain side. The trio made camp for the night to rest for the remaining trek to the top of the mountain peak. Kulla went to gather wood for a fire as Maia changed Fid's bandages.

"What do you think about our new friend?" she looked up from the bandages to him.

"Although I am weary around vampires, I do believe we can trust him," Fid's tone was hushed.

"I don't like him," even after Fid seemed accepting of Kulla, Maia remained defiant.

"Why not?" he asked.

"It seems to me that he's very arrogant. As if he knows everything that needs to be known," she responded.

"He saved my life while you were under the water," Maia looked at him with slightly widened eyes at the revelation.

"He did?" she had stopped wrapping the new bandages.

"Yes," he nodded his head.

"Oh. Well still, he's arrogant and I don't like that. He needs to be knocked down from his pedestal," she went back to wrapping the bandages. Fid gave a small chuckled at her stubborn defiance. Kulla soon returned with the firewood. Fid rose to his feet and helped Kulla set up a fire pit with the wood inside. Fid gathered a small ball of fire in his palm and released it into the pit setting the wood on fire. The three gathered around the fire to warm themselves. Maia sat next to Fid arm in arm with him and rested her head on his shoulder. The three eventually fell asleep next to the warmth of the fire.

Later that night, Fid was woken by tremors in the ground. He thought nothing of it at first, but then it happened once more. He sat up and saw a pair of tall dark figures thirty yards from the fire. He crawled over to Kulla and shook him.

"Kulla. Kulla wake up," his eyes did not leave the dark figures. He woke up and saw Fid looking out into the darkness.

"What is it, Fid?" he raised his head from the ground.

"Shush. What are those out there?" Fid asked quietly while pointing to the enclosing figures.

"Those are Trolls. Very large Trolls," Kulla's eyes widened and was visibly shaken at the sight of these monsters. Kulla strapped his broad sword to his waist and drew it. In the meantime, Fid crawled over to Maia and woke her from her sleep. Maia nearly screamed, but Fid covered her mouth to stifle it. The Trolls drew closer to the trio. They now saw that the Trolls were carrying clubs with spikes protruding from the sides. These Trolls were eight feet tall and pot-bellied with glowing green eyes. Their bodies were riddled with warts and thick hair. They had thick powerful jaws with razor-like teeth. They drew closer and closer to the fire for it was what drew them over to the area. Kulla, Fid, and Maia stood ready with their weapons drawn and ready to defend themselves. The Trolls stopped a short ways from them and stared at them. The trio returned the gaze. They were nervous, Maia more than Fid or Kulla.

"Who are these trespassers?!" one of the Trolls growled.

"No one trespasses on our land!" the other snarled. The first charged at Kulla and lifted its club high and brought it down to crush Kulla. Kulla dodged the attack and slashed at the Troll's side. Kulla's attack did not seem to faze the Troll. The second Troll swung its club at Maia and Fid. Both dodged the heavy club. Fid slashed at the Troll's leg and Maia fired an arrow at the Troll's neck. Neither attacked fazed it. The Troll just pulled the arrow out and roared in anger. The first Troll stomped the ground, causing it to quake and knock the trio off balance while the second swung its club once more. Maia used the power of the Necklace to disarm the Troll. She then used the power of the Necklace to lift a boulder and hurled it at the Troll. The boulder smashed against the Troll's chest, throwing it backwards several feet. The other Troll roared seeing his kin thrown. It swung its club at Fid, but he jumped out of the way and ran along the club and up the Troll's arm. With blade drawn, Fid slashed across the Troll's eyes. A squeal of pain escaped the Troll's mouth as it swung its club violently attempting to hit anything that was close. Blood poured down its face from the deep slash Fid's blade left. Kulla jumped high into the air and stabbed his sword into the Troll's skull, killing it. The other Troll regained its composure from having a boulder thrown at him. As the Troll rose to its feet, it saw Kulla kill his brother and now grew angrier than before. He began to pick up rocks and boulders to throw them at the three. Fid sheathed his blades and threw balls of flame at the boulders reducing them in to piles of mere pebbles while Maia placed an energy barrier to block the boulders. Growing more and more with rage, the remaining Troll pulled up a tree stump and charged at the three with it. Maia used the power of the Necklace of Isis to disarm the Troll. Fid then threw fire orbs at the Troll's knees. The Troll roared in pain feeling its skin burn and blister from Fid's intense fire. Kulla put the Troll out of its misery as he rushed in and swung his broad sword to cleave his head from the rest of his body. All three were breathing heavily from the fight. Kulla cleaned then sheathed his blade. He looked back to see if Fid and Maia, "Are you both alright?".

"Yes. I believe so," Fid responded walking over to Maia, who was on her knees breathing heavily. Fid knelt beside her trying to comfort her. Kulla walked back and sat by the fire.

"This must be Troll territory," Kulla looked to their surroundings.

"Then we must get moving at first light to avoid anymore encounters with them," Fid said.

"We must also put out the fire. It is what attracted the first two here," Maia looked to them both for approval.

"I agree," Fid said. Kulla nodded and stomped out the fire.

Fid, Maia, and Kulla awoke as the sun rose over the horizon with its rays kissing and caressing their faces. Kulla was the first to awake and greet dawn. Fid and Maia awoke a few moments later with Maia yawning and stretching. She scanned the area around them and found the bodies of the Trolls were gone. Her eyes widened and yanked on Fid's sleeve to show him.

"Something, or someone, must have picked up the bodies in the middle of the night. Possibly to bury them," he said.

"I thought we would have heard footsteps or felt the earth shake," her ears had flattened against her head.

"Mountain Trogs," Kulla uttered.

"What are those?" Fid looked to Kulla with furrowed eyebrows.

"They are the equivalent to the vultures and condors on Earth. The difference being they are much larger in size. These birds of prey only come out during the night for they can only see in low light or total darkness. The light hurts their eyes. They eat flesh and use the remaining bones to build their nests," Kulla replied. Maia shuddered at the thought of a bird's nest made entirely of bones.

"I see," it was a disturbing thought to Fid, but that was the way of Rhydin's nature.

"We better press on further up the mountain. We want to beat any one of Sekmet's Generals from reaching the Scepter. After our fight with Ivy, I fear who else he may have waiting for us," Kulla looked up to their path up the mountain.

"I agree. We best be on our way," Fid responded. The three rose and summoned their horses. Fid and Maia mounted Sundancer as Kulla mounted his horse. They made their way to the top of the mountain. On the way up the mountain side, Maia spotted a berry bush. She used her Necklace's power to retrieve handfuls of the berries. She stuffed her mouth with them and fed some to Fid.

As the day went on, the three climbed higher and higher up the mountain. A coating of light snow covered the ground. The air became cooler and crisp. With Maia beginning to shiver, Fid handed her his long coat to keep warm. With his long coat off, Fid found the cold of the mountain air did not affect him. The trio reached the top of the mountain peak and found the altar where the Scepter of Osiris rested. It was a simple stone altar where the golden Scepter rested. They dismounted their horses and made their way toward the altar. They drew within thirty yards of the altar and several explosions were set off in front of them.

"It is a trap!" Fid crossed his forearms in front of his face. With his warning they drew their weapons. They stood back to back as they looked for their adversary. So far, they could not find any sign of Orcs, nor any of Sekmet's Generals. They then slowly made their way to the altar while keeping an eye on any more attacks. Twenty yards from the altar the ground gave away and they fell into a ten foot pit.

"This was definitely a trap," Kulla winced.

"What gave you the first clue," Maia responded sarcastically as she got to her feet.

"I thought cats landed on their feet not on their bottoms," Kulla retorted. Maia hissed at him.

"Will you two stop?! You both sound like squabbling children. Instead of arguing let us find a way to get out of here," Fid interjected. Maia and Kulla glared at each other then looked up the pit hearing an evil laugh. Around the edge of the pit, they saw Orcs with arrows aimed at them. They then saw who seemed to be another General of Sekmet. He wore dark armor and a dark cape. From underneath the helmet all they could see were his crimson red eyes. Fid noticed there was a dragon emblem on their attacker's chest plate. Much like the one they saw on Ivy.

"It would seem that we have caught our prey," his tone was dark.

"Who are you?!" Kulla yelled up.

"I suppose you would want to know the name of your killer so that you may remember it in the afterlife. My name is Naafar," he responded with a sneer.

"And I suppose you are here for the Scepter," Fid interjected.

"How observant of you, but I am not here only for that. I am for your heart as well, Bearer of the Dragon Essence," he responded. He was about to give the signal for the Orcs to fire their arrows when something came over Fid as if he were possessed. His eyes glowed white and the Bracelet of Ra glowed a bright gold.

"Cover your eyes," Fid told Maia and Kulla in a hushed tone. They did so immediately. "Solar Flare!" Fid pointed the Bracelet at the Orcs and Naafar and a flash of blinding light emitted from it. The Orcs fell to their knees in pain and Naafar covered his eyes since the only thing he could see was white. At that moment, Maia threw her short sword, bow and quiver of arrows high into the air. She then transformed to her panther form and jumped from wall to wall of the pit making her way to the top. As she reached the top, she transformed back to her human form catching her weapons and landing on her feet at the top. Kulla followed and on the way up slashed at an Orc and a few more once he landed. Fid jumped toward the wall of the pit and kicked off of it to the other and then back until he was at the top with his eyes glowing and a golden aura enveloping his body. As Fid drew his blades they flared like the embers of a fire. Energy surged within his body as well as the blades. The Orcs regained their vision as did Naafar to find Maia, Kulla, and Fid standing in front of them with weapons drawn between them and the Scepter.

"Kulla, get the Scepter. Maia and I can handle them," Kulla nodded at Fid's strategy and turned to retrieve it. Naafar ordered the Orcs to fire a volley of arrows at Fid and Maia. Fid used the blades to block the arrows and Maia placed an energy barrier in front of her. While they were occupied with blocking the arrows, Naafar leapt to the air and pursued Kulla. As Kulla was about to take the Scepter, Naafar threw his shoulder in to the back of Kulla, knocking him off balance. At that point, Kulla drew his sword and Naafar drew his twin sickle blades. Naafar slashed at Kulla's neck and chest going for the kill right away. Kulla countered and blocked these attacks. Kulla attempted to leg sweep him, but Naafar jumped over it and slashed at

Kulla with both sickles. Kulla avoided the slash by bending his body backwards, then rolled forward to position himself behind Naafar. Kulla threw a kick at Naafar, but his foot was caught and was thrown into a boulder. After regaining his composure he saw Naafar making his move to retrieve the Scepter.

"Energy of my soul, repel my enemy," Kulla chanted with his palm held outward. A small orb of energy formed within his hand after his incantation. After the energy gathered and intensified, Kulla released it to hit him and throw him to the ground. Kulla took the opportunity to run for the altar to obtain the Scepter. Naafar got to his feet just in time to see Kulla running for the Scepter. Naafar threw a dagger at Kulla hitting him in the shoulder. Kulla kept his focus as the dagger pierced his skin. He dove to grab the Scepter of Osiris, landing on the ground. After a few moments passed, Naafar saw Kulla rise with the Scepter in his right hand. Naafar's crimson eyes flashed with rage and frustration. He swung his sickle blades to release crescent shaped beams of dark energy. Kulla spun the Scepter between his fingers to deflect the dark energy. Naafar continued the onslaught of energy to no avail. Kulla continued to block the orbs with the Scepter and began walking toward him. He then deflected a crescent of energy back at Naafar to knock him off balance. Kulla pointed the Scepter at Naafar. The Scepter began to glow and throb with its energy. The aura of energy surged through the Scepter and throughout Kulla's body. Kulla's eyes were flushed white with the Scepter's energy seeping from them.

"Soul Spark!" Kulla released several sparks of energy from the Scepter's jeweled head. The sparks of soul energy struck Naafar in the chest plate sending him backwards into the very pit in which he set the trap for the trio. Kulla looked to Fid and Maia to see if they were alright. He found Fid and Maia finishing off the last of the Orcs.

With the last of the Orcs finished off, Fid, Maia, and Kulla walked to the edge of the pit. Looking down they saw the unconscious Naafar.

"Are you two alright?" Kulla looked to them both.

"We are fine," Fid said in between deep breaths.

"What do we do with him?" Maia continued to look in to the pit to make sure Naafar would not make any desperate moves.

"We leave him here to lick his wounds," Fid turned his back on the pit. Kulla nodded his head in agreement. They whistled for their horses and mounted them.

"Where do we go now, Fid?" Kulla steered his horse to be beside Sundancer.

"My brother said we were to meet him, Paige, and Demus at the palace in the Western Province. That is where we will go," he responded. Kulla nodded as he spurred his horse to move down the mountainside.

Fight for the Western Palace

O N THE WAY DOWN, KULLA thought back to the way Fid looked and reacted in the pit before using the Bracelet of Ra's power. He pulled his horse to be beside Fid, "Fid, think back to the pit. What was it that came over you? It was as if you were possessed". Fid thought for a moment with Maia leaning her head on his shoulder awaiting an answer as well.

"I do not know," he thought for a moment. "Yes, I do believe I was possessed, but by what I do not know. One moment I find myself at the bottom of the pit and then the next I am fighting Orcs," his confusion was evident in his eyes. It was at that moment he heard a faint voice in the back of his mind calling to him, "Fid…..Fid," the voice echoed as if it were in a cavern. Fid suddenly became very distracted looking to see where the voice was coming from. To Kulla and Maia it seemed Fid was going temporarily insane with his eyes and head darting from side to side.

"Fid?" Kulla called his name in attempts to gain his attention. The voice continued to speak to Fid, "*Fid… I will always be with you…I am a part of you*".

"W-who are you?!" Fid grabbed at his head.

"*I am here for you,*" the voice soon faded. Kulla and Maia increasingly became more concerned for him.

"Fid," Maia called to him shaking him a bit.

"Stop talking to me! Get out of my head!" Fid's eyes were tightly closed trying to block out the voice that spoke to him.

"Fid!" both Maia and Kulla yelled to Fid. He finally regained his focus with heavy breaths. Blinking his eyes several times he looked to Kulla and Maia. Both looked upon him as if he had gone mad.

"What happened?" Maia's concern for Fid's mental wellbeing was in her eyes.

"There was a voice in my mind saying that it will be with me always," his hands trembled still feeling weary from the encounter.

"Perhaps we should hurry to the Palace. It seems as though you are under a lot of mental rigor. It all may be getting to your head," Kulla placed his hand on Fid's shoulder.

"Perhaps," Fid gave a nod of his head.

Ever since the believed bout of insanity of Fid, Kulla and Maia kept a watchful on him. Since then, Fid seemed to have calmed down. He was even humming a lively tune. Maia and Kulla looked to each other and continued to watch him. Several miles past the base of the mountain Fid brought Sundancer to a halt and looked off into the distance.

"What is it?" Mai's attention perked hwen they stopped.

"What do you see?" Kulla looked back to him. Fid took a moment to answer.

"Smoke comes from the palace in the Eastern Province. It is on fire and overrun with Orc," he said as his voice trembled with sorrow and anger.

"Are there any signs of survivors?" Maia asked with concern.

"I see none," he lowered his head.

"Should we search the remains?" Kulla grew worried as well.

"No. We must move on to the palace in the Western Province," Fid had to resist the urge to return to the Eastern Palace.

"Do you not want to see if Aero, Paige, and Melina survived or not?" it was as if Maia was attempting to urge him to return to the Eastern Palace.

"Knowing them they are on their way to the Western Palace," Fid forced himself to turn Sundancer away from the path to the Eastern

Palace. Both Kulla and Maia nodded and rode on heading toward the woods.

Dusk began to fall and the trio rode deep in to the forest. The light from the moon shone through the forest canopy. The serene state in which Fid was in was interrupted by a suspicious feeling that overwhelmed him. Arrows were fired from the trees in front of the horses causing them to rear on to their hind legs. Maia was thrown from Sundancer, but she quickly got to her feet with bow and arrow drawn. Fid and Kulla drew their weapons. From the trees, an army of cloaked figures jumped from the branches with swords and arrows aimed at them. Fid recognized the make of the bows and swords the cloaked figures wielded.

"Wait. We are friends of Paige. I am her half-brother," Fid lowered his blades. The figures hesitated to lower their weapons as they looked at each other. One of the cloaked figures lowered their bow and stepped toward the three. He pulled back his hood revealing that he was an Elf of the Woodland Realm.

"Who are you?" his eyes examined the trio that crossed their path.

"My name is Fid. I am Aero and Paige's half-brother. This is Kulla, Prince of the Southeast Vampire Coven, and Maia," Fid presented his companions to the Elf. The Elf then turned his head to the others and gave a nod to them. They then removed their hoods revealing their Elf features.

"My name is Aldar. I am the Lieutenant of the Woodland Realm," he turned his attention back to Fid.

"It is an honor to meet you. Have you news of Paige, Aero, and Melina?" Fid's concern for them resurfaced when Aldar introduced himself.

"Follow me," Aldar turned to lead them deeper in to the realm. Fid, Maia, and Kulla followed Aldar with the other Woodland Elves escorting them.

As they reached the western region of the forest, they began to see wooden bridges and rope ladders connecting high within the trees. As they walked further, they saw huts built in the trees, watchtowers were built high in the branches, and torches illuminated this Woodland City. The Woodland Elves climbed ladders leading the three up in to the Woodland City. Aldar led them to a hut at the center of the Woodland City while a few others led Sundancer and Kulla's horse to their stables. As they entered the hut, they found Aero, Melina, and Paige sitting in the far corner with guards by their side. A wide smile came across their faces as they rose to their feet and gave a loving embrace to Fid and Maia. Their attention then turned to Kulla. Aero placed his fist over his heart and bowed his head slightly in reverence to Kulla. Kulla returned the gesture to Aero, Melina, and Paige.

"What happened to the palace?" this thought had been at the forefront of Fid's mind ever since he saw what happened.

"While we cut off the Orcs heading through the forest, we were flanked by another platoon of Orc led by a General of Sekmet's," Aero gave a sigh a defeat.

"Did the General reveal himself?" Kulla asked.

"Or herself," Maia interjected with glare and Kulla returning it.

"My goodness. Have they been like this the whole journey?" Melina asked.

"I am afraid so," Fid sighed and gave a shake of his head.

"To answer your question, the General did not reveal them self," Melina responded, "The General wore dark armor, a helmet and mask, and wielded twin maces," she closed her eyes to remember what details she could. Fid nodded and sat in a chair next to a table.

"What do we do now? The Orcs and that General took over the Eastern Palace. Where are we to go?" Kulla looked to Aero and Paige for the answer.

"At first light, we will head for the Western Palace. There is an army there guarding its gates. We must get there as soon as possible. I fear that another regiment of Orc is heading to invade those walls as well," Aero still held hope in his voice despite losing the Eastern Palace.

"But for now, we rest to regain our strength. I have a feeling we will need it tomorrow," Paige interjected.

"I agree," Maia gave a yawn and stretched.

"Aldar will show you where you will sleep for the night," Paige gave a nod to Aldar to carry out her request of him.

Late in to the night, Fid laid in bed restless. He thought back to the voice that spoke to him on the mountain side. Where did it come from? Was it connected to the Relics being found? Why was it speaking to him now? Many other questions ran through his mind. He turned his head to look at Maia, who seemed peacefully asleep. He rose out of bed carefully as not to wake her. He put on a robe then walked out to the catwalk. He inhaled the fresh air of the forest and looked upon the Woodland City.

"Admiring the view?" Aero stepped from the shadows of the huts smoking a pipe.

"I am. It is so peaceful and quiet. It seems that it is far away from the war that is waging. It reminds me of home almost," he turned his head to Aero.

"These are troubled times Brother, but you must not lose hope. We are all here for each other, no matter what," Aero said.

"Thank you," Fid said as he turned to look up through the forest canopy.

"There is something else that is troubling you, I am sensing," Aero slightly tilted his head.

"How could you tell?" a hint of sarcasm was in Fid's voice.

"What is wrong?" Fid took a moment to answer while looking down at the Bracelet of Ra as the moonlight gleamed off of it.

"A strange occurrence has me perturbed. On our journey down the mountain, after obtaining the Scepter of Osiris, a voice in my mind spoke to me," Fid hesitantly said. Aero tilted his head to the side and looked at Fid as if he were insane. "I know what you are thinking and I am not insane, Brother," Fid said defensively.

"What did the voice say?" Aero sensed Fid was telling the truth.

"That it will always be with me and that it would never leave me," he then paused for a moment in thought, "Perhaps the incident where I was temporarily possessed is connected to the voice".

"Are you saying the voice who spoke to you is the entity that possessed you?" Aero raised a skeptic eyebrow.

"Perhaps. When I was possessed I did not know what was happening. I felt a sudden surge of energy. I blacked out and then woke up moments later fighting Orcs. That may be also the reason why I know how to wield the Bracelet of Ra," Fid said.

"Perhaps this voice is trying to help you. I sense no malicious entity or aura surrounding you," Aero looked at Fid from toe to head

"That is possible. All of this is happening too quickly. What if I am not ready to take on the responsibility," doubt was slipping in to his voice and it was obvious to Aero.

"The Great Red Dragon Tufar would not have given you a portion of his Essence to you if he did not believe you were capable of handling the responsibility. Yes, this journey is long and treacherous, but you do not have to go it alone. Paige, Kulla, Maia, Melina, Demus, Aldar, and I are all here to help you until our death. We all strongly believe in you Fid," he placed his hands on Fid's shoulders. Fid looked into Aero's eyes and grinned knowing that he had the support of Aero and the others.

"Thank you, Brother," Fid said with a smile across his face.

"Now then, you should get your rest. I believe you will need it for tomorrow," Aero gave a couple pats to Fid's shoulder.

"I will," Fid responded. Both nodded to each other and Aero emptied his pipe and left to go back to his hut. Fid stayed for a few more moments to look off in to the forest.

Daylight shone through the canopy of the forest and through the window of the hut awakening Maia. She opened her eyes, rubbed them, and stretched her body. She walked outside to find Fid in the same place as he was that night. It was as if he were in some sort of meditative state. She walked up behind him and wrapped her arms around his waist. Leaning her head against his back, she began to purr quietly. Fid placed his hands over hers and then turned to face her. Both were in each other's embrace being touched by the warmth of the sun. They looked deep into each other's eyes getting lost in each other.

"General Fid," Aldar called to him. Fid and Maia let out a sigh.

"Yes, Lieutenant?" Fid pulled his gaze from Maia.

"Your presence, as well as Maia's, is requested in the main hut. It is quite urgent," he said.

"Take us there," Fid followed him and led Maia by the hand.

The main hut was located at the center of the Woodland City. As they reached the main hut they saw the carvings of King Cretus and King Tidus on each of the wooden doors. Both Kings were in full armor with swords drawn. Above the two kings was the sun shining down on them. The carving depicted them heading into battle. Aldar pulled the door handle to lead Fid and Maia in to the hut. As they entered the room they found a large, wooden round table at the center with the Elf Crest carved in to it. They found Aero, Paige, Kulla, Melina, and Demus already sitting around the table.

"Good morning, Fid and Maia. Please sit, we have some urgent news," Melina gave a graceful gesture for them to be seated. Fid and Maia immediately took their seats and turned their full attention on Aero.

"Bad news has reached us. Word has reached us of a regiment of Orc, led by a General of Sekmet's, making a marching toward the walls of the Palace in the Western Province. It was said this General is massive in stature, at least seven feet in height. He wears iron gauntlets on his wrists, wears bear skin pants, and leather tunic with a chain mail. He wields a massive iron war hammer. He wears an emblem of a dragon on his tunic," Aero stated. The room fell silent for a few moments. Fid thought back to the emblems of Ivy and Naafar. They were all the same, but why were they wearing dragon insignias?

"What can we do?" Maia's ears had flattened against her head with this revelation of bad news.

"The forces at the walls can hold, but only for a little while before Sekmet's forces breach the gates," Paige responded.

"Do we have enough time to give aid?" Fid asked.

"If we leave now and make it there with much haste," Aero answered.

"What are we waiting for then? The Western Palace needs our help," Kulla interjected.

"Demus, Aldar. Gather the troops. Prepare them for battle," Aero ordered. Demus and Aldar placed their fists on their hearts while bowing their heads and took their leave.

"Everyone else should prepare yourselves for battle. This will be a difficult one," Paige stated. Fid, Kulla, Maia, and Melina stood and left to gather their weapons.

Finishing strapping on his armor, Fid turned to see Maia standing in the doorway holding her bow in one hand, a quiver of arrows on one hip and her short sword on the other. The Necklace of Isis clasped around her neck gleamed in the sunlight. He walked toward her and gently placed his hands on her shoulders. Her body was tense and her tail did not sway as it normally did. Worry was in her eyes. This would be her first major battle.

"Are you nervous?" his voice was calm.

"Yes," she answered in a timid voice.

"I will protect you. I am not going to let anything happen to you," with that vow to her, Maia was compelled to raise up on her toes to kiss him on the cheek.

"You still owe me for saving your life," she smiled and turned to saunter out of the hut. Fid shook his head with a grin on his face and walked outside. He found Maia standing at the edge of the deck with her mouth gaping and eyes widened, focusing toward the ground.

"What is it?" he looked at her. Maia pointed toward the ground and standing there was a massive army of Elves mounted on horseback awaiting him. Fid shared in Maia's awe. They slowly made their way down a spiral staircase that put them in front of the army. Fid then saw Aero on horseback holding the reins of Sundancer along with

Kulla, Paige, Melina, Demus, and Aldar. Fid and Maia walked toward them and took the reins of Sundancer. He hoisted Maia onto the saddle and then swung himself behind her. Fid turned Sundancer to face the rest of the army. He gazed upon them nodding his head in approval of its size. He also noticed the Rangers from Earth who Paige and Demus called upon. Fid looked over to Paige to give an approving nod. She gave a grin to him knowing that he approved of the Army of Rangers. Looking to the army he drew one of his blades and raised it to the sky with the light from the sun gleaming off of it. Each and every one in the army gave a war cry. Fid reared Sundancer to his hind legs and led them into battle.

Closing in on high noon, miles from the western border of the forest, a massive army of Orcs and Ogres led by their giant of a General, Kain, marched upon the walls of the Western Palace. At the head of the army was Kain on horseback with his war hammer in hand. He looked upon the walls with a grin of malice.

"This will be yours, Lord Sekmet," his voice was low and raspy. He then turned to face the army of Orcs behind him. "Ready the catapults!" he barked. At that order, Ogres hoisted massive boulders onto the catapults. The Elf Lieutenant on the wall ordered for two ranks of archers at the wall and for other soldiers to ready the catapults. The gates to the palace were braced from the inside as to not let any Orc or Ogre set foot in the walls.

"Let's take it down!" Kain hoisted his heavy war hammer in to the air. The Orcs gave a thunderous roar and charged for the main gates. The catapults released the massive boulders at the palace walls. The boulders destroyed portions of the wall as well as crushing several Elf guards.

"Fire!" the Elf Lieutenant ordered. The guards at the gate released their arrows and boulders were released from the catapults. The boulders hit and rolled over Orcs. Some boulders destroyed the enemy catapults. Kain grew angry and impatient. He ordered for the battering ram. Eight Ogres, with four on either side of the battering ram, were flanked by Orc's with crossbows emerged from the army

and started their charge for the gate. As they made their charge, the
Orc bowmen fired volleys at the gate guards killing them one by one.

"Take them down, take them down!" the Elf Lieutenant yelled.
Firing arrow after arrow the gate guard could not bring down the
Ogres or the heavily armored Orc bowmen. The gate began to weaken
as it was repeatedly rammed in to by the massive battering ram. Kain
gave an evil grin as he could taste victory.

"Brace the gate!" the Elf Lieutenant yelled down to the guard.
Wood from the gate began to break from the numerous hits it had
taken. Several rows of archers waited several yards from the gate
with arrows aimed at the door. After several more hits to the gate it
burst open and Orcs and Ogres with armor and clubs came charging
through. Volleys of arrows were fired, but it was not enough to stop
the wave of Orcs and Ogres flooding through the gate. Kain gave a
triumphant laugh as he saw the gate break open and ordered for more
Orcs to enter the gates. At that moment, a bellowing horn sounded
in the distance. It was not any Orc horn Kain had ever heard. He
turned, as did the Orc army, to find an army of Elves and Men led
by Fid, Maia, Kulla, Aero, Melina and Paige. Kain's eyes widened at
the sight of a surviving Elf army that was marching from the woods.
Growing angry he ordered half of the Orc army to charge them.

"Over one thousand Orc against eight hundred Elves and Men,"
Aero said to Fid.

"Hardly seems fair," Fid replied with a slight grin on his face.

"Too bad for them," Paige smirked as she drew her short swords.

"Fid, it is high noon," Kulla looked up to the sky. Fid looked up
to the sun as it was at its highest point where it shone brightest and
was the warmest. High noon was when the sun was at its strongest.
Seeming to absorb its rays, he closed his eyes for a moment. As he
opened them again they glowed a bright flushed white. He drew his
blades that were glowing with a vibrant red aura.

"Aldar…. Demus, sound the charge," Fid ordered. As they
sounded the charge, all readied their weapons. "Sundancer Ignite!"
Sundancer reared on to his hind legs. Stomping his hooves to the

ground, Sundancer was slowly engulfed in flames. Fid led the charge toward the army of Orcs and Ogres. The Orc army continued their charge toward the Elf army. The front lines of the Orc Army carried heavy iron shields and brandished long spears.

Seeing the Orc Army charge toward them, Melina closed her eyes, lowered her head, and folded her hands in front of her face as if in prayer. A faint blue aura rose from her body as she focused her energy. "Head of a Bull... Body of a man...Strength of ten men.... Minotaur, I summon thee. Aid us in this battle!" when she opened her eyes, an ancient seal with many intricate runes appeared on the ground in front of the Elf army. From that seal, a light burst from it. As the light faded, a giant Minotaur wielding a large battle axe roared. Its eyes glowed with rage when it saw the front lines of the Orc army. The Minotaur pawed the ground, kicking up dirt. The eyes of Fid, Maia, and Kulla widened when they saw, for the first time, Melina's summoning magic. Aero and Paige only grinned at it. With a heavy outward breath and grunt, the Minotaur fearlessly charged at the frontlines of the Orc army with his head lowered. Fid gathered his focus and led the Elf army to charge upon the Orc army close behind the Minotaur. The Minotaur crashed upon the shields of the Orc frontlines, throwing many aside. This weakened the Orc frontline, allowing for the Elves and Rangers to easily break in to the ranks of the Orcs. Orcs were trampled over by the horses, Elves and Men were thrown off their horses by Orc bolts and Orcs slashing at the legs of their horses. The clashing of swords and axes sounded throughout the western region. Fid was slashing at charging Orcs while Maia was releasing arrow after arrow. Kulla was thrown off his horse by an Orc who leapt and tackled him to the ground. Kulla quickly deposed of that Orc by stabbing it through the head. Using the Scepter of Osiris, Kulla summoned sparks of soul energy and released it toward a small group of Orcs charging at him. Paige too was thrown off her horse by an arrow piercing her horse's leg. With both her short swords drawn, like a whirlwind, she fought her way through a horde of Orcs surrounding her. Aldar and several rangers rushed to her aid. Demus was shot through the shoulder with an arrow throwing him off his horse. Finding himself surrounded by Orc he drew his short sword along with having his broad sword in the other hand. Violently slashing at Orcs, Demus fought his way to Kulla's side. Aero, along with other Elf soldiers fought their way to the gate where they came face to face with Kain. Leaping from his horse, Kain brought his massive war hammer above his head and slammed it to the ground causing a seismic quake. The quake threw Aero and the other Elf soldiers off their horses. Kain charged through the Elf soldiers and swung his war hammer at Aero. Aero blocked the attack with his sword. Kain took several more deadly swings at him, but Aero dodged and blocked each of the attacks. Aero threw kicks and slashed at Kain, but they were easily blocked. Kain gave a bone crushing punch to Aero ribs and then hit him in the face with the hilt of his war hammer knocking Aero backwards on his heels. Spinning with his war hammer outstretched, he hit Aero's ribs sending him into the gate wall causing an impression. Aero was doubled over and gasping for air. Looking up, he saw Kain coming in for another charge. As Kain drew within a few yards of him, Aero flipped over him. In mid-air, Aero charged an energy orb in his hand and threw it at Kain's back sending him face first into the gate wall. Kain slowly got to his feet and turned to face Aero. He saw Aero doubled over and gasping for air. Kain knew Aero was severely hurt. It was like a predator smelling the blood of its prey. Kain swung his war hammer and hit Aero's chest. Aero was laid out on the ground with blood trickling from his mouth. Kain stood over Aero with an evil smile on his face. He lifted his war hammer above his head about to give a smashing blow to Aero to finish him off. Fid saw Kain standing over Aero. He veered Sundancer toward Kain.

"Get ready with an arrow, Maia," he told her. Immediately, Maia drew an arrow and took aim. As they drew closer, Kain brought the hammer down toward Aero's head. "Now!" Maia released the arrow and it struck Kain's shoulder. The war hammer landed inches beside

Aero's head. Kain turned to see Fid and Maia charging toward him on a flame engulfed Sundancer.

"All units retreat!" Kain yelled to the remaining Orc army. All Orcs, Ogres, and Kain retreated into the hills towards the south. Some Elves and Rangers were in pursuit.

"Let them run!" Fid yelled to them.

"Gather the wounded and take them in to the palace. Bury the dead in the cemetery," Aldar ordered the soldiers. Fid, Melina, and Paige rushed to Aero's side who laid there with blood trickling from his mouth. Fid looked at Aero's wounds. Aero lied on the ground, gasping for air.

"Will he be alright?!" Melina was hysterical seeing her husband badly injured.

"Several of his ribs are broken and there may be some internal bleeding," Fid said grimly.

"We need to take him inside now," Paige said urgently. Several Elves and Rangers gently hoisted Aero from his legs, waist, and arms and carried him in to the palace. They cleared a table in the foyer and placed him there. Paige began to mend the cuts on his body and wrap his ribs.

"We cannot stop the internal bleeding," Paige said.

"Is there anythin' I can do?" a voice said from behind them. Fid, Paige, Maia, Melina and Kulla turned to see Rosey.

"Rosey?" Fid looked in disbelief.

"Aye, m' lord," she nodded her head to him.

"What can you do to help Aero?" Paige asked. Rosey walked to the table side and held her hands over his chest and closed her eyes. A warm glow emitted from her hands. It grew more vibrant and pulsed the more she concentrated. A few moments passed and Rosey stepped back from Aero. His eyes slowly opened and all who were there breathed a sigh of relief. Melina wrapped her arms around him, happy to see that Aero was healed and out of mortal danger.

"Thank you, Rosey," Paige said. Rosey bowed and turned to take her leave. Fid followed her down the hall.

"Rosey," Fid called to her. She turned to face him, "Yes m' lord. Is there anythin' else that I am needed for?".

"There is much more to you than you want to admit," Fid stated.

"I thought I have already told you that," she responded with a grin.

"What else should I know about you," he asked. She paused for a few moments before answering him. She folded her hands in front of her chest and looked down at them as if she were deciding whether to tell him or not. She then inhaled a deep breath.

"There are a few things that I have not told you or many people," she responded. Fid nodded and folded his arms. "I told you that I'm a spy for your brother and sister. And you just saw the demonstration of one of the skills that I possess. There is something else that I do not tell many people," she paused.

"And that is what?" Fid asked trying to coax her in to revealing her secret.

"At a young age, I trained to be an assassin, but then I came to Rhydin and became a Shadow Shinobi," she finally said. She then looked back up to Fid biting her lower lip nervously to see how he would react to the secret. Fid's eyes widened slightly and found himself speechless. Fid was told stories of the Shinobi Tribes on Rhydin by Master Chen Shun, who learned all of the Shinobi Arts. There were five Tribes in all. These Shinobi Clans practiced the Art of manipulating a particular element. There was an Earth Shinobi Tribe, a Shadow Shinobi Tribe, a Fire Shinobi Tribe, a Water Shinobi Tribe, and a Wind Shinobi Tribe. Each of these people had their own culture and philosophies on how to practice their Arts.

"That is a great secret that you have kept for a long time. How long have you been a Shadow Shinobi?" he asked. She again looked down toward her feet and a tear dropped to the floor. Fid walked over to her and placed his hands on her shoulders.

"Ever since my village was ravaged and destroyed by a horde of vampires, years ago. I was thirteen then. I was almost killed that night, but you saved me," she looked from the floor in to his eyes. Fid took a step back in shock. This was the girl he saved in his Appalachian village. "But then you left in search of the horde to gain vengeance. I swore the same vow. I trained under Raoko Shun," She stated.

"Raoko Shun. Is he not the brother of Chen Shun?" he asked.

"I do believe so, m' lord," she responded with a nod and a sob.

"This is all so sudden," Fid's eyes were still wide with shock.

"I'm sorry that I surprised you like this, m' lord," her voice softened.

"It is fine Rosey. Do not worry about it. It is actually a pleasant surprise. I am glad to find someone who is from my village and knows the pain that I have endured," he gave a smile of relief.

"I'm here if you need me, m' lord," she placed her hand on his shoulder.

"Thank you," he responded.

"You're welcome. I believe I ought to take my leave if there is nothin' else that I am needed for," she said.

"There is nothing else, Rosey," he responded. She then bowed and made her way to the kitchen. Fid took a seat in that hall for several moments before Paige found him there.

"Is everything alright, Fid?" she asked.

"Oh… yes Paige. I was just thinking," he responded snapping out of his train of thoughts.

"Good. Aero would like to speak to you," she said. He nodded and followed her down the hall. This palace reminded Fid of the Eastern Province Palace. The walls were made of brick and lined with candles and the portraits of past kings of the Elf race.

"The palace looks much like the Eastern Province," Fid observed.

"Yes, it does. They were designed to be the same. They are often called the Twin Palaces," Paige told him.

"I see," even though he walked the halls of the Eastern Palace many times, he still was in awe of what the Western Palace held. Paige led him up a staircase leading to another hall lined with suits of various armors. At the end of the corridor was an arched wooden door. On either side of the door were suits of armor with the family crest above the doorway. Both Paige and Fid entered through the door to find Aero lying down in the bed resting. Melina was sitting by his side in a chair tending to his needs. Fid walked to the bedside as Aero opened his eyes.

"How are you feeling Aero?" Fid asked in a softer tone.

"Like I have been hit with a solid steel war hammer several times," he replied with a grin on his face. Fid and Paige grinned as well.

"You wanted to see me?" Fid asked.

"Yes I did. While I am healing, I want you to take over as the Head General of the army," Aero said as he sat up.

"Are you serious?" Fid was reluctant to take on such an important role in this fight against Sekmet.

"I could not be more serious, Brother," Aero looked in to Fid's eyes.

"But why?" it seemed that Paige would be a better choice, he thought.

"You have given us all hope. You led us to victory in this last battle. We all know you are the one who possesses the Essence of the Red Dragon," Aero said with conviction.

"We all believe in you Fid," Melina looked up to him. It was evident in Melina's eyes that she believed that Fid brought hope to the Elf Kingdom.

"I do not know if I will be able to do it, Aero," Fid responded.

"I will help you," Paige placed a hand on his shoulder.

"I need you to do this, Brother," Aero said almost pleading with him. Fid looked at Aero, Paige, and Melina.

"I will do it," he finally said. Smiles grew on the faces of Paige, Aero, and Melina.

"Excellent," Aero rejoiced.

FIGHT FOR THE EASTERN PALACE

I N THE DOJO OF THE palace, Maia was refining her technique
wielding a short sword. She tried to imitate the movements of Fid,
but had no success. Maia lost her grip on the blade many times. She
was thrown off balance and fell often. But after each time she rose
to her feet and continued. She was determined to become a better
fighter with a blade in her hand. She knew she could shoot an arrow
accurately, but her skills with a blade were mediocre. She stayed in
that dojo for hours and with that time she improved. She became
more graceful and quicker. She found that trying to imitate another
was not working for her but to find her own form was best.

In the shadows of the dojo, Rosey watched and admired the
dedication and determination Maia demonstrated. Maia sat down in
the middle of the dojo with sword in hand, breathing heavily.

"You have some skills with a blade, Little Kitty," Rosey smiled
as she emerged from the shadows. Maia rose to her feet and turned
towards her.

"Thank you," she responded breathing heavily.

"But how are you against a real opponent?" a mischievous grin
grew on her face.

"What do you mean?" Maia had lowered her weapon. Seeing she
was vulnerable, Rosey threw several shuriken at Maia. Maia spun out
of the way of the shuriken, "What are you doing!?".

"Testin' your skills, Little Kitty," Rosey jumped toward her with
kunai in both hands. Maia rolled out of the way of Rosey's attack.
Rosey slashed and stabbed at her, but Maia was too agile with cat-like

reflexes. She dodged and blocked every attack Rosey threw at her. Maia threw kicks and slashed at Rosey, but she too was very agile and dexterous that a blow did not land. Rosey and Maia landed a kick at the same time sending each other backwards. Both kipped up to their feet and stared each other down. With their eyes locked on to the other, they circled the room crouching in attack ready stances. With a grin on her face, Rosey charged at her and leapt in to the air. Maia braced herself for the oncoming attack. Within feet of Maia, Rosey vanished in a cloud of shadow and then reappeared behind Maia and kicked her in the back sending her rolling forward.

"You don't fight fair," Maia growled looking back at her.

"Who said that I did," Rosey retorted with a smirk on her face. Maia charged at her about to slash, but Rosey vanished once again. Maia missed her attack and was tripped by Rosey when she reappeared in her blind spot. Maia fell backwards and was about to be stabbed, but she rolled out of the way and kipped up to her feet. Remembering the power of the Necklace of Isis, she focused her energy and formed a protective aura her body. Rosey threw a shuriken at Maia, but it ricocheted off and stuck to the wall. Maia grinned and walked toward Rosey. Rosey threw more shuriken and all shattered when they hit Maia's barrier. Maia then charged at her and slashed. Rosey jumped away and vanished in to a cloud of shadow. Reappearing behind Maia, Rosey threw a kick but was thrown backwards when her foot hit the protective energy aura. Maia leapt to the air about to strike when Rosey slipped a very small orb from her waistline and dropped it to the floor. A thick black cloud of smoke burst from the orb. It caused Maia to cough and lose her concentration. The protective aura faded leaving her open to attack. Rosey seized the opportunity and threw a kick to Maia's stomach sending her backwards. Maia saw Rosey charging for her again. She leapt to the air over Rosey and focused energy from the Necklace into an orb. When thrown, the orb hit Rosey in the back throwing her forward onto her face. Rosey growled under her breath while looking back at Maia who grinned and motioned for her to attack. Rosey quickly rose to her feet, then slashed and stabbed at Maia. Maia blocked and countered the attacks, then swung at Rosey with her blade. Rosey blocked the strike with her kunai and spun to slash at Maia. Maia also spun and slashed at Rosey. Both blades stopped within inches of each other's throat. They stood staring at each other breathing heavily.

"That was very impressive, Little Kitty. You were able to hold your own against a trained Shadow Shinobi," Rosey finally said with a grin.

"It's what I have been training for," Maia responded. Soon Lieutenant Aldar entered the room. Both Maia and Rosey turned their attention to him without removing their blades from each other's throat. Aldar then cleared his throat. Both smiled and removed the blades.

"Your presence is requested in Aero's bed chamber," he said. Maia and Rosey nodded and followed Aldar.

Once in Aero's bed chamber, Maia took her place by Fid's side and Rosey stayed on the outskirts of the gathering by the doorway. Paige, Fid, Kulla, Melina, Lieutenant Demus, Lieutenant Aldar were all gathered around Aero as he laid in bed.

"I have called this meeting because word has reached us that the town of Belnar has been overrun with Orcs. They seized the palace a few days ago and then took over the town," Aero stated grimly.

"What of the townspeople?" although this was grim news, Fid was more concerned for the people.

"They all fled just before the Orc army moved in. The townspeople are now taking the mountain pass to the nearby village. The townspeople will arrive within a few hours," Aero responded.

"That is a relief," Melina said.

"Yes it is. We now need to devise a plan to take back not only the village but also the palace," Paige said.

"Can we not take a small army and take back the town?" Aldar interjected.

"No. They will be expecting a frontal assault and we do not have enough man power to launch such an attack," Aero gave a shake of his head.

"What should we do then?" Kulla asked. Silence filled the room for several moments.

"Perhaps a night attack. Not with an army, but a small group," Fid finally suggested.

"Explain this plan," Aero said.

"Kulla, Maia, Paige, Demus, Aldar, and I will sneak into the town and sweep through it unnoticed. We then make our way into the palace through the underground door to the stables and send a signal to an awaiting army, led by Melina, and let them in to the palace," Fid looked to everyone as they listened attentively. Aero nodded and smiled in approval of the plan.

"There is one problem. Where are we to get the equipment for a night raid?" Fid would answer Kulla's question by looking to Rosey, who still was standing in the doorway. Everyone else's eyes followed Fid's and fell upon Rosey. Her eyes widened when the attention of everyone turned to her. 'What am I expected to do?', she thought to herself.

"Rosey, you are a Shadow Shinobi and a trained assassin. Where did you keep the equipment that you used on your covert missions?" Fid stepped toward her. She lowered her gaze to the ground as she was reluctant to tell.

"I will take you there," she closed her eyes as if pained to do so.

"Thank you," Fid placed a hand on her shoulder. Maia noticed that Rosey had lowered her head almost in shame. What was bothering her? Did it have anything to do with her background as an assassin?

"The small party will follow Rosey to retrieve your equipment, while Melina works with the Captain of the Rangers to gather a small army. Both will await your signal near the edge of the woods," Melina nodded her head, understanding her role in the assault. "Go and may you be blessed with victory," Aero said. All bowed and left the room. Maia did not see Rosey in the doorway. She was found huddled in a dark corner of the hall. Maia walked to her stopping a few feet short.

"What's troubling you, Rosey?" Maia asked reaching a hand out to her. Rosey looked to her with tears in her eyes, "I tried to get away from the life of an assassin".

"What happened?" Maia's ears flattened against her head seeing the pain in Rosey's eyes. Rosey looked up to Maia and then back to the ground, "Years ago, a warlord came to me and wanted to hire me to kill the mayor of a nearby town. I told him that I would not because he was an innocent and committed no crime. I told him that I only killed those who had committed misdeeds. He pushed me again and again," her teeth were clenched, "I refused. He then threatened to kill my family if I did not do as he said. I had to comply. That night I gave the mayor a fast and painless death. That memory of him looking at me before I killed him still haunts my memories," a stream of tears running down her flushed cheeks. Maia knelt down to embraced her, "I'm truly sorry to hear that story, but it was not your fault. You had no choice. You had the choice of killing the mayor or having your whole family killed. I believe that many of us would have made the decision you did. This mission can redeem you of that deed".

"Thank you, Little Kitty," Rosey said in between sobs.

"You're welcome," Maia responded with a smile.

"I am supposin' I should lead you all to get your equipment," Rosey forced a smile. Maia nodded with a smile on her face. They both walked down the hall and down the stairs to meet the small party. Once downstairs Fid, Kulla, Paige, Melina, Aldar, Demus, and the Captain of the Rangers awaited them.

"Is everything alright?" Fid asked. Rosey looked to Maia and Maia looked back with a smile.

"Yes. Everythin' is alright. Is everyone ready?" Rosey asked.

"Yes," all answered in unison.

"Let us be off then," she said. They all then made their way to the stable and mounted their respective horses, then rode on out of the palace. The small party headed east in to the woods while Melina led the army of Rangers rode farther south.

The small party of Rosey, Paige, Fid, Maia, Kulla, Aldar, and Demus rode farther and farther in to the woods. The day began to turn to dusk as the riders were nearing their destination. They soon came to a clearing which was familiar to Fid. The smell in the air was very distinct to him. At the edge of the clearing was the Red Dragon Inn, the first place Fid had been on Rhydin all those months ago. The riders dismounted their horses and tied their reins to a post, then entered the inn. The familiar smell of ale, whiskey, and beer filled the nostrils of Fid and the others. Rosey led the group behind the bar counter in to a room where shelves were stocked with all brands and makes of whiskey, ale, wine, and beer. Rosey walked to the far end of the room and reached behind a shelf. Pulling a lever behind the shelf, one of the shelves creaked and slid open. There was a dimly lit opening behind the shelf. It led to a lower level of the inn. Rosey motioned for the others to follow her down the dimly lit stairway. The stairway was lined with cobble stone. Cobwebs lined the walls and ceiling. The air was stale and dust coated the stairs. The staircase led to a smaller room. There was just enough room to fit ten people. The room was mostly made of stone. One side of the wall was lined with katana, kunai, sai, shuriken, daggers, arrows, bows, rope, and bead-like orbs. The opposite side of the room hung dark clothing. Dark body suits with hoods, masks, light wrist gauntlets, shin guards, and light chest plates. "Take what equipment you need. I suggest you wear dark clothing as to not be seen by the enemy," Rosey looked to everyone. The small party did so. The material of the body suits was light yet durable. It stretched to fit the form of its wearer. The mask left only the eyes of the wearer visible. The wrist gauntlets, shin guards, and chest plates were made of a light tempered steel. An arrow could not even pierce this tempered armor. Fid took a considerable amount of shuriken attaching them to his belt and took a few daggers strapping them to his thigh. Fid found a belt that allowed for him to strap the Twin Dragon Blades to his back. Maia took more arrows for her quiver and strapped a few daggers to her hip. Kulla added a short sword and daggers to his arsenal. Paige also added shuriken and daggers to her arsenal of weaponry. Aldar and Demus added coils of rope, daggers, to their arsenal of bows, arrows, and their swords. Once they were ready, Rosey led them through a small corridor. It seemed as though the corridor was dug under the surface of the earth. It was small enough for an average sized adult human.

"Where does this tunnel lead?" despite being one of the smallest in the party, Maia seemed cramped in the corridor.

"This tunnel leads to the eastern border of the woods, just under two miles from Belnar, Little Kitty," Rosey responded. Maia nodded in acknowledgment. One by one they entered the narrow tunnel.

They later reached a dead end in the tunnel. There was a ladder that led to the surface. One by one they each climbed the ladder to the top. Rosey was the first to climb. She opened a disguised trap door to the outside. It was late at night. It was cool and there was a breeze blowing about. A thick fog hovered over the ground. It would give some concealment to the small party. Belnar was in sight, but the details of the town were vague.

"Fid, what do you see?" Kulla asked. Fid focused his vision, "There are Orcs posted on the wall. They are armed with iron crossbows. They also have broad swords and thick armor. The armor is weak at the neck and stomach. Each Orc has a horn as to warn others if they spot a threat".

"We need to move quickly and quietly as to not let the guards at the wall rouse the others," Paige stated.

"Agreed. We do not need to rouse a small army," Kulla said.

"It would seem as though there is one guard on each wall," Fid observed.

"So four wall guards all together," Aldar said to clarify. Fid nodded his head.

"Little Kitty, can you shoot the wall guards?" Rosey turned to Maia. Maia nodded with a smirk on her face as if that were not a difficult task.

With the fog covering their movements, the small party moved in closer to the town walls without causing any noise. They could not even hear each other breathe. When they were within twenty yards of the walls, Rosey signaled for Maia to take careful aim. Maia did so. With one arrow she took aim at one of the guards. She released the arrow to the skull of the guard. The Orc did not see it coming and as soon as the arrow pierced his thick skull he dropped forward to the ground. Rosey nodded to Maia in approval of the shot. They then moved around the perimeter of the town and came to the next guard. The whole party, with the exception of Maia, laid flat on the ground under the cover of the fog while Maia took aim and released another arrow through an Orc's skull. The next two Orcs were killed in the same fashion as the first. Aldar and Demus attached their length of rope to two of Maia's arrows. Maia shot both arrows to the top of the wall. The small party started to quietly climb to the top of the wall. Once at the top, Rosey motioned for Fid and Maia to follow her while Paige, Kulla, Aldar, and Demus took care of the other side of town. Fid, Rosey and Maia took the eastern side of town while Paige, Kulla, Aldar, and Demus would sweep through the western side of town. Rosey, Fid, and Maia looked down at the stone houses. They observed Orc guards patrolling the streets. Rosey gave a grin under her mask. She vanished in to shadow and then reappeared behind the Orc guards stabbing them in the back of the neck with her kunai. Both Fid and Maia jumped down to the nearest roof and entered quietly through the window silently killing the Orc guards inside. Moving from house to house and building to building, the small party silently killed the Orc guards within the town. The small party met at the center of the town and moved south toward the palace, moving silently in the shadows. After killing the rest of the Orc guards, the small party made their way to the palace under the cover of the fog. The party stopped a short way from the palace walls to huddle together.

"How should we get in to the palace?" Rosey's tone was hushed.

"It must be quietly and carefully. Orc guards will be everywhere. Thankfully these bodysuits mask our scent," Kulla said quietly.

"There is a door that leads to the stables below the ground level of the Palace," Paige interjected. They all look at each other and nodded.

"Lead us there," Rosey whispered. Paige nodded and took the lead of the party. Moving quietly and swiftly as to not be seen by the Orc guards at the wall, they moved along the Palace walls. As they reached the corner of the wall, Demus crouched down and reached for a handle. Pulling up on the handle, Demus opened a trap door leading to an underground tunnel. There was no brick, no stone, and no wood lining the walls of the tunnel. There was nothing but dirt and some roots dangling and lining the ceiling of the tunnel. Every twenty feet there was a dimly lit torch lighting the tunnel. The dirt tunnel led the party to a dead end. Leaning against the wall was a ladder leading to another trap door. Rosey was the first to climb the ladder. When she reached the top of the ladder she slightly opened the trap door so that she could see if there were Orc guards patrolling. The area was clear and she motioned for the others to follow. All climbed the ladder and into the stable. Looking down the hall, Maia noticed two Orc guards approximately thirty feet away side by side along the near wall. She motioned for Aldar to take a shooter's position. He took careful aim and then released the arrow. It pierced through one Orc's head and stuck in the other's. A smile of triumph came across his face and then motioned for the others to follow. Paige, Aldar, and Demus led the way through the dimly lit halls of the Palace. There were several close encounters with Orc guards noticing the party. Paige, Demus, and Aldar threw their shuriken and released their arrows at patrolling Orc guards. Fid, Kulla, and Maia dragged the Orc corpses to dark corners and small rooms as to not give evidence they were present in the palace.

They were outside and were drawing getting closer to the mechanism that opened the gate when Fid's ears twitched. He looked up and saw a shower of arrows about to rain down upon them.

"Look out!" he warned the others. They all looked up. Rosey vanished in to shadow to avoid the arrows. Paige, Demus, and Aldar leaped out of the way. Maia placed a barrier in front of her to deflect the arrows. Fid's hands burned with fire. He unleashed an inferno up to the oncoming arrows turning them to ash. Kulla used the Scepter of Osiris to summon sparks of soul energy and launched them toward the arrows to burn them. There were a few that were not destroyed. One grazed Fid's shoulder and another pierced Kulla's leg. Kulla winced as he pulled the arrow from his leg. The whole party gathered back to back and saw the gate wall littered with Orc archers and Orc ground troops poured out of the Palace's main door. They pulled back their masks seeing as though it did not matter that their faces were hidden. More Orc archers were in the windows. At that moment, Fid lost his focus and the same voice that spoke to him, again made its voice heard, *"Trust in yourself. Believe in your power, your abilities, and most importantly yourself. Look deep within your heart. That is where your true power lies"*. Fid then regained his focus. The Orc ground troops had surrounded the party with spears and swords pointed at them. Then an armored figure emerged from the horde of Orc guards. His armor was dark and thick. His long cape blew with the breeze. Two maces were strapped to his waist. Fid noticed the same dragon emblem he saw on Ivy, Naafar, and Kain. He stood before the party of seven with arms folded and gave an evil laugh.

"Here I have the Elf Ruler of the Woodland Realm, her two lieutenants, the only Day Walker in the South East Coven, a human girl, a cat girl, and the Bearer of the Red Dragon Essence. The question is, do I turn you all over to Lord Sekmet alive or kill you where you stand. This Bearer of the Dragon Essence is worth a lot to Lord Selmet alive," he said.

"Who are you?" Fid asked in a demanding tone.

"You will hear my name when Lord Sekmet praises me for taking you to him alive so that he may slay you and take your heart and your power, Dragon. Lord Sekmet has slain many Dragons, but your power is the greatest of all," he said. Fid then figured out that Sekmet and his General's were in fact Dragon Slayers.

"Come and try to take him," Maia drew her short sword as did the others. The armored man walked up to Maia looking deep into her amber eyes.

"You have spirit, Little Kitty. Maybe I will keep you for myself," he said with an evil grin under his helmet. Maia spat in the eye slit of the man's helmet.

"You will regret that," he growled.

"*Trust your instincts, Fid*," the voice spoke to Fid again. With a deep breath and closed eyes, Fid began to focus his energy.

"Kill them. Leave the Red Dragon alive," the armored man turned to walked through the Orc army. The Orc archers took aim and the ground troops stepped closer to the party ready to strike.

"Rosey can you take more than one person with you in to the shadows?" Fid asked in a hushed tone.

"Yes," she responded.

"When I tell you to, take everyone to the gate and open it to let the awaiting army in," Fid said. Rosey nodded and motioned for everyone to get closer to her. Fid focused his power and energy. Flames began to engulf one of his fists. Fid's eyes glowed a crimson red, "Now Rosey!" Rosey did what she was told to do. She carried the group through shadows to the gate. When they reappeared, Paige ran to the lever and pulled it to open the main gate. The Orc archers released their arrows. Fid threw his fire engulfed fist to the ground creating a dome of fierce flames. The dome of flames radiated and expanded from his body setting the surrounding Orcs on fire. At that moment, Melina, with a giant dire wolf she summoned by her side, led the small army of Rangers to sweep through the gates killing the remaining ground Orc troops. Aldar and Demus shot at the wall guards. Maia looked to Fid and saw him drop to his knees. She rushed to him and found that an arrow had pierced his stomach. She let out a horrifying scream. She held him and tried to pull the arrow out but it was deep inside of him. Blood trickled from his mouth. There was a blank stare in his eyes. He then slowly looked in to her eyes. Tears welled in her amber eyes. He wiped away the tear that streamed down her cheek and forced a smile.

"Don't do this to me. Don't leave me, please," Maia implored with tears streaming down her cheeks.

"I have…a feeling…that…we will….see each other…..again," Fid gasped for air. His eyes slowly closed as he exhaled his last breath.

"No! No don't leave me Fid! You cannot die on me! I love you!" a tear rolled from her cheek and fell on Fid's forehead. While carnage ensued around her, Maia held Fid's lifeless body. Moments later, anger began to swell within her. The Necklace of Isis glowed vibrantly. She used its power and lifted herself in to the air with bow in hand. She reached for her quiver of arrows and drew three. She aimed and released three into a retreating Orc soldier. Maia released arrow after arrow into Orc troops and archers. Maia noticed the armored General retreating through the gate and was riding toward the border of the woods. On the General's back she saw the arrows in his quiver were the same make of arrow that pierced Fid's stomach. She took aim with one arrow and concentrated the Necklace's energy into the arrow's head.

"Arrow of Isis!" she yelled as she released the charged arrow. The arrow pursued the mounted General leaving a trench in the ground and destroyed all in its wake. The arrow exploded as it hit one of the hills with a thunderous explosion. There was nothing but a ditch in the ground and a cloud of dust and ash. She lowered herself to the ground and held Fid's lifeless body once more. All gathered around and shared in her grief.

A Dragon Reborn

ONE MONTH PASSED SINCE THE night Fid was killed by one of Sekmet's Generals. Many battles were fought across the land since that tragic night. Those battles were the most violent and bloodiest of this war. Many were lost, but the Elf Empire suffered the most. The Elf Empire lost precious manpower forcing the Elves to spread their forces thin to protect their boundaries. Melina was charged with the defense of the Western Palace while Paige and Aldar were to return to the Woodland and protect its borders. Despite Sekmet conquering most of the southern lands of Rhydin, the Elf Kingdom was able to stop them from spreading any further, but they were unsure of how long they were to last.

Fid's body was buried outside of the Eastern Palace walls along with the Twin Dragon Blades, and the Bracelet of Ra still on his wrist. The headstone faced to the west. The head stone read, 'Here lies Lord Fid, The Bearer of the Red Dragon Essence'. Lilacs, chrysanthemums, and roses decorated the head stone. His face was engraved into the marble head stone. Maia was on her knees in front of the head stone with her head bowed and tears flowing from her eyes down to the headstone. Aero had been standing several feet behind her not wanting to disturb her moment of grief. After a few moments, he joined Maia and knelt beside her. He placed his hand on her shoulder to comfort her.

"We all loved him," he said quietly choking back the tears welling in his eyes.

"He was all that I had in my life. Before I met him, I had nothing. My family had been killed by the tyrant Duke Thaius, then he enslaved me. I was nothing but a plaything to that bastard," she spat through her cat-like teeth." Then, Fid came to the forest, I felt warmth in him. The way he looked at me and talked to me made me forget all the worries and troubles that burdened my life," Maia's voice trembled with sadness.

"Yes, he was special to us all. Not only was he a great man, he was a great warrior. The most powerful I have ever seen. He gave us all hope. But now, we do not know how we can win this war without his power," Aero said. Maia's ears perked up and frustration overtook her grief.

"Was that all he was to you?! A weapon for this army to use?! He was much more than that!" she said quickly rising to her feet then stormed away. Aero's eyes followed her and sighed.

"No. He was much more than that. He was my brother," he said to himself. He then rose to his feet and made his way back to the Palace. As he was about to enter the Palace, he heard the hooves of a galloping horse behind him. There was a man on the horse riding toward the palace. He wore dark pants and leather tunic. His hair was short and dark. His eyes were dark and somewhat shifty and suspicious. The man rode up to Aero and dismounted his horse. Aero looked him up and down wondering who he was and what his business was. Aero saw that he was not very tall, maybe five feet and six inches. He was of an average build.

"Greetings, I am Anaius," he introduced himself with a bow.

"I am Aero. The Elf Ruler of the Eastern Province," Aero returned the bow.

"I am from Earth and am an old friend of Fid. Is he here?" Aero lowered his head and pointed to the headstone. Anaius' eyes widened and sighed, "How did this happen?".

"A month ago, this palace was taken over by a General in Sekmet's army. A small party of our army took it back but was ambushed. Fid took an arrow to the stomach from that General and died," Aero grimly informed him.

"That is rather unfortunate. He did die honorably though," Anaius said as he walked over to Fid's grave.

"How do you know Fid?" Aero watched Anaius as he stood over Fid's grave. Not a tear was shed by him over the news of Fid's death.

"We were students under Master Chen Shun on Earth. We were his most advanced students. Fid was favored by Master Shun, b-but that did not bother me. It drove me to do better and focus more on the studies and techniques," Anaius turned to face the grief stricken Elf Ruler.

"I see," Aero nodded. Anaius turned to face the headstone then dropped to his knees to whisper a brief prayer.

"We can accommodate you in the palace if you would like to stay," Aero offered.

"That would be much appreciated. Thank you," Anaius responded getting to his feet. Aero first led Anaius in to the stables to rest his horse, then in to the Palace. As they both walked through the corridor, Maia was perched on the railing of the staircase. She jumped down and landed in front of Aero and Anaius.

"Who is this?" she asked with curiosity in her voice, sniffing at him. His scent was familiar to her.

"This is Anaius. An old friend of Fid's," Aero said. Anaius bowed his head slightly with his eyes still on her and a grin on his face. She cocked her head to the side with more curiosity and suspicion.

"A friend of Fid's?" she further asked. It was odd to her to find a friend of Fid's at this time. Anaius nodded his head still grinning.

"I was showing Anaius the Palace," Aero stated. Anaius looked upon Maia with lustful eyes as he passed. Maia shuddered as he gazed at her. Kulla walked down the stairs to Maia's side as she glared at Anauis.

"Is there something wrong?" Kulla asked.

"I don't trust him," she growled.

"I see. And why is that?" he mocked. She glared at him and looked back down the hall toward Aero and Anaius.

"His scent is familiar. And there is an air of evil around him," her growled deepened.

"What are we suppose to do about it? Expose him to everyone?" his tone was sarcastic and skeptical.

"No. Just keep an eye on him," she snapped at him looking deep in to his eyes. Kulla looked back at her and nodded. At that moment, Demus rushed in behind Kulla and Maia breathing heavily. Kulla placed his hand on his shoulder, "Are you alright Lieutenant Demus?".

"Where is….Lord…Aero?" he gasped for air.

"He walked down the hall and went in to the room to the right," Maia answered him as she sat back on her haunches. Demus rushed down the hall and entered the room. Kulla and Maia looked to one another and walked to the room to listen to the conversation inside.

"How many are coming?" they heard Aero's voice ask.

"They come by the hundreds Lord Aero. All with broad shields and swords," Demus' voice responded.

"There is an Orc army headed our way," Maia whispered to Kulla with her ear against the door.

"How far away are they?" Aero asked.

"They are crossing the southern border of the province," Demus responded. There was a moment of silence.

"Gather what troops we have. Post the archers on the walls and ground troops fifty yards outside the gate," Aero finally said. Maia heard footsteps walk toward the door and she moved aside as did Kulla. Demus walked passed Maia and Kulla to the wall and pulled a rope hanging from the ceiling to sound the alarm. Aero and Anaius walked out of the room as well.

"Allow me to help you in this fight," Anaius said almost pleading with him.

"Very well," Aero gave a nod. Anaius looked at Kulla and then to Maia with those lustful eyes again. Maia shuddered in disgust and Anaius gave a grin. He followed closely behind Aero. Kulla walked beside Maia, "I am starting to understand what you were referring to". She nodded and shuddered again at the thought of Anaius.

"Come. Let us get ready for this battle," Kulla urged. She nodded and walked to her bed chamber to retrieve her weapons, as did Kulla.

Hours later, Aero, Kulla, Demus and Anaius were on horseback in front an army of Elf ground troops. Elf archers were on the gate walls along with Maia. Her bow and quiver of arrows were at the ready. The Orc army emerged from over the hills. Their footsteps and clanging of their armor could be heard by the Elf army. The Orcs halted their march one hundred yards from the Elf army. Maia ordered the Elf archers to take aim as she did the same. The Orc army drove the butts of their spears into the ground. The clanging of the armor and the thunderous sound of the spears sounded throughout the eastern hills. Aero ordered for the ground troops to draw their swords and ready their shields. The Orc front line lowered their spears and began a charge for the Elf army. The Elf line prepared themselves by stepping forward and placing their shields side by side to repel the onslaught. The Orcs crashed into the Elf shields. The Elf soldiers did not let them pass and drove them backwards. Maia ordered the archers to release their arrows. Each Orc fell to an arrow. At that moment, Aero, Kulla, Demus and Anaius dismounted and took positions behind the shield bearing Elf soldiers.

"Forward!" Aero ordered the soldiers. A second wave of Orc troops charged for the Elf frontlines. Again, the second wave could not penetrate the Elf wall of shields. The archers once more released their arrows in to the Orc soldiers killing many of them. There were few that survived the shower of arrows. Aero, Kulla, Demus, and Anaius stepped from behind the Elf shields and cut them down. Anaius' fighting style reminded Aero of Fid. One last wave charged for the Elf wall of shields. Kulla raised the Scepter of Osiris to the air and unleashed bolts of soul energy onto several of the charging Orc troops. The Orc troops turned to ash as the bolts struck them. Once more they failed to penetrate the wall of Elf shields. The Orc

troops were pushed back several feet and were shortly killed by Elf
arrows and blades. The surviving Orc troops retreated to the south.

"Victory!" Aero declared raising his sword to the air. All the Elf
troops cheered in unison. Kulla walked to Aero's side, "Do you find it
most peculiar that the Orc troops attacked a palace with no General
to lead them?".

"It is rather odd," Aero gave a nod to Kulla's thought. They looked
back and saw Anaius surveying the Orc casualties. He looked up at
Kulla and Aero with a grin on his face.

"Lieutenant Demus," Aero called.

"Yes, Lord Aero?" Demus came and stood at attention.

"I want you to post platoons of soldiers in Belnar, at the borders
of this Province, and the Western Province. I will go to tell Paige and
Melina to post platoons at the southern borders of the Woodland
Realm," Aero stated.

"Yes, Lord Aero," Demus placed his fist to his heart and bowed
his head. He then took his leave. Aero then turned to Kulla, "I am
leaving you in charge of the Palace," Kulla nodded his head. Aero,
Kulla, Anaius, and the Elf soldiers took their leave of the battlefield
after burning the corpses of the slain Orc troops.

Later that night, Aero mounted his horse and rode to the
Woodland Realm. Demus left at the same time along with Elf
troops to make camps along the borders of the Western and Eastern
Provinces. Maia sat on the edge of her bed on her haunches thinking
about Fid. Every night the past month, she had cried herself to sleep.
A tear rolled down her cheek. She then heard the door creak open.
She quickly wiped the tear from her face. She saw in the doorway
Anaius leaning against the doorframe.

"Oh, it's you," contempt was in her voice.

"Why do you hate me so, Little Kitten?" his attempt to sound
innocent was obvious.

"I don't trust you," she hissed.

"You don't even know me," he took a few steps closer toward her.

"I know enough," her hand crept to her short sword that laid next to her on the bed. He took a few more steps toward her. She suddenly leapt toward him and held the blade to his throat.

"You were in love with him, weren't you?" his lips curled in to a grin.

"That is not any of your concern," she growled.

"He always received the praise of everyone around him. He was loved by everyone," contempt was in his voice.

"It would seem that you were jealous of Fid," it was her turn to taunt him. He bore his clenched teeth and reached for one of his maces. It was then that Kulla walked to the door and peered in to the room, "Is everything alright?". Anaius growled under his breath. There was a scowl on her face as she glared daggers at him. She did not lower her blade from his throat. He returned the glare, then turned to walk toward the door. His shoulder bumped in to Kulla's on his way out of the room. Kulla's eyes followed Anaius down the hall and down the staircase. Maia walked to Kulla's side, "I now know of what you spoke before. He is indeed suspicious". Rosey then walked up the stairs and toward Maia and Kulla.

"Who was that?" Rosey pointed back toward the staircase.

"No one of any significance," Maia walked to her bed to sheathe her sword.

"I see. There's an older man downstairs. He wants to see the head of the palace," Rosey said. Maia and Kulla looked at each other with a look of confusion on their faces.

"Take us to him, Rosey," Kulla said. Rosey nodded and led them downstairs. When they entered the foyer, they saw middle aged human man sitting in a chair. He wore a round braided hat that hid his face. He wore a dark red cloth robe and carried a wooden staff with five symbols engraved into it. They could see the man had a full, black beard with speckles of gray in it. Kulla, Maia, and Rosey stood in front of the man. The man looked up at them with his almond shaped eyes as if he were examining them.

"Who are you?" Maia finally asked. The man looked to Maia and then rose to his feet. He was of average height for a human man. His was slender, yet his body was strong and solid.

"I am Chen Shun. I am Fid's Master," he responded in a mellow voice. Kulla's, Maia's, and Rosey's eyes widened when he spoke.

"You are Fid's teacher?" Kulla asked.

"I am. Where is Fid? I have much to discuss with him," Shun looked at them with patient eyes.

"There is something you should know then," Maia stepped toward to him. Shun turned his attention to the young were-cat woman.

"Fid was killed during battle a month ago," her voice was soft and held the grief she felt. There were several moments of silence.

"How was he killed?" Shun finally asked.

"An arrow pierced his stomach," Kulla replied.

"His heart was not taken or damaged?" Shun there was glint of hope in Shun's voice.

"No," Rosey shook her head.

"There is still hope then," Shun stated.

"What do you mean?" Maia's eyes were wide and her heart began to beat faster.

"Where is his body buried?" Shun asked.

"Outside of the Palace walls, Master Shun," Kulla answered.

"Take me there," Shun said. "And bring a shovel," Kulla, Maia, and Rosey all looked at each other with a look of confusion on their faces. They did as Chen Shun asked. Kulla went to find a shovel while Maia and Rosey led Shun to Fid's grave. Once outside, Maia and Rosey led Chen Shun to Fid's grave. He looked upon it and then closed his eyes for several moments as if meditating. Maia and Rosey looked to each other not knowing what Master Shun was doing. At that moment, Kulla arrived with shovel in hand. Chen Shun slowly opened his eyes and looked to Kulla, "Dig," Shun pointed to the grave.

"Excuse me?" Kulla asked as if he did not understand.

"I said, dig," Shun said more articulately.

"Why are we digging up his body?" disgust was in Rosey's voice.

"Can you not sense the energy emitting from his body?" Shun furrowed his eyebrows in disbelief of their ignorance.

"What energy?" Maia looked from Shun to Fid's grave not knowing what energy he was speaking of.

"Complete novices," Shun mumbled under his breath shaking his head.

"Are you saying that Fid's body is emitting energy?" Kulla asked.

"Yes, I am saying this," Shun's waning patience was heard in his voice. Kulla looked to Maia and Rosey. They both nodded their heads to him and he began to dig.

After Kulla came to Fid's casket, he hoisted himself out of the six foot hole. Maia then, with the power of the Necklace, lifted the casket from the grave. She carefully placed the casket to the side of the grave. Shun walked to the casket and unfastened the clasps then slowly lifted the lid. There they saw Fid's body surprisingly unspoiled by decomposition. Shun placed his hand to Fid's face, then looked to Kulla, Rosey, and Maia. They all looked at him in anticipation.

"His face is still warm," Shun finally said. Kulla, Maia and Rosey all looked at each other in amazement.

"How is that possible?" Kulla asked.

"Fid is the Bearer of the Essence of the Red Dragon. The only way to kill him for good is to take his heart from his chest and take his power by consuming it. The power within him is sustaining his body. But like all when they die, his soul has left him. His body is now an empty shell," Shun looked from Fid's body to them. Maia, Kulla, and Rosey were rendered speechless for several moments.

"You're saying that he can be brought back to life?" Maia's eyes were bright with hope.

"Yes, my child," Shun answered. Tears came to Maia's eyes and her heart raced with joy. She suddenly embraced Shun in her excitement.

"Oh thank you, Master Shun!" Maia squealed.

"Do not thank me yet, my child. We have yet to take his body to the Keshnarian Ruins to perform an Ancient Ritual called the Ritual of Life," Shun stated.

"The Ritual of Life? What is that?" Rosey asked.

"During this Ritual two souls are summoned. One of which is the body's original soul and the other another unknown soul. These two souls fuse into one entity and go into the empty shell to create a somewhat new entity. The person retains their original memories in addition to the memories of the other soul," Kulla explained.

"Very good Kulla, but you forget the person also gains the life force and energy from the second unknown soul," Shun added. Kulla nodded.

"Is it not dangerous because we do not know who the second soul is? It could be an evil soul and could that not cause Fid to turn evil?" Rosey asked.

"That is quite possible, but I have faith there is a higher power that watches over Fid's soul," Shun gave a confident smile. Kulla, Maia, and Rosey all looked to each other and nodded.

"What should we do?" Rosey was ready to get on with whatever task it was they had to do.

"Place the casket on my wagon and retrieve your horses. We are going to the Keshnarian Ruins," Shun told them. Kulla, Maia, and Rosey nodded their heads to Shun and began right away. Maia once again used the power of the Necklace to lift the casket and carry it. Shun led her to the front of the Palace where he left his horse and wagon. The wagon was simple. It was made of redwood and a canvas was rigged like a dome to cover the wagon. Maia placed the casket in to the wagon. She returned to the Palace and made her way to the stables. She thought about taking one horse, but looked to Sundancer who was in the dark corner of the stable. She let the reins down of the other horse and walked over to Sundancer. She stood in front of him for a few moments and looked into his eyes. Sundancer looked at her as well. Maia took a step forward to him, but Sundancer took a step away from Maia. Maia gave a sigh.

"Sundancer, I know I'm not Fid, but can you please cooperate with me. I will take care of you, I promise," Maia pleaded with him. Sundancer hesitantly took a few steps toward Maia and outstretched his neck to her. Maia tried to interpret his body language. She slowly reached out and placed her hand on his head and then ran her fingers though his coarse mane. She smiled and mounted him. They rode out of the stable to meet Kulla, Rosey, and Shun. They made their way to the woods. Anaius watched the events transpire from a window with a scowl on his face.

"They will not succeed in bringing that bastard back to life," he growled.

The Sun was just rising the next day as Shun, Kulla, Maia, and Rosey were resting before moving on to the Keshnarian Ruins. The Sun's rays illuminated the woods through the morning mist and dew of the woods. Maia looked up and saw there were apple trees growing in this part of the woods. Rosey, Kulla, and Shun looked up and saw the fruit also. Maia grinned and shifted to her panther form and climbed to the higher branches to retrieve the apples. She shifted back to her human form and perched herself near the apples to pick them. She dropped a few down to Kulla, Maia, and Shun. They all caught them and began eating. Maia dropped an extra apple on Kulla's head. Kulla looked up to her and growled.

"Young people," Shun mumbled under his breath shaking his head. Once they finished, they moved on further to the Ruins of Keshnar. Maia's ears perked up and looked behind her. Rosey stopped alongside her, "Is something the matter?".

"I don't know. I thought I felt someone following us," Maia looked over her shoulder once more to look behind them. Rosey looked back as well but saw nothing.

"Perhaps you are just bein' anxious about bringin' Fid back," she suggested.

"Possibly," Maia looked behind her several times before reassuring herself nothing was following them.

The day grew to almost high noon. The Sun was hot and its rays shone through the canopy of the redwood trees. Shun, Kulla, Maia, and Rosey were now on the outskirts of the Ruins. They saw the rubble and remains of the pyramid-like structures of what was once the city of Keshnar. Vines and weeds grew from the cracks in the brick on the ground. The walls of the city were crumbling and were very weak. Maia, Kulla, Shun, and Rosey made their way to what was the Sun Temple near the center of the city. At the top of the Temple was a golden disk with the Eye of Ra engraved on it. It reflected the rays of the Sun as it climbed higher in to the sky. Kulla, Maia, Rosey, and Shun dismount and prepared to carry Fid's casket in to the Temple. Maia used the power of the Necklace of Isis to lift and carry the casket in to the Temple. The entrance corridor was dark and the air was stale. Clouds of dust flew up with every step they took. There was no sign of light at the end of the corridor. Shun closed his eyes to concentrate his energy. The top of his staff flared with fire to illuminate the corridor. They walked further down the corridor and saw the end. Once at the end of the corridor, they saw it led to a rather large room. At the center of the floor was the Eye of Ra in gold plating. Directly above the Eye was an opening in the ceiling. There was also a very small stone pedestal with a tattered book on top of it. On the opposite end of the room was an upright coffin against the wall. It was made of what seemed to be iron and the Eye of Ra was engraved in gold on it. On either side of the coffin were doorways that seemed to lead in to eternal darkness. Shun turned to look to Maia and nodded to her. She let the casket down and unfastened the clasps. She opened the lid and looked upon Fid's face. She gently placed her hand on his cheek and felt his warmth.

"We will be together once again very soon," she said quietly.

"Place him inside of that coffin," Shun said pointing to the upright coffin. Kulla and Maia nodded and carefully hoisted him from the casket. They carried him to the coffin and carefully placed him in it along with the Twin Dragon Blades. Maia looked upon him, kissed the palm of her hand and tenderly placed it upon Fid's cheek. She then stepped back and closed the door of the coffin. At that moment, an arrow flew passed her ear and in to the wall. She noticed the arrow was identical to that of the one that killed Fid fired by the Armored General that fled the battle over a month ago. Maia, Shun, Kulla, and Rosey sharply looked behind them drawing their weapons. They found Anaius with bow in hand and behind him was a platoon of Orc.

"Why now?!" Maia exclaimed.

"You will not resurrect that bastard, Master Shun," Anaius said with anger and contempt in his eyes and voice.

"Anaius, what is the meaning of this?!" Shun exclaimed.

"You always praised him. You favored him. You paid more attention to him than you did me or your other students. He was your prized pupil. The other students didn't care, but I did. I always did what you wanted me to do, but it was not good enough for you, Old Man!" Anaius's grip on his bow tightened.

"I pushed you because I knew you were not working as hard as you could have. If you worked as hard as I believed you could have, you would have been as skilled as Fid," Shun slammed his staff in to the stone floor creating a small gust of wind.

"Don't lecture me, Old Man. Fid had an advantage because he bears the Essence of the Great Red Dragon, Tufar. All because at birth he had a bad heart!" Anaius spat from between his clenched teeth.

"That is enough, Anaius!" Shun demanded.

"Very well. Once I take this bastard's body to turn over to Lord Sekmet, I will personally kill you. And I will enjoy it," Anaius growled as he threw aside his bow and drew both maces.

"You will not touch him," Maia drew her short sword. Kulla readied his broad sword and the Scepter and Rosey readied both kunai and stood next to Kulla. Rosey took a quick glance at Kulla from the corner of her eye and felt his intensity. Her focus was shaken a bit looking at him, but quickly regained it.

"So it is the hard way. That is fine with me. Orcs attack!" at Anaius' command, the Orc troops charged for Kulla, Rosey, Shun and Maia. Kulla and Rosey stepped up between the Orc troops and Maia and Shun.

"Perform the Ritual quickly. Rosey and I will divert the Orc troops," Kulla yelled back to Shun. Shun nodded his head and turned to stand in front of the small pedestal. He flipped through the torn and tattered pages of the ritual book. Anaius leapt toward Shun, but Rosey appeared from a cloud of shadow in front of him and kicked him back to the ground. Rosey shook her head at Anaius.

"Maia, come here my child," Shun told Maia. She leapt to his side.

"What should I do, Master Shun?" she asked anxiously as the fight ensued behind them.

"I want you to place your hands above the book as I read the spell. Your thoughts of Fid will lead his soul to the gate," Shun told her. She nodded and held her hands above the book Shun began to read the spell from the book.

"Spirit Realm, we plead to thee that you release the soul of Fid and that you lead him back to the land of the living...." Shun began reading.

"No!" Anaius yelled. He once more leapt toward Shun and Maia. Kulla released a bolt of soul energy from the Scepter at Anaius. The energy crashed in to Anaius's chest sending him back in to the wall, cracking it more than it already was.

"We furthermore ask that you send another soul from your realm to complete the Fusion of the two souls," Shun recited. Maia concentrated hard. Her hands began to glow as did the Necklace of Isis and Kulla's Scepter of Osiris. The fighting stopped as the two Relics glowed and a beam of light emitted from them and hit directly in the Eye of Ra. At that moment, a bright white light emitted from the doorways next to the coffin. The light illuminated the entire room as well as the corridor leading out of the Temple. All covered their eyes as not to be blinded by this explosion of pure light. Moments later, the soul of Fid emerged from the doorway to the right of the coffin. It was white and transparent. It seemed that his face was at peace as it looked upon them. Maia looked back to him and reached out to him. Fid's soul looked in to her eyes and reached out to her as well. Then another soul slowly emerged from the opposite doorway. The soul wore armor that would be fitting for a Knight. His face was hidden by his helmet and face mask. He bore a Dragon Emblem with the Eye of Ra above it on his chest plate. It was not the same as the Generals of Sekmet's army. The unknown soul looked at Fid and nodded, "*I told you that I will always be with you,*" his voice echoed throughout the Temple. Fid smiled and nodded once more to the unknown soul. They then walked toward each other and began to merge into one. A bright light emitted as the two souls fused in to one entity. The fusing entity floated and faded in to the upright coffin. With thunderous rumbles and bright lights emitting from the coffin, the door of the coffin violently swung open. Smoke emerged from the coffin as all saw the figure that stood before them with his head bowed slightly. He slowly lifted his head and opened his eyes. His eyes did not hold their dark brown hue, but a shimmering silver that saw who came to revive him and then to those who came to stop this Ritual. He stood in the coffin wearing a dark tunic underneath a light weight chest plate. His dark, loose fitting pants were tucked in to his dark boots. A light weight gauntlet was worn on his left forearm while the Bracelet of Ra was fastened on to his right wrist. The Twin Dragon Blades were strapped on to his waist. His dreadlocks lightened in color from black to a dark brown.

"F-Fid. Is that really you?" Maia asked in disbelief that he stood before her.

"I am, but I am not Fid. I am a new being," he simply said as he smiled and lightly caressed her cheek. She closed her eyes and purred lightly.

"No matter who you are. You will be destroyed!" Anaius yelled as he released an arrow at him. The new being stepped in front of Maia and caught the arrow by its shaft within inches of his face. Anaius grew angrier and frustrated.

"Orcs, kill them all!" Anaius ordered. The remaining Orc troops charged for the newly fused Being. He drew both Blades standing in front of Maia. As he focused on the enemies in front of him, a faint aura of flame surrounded his body and his dreadlocks flared like a wildfire with embers sparking from each lock. He dashed pass Kulla and Rosey charging toward the Orc troops cutting each one down as he passed them. His eyes flared red as he looked up at Anaius who stood in fear of him. He sheathed both Blades.

"It is high noon," Kulla said to the new being. As he stood in the middle of the Eye of Ra, He looked to the opening in the ceiling above him as the Sun's rays shone down upon him. The Bracelet of Ra glowed vibrantly gold.

"Anaius, your deeds will not go unpunished. By the power of Ra, I am banishing you for all eternity to the Shadow Realm!" his voice was thunderous and resonated throughout the Temple. He then held his hand out with his palm facing outward. A bright gold aura radiated from his palm. He released an intense beam of energy at Anaius. Anaius let out a blood curdling scream as the beam hit him.

"Curse you, your allies, and your children!" these were the final words of Anaius before he faded in to the shadows. After the smoke cleared, he stood there and watched the surviving Orcs retreat. Kulla, Rosey, and Maia stared in amazement at the physical change Fid had undergone. He was a bit taller; his eyes became more focused and intense; and his hair turned from its dark color to a dark brown, but seemed to flare when his energy was focused. His muscles seemingly became more broad and stronger.

"I am amazed at the transformation you have undergone," Kulla looked upon him.

"It is like the caterpillar turning in to a butterfly," Shun commented.

"What should we call him?" Rosey asked as she stood by Kulla's side and looked upon him.

"I do not know," Kulla responded. All took a moment to think.

"I like the name Zidane," Shun finally said.

"Why that name?" Maia asked.

"Zidane was the name of one of the greatest warriors in the history of Earth. Not only was he a skilled fighter, but he was a fair and benevolent Ruler of his era. He was the one who united Asia under one banner. He himself was not from any region in Asia. He was an outsider, much like Fid was when he first came to Rhydin. I feel that Fid, now Zidane, will be the one to unite Rhydin under one banner," Shun proudly looked at Zidane.

"I like it," Kulla stated. Maia and Rosey nodded in agreement.

"Zidane, what's that on your wrist?" Rosey asked looking at the markings she just now noticed. Zidane lifted his arm and followed the markings that coiled around his wrist. It was the image of a Dragon coiling around his wrist. Its head rested in his palm and was breathing an inferno that reached to his fingertips.

"It appears to be a Dragon. Why I have it, I do not know," Zidane looked at it curiously.

"I believe the answers about your past, present, and future will be revealed to you in time young Zidane," Shun said with a reassuring nod. Maia approached Zidane and wrapped her arms around his waist and rested her head against his chest. He returned the tender embrace.

"I heard you call my name each night. I felt the tears you shed as they fell on my grave," Zidane looked into Maia's amber eyes.

"Is that really you in there Fid?" she gazed deeply in to his silver eyes. All he did was stand there and smile at her. She gazed more deeply as if she were looking for something she had lost. Her eyes then widened and a big smile came across her face.

"There you are!" she tightened the embrace she had on his waist as she squealed in excitement. They then looked in to each other's eyes and slowly gave each other a tender kiss. The light from the Sun shone down upon them. Kulla, Rosey, and Shun looked on them and smiled.

"It is about time this happened," Kulla whispered to Rosey. She nodded in agreement. She glanced at Kulla once more and bit her lower lip.

"Young love is a beautiful sight to behold," Shun said as if he were refreshed to see this spectacle. Zidane and Maia then looked in to each other's eyes once more before they departed arm in arm from the Temple with the others close behind.

THE TRINITY

WEEKS PASSED SINCE THE REBIRTH of Fid, now renamed Zidane. Since his rebirth, the Elf Army began to gain ground and win more battles and more territory over the forces of Sekmet. Zidane, Kulla, and Maia led many of the battles and worked as a single cohesive unit. They were flawless in their tactics. With the powers of the Bracelet of Ra, the Necklace of Isis, and the Scepter of Osiris being wielded by Zidane, Kulla and Maia, the Elf Army seemed invincible. Sekmet scolded his Generals after failing time after time to eradicate the Elves. His anger grew with each defeat. He knew that Zidane was the key to the success of the Elf Army. There was nothing more he wanted than the three Ancient Relics and Zidane's heart.

Early one morning, Maia awoke to the first light from the Sun caressing her face. Her eyes fluttered open and she yawned. She rose and stretched in a cat like manner. She looked to her side and saw that Zidane was not there. She rose from the bed, placed a red satin robe on, and walked down the hall and down the stairway. In passing the Study, she found Kulla attentively studying parchments that laid on the table in front of him. She stood in the doorway for a few moments before saying anything, "What is that you are studying?". Kulla looked up to her. He had dark circles under his eyes. They were dull and lacking life. His hair was unkempt.

"These are documents on the Ancient Relics. They tell of where they originated and who were the wielders. From what I found, the one who possessed the Bracelet of Ra before Zidane was a Dragon

Knight by the name of Giltia," Kulla held each parchment to show Maia.

"Have you been up all night reading and studying those?" she asked almost in disbelief.

"I have," he responded.

"That would explain why you look like a wreck," she said with a sarcastic grin on her face. Kulla said nothing but glared at her and went back to reading. Maia walked to the table and peered over Kulla's shoulder. Kulla sensed she was behind him and let out a deep breath.

"Is there something that you want?" he asked impatiently.

"Do you know where Fi-, I mean Zidane is?" she asked.

"He is in the dojo with Master Chen Shun," he responded.

"How long have they been down there?" she asked.

"A few hours," he was growing more and more impatient with her disruption.

"Thank you," she messed his hair even more with both of her hands. Kulla growled under his breath. She smiled and walked to the door and turned to walk down the hallway. Kulla went back to reading the parchments in front of him. Maia then peered her head in to the Study. Kulla looked up once more and saw nothing but Maia's head peeking in.

"What?!" he said impatiently.

"I just wanted to ask you to bathe because you smell like a pig right now," she said sarcastically.

"GO!" Kulla exclaimed.

"Humph," Maia walked down the hallway and down the stairs toward the dojo. As she walked down the stairs she heard the voice of Chen Shun and the grunts of Zidane. As she stood in the doorway she saw Shun circling Zidane as he underwent rigorous exercises. Maia quietly made her way in to the shadows of the dojo as not to disturb the exercises of Zidane. Shun's voice and commands echoed throughout the dojo.

"One!" Shun ordered and Zidane threw a forceful punch that cut throw the air like an arrow in flight. "Two!" Shun once again ordered. Zidane threw another punch with the other fist. "Three!" Shun exclaimed. Zidane threw a forceful roundhouse kick with a flare of fire bursting from his foot. "Four!" Shun once more ordered. Zidane did a back flip and crossed his forearms in front of his face in a defensive position. His feet were set to the floor. Beads of sweat ran down his forehead and cheeks. His shirtless torso glistened as the Sun's rays from the windows touched his body. He was breathing heavily but his silver eyes retained their intensity.

"Very good, Zidane," Shun said as he walked passed Zidane toward a table with what seemed to be a pile of clay discs. Shun walked behind the table and flatly held his hand out above the discs.

"Defend yourself!" Shun yelled. Shun used tiny, but potent, concentrations of air gusts to levitate and throw them at Zidane. Zidane threw small orbs of fire shattering the small clay discs. After several discs, they started to come at him more frequently and more quickly. Zidane threw punches and kicks smashing the discs in to small fragments. Disc fragments and dust began to accumulate around his feet as he destroyed more and more discs. Maia smiled but restrained her glee still attempting to not disturb the exercises. As the discs were thrown even faster, an aura began to build around Zidane as he pushed his energy farther. Shun then threw a larger disc at him. Zidane gathered energy into his fists as he clenched it. Fire formed around his fist. His eyes and hair flared a fiery red. His eyes grew more intense as they focused on the target. He threw his fire engulfed fist in to the disc and obliterated it. Zidane was breathing heavily. His muscles were tense and flexed. The aura around his body faded and his eyes and hair returned to their natural color. His eyes retained their focus even after destroying the last of the clay discs. Shun nodded his head and walked from behind the table toward him. Zidane began to relax his muscles.

"Well done, Zidane. Your skills have improved greatly since our last training session. Your fundamentals are still intact I see. Your focus has improved seeing as a certain someone has entered the dojo," Shun stated as he looked toward the dark corner in which Maia stood. She smiled sheepishly and waved to both of them. Shun shook his head while Zidane's eyes did not waver.

"Thank you, Master," Zidane said as he bowed. Shun bowed as well.

"We will continue your training tomorrow morning," Shun said as he turned to walk out of the dojo. Zidane turned to walk toward Maia. A smile came across her face as she saw the man who had her love walked toward her. He took a few steps to her but a sudden sharp pain coursed through his body. He dropped to his knees holding his ribs. His teeth clenched and his eyes closed tightly shut as the pain radiated throughout his body. Maia ran to him and knelt by his side. Shun turned and saw him on his knees in excruciating pain.

"Zidane?! Zidane, what's wrong?!" a look of concern was on her face and worry in her voice.

"There is a...burning pain... coursing through....my....body," Zidane forced from his lips. A mark appeared along his back from his left kidney to his right shoulder blade. The Dragon mark on his wrist faintly glowed red as the fiery pain radiated throughout his body. The pain soon subsided and Zidane was left there breathing heavily. He caught himself from falling over. His body glistened from the sweat that covered his body. A light steam rose as heat met the moisture on his body.

"Are you alright, Zidane?" Maia asked with worry still on her face and in her voice.

"I....believe so," he responded taking deep breaths.

"What did the pain feel like?" Shun asked as he walked over toward him.

"It was a burning sensation. It radiated throughout my body, as if a wildfire was set to my insides," Zidane explained continuing to breathe heavily.

"Do you know why he had this pain?" Maia looked up at Shun. Shun shook his head 'no' with a bewildered expression on his face.

Maia looked upon Zidane and helped him to his feet. She placed her hand on his back and felt the marking on his back.

"Zidane, what is this?" she ran her hand over the marking. It felt like the markings were burned into his skin.

"I do not know. It was not there before the training session," Zidane stated as he slowly got to his feet. Shun walked closer to Zidane and examined the markings.

"They appear to be scales," Shun observed.

"Scales?" Zidane furrowed his eyebrows at Shun's discovery. Shun nodded his head. At that moment Kulla rushed in to the dojo breathing heavily.

"Zidane! There is trouble… at the camp… on the southern border," he said out of breath. Zidane looked at Shun and Maia.

"How many Orc?" Zidane asked.

"There are two hundred," Kulla responded. Zidane sighed heavily.

"Get ready Kulla and Maia, they need our aid," Zidane stated. Maia and Kulla nodded and immediately took their leave.

"Master Shun, I am going to ask you to look after the palace along with Rosey just in case something is to arise. And thank you for the training," he said as he bowed. Shun bowed his head slightly and then Zidane took his leave.

Once upstairs, in his bed chamber he strapped on his armor and his blades to his waist. Maia was sitting on her haunches with her short sword and quiver of arrows strapped to her hips and her bow beside her.

"Are you ready?" Zidane turned to her. She nodded her head and they made their way to the stables. Kulla met with them in the stables. Zidane hoisted Maia onto the back of Sundancer and then swung himself onto Sundancer's back. Kulla hoisted himself onto his horse and rode south toward the post on the southern border of the province.

At the southern border, a mix of Elf troops and Rangers from Earth readied themselves for the oncoming onslaught of the Orc army. The Elf troops made two lines with tower shields lined next to each other and the archers several paces behind them. Orc troops were seen marching over the hill.

"Steady!" ordered the Elf Captain. The Orc troops marched closer and closer. They then began a steady charge toward the barricade of tower shields. The Elf and Ranger platoon was at a severe disadvantage for they were half the size of the Orc army.

"Stand your ground!" the Captain ordered once more. The Orc troops steadily gained ground on to the barricade. "Fire," the Captain ordered the archers to fire upon the charging Orc troops. The archers released a shower of arrows upon the Orcs. The Orcs who fell victim to Ranger and Elf arrows were trampled by the other charging Orcs. The Orc troops continued to charge toward the barricade. The Orcs crashed onto the tower shields like the waters of the ocean onto rocks of the shore. The Elf troops did their best to hold the Orc troops back, but soon the Orcs pushed back and broke through the line. The Elf and Ranger troops were fighting for their lives and to not allow the Orc troops to take over the post. The fighting could be heard throughout the western hills. Zidane, Maia, and Kulla saw the Elf and Ranger platoon fighting off the Sekmet's troops.

"Kulla. Summon the power of Osiris to separate the two armies," Zidane said. Kulla nodded and raised the Scepter of Osiris to the sky. The head of the Scepter glowed with the vibrancy of the soul energy it commanded. A chain of soul orbs were launched from the Scepter and hit in front of the Orc troops sending them reeling backwards. The Ranger and Elf troops looked back and saw Zidane, Maia, and Kulla riding toward them at full gallop.

"It's the Trinity!" the Captain yelled and rejoiced.

As of late Zidane, Kulla, and Maia have been known as The Trinity since they began to fight as one, wielding the powers of the Ancient Relics with great skill. These three gave the army hope and kept their morale high.

"Maia, I want you to use the power of the Necklace to launch me in to the Orc horde," Zidane told her.

"But...," she started to say.

"Please trust me," Zidane said. Maia bit her lower lip and nodded her head. She kissed his neck.

"Be careful," she said. He looked back and nodded to her. He then stood on Sundancer's back and jumped to the air. Maia guided Zidane through the air toward the Orc troops with the power of the Necklace. Once in the air, the Orcs spotted him and began to throw spears and fire arrows at him. Zidane spun while in the air with flares of fire bursting from him and burning the spears and arrows. The Bracelet of Ra began to glow a vibrant gold. He held his hand down toward the ground troops.

"Solar Flare!" he yelled. A blinding light emitted from the Bracelet blinding the Orc troops. They yelled in agony covering their eyes. Zidane landed on his feet drawing both Dragon Blades, cutting down Orcs all around him. Maia and Kulla rode in to join the fray with Maia firing arrows at Orcs and Kulla slashing at them with his broad sword. There were several remaining Orc troops and they retreated. Zidane, Maia, and Kulla watched them retreat over the hill.

"Victory!" the Captain declared. The other troops rejoiced, but drums were heard over the hills. They then saw Ogres marching toward them with heavy armor and giant clubs in hand. There were more than the small platoon could handle.

"General Zidane. What shall we do?" fear and doubt were creeping in the Captains mind. Zidane closed his eyes and focused his energy. He dug deep within himself, searching for strength.

"Stand back," he responded as he opened his eyes. His eyes were glowing red with fire and intensity. Each strand of his dreadlocks burned like the embers of a fire. A new energy and strength swelled and surged throughout his body. He felt this new power just after he felt the burning sensation in the dojo. It was a power that seemed to have mingled with his Red Dragon Essence. He did not know where it came from, but it was a power that will be of great use to him.

With this new power flowing within him, his hands began to glow white as he clenched his fists focusing this new found energy.

He cupped his hands to his side and lightning began to gather in his palms. The intensity of the lightning in his cupped hands grew and throbbed. The streaks of lightning swirled together to form an orb of pure lightning. "White Lightning!" he yelled. He released several streaks of lightning at the oncoming Ogres. There was a tremendous explosion as the Ogres were turned to ash from the lightning attack. After releasing that tremendous amount of energy, Zidane was left breathing heavily slowly lowering his hands to his sides. The markings on his hand and back were glowing from under his tunic and armor. The marking on his back burned him slightly, but it bothered him not. Kulla and Maia rode to his sides.

"Are you alright, Zidane?" Maia jumped from Sundancer's back to his side.

"Zidane. How did you release that amount of energy? And how did you conjure lightning?" Kulla was perplexed and fascinated at the same time.

"I do not know," Zidane responded as he looked from his hand with the Dragon mark and then up to Kulla.

In the throne room of Sekmet's dark fortress, Sekmet called his Generals. His was none too pleased at their lack of victory in the recent battles. The Elf Kingdom had all three of the Ancient Relics in their possession; many of the battles that waged on the past weeks were lost; one of his Generals was lost to the power of the Bracelet of Ra and was unable to stop the resurrection of the Bearer of the Red Dragon Essence. The numerous failures only angered the Dark Warlord.

"Anaius was unable to stop the resurrection of the Red Dragon Essence Bearer," he said in a thunderous voice.

"Yes that is correct, Lord Sekmet," Naafar responded in a quivering voice.

"What happened to Anaius?" Sekmet demanded.

"Several Orc troops informed us that he was banished to the Shadow Realm by the power of the Bracelet of Ra," Ivy responded. Sekmet slammed his immense fist on to the armrest of the throne.

His eyes flared red as the anger and frustration grew within him. Ivy, Naafar, and Kain trembled as the floor quaked. Sekmet rose from the throne and walked toward the three generals.

"No matter, I do have a plan. We have been weakening their camps on the borders significantly. We will continue to wear their forces down. And then attack with our full force," he thought out aloud.

"Yes, Lord Sekmet," Kain responded.

"On another matter, Naafar, I want you to send more Orc troops to hunt down Craven and his pack and bring them here. He has been able to elude us since he failed to bring the Red Dragon to me. He will be severely punished," Sekmet ordered.

"Yes, Lord Sekmet," Naafar responded.

"Get out of my sight, all of you," Sekmet ordered. The three Generals hurriedly rose to their feet and left. Sekmet returned to the throne with his eyes flaring red. He was deep in thought. "The power of the Red Dragon Essence will be mine".

In the dojo of the Western Palace, Zidane was sitting on the floor in the lotus position in front of Shun, who also was in the lotus position. They were in a state of meditation. A bright, vibrant aura surrounded both of their bodies and they slipped deeper and deeper in to meditation. Memories began to flash within Zidane's mind. He saw the Sun. The Sun was setting over the Western Mountains. He then saw shadows off in the distance. They were flying. There were many almost blotting out the Sun's light. They flew closer and the details of the flying figures became clearer. They in fact had wings. Some were smaller than others, but toward the front was the largest. As they drew closer, he could tell they were Dragons. A whole fleet of Dragons was flying east, away from the Western Mountains. On top of the Dragons rode figures with heavy armor. They wielded spears and tower shields, battleaxes, and broad swords. On top of the largest Dragon, who appeared to be a fiery red color, rode Giltia the Dragon Lord. In one hand he held a massive lance and in the other a broad shield. A large broad sword was sheathed on his right hip.

The emblem of the Red Dragon was engraved onto the breastplate. Around his neck, dangled a jade crystal clasped to a gold chain. Zidane awoke with a loud gasp from the memory that flashed within his mind. Shun opened his eyes, interrupted by Zidane's utterance. Zidane's eyes were wide and wild. Confusion ran through his head.

"What is wrong?" Shun asked as he rose to his feet. Zidane was breathing heavily and seemed to be in a daze. "Zidane!" Shun called to him. Zidane snapped out of the daze and looked up at Shun still with wide eyes. "What is wrong?" Shun asked once more.

"I had a flashback of a memory. I do not know why I am having them. I use to have them when I was Fid and Giltia was trying to send me messages," Zidane said in between deep breaths.

"Perhaps Giltia's memory is still trying to tell you something. His memories are now yours. You possess memories that are from one thousand years ago," Shun's face and voice showed that he was curious about this flash of memories. Zidane nodded his head, but was still perplexed as to why he had that specific memory flash. Was Giltia still trying to tell him something? Was there something for him in the Western Mountains? Many questions raced through his mind. Shun then offered his hand to Zidane. Zidane took it and was helped to his feet.

"Let us train," Shun said, Zidane nodded and took a ready stance.

Reinforcements

THREE MORNINGS LATER, ZIDANE WAS standing in front of the bay window of his bed chamber. He wore a dark velvet robe with the emblem of a Red Dragon embroidered on the back. The Sun's rays touched his face making his ebony skin seemingly glow. His eyes shimmered brightly as the light from the Sun reflected off of them. He gazed toward the Western Mountains as if he were searching for something. As if something was there for him to discover. His eyes searched and searched, but found nothing. Behind him on his bed laid Maia. She laid comfortably on the bed, quiet. She was sleeping soundly. Her tail swayed lightly as she slept. Her ears twitched as if flicking a fly from the air. Zidane looked back at her and admired the beauty that radiated from her being. He walked to the bed and sat on the edge next to her. He ran his fingers through her thick, dark, wavy hair. She stirred in her sleep and purred lightly feeling Zidane's fingers intertwine with her hair. She turned to face him. Her eyes slowly fluttered opened and looked at Zidane. Her eyes glowed as the sunlight touched them.

"Good morning, my love," she said with a smile.

"Good morning," he returned the smile and leaned to kiss her forehead. She purred lightly and nuzzled her nose to his neck. He smiled and caressed her face. She curled in to his arms and rested her head on his chest. He held her closely to him and rested his head on the top of hers.

"I wish this war was over. No more fighting. There would be no more dying. No more pain and suffering. We all would be at peace," an air of hope was in her voice.

"Rhydin would be a more peaceful and more beautiful place. The grasslands would not be littered with the corpses of Orcs, Elves, Humans, and Ogres," Zidane said. She nodded and sighed. They sat on the bed in each other's arms for the remainder of the morning indulging in each other's caresses and embraces.

Mid-day approached, Zidane and Maia remained in their bedchamber. A knock was heard at the door. Zidane rose to his feet and opened the door. Rosey was in the doorway.

"Yes, Rosey?" he opened the door and leaned against the doorway.

"Lord Aero and Lady Paige are here. They wish to speak you," she said.

"Very well. Thank you, Rosey," Rosey nodded her head and left. Zidane turned and threw off his robe onto the bed. He put on a dark tunic and strapped his blades to his waist. He walked to Maia and kissed her on the forehead.

"I will return soon," he said with a smile. She purred and lied back down on to the bed. Zidane walked down the hall and down the staircase. Rosey awaited him at the bottom.

"Where are they?" Zidane asked.

"In the war room," she responded.

"Thank you," he continued to walk down the hallway, followed by Rosey. He opened the wooden door and entered the room. Aero and Paige were sitting on the other side of the round table side by side. On the table top a map was laid out. It was a map of Rhydin. Aero and Paige rose to their feet and walked over to Zidane. Zidane and Aero clasped each other's wrist and Zidane and Paige shared an embrace.

"It is good to see you again, Brother," Aero stated.

"And in good health," Paige added.

"I share the same sentiments of you two," Zidane said. They all smiled at each other.

"Let us get to the matter at hand, Brother," Aero said. Zidane nodded. Aero walked back to the other side of the table and looked down at the map of Rhydin with a grim expression upon his face. He then looked up to Zidane and Paige.

"We are fighting a losing war, Zidane. We are losing soldiers by the hundreds. Sekmet's forces are too strong and too many. Wave after wave of his troops attack our outposts of the southern borders of the Western and Eastern Provinces and the Woodland Realm. Our numbers are dwindling. We need more support," urgency was in his voice as he pointed to the regions on the map.

"Where are we going to get such aid?" Zidane asked. Moments of silence passed as they looked at the map.

"There is a Tribe of Earth Shinobi in the Northern Mountains, as well as several communities of Dwarves in the mountains," Paige finally stated as she pointed to the region on the map.

"There is one problem with calling upon them," Zidane stated grimly.

"And what is that?" Paige asked.

"That is Troll territory and Mountain Trogs rule the skies of the Northern Mountains. That mission is very perilous," Zidane said. The heads of Paige and Aero dropped at the discovery of this.

"We still have to try. It is our only hope," desperation was on Aero's face.

"I will take Maia, Kulla, Master Shun, and Rosey," Zidane gave a sigh.

"Why Shun and Rosey?" Paige asked.

"Shun and Rosey have experience dealing with the Shinobi. Rosey is a Shadow Shinobi and Master Shun has spent much of his life on Rhydin. There is a good chance that he has had dealings with the Shinobi," Zidane stated. Aero and Paige nodded their heads.

"Good, in the mean time, Paige will move the Ranger platoon from Belnar to the southern border of the Eastern Province and I will ask for aid from Lord Zell and his coven. His lands have been under siege by Sekmet's armies as well," Aero stated. Zidane nodded.

"When can you be ready to depart?" Paige asked.

"As soon as possible," Zidane responded.

"Gather the others then," Paige said. Zidane nodded his head. He turned to walk out of the door.

"Zidane, good luck," Aero called to him. Zidane turned to face Aero and Paige.

"Thank you," he placed his fist over his heart and bowed slightly. He then took his leave and walked down the hall.

"Do you think they will succeed?" Paige turned to Aero.

"For all of our sakes, I pray they do," Aero responded.

Zidane was met by Rosey who waited in the corridor for him. She was leaning against the wall with her arms folded in front of her chest.

"What are we to do m' lord?" she asked.

"We are riding to the Northern Mountains to ask for aid from the Dwarf civilization there and the tribe of Earth Shinobi. You, Kulla, Maia, and Master Shun are to accompany me on this mission. Please rouse Kulla and Master Shun and inform them of these events and tell them to meet us in the stables," Zidane stated.

"I will," Rosey hesitantly replied. She walked down the corridor and down the stairway. Zidane sensed her hesitation, but quickly dismissed it from his mind.

Zidane walked down the hall and up the stairs toward his bedchambers. Zidane walked through the door and found Maia curled up in a little ball. Her eyes were closed, her tail swayed lightly and her ears were perked up. Her breathing was light and calm. She was at peace. Zidane quietly walked to the bed and placed his hand on her shoulder. She stirred and her eyes fluttered open. She looked up to Zidane and smiled. He returned the smile.

"I am sorry to say this, but we have a mission," he looked in to her amber eyes. Maia groaned and slowly rose. She leaned her head against his shoulder.

"What is it this time?" she was reluctant to get out of the bed, let alone leave the Palace to accomplish a task for the Kingdom.

"We have to travel to the Northern Mountains to ask for aid from the tribe of Earth Shinobi and the Dwarf civilization in the mountains," Zidane said to her softly.

"Why?" she groaned once more.

"Our army is dwindling and we need to ask for help," Zidane explained. Maia sighed and rose to her feet. She stretched and walked to her wardrobe. She took out a knitted skirt that reached down to her knees with slits on either side. Mythril was knitted onto the skirt. She then took out a leather, sleeveless tunic. She strapped her short sword to her hip and quiver of arrows to her other hip. She grabbed her bow and turned to look to Zidane. In the meantime, Zidane strapped on his wrist gauntlet, greaves, and chest plate with his blades strapped on his waist.

"Are you ready?" he turned to face her.

"I believe so," she answered with a sigh. He walked to her and held her in his arms for a moment. She trembled for a moment, but was then calmed by the warm she felt from Zidane.

"You have been in many battles and yet you still tremble," he said with a lightness in his voice. She smiled and looked in to his eyes. She reached up and gave a light kiss to his lips.

"I know you will protect me," faith in him was seen in her smile.

"I will never leave you," his tone was soft and calming.

"You still owe me for saving your life. And now for bringing you back to life," she said with a grin on her face. Zidane could not say anything but smile and nod. She grinned showing some of her panther-like teeth and gave one more light kiss on his lips before sauntering out of the chambers with her hips swaying from side to side. Zidane stood there for a few moments with a grin on his face as he watched Maia leave the room. "Are you coming?" she peered her head back in to the room. He smiled and walked out of the room.

At the stables, Kulla, Chen Shun, and Rosey waited on Zidane and Maia. Kulla wore his broad sword on his hip and a chest plate with his long, dark coat over it. The Scepter of Osiris was in hand. Rosey wore her traditional Shadow Shinobi garb with chest, shoulder, wrist, and shin armor. Her mask and hood were lowered. Her shuriken were in a dark leather pouch on her hip and her kunai strapped to her lower back. Master Chen Shun stood there with his staff in hand. He wore his round peasant hat made of straw. He wore a traditional dark robe with a Dragon embroidered on the back and front. Kulla walked toward Zidane with his arms folded in front of him and his eyes fixed to his.

"You know this is a very dangerous mission," he stated in a low voice.

"Yes, I am aware of this. We must try for the sake of Rhydin. Our numbers are rapidly dwindling and we need aid quickly," Zidane replied.

"Very well. We are with you to the end Zidane," Kulla gave a sigh. Zidane took a couple steps toward him and placed his hand on his shoulder.

"Thank you, my friend," Zidane stated. Kulla nodded and turned to retrieve his horse. The others did the same. They mounted their horses and rode out of the stable and toward the Northern Mountains.

It was mid afternoon when the five rode across the rolling valleys of the Western Province. The vast lush green lands and the valleys stretched as far as the Northern Mountains. Zidane looked to the Western Mountains as they passed them off in the distance. The images from his previous memory flash of the fleet of Dragons recurred in his mind for several moments. He shook his head and forced himself to look to the north. He could not help but to glance toward the west as if it whispered, beckoning him to look. Maia noticed that Zidane was distracted, "Are you alright?" she turned her head to look at him.

"Y-yes... I am," he stammered. Shun, who was riding slightly in front of him, looked back to Zidane, then toward the Northern Mountains. He knew there was an internal burden on Zidane's mind, but he could not pin point it. Meanwhile, Kulla and Rosey remained oblivious to the fact.

Dusk crept upon the land and the Sun set behind the Western Mountains. Zidane, Maia, Kulla, Shun, and Rosey stopped to make camp for the night at the foot of the Northern Mountains. Kulla and Zidane went off to the edge of a grove of trees to gather tinder and firewood.

"Zidane, there have been strange occurrences within you. Has anything come together?" Kulla had paused in gathering pieces of wood in to his arms.

"No. Nothing has pieced together. It is all scattered," Zidane replied with a look of focus on his face.

"I have read the memories of fused beings are scattered and that it takes a while for them to piece together the memories to be coherent," Kulla resumed searching for firewood.

"So I have come to find out," Zidane bent over to pick up a few pieces of wood.

"I believe this is enough," Kulla stated. Zidane nodded in agreement and they both went back to the camp they made. They walked back to Rosey, Maia, and Chen Shun who were waiting on them.

"We require food," Shun stated looking at Kulla and Zidane. They both looked to one another as if telling the other to go hunting.

"I will go!" Maia excitedly chimed in. She shifted to her panther form and bounded off in to the grove of trees.

Hours passed and night fell upon them at their camp at the foot of the Northern Mountains. Rosey, Kulla, Shun, and Zidane were gathered around the fire they built. The reflection of the flames danced about in their eyes. Zidane seemed to be hypnotized by the flames. Without even thinking about it, he held out his left hand, with his palm out toward the flames. Kulla, Shun, and Rosey watched him curiously. Zidane focused on the flames and they seemed to dance and spark more with the Dragon mark on his hand and wrist faintly glowing. The flames grew and burned brighter. As Zidane moved so did the rising flames. Then a figure began to slowly form from the flames. The flames began to form the figure of a knight. It was Giltia, the soul with whom Fid's soul fused to form Zidane, that sat before Kulla, Shun, and Rosey. The figure of Giltia turned and pointed toward the Western Mountains. Zidane gazed upon the flame wreathed Giltia and then stared off to the Western Mountains which were barely visible. The flames of Giltia died down and then the four of them heard a rustling in the bushes. They all jumped to their feet and readied themselves to draw their weapons. With the bushes rustling again, Zidane, Kulla, Rosey, and Shun tensed their muscles and braced themselves for an attack. A dark figure emerged from the bushes. It was Maia in panther form carrying the carcass of a freshly killed elk that she hunted. She dragged it to the fire and left it there. All breathed a sigh of relief and relaxed. She shifted back to her human form and walked to them.

"Dinner is here," a satisfying smile was on her face.

After eating the meat from the cooked elk, the party began to unroll their bedrolls and fall asleep. All set themselves around the warmth of the fire. There was a comfortable chill in the air and a slight breeze that was comforting. The sky was clear with no sign of any overshadowing clouds. The stars were shining brightly above them. Zidane lay awake sleepless and restless. The stars seemed to reflect in his eyes and make his silver eyes glow even more. His thoughts were on the flames. Was Kulla correct? Was Giltia attempting to tell him something and help him piece together the memories, thoughts, and abilities from a millennia ago? How is he supposed to tap in to these thoughts and abilities? So many questions raced through his mind that night. The most prominent question being, were the answers in the West?

They slowly began to wake up early the next morning to see the Sun rise in the east. There was a light morning fog hovering over the grasslands of the west. A small cloud of smoke rose from the last of the embers from the night previous. Maia was the first to wake. She stretched in a cat like manner and yawned greatly. She saw that Zidane was still asleep. A slightly mischievous smile grew on her face. Like a cat stalking their prey, she crawled toward him with her amber eyes fixed upon him. She licked her lips and cat like teeth. She leapt to the air and pounced on him. Zidane, startled, tried to get to his feet, but Maia was straddling his ribcage. She had a smile of triumph on her face looking down on him. She leaned her face to his. Her eyes still fixed on his.

"Good morning, Love," she said with a smile. She then lightly licked his lips, purring.

"Good morning to you also," he said as his heart was still beating rapidly in his chest.

"Ahem," they both heard someone clearing their throat. They saw that it was Shun awaking from the night's sleep.

"G-good m-morning, Master Shun. I was just waking Zidane up," her ears sheepishly flattened against her head. Shun neither said anything or did anything but shook his head and rose from his bedroll. Rosey and Kulla arose from their sleep shortly after. They picked some fruit from the nearby bushes and ate them for breakfast.

"It would be best to leave the horses here. The pathways along the mountainside are far too narrow for a horse," Kulla looked up to the mountains and their pathways.

"Agreed," Zidane turned to Sundancer and spoke to him. "Lead the other horses back to the stables. You know the way," Zidane stroked Sundancer's mane. Sundancer seemed to nod and turned to lead the other horses back to the Western Palace. Zidane watched as they disappeared in to the hills.

The air began to grow cool and brisk and the winds became stronger as the small party climbed higher and higher up the mountainside. Maia trudged along the narrow dirt pathway behind Zidane protecting herself from the strong winds of the Northern Mountains. Kulla was at the head of the single file line. He knew best where the caves of the Dwarf civilization were. From where they were on the mountain, a shadow of the Western Palace could be seen. They reached a plateau in the mountain. There were pine trees and a frozen pond. On the other end of the plateau was an opening in the mountain side. As the small party walked closer to opening in to the mountain, they began to see writing around the edge of the cave opening.

"Kulla, what do those writings say?" Rosey asked as she walked to his side and looked in to his eyes. Kulla walked closer to the cave opening, he squinted his eyes to read the worn out Dwarven script.

They were carved into the rock and stone of the mountain. He took a few moments to translate the inscriptions.

"All those.... who are friends... enter.... All enemies be warned," Kulla read the inscriptions with pauses trying to determine the symbols that were almost worn out by the erosion of the earth and rock. "Well we certainly are not enemies," Kulla muttered to himself.

"Shall we enter then?" Shun looked to the others.

"Might I suggest Kulla, Maia, and Zidane lead the way in to the caves. They have the best eyesight in dark places," Rosey stated.

"Agreed," Zidane responded and led the way in to the caves. His eyes seemed to glow a brighter silver as he focused his vision as did Maia's glow a brighter amber and Kulla's pure white. Rosey and Shun followed in closely to them with their hands on Kulla and Maia's shoulder. Zidane was several feet ahead of the rest of the group. The cave seemed to grow darker as they walked deeper in to the dark abyss. Kulla began to sniff at the air taking in the scent.

"What do you smell, Kulla?" Zidane asked as they began to slowly walk down what seemed to be stairs to them.

"Blood," Kulla responded grimly. Maia sniffed the air as well.

"There is a scent of stale blood in the air," Maia agreed.

"For once we agree," Kulla stated to Maia. Maia growled at him bearing her teeth.

"Quiet you two," Zidane scolded.

"We need more light," Shun stated.

"I agree. Not bein' able to see in this dark renders Master Shun and I helpless if anythin' were to arise bein' that Kulla and Maia smell blood," Rosey added. Zidane used the Bracelet of Ra to create a glow that illuminated their path. They found themselves in a huge hall with colossal stone columns lining one end of the hall to the other. Then a shriek was heard from within the group. Maia huddled in to Zidane's chest with a grip of terror around his waist. Zidane felt her trembling.

"What is wrong?" Zidane asked. She pointed at the foot of one of the stone columns. There lay a Dwarf corpse. It was freshly killed.

There was a pool of blood under the body. His axe lay on the floor next to him. Blood stained the blade of the axe, but it was not the blood of the Dwarf.

"Who could've done this?" Rosey crouched down to the corpse.

"These seem to be bludgeoning wounds. His skull had been crushed and sternum caved in," Kulla closely examined the body.

"What could have done this?" Zidane furrowed his eyebrows with a scowl on his face.

"Something of immense size and strength," Kulla responded.

"Look at these bodies," Shun called their attention. The others walked over to where Shun was standing. Twenty feet ahead of them was a line of Dwarf corpses. The stone floor of the chamber was stained with the blood of the Dwarf bodies.

"These Dwarves appear to have been clawed," Kulla looked to a small group of Dwarves, "And these look like they have been bludgeoned, much like the first one we saw," Kulla looked to another pile of Dwarf bodies.

"What creature, or creatures, on Rhydin could leave such carnage?" disgust was in his voice knowing there was a creature that possesses this much malice and bloodlust.

"I hope we do not cross paths with any of them," Maia was still trembling and holding a tight grip around Zidane's waist.

"I share your sentiments. Let us move on," Zidane said with a heavy breath. The group walked farther in to the Dwarf City. They found the grounds of the civilization littered with not only the bodies of Dwarf men, but women and children as well. Tears began to well in Maia's eyes as she saw this horrific sight.

"How could anythin' do such a horrific deed? Slaughterin' defenseless women and children," anger was in Rosey's voice.

"Something with no soul," Shun grimly responded. Kulla knelt down before the corpses. He closed his eyes and focused his energy through the Scepter. The Scepter began to glow. A light mist gathered above one of the corpses. It was a blue light and began to form an identical image of that of the body.

"What is this?" Rosey took a few steps backward.

"It is the power of the Scepter of Osiris. It is reading the soul of this Dwarf. It may tell us what happened here," Kulla stated.

"They came.... Big creatures... Sharp fangs... Five of them... Red lidless eyes... Long sharp claws... They came and destroyed everything and killed everyone," the soul said with fear still in its voice.

"What creatures did this? Where are they?" Kulla was asking the soul, but the soul began to fade away.

"Five big creatures, sharp claws, lidless eyes. What manner of creature is he talkin' about?" Rosey had knelt close to Kulla.

"I do not know," Kulla looked back at the corpse.

"Should we be movin' on? Seein' as though it's goin' to get more perilous," inquired Rosey.

"I think we should as well," Kulla nodded his head. "We can take these caves to get to the village of the Earth Shinobi of the Mountains," he pointed the way with the Scepter.

"Agreed. It will take far too long to exit the caves and then climb to the village. It will take considerable less time to go through the mountain caves," Shun stated.

"Let us keep moving then and try to avoid those horrid creatures," Zidane stated with Maia still clinging to his waist.

"We need more light," Rosey said as they started to walk farther in to the cave.

"I can remedy that," Zidane said as his eyes and hair glowed crimson red. There were torches on each of the columns. He leapt to the air and shot bursts of flames from his feet allowing him to hover in the air. He focused his energy and released balls of flames at each of the torches. Each torch caught on fire to illuminate the halls. Zidane then lowered himself to the ground.

"Thank you much," Rosey said with a smile. Zidane smiled as well and led the group farther in to the cave dwelling of the Dwarves. Venturing further in to the caves, they found more bodies of Dwarf males, females, and children.

"These creatures annihilated this whole civilization," Zidane looked upon the bodies. The ground then shook slightly. Maia's ears perked up as if listening for what it was that caused the quake. She became more alert and gripped Zidane's arm more tightly.

"What is wrong, Maia?" Zidane asked looking down to her.

"Did you feel that?" Maia asked with a trembling voice.

"What is it now?" Kulla asked impatiently.

"The floor shook," Maia responded.

"It is just your imagination. You are just spooked from the corpses and the huge vicious creatures who may still be wandering the caves," Kulla mocked her. At that moment, the floor shook once more.

"Did you feel it that time?!" she rapidly looked from dark corner to dark corner. Her ears were turning this way and that trying to catch another quake to see where it came from. Her grip on Zidane's wrist tightened.

"Yes, I did," Shun responded looking for any sign of approaching enemies. All began to form themselves in a circle back to back with their hands on their weapons ready to draw them. The small quakes drew closer and more frequent. They began to sound more like footsteps. Zidane, Maia, Kulla, Rosey, and Shun took fighting stances and prepared themselves for a possible onslaught. Fifty yards in front of Zidane, he saw dark figures walking toward them. Three seemed to be ten feet tall and broadly built. From what Zidane could make out, they were carrying heavy weapons. In front of the huge figures were what seemed to be huge cat-like figures. From paw to head they seemed to be five feet tall and seven feet from head to tail.

"Everyone face this way. They are coming!" Zidane told the others. They all faced the direction in which the creatures were coming. Their eyes widened at the menacing shadows that stalked them.

"W-What are those?" Maia stammered at the sight of the fearsome creatures.

"Those...are Bugbears," Kulla's hand trembled around the hilt of his sword.

"And those big cat-like creatures?" Rosey asked.

146

"They are known as Hellcats. They say these are the most vicious creatures on the face of this world and on Earth. Rarely does anyone survive an onslaught of these creatures alone. But both creatures are here. Our chances of survival are slim," Kulla's words were grim.

"We can always run," Rosey said.

"No. That is a bad decision. Hellcats can cover distances at a high rate of speed. They would catch us and tear us apart with great ease," Kulla shook his head.

"What are we to do then?" Maia trembled with the creatures stalking them.

"We fight," Zidane drew his blades with his eyes fixed on the oncoming creatures.

At this point, the creatures were thirty yards away and seemed to have spotted the small party. The features of the creatures became clearer. The Hellcats were dark in color; their eyes were grey and lidless. There were chunks of skin missing from their bodies that exposed their muscles. The Bugbears were carrying spiked clubs in their massive hands. Their bodies themselves were massive in size. Thick, scraggly fur grew from their arms and chest. Their hands looked like they could smash a boulder in to dust and thick discolored nails grew from their fingers. They stood ten feet high. They wore torn rags on their bodies. Their eyes were red and menacing. With each step they took, the ground shook beneath them. Zidane, Maia, Kulla, Rosey and Shun drew their weapons and stood their ground. Maia aimed an arrow at one of the Hellcats keeping it in her sights. The five menacing creatures drew closer to them. They were twenty yards away from them now. Maia released the arrow and it pierced the Hellcat in its front leg. The Hellcat growled with its eyes fixed on Maia, as did the other Hellcat. They bore their razor sharp fangs and crouched on their hind legs as if to launch themselves at their target. Maia cringed as the Hellcats growled at her and took a few steps back. The Hellcats launched themselves at their prey. Zidane and Kulla stepped forward with swords drawn, but the force and speed of the

Hellcats knocked both Zidane and Kulla to the side. Maia ran as fast as she could away from the Hellcats.

"I'll help her," Kulla quickly rose to his feet to pursue the Hellcats and Maia.

"We're fine with leftovers," Rosey said sarcastically as she readied her kunai. Zidane, Shun, and Rosey stood before the three Bugbears who drew closer with their spiked clubs clenched in their massive hands. Zidane charged toward the Bugbears with blades drawn. One Bugbear swung at him. Zidane ducked under the club and then launched himself off from a column and threw a kick at the Bugbear's head. The kick had no effect on the Bugbear. It then threw its fist into Zidane's sternum sending him in to a wall, leaving a crack in it. Shun raised his staff and slammed it to the ground causing the ground to quake throwing the Bugbear off balance. Rosey leapt toward one Bugbear. It swung its club at her, but she vanished moments before it made contact with her. She appeared behind it and stabbed a kunai at the back of its knee. The Bugbear roared and slammed its fist into Rosey knocking her backwards. Shun spun and sent several lashes of fire from his staff sending one Bugbear reeling backwards in to a stone column. Zidane ran in behind one and slashed at its knees bringing it down. Rosey then leapt to the air and stabbed that Bugbear in the temple with her kunai. That Bugbear dropped dead. This infuriated the two that remained. They began to swing their spiked clubs wildly with no concern of what they hit. Zidane leapt out of the way of the swings while Shun and Rosey vanished in to clouds of shadow dodging each swing. Shun leapt backwards as did Zidane. Shun whirled his staff in front of his body and began to create a small funnel of wind. It grew the faster Shun whirled his staff. Zidane concentrated his energy and fire emitted from his clenched fists. He unleashed a ball of fire into the growing funnel of wind. The funnel was set ablaze and fused together and formed a funnel of flames. Shun unleashed the funnel onto the two remaining Bugbear. One sidestepped the oncoming funnel while the other was caught in it and burned. Zidane cupped his hands to his side and gathered white lightning in to his palms.

"White Lightning!" Zidane cried as he unleashed streaks of white lightning to the burning Bugbear who was reduced to ash after being hit by the streaks of lightning. The remaining Bugbear roared in anger. Its muscles tensed, its eyes glowed violently, and it clenched the spiked club more tightly. Rosey leapt to its back and stabbed her kunai into its back. The Bugbear growled and threw her aside. Shun unleashed several gusts of wind at it pushing it back only a few feet before it braced itself against the ineffective gusts. Zidane charged it with blades readied. Flames flared from the blades' steel. The Bugbear was about to deliver an overhead smash onto Zidane when he sidestepped the blow. The club cracked the stone floor. Zidane ran up the club and the Bugbear's arm. As he did this, Zidane leapt from the Bugbears shoulder, spun and severed the Bugbear's head from its shoulders.

Maia was running as fast as she could with the Hellcats only several yards behind her and closing in for the kill. Kulla was running several yards parallel to Maia and the Hellcats. One Hellcat leapt at Maia and swung its massive paw at her. The Hellcat hit Maia's shoulder knocking her forward. She rolled, then quickly got to her feet and tried her best to resume run. The other Hellcat gained ground on her and was about to attack when Kulla leapt onto its back. The Hellcat tried to throw Kulla off, but he hung on to its neck. It ran and then rammed Kulla into a stone column knocking him off. The Hellcat veered around and charged at Kulla. Kulla rose to his feet with his sword drawn. The Hellcat leapt at Kulla with razor sharp claws ready to shred at his flesh and teeth ready to bear into his throat. Kulla rolled backwards and in doing so, got under the belly of the Hellcat while it was in midair. Kulla thrust his blade into the stomach of beast. The Hellcat fell on its side dead. In the meantime, the remaining Hellcat was continuing its pursuit of Maia. Maia launched herself from columns and walls evading each claw slash and bite. Maia was heading for a wall and began to run faster

Aaron Gooding Jr.

toward it. She ran up the wall and drew her bow and an arrow as she was in mid air. She flipped backwards over the head of the Hellcat and released the arrow in to the Hellcat's skull killing it. She landed on her feet behind the body of the Hellcat breathing heavily. Kulla met her to see that she was still alive.

"Still alive I see," he said jokingly.

"Would you expect anything else," she quickly responded. They exchanged a smirk and left to meet the others. Kulla and Maia met up with Zidane, Shun, and Rosey near the corpses of the Bugbears.

"Is everyone alright?" Zidane looked to everyone.

"It would seem so," Kulla was still breathing heavily.

"Let us move on then and leave this horror behind us," Shun stated.

"I agree. We do not need to stay here," Maia responded quickly as she held on to Zidane's arm.

"Our asking the Dwarf civilization to help us in the war was thwarted," Kulla's hope was dashed with this horror.

"At least we still have the Earth Shinobi Tribe to ask," Maia said.

"As far as we know. Let us hope that the Trollss and Mountain Trogs have not attacked them," Kulla stated.

"Agreed. Let us make haste," Shun replied.

They traveled throughout the caverns of the mountains. The caverns became darker and the air became even more stale. Zidane, Maia, and Kulla were in front with Shun and Rosey close behind them being led through the veil of darkness. For two days, they traveled through the mountain's labyrinth of caverns and small corridors. Toward the end of their second day of traveling, the air smelled fresher and there was a small glint of light that vaguely shone through the caverns.

"Is that moonlight that I am seein' up ahead?" Rosey strained her eyes in attempts to see..

"It would seem so," Zidane responded. The light grew brighter as they drew closer.

"It is the end of the cavern," Kulla said. They exited the caverns and found themselves in a forest of pine trees and the ground was covered in a light coating of snow. From what they could tell, it was late into the night. They walked fifty yards from the opening of the mountains and stopped.

"I suggest we make camp for the night here," Zidane turned to look at the others.

"Yes, I agree. We need to rest and wait for the light of day to explore," Kulla looked to their surroundings making sure there was no danger nearby.

"Kulla, come with me to gather wood," Zidane turned to head further. Both of them disappeared into the forest of pine leaving Shun, Rosey, and Maia to guard their camp.

"Master Shun, have you noticed that Zidane has been distracted?" Maia asked in a hushed tone for fear of Zidane hearing her.

"Yes my child. You were not there when the image of Giltia formed in the flames at the camp we set at the base of these mountains. You were in the woods hunting," Chen Shun took another moment to think on what he had seen from Zidane, "Furthermore, I observed him looking toward the Western Mountains. I believe there will be a time when he will go off to search there. That time may be sooner than we all think. And we must let him go alone. What may be out there is for him and him alone to find and accept. Do you understand child?" Shun knew Maia's love for him and he wanted to make sure that she would understand.

"Yes Master Shun," she responded with a sigh and a flattening of her panther ears against her head. Rosey sat at the base of a tree in the darkness. She sat there in seemingly deep thought.

"Rosey!" Maia called to her.

"Huh? Yes?" her body straightened and her eyes widened at the call of her name.

"Are you alright? You seem to be deep in thought," Maia asked.

"Aye, I am quite alright. It is just that the Shinobi of the Shadow, my tribe, and the other tribes of Shinobi never really got along very well. We were always thought of as thieves and assassins. We were thought of in that manner because of those the Shadow Shinobi call Rogue Shadow Shinobi. One becomes a Rogue Shadow Shinobi when they succumb to their darkness during their trainin' in the Shadow Arts. The other Shinobi Tribes see what the Rogues do and believe that all Shadow Shinobi are like that. In my case, I was an assassin, but that was not my fault. Now I am tryin' to make up for the pain and sufferin' that I personally caused," Rosey tightened her fists attempting to fight back the welling tears. Maia sat beside her and hugged her trying to comfort her. Shun bowed his head down seemingly in prayer. He mumbled a few words to himself. At that moment, Zidane and Kulla returned with armloads of wood. They built the wood up in a teepee form. Zidane inhaled a deep breath and blew fire onto the wood. The flames shot a few feet from the ground.

"When did you learn to do that?" Maia's ears perked up when she saw what ZIdane had done.

"Just this moment," Zidane gave a shrug of his shoulders. They all were soon asleep for the night comfortably under the pine trees.

The next morning greeted them with a cool mist hovering over the ground. The Sun was just rising over the horizon and illuminated the skies. Maia was again the first to wake. She stretched in a cat-like manner and yawned. She rose to her feet and looked around. She saw Zidane, Kulla, and Shun still asleep in their make-shift beds made from soft pine branches. But where was Rosey? She looked around the forest and saw no sign of her.

"Rosey?!" she called out. With attentive ears listening out for Rosey, Maia walked into the forest of pine and called out to her a few more times thinking Rosey had gone out to gather some food. Still there was no sign of her. She looked to the ground and saw footprints going to and coming from the camp. She let out a yelp and hurried back to camp.

"Wake up, wake up, wake up!" she pounced onto Zidane's chest. Zidane quickly rose throwing Maia off his chest. Everyone else rose quickly.

"What is it Maia?" Zidane's eyes were wide from being jarred awake.

"Rosey is gone I do not know where she went I went to go see where she had gone and there were tracks coming to the camp and going from the camp," she said rambling on without taking a breath.

"Slow down, Maia. We cannot understand what you are saying," Kulla put his hands on her shoulders to slow her down.

"I understand," Zidane looked to him. "Rosey was abducted and there are tracks leading to and from the camp," Zidane paraphrased the message.

"Lead us to the tracks," Shun looked to Maia. She nodded and darted off leading the others to the tracks in the forest of pine. She stopped short of them and pointed. Zidane walked forward and examined them.

"What do you see, my son?" Shun leaned on his staff while they were stopped. Zidane took a few moments to answer.

"There were six of them. They were not carrying much. They seemed to have been patrolling this area when they saw her from this point. They walked silently toward her. There was no struggle. Then they carried her off East from here," he said as he followed the tracks from where Maia found them. The tracks led back to their camp and then further in to the forest.

The four of them walked for miles with Zidane in front following the tracks when they came to a clearing in the forest. At the center of the clearing, there was a village of wooden huts and cabins. A tall, wooden wall was built around the village with a watchtower on the east, south and west sides of the wall. The entrance to the village was at the south wall. It was a huge wooden gate that opened out away from the village. Maia, Zidane, Shun and Kulla huddled together and whispered amongst each other.

"What should we do?" Maia asked.

"We could always sneak in," Kulla suggested.

"There are guards on each wall and we do not want to rouse suspicion of the ones we are asking aid from," Zidane shook his head.

"There is always the direct approach," Shun added. All looked at each other and nodded. They emerged from the forest of pine and cautiously walked down toward the south gate of the village. As they came within twenty yards of the gate as voice yelled to them, "Halt! Who approaches the gate!?"

"I am Zidane. Elf Ruler of the Western Province," he stepped forward.

"Who travels with you!" the guard demanded.

"Master Chen Shun from Earth, Maia from the Woodland Realm, and Prince Kulla of the Southeast Vampire Coven," Zidane presented each of his comrades. As each name was announced each person bowed their head slightly.

"What is your business here!?" the guard's demanding tone softened, but was still strong.

"We wish to speak with your leader. We are asking for aid from your tribe," Zidane responded. The guard took a few moments and looked upon the four seemingly to examine them. He turned his head and nodded to someone behind the gate. At that moment, the doors of the gate creaked and began to open. Seven ebony skinned guards rushed out and surrounded Zidane, Maia, Kulla and Shun. They carried no weapons and wore no armor of any sort. They wore dark green cloth tunics and brown leather pants. They wore a sash around their waists. They also wore leather wrist bands.

"We ask that you hand over your weapons," one guard looked to the heavily armed travelers.

"You want us to hand over our weapons?" Kulla was skeptical of such a request.

"Think of it as an act of trust," the guard responded. They all hesitated and then finally un-strapped their weapons and handed them over to the guards. A guard looked at Shun and at his redwood staff. Shun looked back at the guard.

"I am in need of this walking stick," Shun seemingly pleaded with the guard. The guard sighed and left him alone. The guards encircled the group and led them through the gate.

"It is odd they carry no weapons," Zidane whispered to Shun.

"You do not know the extent of the Earth Shinobi Arts," Shun responded.

"It would appear that I do not," Zidane looked to the Earth Shinobi that escorted them in to the Village.

"Their Art is not just making the ground quake under the feet of their enemy, but they are able to command and shape it with their strong wills. They can rouse large chunks of earth from the ground and they can form seemingly impenetrable walls of solid rock. The Earth Arts have the strongest defense out of all of the Shinobi Arts," Shun explained.

"Living in the mountains gives them a great advantage against their enemies," Kulla interjected.

"Quite right," Shun gave a nod of his head.

"How do you know so much about the Rhydin Shinobi, Master Shun?" Zidane asked.

"Do you remember when I told you I spent several years of my life on Rhydin?" Shun asked.

"I do," Zidane nodded as he recalled the conversation.

"I spent several years living with each Shinobi Tribe and mastered their disciplines. In doing so I became one of the rare Shinobi Saints in the history of Earth and Rhydin," Shun responded as he showed him his Staff where the odd symbols were etched in to it. "Each symbol represents one of the Shinobi Tribes. It shows that I have mastered their Art," Shun said.

As they entered the village, there were men, women, and children going about their business. The Earth Shinobi people were all of the same complexion as Zidane, the color of the earth. Their hair was of the same texture as well. There were even those with locked hair like Zidane within the village. These people reminded Zidane of his father and aunt. All were with brown eyes, full lips, and high cheekbones. There were Earth Shinobi outside cleaning and hanging cloths outside of their huts. Young children were running in and out of huts playing.

"Is everyone an Earth Shinobi in this village?" Maia asked as she hung onto Zidane's arm.

"Yes. Even the children are trained to be able to manipulate the earth," one guard responded. At that moment, the four saw a father and son next to their hut training. The father demonstrated a technique to the boy. The father executed a low, strong stance bending at the knees and his feet were shoulder width apart. He took several deep breaths from his stomach. After several breaths, he stomped on the ground and a chunk of earth rose from the ground and hovered in front of him. The father then held out his hands to the chunk of earth and split it into two chunks then four chunks. He then lowered the chunks of earth back into the ground. The boy watched intently and did as his father did. The boy took his low stance and stood firm. The boy stomped on the ground as his father did and a small chunk of earth rose from the ground. The boy struggled to keep the earth hovering, but he could not. The boy got frustrated and stomped at the ground causing a small quake. The father knelt down and placed his hand on the boy's shoulder.

"It is alright. You will only get better with practice. I could not keep a chunk of the earth hovering for long at your age," the father said.

"Really?" the boy asked with brightened eyes.

"Yes," the father responded with a smile. They both hugged and returned to practicing. Zidane saw this and a tear formed in his eye, but it did not fall. As they walked further into the village, they began to attract attention. People stopped what they were doing and looked upon the four strangers.

"Why are they staring at us?" Maia started to feel uncomfortable.

"We are strangers on their land. They are curious," Shun gave the simple answer.

"Or maybe they think you look odd," Kulla added. Maia growled and stuck her foot out in front of Kulla causing him to stumble almost falling on the guard in front of him. They both glared at each other.

"Will you two stop?! This is not the way to represent the Elf Kingdom," Zidane scolded them. A few moments later, they arrived to the center of the village and there was a large wooden hut. Outside of the hut, a few men awaited them. They wore white beards with no hair on either of their heads. They wore simple woven robes. To the four, these men seemed to be frail old men leaning on walking sticks. The guards stopped in front of the older men and lined themselves behind Zidane, Maia, Kulla, and Shun. One man stepped forward, "I am Karfi, one of the Elders of the Earth Shinobi. This is Igboya and Roho. We are the Council of this village. We understand that you have a matter of business you wish to discuss with us".

"Yes, we do. Two matters in fact. The first being we ask for your aid. As you might be aware, the forces of Sekmet are closing in on the southern borders of the Eastern, Woodland, and Western provinces. Our forces cannot keep them at bay for very long. We need help. We have gone to ask one the Dwarf civilizations of the mountains, but they were all slaughtered by Bugbears and Hellcats. You are our only hope for any other alliance," Zidane looked to the Elders with earnest eyes. The Elders looked to one another.

"This matter we will consider," Karfi gave a nod to Zidane.

"And the second?" Igboya asked.

"There was a fifth traveler with us. We believe that she was taken by members of your Tribe. There were tracks in the snow that led us to your gates. Would you know if anyone has brought in any strangers?" Zidane's ears awaited their answer. The Elders all looked to each other once more.

"We are assuming she is a companion," Roho stated.

"She is," Zidane nodded.

"She is being held as prisoner," Karfi replied.

"But why?" Maia stepped forward.

"What are her crimes?" Kulla demanded.

"She is a Shinobi of the Shadow. They have all committed crimes against our tribe," Igboya's voice was raised as if countering Kulla's demand.

"But what has she done?" Zidane saw no sense in Rosey's imprisonment.

"She is a Shinobi of the Shadow. That is her crime," Roho said with his eyes growing more intense.

"Now if you would like to discuss the terms of our alliance, I suggest we move to the main hut," Karfi said as he and the other two Elders turned to walk to the main hut. Zidane stood there with tensed muscles and his eyes flashing silver.

"What are we to do?" Maia looked to Zidane and Kulla with desperation in her eyes.

"What can we do? They are not going to release Rosey. They are stubborn old fools. Just for the fact that Rosey is a Shinobi of the Shadow they will charge her for the crime," disgust was in Kulla's voice.

"*Shitara!*" Zidane called out with his eyes flashing brightly. Karfi, Igboya, and Roho all turned in unison.

"What did you say?" Karfi asked in disbelief.

"I said Shitara," Zidane growled with flared nostrils.

"What is a Shitara?" Maia asked Shun in a soft tone.

"Zidane is challenging them. It is an old Shinobi tradition, supposedly more peaceful than having an all out battle. Two people from opposing sides fight. Whichever side wins, their terms are met," Shun responded.

"But how would Zidane know about it?" Maia's eyebrows furrowed in confusion.

"Perhaps it is a memory from Giltia," Kulla said. "Giltia may have had dealings with the Shinobi when he was alive," he added.

"It has been years since someone has called for a Shitara," Karfi calmly walked toward Zidane.

"You must honor the Shitara," Zidane said more intensely.

"What are your terms?" Igboya asked.

"I fight your best Earth Shinobi. If I win you join us and you release Rosey to us," Zidane said.

"And if our best Shinobi bests you?" Roho asked.

"We leave in peace and never bother you again. And you keep Rosey to do what you will," Zidane responded.

"We will discuss this matter amongst ourselves," Karfi responded. The three Elders walked into the main hut. In the meantime, the people of the village began to gather around Zidane and his comrades.

"How are you going to fight an Earth Shinobi?" Maia had seen Zidane fight many enemies, but no one who had the ability to bend the earth to their strong will.

"The only way I know how to fight. With all of my heart," he gave a reassuring grin.

"The heart of a Dragon," Shun added with a proud smile.

"Yes. The heart of the Red Dragon," Zidane nodded to Shun.

Moments later, Karfi, Igboya, and Roho emerged from the hut walking toward the four along with Rosey behind them. Her hands were tied behind her back and her head bowed to the ground.

"Rosey, are you alright?" Zidane called to her.

"I am fine, m' lord," Rosey raised her head to behold her comrades.

"Have they harmed you?" concern was clearly heard in Kulla's voice.

"No, they have not. Not yet anyways," she responded with a slight smile looking into Kulla's eyes.

"Zidane will free you soon," Maia called to her.

"Please do. This rope is quite uncomfortable on my wrists," she periodically adjusted her wrists within her binds in attempts to make it more tolerable.

"We accept your terms, Lord Zidane. We would like to introduce your opponent, Raziel," Igboya stepped forward to say. Raziel stepped from the crowd of gathered spectators. He was the same height and build as Zidane. Raziel was appeared to be the same age as Zidane, which seemed curious to Shun. One would think that becoming the better of the Tribe's Art that they would be of an older age. Shun looked upon the young man and saw what seemed to be a birth mark on the inside of his wrist. It was a circle with two sets of parallel lines intersecting in the middle. At the center of the circle, the point where the lines crossed each other, was a smaller circle. Shun looked from the young man's mark to the same exact symbol that was etched on to his Staff. Shun then came to realize that this young man was the Earth Shinobi Master.

Raziel's head was clean shaven, not even a stubble of hair grew from his scalp. Raziel's skin was almost the same complexion as Zidane's, but only a bit lighter. His eyes were as dark as a bottomless abyss. He wore a dark green cloth tunic with pants made of animal skin. He also wore leather wrist bands. His intense eyes met with Zidane's. There was an air of tension between the two. Zidane threw off his hooded long coat and took a fighting stance.

"I suggest that you distance yourselves from us," he called back to Shun, Maia, and Kulla. As he said this Shun, Maia, and Kulla stepped from behind him and joined the crowd. As Raziel crouched down into a deep fighting stance, several of the Earth Shinobi men and women began to play on goblet shaped drums. The heads of the drums were made of the hides of animals and seemed to be tuned with rope that laced up and down the sides of the drum. Some were higher in pitch while the others were lower in pitch.

"You have no chance of winning, Lord Zidane. What skill do you have to match the power of the earth," Raziel taunted him.

"I can do this," Zidane responded as he leapt to the air and pounded his fist to the ground. As his fist was driven in to the ground, a wall of flame five feet high and six feet wide emitted from it and roared toward Raziel. His eyes widened as the wall of flames rushed to him. Raziel leapt backwards. When he landed on his feet, he stomped on the ground and a wall of earth and rock rose to disperse the wall of flame. He then lowered the wall of earth back to the ground.

"It would seem that you possess some talents," Raziel smiled seeing there was a true warrior in front of him.

"I can do much more," with a grin on his face, Zidane leapt toward Raziel. Raziel stomped at the ground to rouse several chunks of solid earth. With several strong motions of his arms, he hurled the chunks of earth at Zidane while he was in the air. Balls of fire and orbs of lightning flew from Zidane's palms at the barrage of earth. When he landed in front of Raziel, Zidane threw flame engulfed punches at him. Raziel motioned with his hands to rouse a series of small walls of earth to block the punches. With a powerful stomp to the ground, the ground quaked underneath Zidane's feet causing him to be thrown off balance which left him vulnerable to Raziel's attacks. With Zidane's defense down, Raziel threw thunderous kicks and punches at Zidane. A few punches landed to Zidane's ribs, but others were dodged and blocked. Zidane caught one of Raziel's kicks and threw him backwards. Raziel flipped to land on his feet. While raising his head, he found a ball of flame being thrown at him. He crossed his forearms in front of him. The ball of fire hit him and pushed him backwards. They then glared at each other breathing heavily and taking fighting stances.

"You are quite skilled, Raziel," Zidane stated.

"So are you, Lord Zidane," Raziel responded.

Moments passed as they waited for the other to make a move. Neither flinched nor took their intense eyes from each other's. The crowd of villagers fell silent, while the drums still played, as they were in awe of the raw power that was demonstrated. Both Zidane and Raziel were evenly matched.

"I have never seen Zidane fight like this. Even without the Twin Dragon Blades, his power is incredible. You must be proud, Master Shun," Kulla looked to Master Shun.

"Indeed, I am," Shun gave a nod, "But he is not fighting at his full potential," Shun had been carefully watching his pupil throughout this entire fight.

"What do you mean?" Maia gave a tilt of her head.

"He is much more powerful than this display of power," Shun responded.

"Zidane is holding back?" Kulla furrowed his eyebrows not knowing the reason as to why Zidane would do such a thing.

"It would seem so," Shun concluded.

"But why?" Kulla looked from Shun to Zidane and Raziel.

"I do not think he knows he is holding back. I do not believe he knows the full extent of his powers and abilities," Shun stated. Maia and Kulla stood in awe at the fact that Zidane may be even more powerful than the display he has been showing thus far.

Raziel and Zidane charged at each other. Raziel threw mounds of earth at Zidane while Zidane threw fireballs. Each dodged and blocked each other's attacks. When they got within a few feet of one other, Raziel motioned for the earth beneath him to launch him to the air. Landing behind Zidane, Raziel stomped at the ground and roused chunks of earth and hurled them at Zidane. Several hit him in the jaw and torso. The biggest chunk hit him in the chest to throw him backwards. With a dull *thud*, he landed on his back. Raziel stood proud of having the upper hand. Zidane slowly rose to his feet holding his ribs. Raziel was surprised at Zidane's resilience and readied himself. Zidane took a few steps forward, but a sharp, burning pain radiated throughout his body. Zidane dropped to his knees. Raziel, confused at this, relaxed his body and took a few steps forward, but was hesitant to do so thinking it was a ruse to draw him closer. The excruciating pain continued to radiate throughout Zidane's body. He let out a scream that echoed through the village. Flames then burst from with, engulfing his entire body. The flame shot from his body five feet above him. Everyone who encircled them stepped backwards, even Shun, Maia, Kulla, the Elders, and Raziel. The flames soon subsided and Zidane was left doubled over clutching his ribs. The Dragon mark on his wrist and hand glowed red, then faded as the flames did. His head was lowered and was breathing heavily. Everyone in the crowd, even Raziel, was concerned over Zidane's well being. Zidane rose his head with his eyes flashing silver. Raziel stepped backwards with his guard up. Zidane rose to his feet clenching his fists. With a deep breath, he crouched down into a deep fighting stance. Each vibration of the earth beneath his feet he felt. With this new sensation, he felt strong, immovable, and deeply rooted to the earth. Raziel eyes widened at the sight of something within Zidane changing. Not knowing what it was, Raziel took steps backwards. Zidane gave a grin, "Let us see where this goes," he said in a soft, yet intense, tone. A fiery aura began to gather around his body. Raziel regained his focus and made a charge at Zidane. Zidane stayed firm in his stance as he watched Raziel charge at him.

"What is he doing?" Maia's ears flattened against her head while she nervously tapped her fingers against the side of her thigh.

"Patience," Shun responded. Maia looked over to Shun and he nodded to her for reassurance.

As Raziel drew within several feet of his adversary, Zidane stomped the ground causing the earth to quake under Raziel's feet. Raziel was knocked off balance and then Zidane then motioned for the ground to lift him over Raziel's head. When he landed on his feet, Zidane threw a flaming kick to his back. Raziel was knocked forward. Raziel quickly spun up to his feet and found several chunks of rock and earth being hurled at him. He blocked a few by motioning the earth beneath his feet to block them. The last few chunks came at him too fast that he could not stop them in time. The last few chunks hit him in the ribs and chest. Zidane then took this chance to rouse an immense chunk of earth. It levitated in front of him as he began to gather fire in his hand. His fist was soon engulfed in flames. He then looked from his fist to the piece of earth that hovered in front of him. Zidane threw his fist in to the piece of earth setting it ablaze. The flaming chunk of earth was hurled toward the Earth Shinobi Master. Raziel was doubled over in pain from the previous onslaught when he saw the comet-like object rushing toward him. The flaming piece of earth exploded on contact a few feet in front of Raziel sending him backwards, almost in to the gathered crowd. He landed on his back with his head bouncing off the ground. He was knocked unconscious for a few moments. When he awoke, he found Zidane standing over him.

"You... win," Raziel declared the drums ceased in their varying, yet harmonious, rhythms when the winner was declared. He laid there with his torso covered in dark soot from the explosion. Zidane extended his hand to Raziel. Raziel looked at him for a moment but then took it and was helped to his feet. When he got to his feet, Raziel bowed to Zidane in recognition of the victory. Zidane returned the bow in respect.

"It would seem that you have won the Shitara, Lord Zidane," Karfi approached from the crowd.

"In that case, we must honor your terms," Igboya turned to nod to one of the guards to untie the bindings around Rosey's wrists. When she returned to the group her eyes met with Kulla's for a moment.

"I thank you on the behalf of the Elf Kingdom," Zidane gave a bow to the Earth Shinobi Elders.

"How many Earth Shinobi do you require?" Roho asked.

"As many as you can spare," Zidane responded. The three Elders then looked at each other.

"There are smaller, neighboring villages of Earth Shinobi. We will need to convene with the Elders of those villages to come to an agreement of how many Shinobi we can spare to send to war," Karfi stated.

"We ask that this matter be taken care of as soon as possible. Our armies cannot ward off the army of Sekmet for very long," Zidane said.

"We understand. This war affects us all," Igboya responded.

"We will leave immediately," Roho stated. The other Elders nodded in agreement.

"That would be most appreciated," Zidane responded.

"Raziel, signal the neighboring villages that we are on our way and that it is a matter of urgent business," Karfi said.

"Right away," Raziel went off to the edge of the village to a pile of wood. There was a torch that sat near the fire in which he used to set the pile of wood on fire. Along with other Shinobi, Raziel used a large canvas to gather smoke from the fire under it and released clouds of dark smoke in to the air. Miles off in the distance of the mountains, another set of smoke signals was seen from the neighboring Shinobi village. And then farther off in the green of the pine forests, other sets of smoke signals were seen rising in the air. Raziel ceased raising the signals and went to find the Elders. The Elders, along with Zidane, Maia, Kulla, Rosey, and Shun, were found sitting around a long table in the main hut.

"The signals have been raised and the other villages have been notified," Raziel entered and bowed to the Elders.

"Very good Raziel. Ready the covered wagon and an escort," Karfi stated.

"Right away," Raziel bowed and took his leave.

"Am I correct in assuming that Raziel is your General," Kulla inquired.

"You would be correct, Kulla. Like we stated earlier, he is our best Earth Shinobi," Igobya replied.

"Will he be the one to lead the Earth Shinobi alongside with us against the Army of Sekmet?" Zidane asked.

"It would be in your best interest to take him," Roho said.

"I agree. A young man with those abilities and potential should be in our army. The Earth Shinobi should be placed at the borders for defensive purposes since they are able to control the earth beneath the feet of the Orc army," Shun stated.

"I agree, Master Shun. Having the Earth Shinobi on the borders will enable us more time to search for more allies in our cause," Zidane stated.

"Where else are we to look, m' lord? Most of Rhydin is under the thumb of Sekmet's Army. Kulla's coven has taken refuge in the Eastern Palace, the Rangers from Earth are at the borders as well as your Army, and one the Dwarf civilizations has been destroyed. Right now, all we have are the Earth Shinobi. Our chances of winnin' this war is lookin' bleak," Rosey stated. At that moment, Raziel entered the hut, "Everything is prepared".

"Thank you, Raziel," Karfi said.

"We hope and pray that you find more aid in your fight against Sekmet. In the meantime, the council of Earth Shinobi will convene on the matter of how much aid we can spare," Igboya stated as the other Elders rose from their seats and made their way out of the hut.

"What are we to do? Rosey is correct. We do not have many options and are running out of what we have," Maia looked to her comrades for any glint of hope.

"We have a chance," everyone perked up in their seats to hear what Kulla had to say, "Maia, do you remember the morning you came by the Study and I was reading all of those scrolls and documents?" she nodded in response. "I found in those ancient documents a weapon, much like the Bracelet of Ra, Necklace of Isis, and the Scepter of Osiris. It is called the Sword of Ages," he stated.

"What does it do?" Rosey leaned forward in her seat.

"It is a sword of Kings. It was forged by Rulers and Kings from Egypt, Asia, Sparta, and England with the aid of the Ancient Guiding Spirit of the Twin Planets, Mesnara. Each Ruler contributed a fragment of metal that was in turn forged together by the flames of the Heavens, by Mesnara, to form the blade. The hilt was made of star metal. Star Metal is an ore that was found on a rock that fell from the stars above. Mesnara took the fallen rock and harvested the ore to form this hilt. The one who wields this sword commands the greatest army of men from the nations that forged the blade," Kulla said.

"Magnificent," Rosey's eyes widened in amazement.

"Where can the Sword of Ages be found?" Shun asked.

"It is found during a solar eclipse on Earth in the middle of Stone Island. The halo of the eclipse reveals the Sword at the center on a pedestal," Kulla said.

"When is the next solar eclipse on Earth?" Zidane asked.

"Exactly one month. It is the same here on Rhydin," Kulla responded.

"We do not know if we will be alive in one month," Maia frowned.

"Yes we will. Rosey, Maia, and Kulla, you will go retrieve the Sword of Ages. You will have to leave immediately after our business here has concluded. Master Shun and I will support the borders of the Elf Provinces along with the Earth Shinobi," Zidane said.

"Where is the nearest Gate of Caelum to Stone Island?" in her voice, Zidane heard that Maia did not like the plan of them separating yet she was willing to do what needed to be done to save Rhydin.

"I believe the nearest Gate of Caelum is in the Caribbean. You will need to hire someone to transport you to Stone Island. And preferably someone who has a fast ship," Zidane responded.

"We understand Zidane," Kulla nodded.

Dusk came across the land, the air began to chill and a light fog hovered over the grass. A frost coated the grass and reflected the rays of the setting Sun causing the fog to appear to faintly glow a fiery orange. Maia stood at the entrance of the village looking out toward the west watching the Sun set over the Western Mountains. The image of the setting Sun gleamed in her amber eyes. Her arms folded in front of her chest trying to keep herself warm. Zidane walked behind her and wrapped his arms around her. She felt the warmth from his body and purred lightly closing her eyes.

"When will this war end?" Maia asked.

"I wish I knew," Zidane replied in a soft tone. Zidane began to stare off into the west as well, gazing upon the setting Sun behind the Western Mountains. They stood for several moments in silence listening to their surroundings, watching a light flurry of snow fall onto the ground and the pine.

"Zidane, what is happening to you?" Maia slightly turned her head.

"I believe my inner abilities are awakening. Somehow I am evolving into the person or being I am meant to be. These flares of pain are abilities rising to the surface," he replied.

"How much longer must you endure these changes?" she turned to face him. She placed her hands on his back and lightly caress. She then seemed puzzled and began to feel the same place on his back. "Zidane, the markings on your back," her ears flattened and her eyebrows furrowed, "There are more of them," her voice held confusion as her fingers gently ran across the markings.

"There are?" he seemed puzzled as well.

"Turn around and take off your tunic," he did so and she found there were more of the same markings on his back. It was as if someone had burned more of these markings into his back. They began to form something. She still could not tell what it was. She could tell some of the markings formed scales of some sort and then there were scattered markings around the centermost markings. The markings spanned from his right shoulder to the lower left side of his back.

"What do you see?" Zidane turned his head to look over his shoulder.

"I still cannot make out the markings. They are beginning to form something. Something big," Maia responded as she ran her fingers along the markings. He then turned around and slipped the tunic back on. Soon after, Kulla, Rosey and Raziel approached Zidane and Maia.

"Zidane, the Earth Shinobi have reported spotting a platoon of Orcs traveling through the woods," Kulla stated.

"How many were seen?" Zidane asked.

"Nearly fifty," Raziel answered.

"Alright. Kulla, you are to stay here and wait to hear from The Elders. Raziel, Rosey, Maia, and I will scout the Orc platoon and follow them to see what they conjuring. We are going to need our weapons Raziel," Zidane said.

"I will send for them right away," Raziel responded as he hurried back to the village.

"What do you think they are up to?" it was odd to Maia that an Orc platton would be seen this far north.

"They are not looking for a battle. Otherwise there would be a larger number of them. Where they heavily armed?" he asked.

"From what the scouts reported, they carried broad swords and wore light armor. And they carried manacles with them and crossbows and arrows with silver heads on them," Kulla responded.

"They are looking to capture something. Something big," Zidane thought aloud. Raziel returned with two other Shinobi carrying their weapons. Rosey, Zidane and Maia strapped on their weapons.

"Where were the Orcs headed?" Zidane looked to Raziel.

"They were headed East through the pine forest. By now, they are at least fifteen miles from here," Raziel replied.

"We must be off then," Rosey stated strapping her kunai to her lower back.

"I agree with the Shadow Shinobi," contempt for Rosey was heard in Raziel's voice. Rosey shot a glare at Raziel, but she held her tongue. The four rushed off in to the pine forest. Maia shifted to her panther form and ran off in to the forest, while Zidane, Raziel, and Rosey jumped to the trees and leapt from branch to branch heading east.

With armor and weapons clamoring, and labored grunts and loud footsteps, the Orc platoon traveled swiftly through the forest of pine. They did not travel in one horde, but were fanned out. The Orcs in front carried the crossbows with silver tipped arrows. Close behind them were the Orcs who carried the manacles. They were on the hunt for something. One of the Orcs up front stopped and sniffed the air. It then looked down to the ground and saw footprints in the snow and in those footprints were bits of hair. The Orc knelt down and picked up the hair and sniffed at it.

"What is it?" one Orc growled.

"Wolf hair. We are on their trail. Keep moving!" the Orc yelled. They quickened their pace in their pursuit of their prey.

Leaping from tree branch to branch, Zidane, Maia, Rosey, and Raziel were closing in on the Orc platoon. Zidane stopped in one of the higher branches of the pine. He looked off in to the forest of pine. Raziel and Rosey stopped in the branches when they saw Zidane stopping. Maia looked up and saw they had stopped as well. She slid to a halt and looked up to them.

"What do you see?" Rosey asked.

"I see the Orc platoon. They have stopped and began to struggle with some creatures. I cannot determine what the creatures are. There are a few of the creatures dead and several Orc soldiers dead," Zidane focused his vision to look off in to the forest.

"Shall we help the creatures then? They are obviously enemies of the Orc," Rosey said.

"I agree Rosey," Zidane nodded.

"For once, intelligence from the likes of a Shadow Shinobi," Raziel mocked.

"Hold your tongue 'less you want me to cut it out for you," Rosey spat.

"This alliance will not hold together if you two continue to verbally attack each other," Zidane scolded.

"What are we doing?" Maia called up as she shifted back to human form.

"The Orc platoon is attacking creatures that I cannot determine what they are. The trees are in my line of sight. They are just ahead of us," Zidane called down.

"We best make haste then," Rosey said. Zidane motioned for them to hurry ahead. Raziel, Zidane, and Rosey made haste and leapt from branch to branch quicker. Maia shifted back to her panther form and tore through the forest.

The Orc platoon had snared and bound many of the creatures. They left few dead in their own blood. They struggled to keep some of the creatures in their binds while others struggled to put binds on others. It took at least five Orc soldiers to hold one of these creatures down.

"Hold him down!" one Orc ordered as he attempted to fasten manacles on the creature. This one was the largest of all of them. It seemed to be the leader of the group. He threw Orc soldiers in to trees snapping the branches and cracking the trunks of the trees. An Orc was about to fire an arrow from his crossbow when a shuriken pierced his neck dropping him to the ground. The other Orcs looked up and saw Zidane, Raziel, and Rosey leap from the branches above them. Other Orcs were victims of Maia in panther form as she pounced, clawed, and tore into them. Zidane drew his blades and slashed through a few Orcs as did Rosey. Raziel used the earth to knock the Orcs off balance and to crush them. Zidane, Maia, Rosey, and Raziel now stood between the creatures that stood in the shadows of the pine trees and the remaining Orc troops who stood with weapons drawn and crossbows were aimed at them.

"We do not let one Orc scum passed us," Zidane sternly said with blades drawn and glowing red. They and the remaining Orcs stood in attack ready position for several moments waiting for the other to make their move. All were tense and focused. The Orcs flinched first and charged at them. Raziel leapt forward and stomped on the ground causing a small seismic quake knocking the Orcs off balance. Rosey leapt forward while the Orcs were off balance and vanished in a cloud of shadow. She reappeared and slashing at the necks of the Orcs. The Orcs carrying crossbows fired their silver tipped arrows to the air with intentions of hitting the creatures. Maia placed a barrier of energy to deflect the arrows. Zidane quickly sheathed the Twin Dragon Blades and released several small orbs of fire at the arrows to incinerate them. Both Zidane and Maia looked at each other and nodded. Maia leapt to the air and used the power of the Necklace of Isis to guide her to the archers and Zidane made a tremendous leap to launch himself over Raziel, Rosey, and some Orcs soldiers. Maia and Zidane landed on their feet next to each other and immediately cut down the Orc archers. Raziel and Rosey finished off the Orc soldiers, but left one badly injured on the ground. Zidane sheathed his blades and gripped the Orc soldier by the collar.

"You will tell me why you are hunting these creatures," Zidane demanded as his eyes flashed silver.

"I would rather die than be interrogated by the likes of you, Red Dragon," the Orc weakly stated as blood ran from his mouth down to his chin.

"That can be arranged," Zidane responded as he raised his fire engulfed fist and brought it down with full force on to the skull of the Orc crushing it. Zidane rose to his feet and checked on the health of his companions. All were well.

"I can tell you why they pursued us," a voice from the shadows said. Zidane and the others turned their attention to the tall figure that was emerging from the shadows.

"Craven?" Zidane said in disbelief.

"Yes, it is me Fid. You have changed in appearance," Craven sniffed the air that surrounded Zidane.

"That is story for another time. And I am no longer Fid. I am Zidane," Zidane still could not believe it was Craven and his pack they saved. Craven nodded acknowledging this, even though it was confusing to him. He motioned for the other members of his pack to step out of the shadows. Most were the members of the pack that Zidane and Aero came across on Earth months ago and the others were unknown to Zidane. There were females among them as well.

"Why was this Orc platoon pursuing you?" Zidane saw more clearly that Craven had been wounded during their skirmish with the Orcs.

"I failed to bring you to Sekmet. I did not report back to him as I was ordered to. Sekmet sent this platoon to bring me in and kill all other Lycans in my pack," Craven winced at the pain from his wounds.

"I am truly sorry to hear of this ill news," Zidane responded.

"How do you two know each other?" Maia asked.

"Craven was hired to bring me to Sekmet so that he can kill me and take my powers. He drew me back to Earth by taking over the village in which I grew up. They had rebuilt it after the attack by the Vampire horde. Craven and I made a deal that if I were to defeat him in hand to hand combat he would leave me, Aero, and my village alone. I defeated him and he held up his end of the deal," Zidane said.

"And we helped him?.... Why?" Rosey raised an eyebrow.

"We did not know they were Lycans from a distance and Craven and his people are honorable creatures," Zidane responded.

"On behalf of my people I thank you for your aid Fi-, Zidane," Craven clenched his teeth and clutched his wound more tightly.

"They can come with us. We can take them back to my village where they can get food and have their wounds tended to," Raziel offered.

"What say you, Craven?" Zidane asked.

"We would greatly appreciate that, Lord Zidane," there was a breath of relief from Craven's pack. Zidane nodded and turned to lead the Lycan pack to the village of the Earth Shinobi.

As Zidane, Maia, Rosey, Raziel, and the Lycan pack returned to the village, they were met by Kulla and a few Shinobi guards. Kulla walked up to Zidane and then looked at the Lycan pack.

"What are *they* doing here?" contempt for the Lycans was heard in Kulla's voice. A scowl was on his face.

"We saved them from the Orc platoon. What is the issue?" Maia saw that he bore his fang at the pack.

"There is an uneasiness between Lycans and Vampires," Craven growled as he stared in to Kulla's hateful eyes.

"We cannot have any turmoil within our ranks. First, it was the Shinobi of the Shadow and the Earth Shinobi, and now Lycans and Vampires. If we are to have any chances in winning this war, we all need to work together. Is that understood," Zidane's voice was strong and demanding as he looked in to the eyes of everyone present.

"Understood," everyone was in agreement.

"Good. Raziel, please find some people in the village to tend to the wounds of the Lycan pack," Zidane turned his eyes to Raziel.

"Yes, Lord Zidane," Raziel gave a slight bow of his head. "Follow me, Craven," he motioned for Craven and the other Lycans to follow him. The Lycan men and women followed Raziel in to the Shinobi village. Kulla, Zidane, and Maia watched them enter the village then they turned to face each other.

"Is there any word from the Elders?" Zidane looked to Kulla.

"No word," Kulla shook his head.

"So what is the story between the Vampires and Lycans?" Maia suddenly asked. Zidane gave a sharp look to Maia as if that were a question to avoid.

"No, Zidane, it is fine," Kulla gave a deep breath before explaining the story, "Generations ago, on Earth and Rhydin, Lycans were the daytime guardians for the Vampires as we slept during the day. Some say it was a form of slavery. It depends on who you ask. The

Vampire Princess of the Main Coven on Earth was to be escorted from Earth to Rhydin to meet with the Leaders. Obviously this was a very important mission so they sent the smartest and strongest Lycan to do so. It was night when they were walking through the woods of Rhydin when the Lycan claimed they were attacked by what seemed to be Hellhounds. The Lycan said the Hellhounds overran them both and killed the Princess. There were claw and bite marks on her. The Lycan rushed her to the Southeast Coven where she died. The Vampires present saw the claw marks and blamed the Lycan for committing the crime They did not believe his story of the Hellhounds. The Lycan was whipped and beaten. He was to be executed the next morning, but he escaped and led a revolt against that Coven. Other Lycans caught wind of this revolt and soon they all revolted against their Vampire masters. The Lycans became free creatures. And as a result, there is now bad blood between the two races," Kulla told them.

"Well that's not right," Maia folded her arms in front of her chest. Zidane nudged her with his elbow.

"It does not matter now. Am I to assume they will be joining our side in this war?" Kulla sighed knowing he'd have to put aside his feelings toward the Lycans in order to fight alongside them.

"I would assume he wants revenge on Sekmet for killing off members of his pack," Zidane responded. At that point, an Earth Shinobi rushed towards them.

"What is it?" Kulla looked to the Earth Shinobi.

"The Elders have returned," the Shinobi responded.

"Very good, thank you," Zidane said. The Shinobi guard bowed and took his leave. Kulla, Zidane, and Maia soon followed the guard in to the village.

One by one, Roho, Karfi, and Igboya stepped down from the covered wagon. Their faces showed no expression. The Shinobi from the village began to gather as well as did the Lycan pack. All attention was turned to them as the villagers awaited the decision of the Earth

Shinobi Council. Raziel then approached the Elders and bowed in respect.

"Has the Council reached a decision?" Zidane stepped from the gathered crowd.

"It has," Igboya nodded.

"The Earth Shinobi will answer the call of the Elf Empire and fight alongside them," Karfi said in a boisterous voice. The villagers rejoiced and the Lycan pack looked at each other and nodded in approval.

"Zidane," Craven called to him which also drew the attention of the village.

"Yes?" Zidane responded as he turned to face Craven. Craven and the pack approached Zidane with bandages wrapped around their ribs, arms, and heads.

"We want to join your army as well. We want to avenge the murder of our kin," Craven said as the other Lycans nodded agreeing with him.

"I will allow this," Zidane placed his hands on the massive shoulders of Craven. Craven nodded his head and looked back at the rest of his pack. The pack threw their hands in to the air and let out shouts of joy as did the Earth Shinobi as Zidane, Maia, Kulla, Shun, Craven, Raziel, Raziel, and the Elders stood in the middle of the crowd.

In the darkest region of the southwest, Sekmet was stirring. His anger and impatience was growing as word of failure reached his ears. His three Generals knelt before him as he was pacing in the shadows of his chambers.

"I do not tolerate failure! We have failed to breach the southern borders of the Eastern and Western Provinces, as well as the Woodland Realm. What will it take to overrun these lands?!" Sekmet's eyes glowed furiously.

"Lord Sekmet," Ivy spoke up.

"What is it!" his tone was sharp when he turned it on Ivy.

"I have noticed that the Elf Empire has been successful when The Trinity is together. If they were to somehow be separated from one another we can take advantage of that," Ivy said.

"Well there is a brain inside of that skull of yours. Luckily for you three, the Elf Empire will want to retrieve the Sword of Ages, which is one of the Ancient Relics, to gain more aid for their army. They do not know that only a human male can wield the power of the Sword. The Dragon will want to send a few of his best allies to retrieve the sword and he will stay behind to help ward off our forces. His best allies are the Vampire Prince and his love; the other two sides of this Trinity; the wielders of the Scepter of Osiris and the Necklace of Isis. Kain you will go with a platoon of Orcs to Earth after them. Use the Gate of Caelum at the foot of the Southern Mountains," Sekmet stated.

"I understand Lord Sekmet," Kain's eyes never left the floor.

"Send all of our forces to charge the borders and begin to send wave after wave until you break through their feeble lines of defense. Do not let up on the attack," Sekmet clenched his massive fist.

"Yes, Lord Sekmet," the three Generals responded.

Beginning of the End

Two days passed since the small party arrived to the village of the Earth Shinobi. Zidane, Maia, Kulla, Rosey, Shun, Raziel, Craven, and the Elders were gathered around a round table in the main hut. There were several Earth Shinobi and Lycans that gathered as well.

"We need to organize a plan of action that will end this war," Zidane stated.

"I agree. Our forces cannot hold for very long," Rosey stated.

"What do you plan to do?" Igboya asked.

"I have decided that Master Shun and myself, along with Raziel and the army of Earth Shinobi the Council has graciously offered, and the remaining Lycan pack will reinforce the lines of defense Aero, Paige, Demus and Aldar have placed. They have aid from the Rangers from Earth, and Lord Zell is no doubt helping when he can lend eyes during the night. In the meantime, Kulla, Rosey, and Maia will retrieve the Sword of Ages and summon the greatest Army anyone has ever seen to help finish this war," Zidane stated.

"What shall we, the Council, and the women and children do?" Roho asked.

"You have the choice of staying here or temporarily move to the small town of Belnar. The town has been guarded since it was attacked," Zidane responded.

"I believe it will be in our best interest to move to Belnar. We will be helpless to the attacks of Mountain Trogs and Trolls that dwell in these mountains," Karfi said as the Elders and the Earth Shinobi nodded their heads in agreement.

"Kulla, Rosey, and Maia, you will go to Earth and retrieve the Sword of Ages. When is the next Solar Eclipse, Kulla?" Zidane asked.

"Three weeks to the day," Kulla responded.

"After retrieving the Sword you must hurry back. I do not know how long our forces can hold against the forces of Sekmet," he said.

"Understood," Rosey replied. She then looked to Maia who lowered her head. She did not like the idea of separating from Zidane. Rosey placed her hand on top of Maia's reassuring her that it will all work out.

"Raziel, tell the rest of the Shinobi in the village to pack what they absolutely need. We need to pack lightly and travel quickly. Is that understood?" Zidane instructed.

"Yes Lord Zidane," Raziel nodded and left the gathering.

"Good. Then let us prepare for battle," Zidane looked to those who gathered around him.

Early in the afternoon, when the whole village seemed to be in chaos and disorganization, villagers were scrambling to pack what essentials they needed in to wagons and onto horses and oxen. Members of the Lycan pack were helping the villagers pack their belongings while in their wolf form. Zidane, Kulla, Maia, Rosey, and Master Shun were walking amongst the mob.

"Do you honestly think we have a chance of winnin' this war, m' lord?" Rosey asked while moving aside to let a villager with a heavy load pass by.

"I do believe we can. If you are successful in retrieving the Sword of Ages, you will be able to summon the greatest Army of man ever. Master Shun, Aero, Paige, Craven, Raziel, and I will hold Sekmet's forces off as long as we can until you arrive with reinforcements," Zidane knew this was a great chance he was taking, but it had to be done for the sake and survival of the Kingdom.

"I do not like that we are splitting up, Zidane. You know the three of us are more powerful when we are together, not separated. I just have a really bad feeling about this," the Necklace of Isis faintly glowed gold around Maia's neck. The glow of the Necklace went unnoticed, even by Maia. Raziel then forced his way through the crowd of Shinobi villagers and approached them, "Everyone is almost ready".

"What of the Elders? Will there be an escort for them?" Kulla asked.

"Yes. I and other Shinobi will escort the Elders to Belnar. I will then join Zidane on the front lines," Zidane nodded in approval of Raziel's plan.

"Let us go then," Zidane said as horses were brought to them by Shinobi guards. All mounted and led the caravan of Earth Shinobi and Lycans down the mountain paths and to the Northern borders of the Elf Empire.

Dusk began to fall as the caravan approached the foot of the mountains to the northern borders of the Eastern Province. Zidane, along with Rosey, Maia, Kulla, and Shun, led the caravan. There were Lycans, including Craven in wolf form, fifty yards ahead of everyone to watch out and sniff for any possible assaults on the caravan. Close behind Zidane, Raziel was escorting the covered wagons transporting the Shinobi Council. Behind and around the Council were the Shinobi villagers on foot and in wagons. They soon came to a fork in the road where one path led into the woods off to the west and the other path led due south. Zidane pulled his horse alongside Maia's. She looked off on to the path leading in to the woods then back to Zidane.

"I don't have a good feeling about separating from you, Zidane. I feel that something terrible is going to happen," she said with sorrowful eyes and the Necklace glowing once more.

"We will be fine, Maia. Kulla and Rosey will look after you when you retrieve the Sword of Ages," the tone in his voice was calm to ease the uncertainty in Maia's mind and heart.

"But, what about you? Who will look after you? There will be many Orc and so few of the Elf Empire. It is ten thousand of Sekmet's forces against five thousand of our forces. You barely have any chances of surviving, Zidane," she could not silence the plea in her heart to not separate from him. Zidane placed his forefinger to her lips as if to hush her.

"Have faith. We will prevail," his tone was soft and calm. He gently placed his fingers beneath her chin to give a tender kiss to her lips, then rode off leaving her, Kulla, and Rosey at the fork.

"Come on, Little Kitty. We don't have much time, so we best be off," Rosey urged. Maia nodded and the three rode off in to the woods to the Keshnarian Ruins.

Night fell and further down the path, the caravan came to another fork in the road. This smaller path led east toward the town of Belnar. Raziel and a few of the Earth Shinobi were to escort the women, children, and the Council to Belnar. Zidane turned his horse around to face Raziel and the escort, "As soon as you escort the rest of the villagers make haste to aid us on the frontlines".

"Understood, Lord Zidane. We will hurry," Raziel responded. At that moment, Karfi poked his head out of the covered wagon, "May the blessing of the Heavens aid you in the battle, Lord Zidane".

"I thank you, Karfi. My gratitude to you and the Council for agreeing to this alliance," Zidane respectfully bowed his head. Craven, who led a few of the Lycans to scout ahead, returned to them while transforming back to human form.

"What did you see, Craven?" Zidane turned when he heard Craven's approach.

"The battle has already begun. The Elf Empire is struggling, but are holding on and warding off the forces of Sekmet," Craven's breaths were heavy from the sprint.

"We must hurry then. Raziel hurry," Zidane called to him as he turned his horse around and led the Lycan pack and a handful of Earth Shinobi on to the battle.

On the southern borders of the Eastern Province Aero and Zell were leading Elf and Vampire soldiers against an immense army of Orc. Arrows flew through the air, mounds of earth and rock aflame lit the sky above and the clanging and clashing of swords and shields resonated throughout the eastern hills. All of a sudden white lightning streaked from behind the lines of the Elf and Vampire troops toward the Orc soldiers turning many to ash. Aero and Zell looked back and found Zidane riding at full gallop with Shun, the Earth Shinobi, and Lycans, in wolf form, close behind him.

"I knew he would come through for us," Aero smiled with relief to Zell.

"I had no doubt," Zell was relieved as well. Zidane, along with the troops behind him, formed a line in front of the Elf and Vampire army.

"Aero, Lord Zell, retreat back and recover. The Shinobi, Lycans, Master Shun, Craven and I will hold them back," Zidane called back to him. Aero nodded and sounded the retreat.

"Master Shun, direct the Earth Shinobi to form one line! Craven, order your pack to stand behind the Shinobi and wait for my orders," Zidane yelled out to them. Master Shun ordered the Shinobi to quickly form the line and told them to ready themselves for an onslaught as they saw Orc troops charging for them at full speed. Craven and the Lycan pack crouched down and were poised to rush at the Orc troops. Zidane dismounted his horse and stood beside between two Earth Shinobi. Zidane then looked down the line on either side of him and signaled for them to raise the earth. Each Shinobi took deep stances and roused a chunk of earth from the ground and allowed it to hover in front of them. Zidane looked at the mounds and outreached his arms to his sides with palms out. His hands were soon engulfed in flames as the Orc troops gained ground on the reinforcements. Flames then shot from Zidane's palms and ignited each of the hovering mounds of earth in front of the Shinobi.

"Unleash our fury!" Zidane yelled with his eyes blazing red with fire and his dreadlocks flaring with embers. The Earth Shinobi hurled the flame engulfed mounds of earth toward the charging Orc troops. The mounds of earth exploded when they made contact with the ground. Orcs were launched in to the air while others were either crushed or burned by the flaming mounds of earth and rock.

"Master Shun and Earth Shinobi, give cover! Lycans charge! " Zidane ordered as he drew his blades and led the charge at the Orcs. Under a shower of earth and rock, Zidane, Craven, and the Lycan pack slashed, clawed, and ripped their way through the charging Orc troops. Zidane and Craven fought back-to-back throwing, and slashing at Orc. In the middle of all of this Zidane felt another sharp burning pain in his sides. He dropped his blades and doubled over.

"No, not now. It cannot happen now!" Zidane groaned in agony as he dropped to his knees. The Dragon mark on his hand glowed brightly red with small puffs of smoke rising from it. Craven saw what was happening and stood closer to Zidane along with other Lycans trying to protect him.

"Zidane, get to your feet!" Craven growled to him throwing Orcs to the side.

"Give me some room!" Zidane yelled back at him. Craven looked at him confused.

"Just do it!" Zidane yelled once more. Craven and the other Lycans did so. Zidane was then soon engulfed in an explosion of flames. Orcs and Lycans were thrown back. Craven was thrown forward and looked back to find Zidane in the middle of a column of flames that reached ten feet in to the air. The flames soon subsided leaving Zidane on his knees in the middle of a small crater of ash. He rose to his feet and looked up to the sky. He saw chunks of rock and earth set on fire being hurled toward him and the reinforcements. He looked to his hands and the wind around him began to swirl lightly. He felt the subtle changes in the wind around him. He held his hands palms up and gusts of wind blew from them. He was now able to manipulate the wind. He then looked again to the chunks of fiery rock and earth. He released a cyclone of wind from his palms to the fire set rock and earth. The force of the wind not only put out the flames but redirected the rock and earth away from him and his forces. Zidane then turned the gusts of wind onto the Orc soldiers. They were thrown backwards by the mighty gusts. The intense lashes of wind even tore skin from the bones of the Orc soldiers. This wave of Orc troops retreated, leaving Zidane, the Lycans, and Earth Shinobi standing over the corpses of Orc soldiers. Zidane was breathing heavily and clenched his fist and threw it to the air, "Victory!" he declared. All cheered and the Lycans howled up toward the moon. Craven walked to Zidane's side transforming to his human form, "Are you alright?".

"I am fine. I am now able to manipulate the wind around me," Zidane looked down at his palms.

By nightfall, Maia, Kulla, and Rosey arrived to the outskirts of the Keshnarian Ruins. Kulla was led them in to the center of the remains of this once great civilization. The eyes of Rosey and Maia wandered around the ruins in awe of the great structures and architecture. They did not pay much attention the last time they were in Keshnar as they were rushing to bring Zidane back to life. They shortly arrived at the center of the ruins and came to the Temple in which the Gate of Caelum stood. Maia, Kulla, and Rosey dismounted their horses and tied their reins to branches outside of the Temple. The three entered the Temple and started their way in to the Temple through the long dimly lit corridor. They came to the end of the corridor and found themselves in a large chamber. At the center of this chamber stood the Gate of Caelum and in front of the Gate was a pedestal. All three looked upon the Gate with wide eyes and jaws agape.

"I have always seen the Gates of Caelum in manuscripts and documents, but never up close like this. This is incredible," Kulla's eyes brightened with amazement of the structure.

"Kulla, wipe the dribble from your lip," Kulla growled at Maia's comment.

"Hush you two. Does Zidane have to deal with this squabblin' all the time? It's a wonder how anythin' gets done" Rosey gave a shake of her head. They gave each other a sharp just before Kulla walked to the pedestal and touched the symbols to open the Gate to Earth. As he touched the symbols, they glowed on the pedestal as well as on the Gate itself. After the last symbol was touched, a bright light burst from the Gate's opening. The light was bright and illuminated the whole room and down the corridor behind them.

"Well, what are we waitin' for? We have a world to save," Rosey stepped up to the bright light of the Gate. She stuck one hand in slowly and then took it out. She looked at her hand and then back to Kulla and Maia, smiling. She then stepped in to and disappeared in to the light of the Gate's opening. Kulla and Maia walked up to the Gate and stopped a few feet short of the light.

"Ladies first," Kulla said.

"In that case, after you then," Maia responded sarcastically. Kulla growled and grabbed her by the scruff of her neck and tossed her through. She let out a squeal when he threw her through the Gate. He then stepped through the Gate and disappeared through the light. As soon as he reappeared on the other side, he found Maia face first in the dirt. He chuckled a little and picked her up to her feet. She pushed his hand away and dusted herself off. They found themselves in a cave of some sorts. On the ceiling of the cave were crystalline structures that hung like icicles. Maia looked up and was almost entranced by them.

"What are those," Maia's voice echoed throughout the cave.

"Mineral deposits of some sort," Kulla looked up at them as well. They made their way through a series a tunnels. It was dark and the air was stale and damp. Maia and Rosey caught a whiff of something and quickly covered their noses.

"What is that horrid stench?!" Rosey covered her nose.

"Guano. Bats live in these caves," Kulla sniffed the air and was unbothered by the wretched stench.

"Relatives of yours?" Maia mocked still covering her nose from the stench.

"Hardly," Kulla retorted. Light was becoming more present as they drew closer to the exit. Once out of the cave, the smell of sea water filled their nostrils. It was refreshing to them as they deeply inhaled the air. They found themselves on a beach of white sand and palm trees. The Sun's rays and heat were beating down upon their skin. The water was so clear that one could see directly to the bottom. Maia stepped gingerly through the sand because it was hot to her bare feet. Kulla chuckled at this sight and Maia growled at him in response.

Walking further down the beach, they saw what seemed to be a Port City. It was small and simple. Several small boats and larger ships were docked there. Some of the buildings were made of stone and others built from lumber. Walking through the town, they noticed the people were simple folk. They did not wear elaborate clothing, just simple woven cloth. Some greeted Maia, Kulla, and Rosey with a smile and others shied away from them avoiding eye contact.

"Where are you thinkin' to look for someone to take us to Stone Island?" Rosey looked from building to building hoping to find something promising.

"If I am correct, many Captains can be found in a tavern," Kulla's eyes searched as well. The three walked around the town looking for a tavern and finally found it close to the town's docks. They walked through the doors and found the air to be filled with smoke from pipes and smelled of alcohol and body odor. The tavern fell uncomfortably silent and all eyes were on them for a few moments, then everyone in the tavern went back to minding their own business. Kulla, Maia, and Rosey made their way to the bar counter and sat on the stools. Rosey turned her back to the bar counter to keep a watchful eye on everyone in the tavern. The barkeeper walked over to the newcomers to see what they wanted. He was a short and barrel-chested man with a scraggly, dark beard. His shirt had a stain on the front with a dark cloth apron over top.

"What can I get ya?" he asked Kulla.

"Just some information," Kulla responded and somewhat shuddered when he caught a whiff of the man's body odor.

"What do ya need to know?" the man asked as he wiped out a dirty beer mug.

"Where can we find a Captain who is willing to sail us across the ocean to Stone Island?" Kulla asked.

"What business have ya got there?" the man raised his eyebrow and stopped in his cleaning.

"Our business is our own," Kulla responded calmly.

"I meant no offense by the question. I was just saying that if it is dirty or clean business, I could point ya in a direction of who ya should talk to. You will also need a Captain who is either insane or one who does not care for life," the man said.

"Why does the Captain need to be insane?" Maia tilted her head to the side.

"The waters of the Atlantic is littered with man eating sea monsters and I do not believe any Captain in this tavern, nor this town, will sail ya over those waters," it was at that moment the three felt discouraged as if the only light of hope they had of winning the war had just been snuffed out.

"I'll take them," a man's voice said from under a ragged cloak. The man sat a few stools from the three and overheard the conversation. The man's face was hidden by the hood of the cloak. Only a pipe and a few strands of what seemed to be brown dreadlocks could be seen hanging out from the hood. Smoke billowed from the pipe. The man was holding a small glass with barely anything in it.

"What are you? Insane or have no regard for life?" Rosey turned her head to the stranger.

"No regard for life. I have lost everything. My family and my village. I have no home, I know no one. I am a wanderer of this world," his voice carried the woes of his life.

"What is your name?" Kulla leaned forward against the bar counter in hopes to get a glimpse of the man who offered his services to them.

"Draco," the man responded raising his head to face the three. He removed his hood revealing his face. He was dark skinned with piercing dark eyes. He wore a full beard and long, brown dreadlocks that reached just below his shoulder blades. He wore a dark cloth around his forehead. They could not see what type of clothing he was wearing, but they could see that he carried a broad sword on his right hip. His most noticeable features were the scars on his left cheek. They looked like claw marks. They ran deep and they were not going to fade away.

"How fast is your ship?" Rosey's eyes narrowed on Draco's face. It seemed familiar to her, but she did not know why.

"I can get you across the ocean in a week," Draco responded.

"When will you be ready to cast off?" Kulla asked.

"Whenever you are ready," Draco responded.

"How much do you want in compensation?" Kulla reached down to a pouch attached to his hip.

"I need no coin. I just need your names. It would be unfair for the crew to know their Captain and the Captain not to know the names of his crew," Draco looked to the three who were to be his sailing companions for near a week.

"I am Kulla, Vampire Prince of the Southeast Coven on Rhydin," Kulla bowed his head.

"Rosey is my name. I am a member of the Shadow Shinobi Tribe on Rhydin," Rosey straightened up in preparation to leave.

"And my name is Maia," she hopped to the floor, anxious to leave this place.

"Very good. Now let us be off to the jaws of danger and to flirt with death," Draco rose from his seat and walked toward the door. The three walked in behind him.

"Is he sure he has no regard for life and not insane?" Maia whispered to Rosey. Rosey responded with a shrug of her shoulders. All three inhaled a deep breath as they stepped outside of the tavern.

"It's good to breathe in fresh air and not the stench of men who haven't bathed in weeks, maybe even months," Rosey inhaled a deep breath of the salt water air.

"One gets use to it after a while," Draco looked over his shoulder at Rosey. The four ventured to the docks. Draco led them to a ship that was forty feet in length; the wood was still sturdy and well intact. There was no rotting in the wood. A red tint was in the wood.

"What type of wood is this?" Kulla ran his fingers across it.

"The framework is oak and the planking is mahogany," Draco started to climb onto the ship by rope ladder.

"Where did ya get that wood? It doesn't grow in this part of the world," Rosey waited her turn to climb on to the ship.

"I built this ship up north and I have traveled in it," Draco pulled himself onto the ship.

"By yourself?" Maia then started to climb the rope ladder.

"Yes," he looked down at her. As soon as everyone was on board the ship, Draco took his place at the helm of the ship and Kulla cast off the line.

"Now let us find out what danger lies before us," Draco gave a hearty, maniacal laugh. Kulla, Maia, and Rosey looked at each other and sighed.

ENTER THE BLACK DRAGON

T HE MORNING AFTER ZIDANE ARRIVED with reinforcements, he, Shun, Craven, Aero, Paige, Melina, Raziel, Demus and Aldar gathered in the main tent of the center most encampment.

"Thank the Heavens you were able to get to the borders in time, Zidane.," relief in seeing his brother was heard in his voice, "I do not think we would have held out much longer. Sekmet's forces seem to grow by the day. They were relentlessly sending wave after wave of troops, not allowing us to rest," his voice grew grim with the mention of Sekmet's forces growing.

"I was fortunate in being able to enlist the aid of the Earth Shinobi tribe, and in finding Craven and his pack," Zidane looked to Raziel, then to Craven, "You do remember them, correct?" Aero and Craven nodded to each other with their eyes meeting.

"Where are Rosey, Maia, and Kulla?" Melina asked.

"Zidane and I sent them on a quest to retrieve the Sword of Ages while we came to aid you on the front lines," Shun responded.

"The Sword of Ages? That is nothing but a fairy tale," Aldar's tone was dismissive.

"Did you believe the Scepter of Osiris, the Necklace of Isis, or the Bracelet of Ra to be mere fairy tales as well?" Zidane held up his right wrist to show him the Bracelet.

"Where can the Sword be found?" it seemed that Aero, nor anyone else, knew of the Sword of Ages.

"Kulla said the Sword can be found in the middle of Stone Island. It is revealed during a Solar Eclipse," Zidane replied.

"When is the next solar eclipse?" Craven asked.

"Less than three weeks now," Shun responded.

"That is not much time for them to retrieve the Sword and it is plenty of time for Sekmet's forces to overtake us," Aero sighed.

"We know, Aero, but it is the only chance we have to win this war," Zidane knew this attempt was desperate, but it had to be done.

"What is the Sword of Ages?" Demus asked.

"According to Kulla, it is a sword that was forged from different metals from Egypt, Sparta, Asia, and England with the help of the Guiding Spirit Mesnara. Whoever wields the Sword will be able to command the armies from those nations," Zidane responded.

"Do we have a plan of action?" a glint of hope was in Aldar's voice hearing of the armies.

"I suggest that we have the Earth Shinobi be divided and camped at the various posts along the borders and do the same thing with the Lycan pack. The Earth Shinobi will be able to create barricades of earth and rock and the Lycans are evenly matched with the Orcs in size and strength," Zidane pointed to the borders on the map that was laid at the center table.

"I trust your judgment, Zidane," Aero nodded in approval of his plan.

"Craven, Raziel, I want you both to inform your people," they nodded at Zidane's instructions, "Lieutenant Aldar and Demus, you will escort the Shinobi and the Lycans to their assigned posts," Demus and Aldar bowed and took their leave, leading Raziel and Craven out of the tent.

"I have a question Zidane. What happened to the Dwarf civilization?" Paige recalled the plan for Zidane to recruit the Earth Shinobi and one of the Dwarf civilizations.

"The Dwarves of the civilization we planned to visit were killed by three Bugbears and two Hellcats. They killed and dismembered everyone who lived in that city," Zidane cringed at the memory as he recalled the sight of the Dwarf corpses that littered the grounds.

"That is most unfortunate," Paige grimaced at the image that was painted for her.

"It is, but I have faith the others will return with the Sword of Ages," Shun interjected.

"I agree with Master Shun. We all must have faith that we will win this war," Zidane's hope was heard in his voice with all nodding in agreement.

"With that said, I must go and update Zell and his coven as to what our actions will be. We have built huts in the Eastern encampment that block out the rays from the Sun," Aero rose from his seat, as did the others.

"Zidane and Master Shun. I want you two to post yourselves at the Western encampment. They have no Generals there," Aero said before he left the tent.

"Understood, Brother," Zidane said as he was the last to leave the tent.

"Where shall I go?" Melina asked.

"You will stay here with Paige," Aero said as he mounted his horse. She nodded with a smile on her face

"Good luck Zidane and Master Shun. May the blessings of the Heavens protect you," Paige said as he and Shun mounted their horses. Zidane and Shun rode off to the Western encampment.

Shun and Zidane arrived at the Western encampment as dusk fell. The Captain of the Rangers awaited their arrival with a few other guards with him. Zidane and Shun dismounted and the guards took the reins of their horses to take them to the make-shift stables.

"How are the defenses, Captain?" Zidane, with Chen Shun and the Captain by his sides, walked through the camp with his eyes assessing their strength and resources.

"They are holding firm, Lord Zidane," there was relief in the Captain's voice. "We have ten catapults with plenty of rocks and boulders to launch," in the Captain's hand was the Quarter Master's inventory. "News has reached camp that a platoon of Earth Shinobi will be joining us. They will provide a great defense for the camps along the borders. And also the Lycans will be aligning themselves with us as well. Their brute strength of body and strength of heart is unmatched," the Captain's hope showed in his eyes and was heard in his voice.

"That is something we all can agree with," Shun said.

"Captain, I want you to set up a night watch to warn us of impending night assaults," Zidane ordered.

"Yes sir," the Captain bowed his head then took his leave.

"I suggest you get some rest. You have had a long journey," Shun's words were more of an instruction than a suggestion.

"I am feeling a bit weak," he nodded in agreement. He barely got any rest since he and his companions set out to request an alliance with the Earth Shinobi. "I will need to recover some strength to endure the upcoming battles," his eyes showed his fatigued. They dulled in color and were half closed. Shun respectfully bowed his head then took his leave to one of the tents. Zidane returned the bow to his Master and then started to head for one of the unoccupied tents. Before entering the tent, he looked off to the west to the shadows of the Western Mountains. He took a deep breath and then entered the tent for the night.

Early the next morning, Master Shun awoke to find Zidane standing in the middle of the camp staring off to the Western Mountains. Zidane was wearing his blades on his waist. He was also wearing his wrist guard and the Bracelet of Ra and as well as his chest plate. Shun walked to Zidane's side and inhaled the morning's air, "A beautiful view, is it not".

"I need to go. I need to find out what is out there for me. Those mountains have been calling me," Zidane's eyes were unwavering. Shun sighed deeply then looked to Zidane, "I cannot stop you from what you feel you need to do, but make sure that this is not a personal journey my son".

"This is not just for me. I believe my journey to the west will be of value to us all," there was undeniable certainty in Zidane's voice.

"Then do what you must my son," pride in his pupil showed in Shun's slight smile.

"Thank you, Master Shun," Zidane turned to bow to his teacher. As Zidane turned to leave for his journey, he found Sundancer awaiting him at the edge of camp.

"Sundancer?" Zidane eyes widened in disbelief. Sundancer neighed as if telling Zidane 'Let's go'. Zidane smiled and ran to him. After leaping on to Sundancer's back, they rode off toward the west. Craven saw Zidane ride off with Shun watching him.

"Zidane! Where are you going!? Zidane!" Craven yelled to him. Craven watched Zidane ride westward. With Zidane in the distance, Craven walked to Shun and turned him so that he faced him, "Why does Zidane leave this post? This army needs him".

"Zidane leaves to realize his destiny," Shun plainly responded.

"What madness are you speaking, Old Man?" Craven's voice intensified with frustration.

"Can you not sense the climax of this war?" Shun looked to Craven. "Everything is falling in to place in preparation for the last battle with Sekmet and his dark army".

"I don't see it," Craven shook his head. He was still in disbelief that Zidane left at a crucial point in the war against Sekmet.

"That is because your eyes are not fully opened," Shun said.

"My eyes are opened enough to see the strongest in this army are gone when we need them the most," Craven growled.

"Calm yourself. They will return in time to aid us," Shun's calm demeanor during this crucial situation was disarming to Craven.

"I hope you are correct old man," Craven sighed.

"Have faith. Faith and hope are our greatest weapons in this war," Shun looked to the Western Mountains.

Days passed since Zidane left the post of the Western Province. He and Sundancer rode through the hills and creeks of the Western Province on their way to the Western Mountains. The Sun began to rise in the East as they reached the foot of the Western Mountains.

It was a straight climb to the top and there did not seem to be any foot paths in sight. Zidane dismounted Sundancer.

"I am sorry old friend, but I have to send you back to the post. You cannot follow me up this mountain range. The pathways are too narrow for a horse," Zidane stroked Sundancer's coarse mane. Sundancer lowered his head and then gave a nudge to Zidane as if telling him to go on. Zidane smiled and turned to the mountains and began to climb. Sundancer gave Zidane another nudge up the mountain side.

"Thank you," Zidane looked down to Sundancer. Sundancer looked up at him and then Zidane began to climb higher and higher.

By mid-day, Zidane climbed some way up the mountainside where he found a footpath leading higher up the mountain. He pulled himself onto the narrow path and began to walk it. To him, the path seemed to be seldom traveled. Dusk just began to fall as he walked further and further up the mountainside, the footpath became wider and Zidane began to see more trees and plant growth. As Zidane reached the summit of that mountain, he looked down and saw that the mountain sloped in to a valley lush in forest and plant life. It was as if this were a hidden land. It was secluded from the rest of the lands of Rhydin. It was away from all of the war and anarchy waging below. The moon was full that night and the light shone upon this new land. Zidane ventured down in to the valley forest. The pine of this forest seemed to grow taller than those of the Northern Mountains. He wondered why as he craned his neck to look up at them. The air seemed different; it was clearer and more refreshing with each passing breath. A light fog began to roll in and cover the forest floor. The moon rose to the highest point in the sky and its light shone upon the forest and through the branches. As Zidane ventured deeper and deeper into the forest, he began to feel a dark presence creep upon him as if a shroud of shadow had overwhelmed his being. The forest around him seemed to turn dark with shadows. He looked down to the Bracelet of Ra and it began to glow violently gold. Zidane has not felt this before from the Bracelet. A sense of uneasiness came over Zidane. He began to walk through the forest with more caution and being more aware of his surroundings. Zidane soon stopped and listened to his surroundings. He heard nothing. The forest was void of all sound. Not even a cricket was heard off in the distance.

"Hello, Red Dragon," a dark, ominous voice echoed among the pine trees. Zidane whipped around drawing one of his blades. He saw a cloaked figure in the shadows of the forest. It looked like a dark ghost that was haunting the forest.

"Who are you?!" Zidane yelled out at the shadowy figure. The figure moved from shadow to shadow in the forest around Zidane. Zidane moved to face the figure as it moved as to not show his back to it.

"Quite a shame that I know who you are and you not know me," the shadow mocked as it continued to move from shadow to shadow.

"Why do you not show yourself? Are you a coward to hide yourself in shadow," Zidane retorted.

"Do you fear me?" the shadow taunted.

"I fear no man," Zidane responded through his clenched teeth.

"I am no man. I am the Black Dragon," the shadow emerged from the shadows removing the hood of the long coat from his head. He had dark skin much like Zidane and wore white dreadlocks which were the same length as Zidane. His eyes were a cold, piercing black. Zidane was in awe of the similarities in which they shared. They were both the same height and build.

"You seem surprised, Red Dragon," he took a few steps forward.

"How is this possible? I thought there was only one Bearer of the Dragon Essence," Zidane took a few steps away from him.

"In each universe," the Black Dragon said.

"Explain yourself," Zidane demanded.

"You are saying you do not know about the parallel universes?" the Black Dragon asked.

"I would not ask you if I knew," Zidane retorted.

"There is the universe in which you live now, made of many stars and worlds. And there are four other identical universes beyond this one. They are all connected by an unknown force and this unknown force balances the five parallel universes," the Black Dragon said. There was no doubt that this Black Dragon was telling the truth. Zidane looked to the left hand of his assailant and saw the same dragon mark coiling around his left wrist in to his palm. His dragon mark, however, was not red in color, it was black.

"If that is true, how did you get here?" Zidane's grip on his blade shook when he found it all to be true.

"On the dial of the Gate of Caelum, the outermost ring is not complete. That fourth ring is to set for the five parallel universes," the Black Dragon replied.

"Why are you here?" Zidane's grip on his blade tightened once more.

"The Red Dragon was always the most inquisitive of the Dragons," the Black Dragon mocked.

"Answer the question," Zidane demanded with his eyes flashing silver.

"And impatient. But to answer your question, I have come to claim your powers," his voice grew dark, "By taking your heart, I will have collected all of the powers of the Dragons to become the one true Lord of All Dragons," the Black Dragon's lips curled in to a grin.

"Are you saying we are the last Dragons?" Zidane's eyes widened and mouth agape. The Black Dragon nodded his head with an evil grin on his face. "What is your name?" Zidane's now realized he was the only one who could stop this madman.

"I do suppose you want to take the name of your killer to the afterlife with you. I am Stratos, Bearer of the Black Dragon Essence," he threw off his long coat then drew his blades that were identical to Zidane's Twin Dragon Blades. Zidane threw off his long coat as well and drew the other Dragon Blade. The two circled each other with eyes locked on the other. The forest was silent and tension rose in the air as the two began to concentrate their energy. Each other's eyes began to glow as well as the Twin Dragon Blades of both of the wielders. They lunged at each other and with strong swings, the blades of their swords clashed. A shockwave of energy surged outward from the blades. The two were locked in a toggle of strength. They pushed from each other and lunged at each other once more, slashing at and countering each other. Zidane's blades were glowing red and Stratos' blades were glowing black. Sparks flew as the clashing of steel against steel was heard throughout the mountain valley. Zidane was being pushed back by the raw strength of Stratos. Zidane threw a kick to the sternum of Stratos knocking him back a few feet. This allowed Zidane to launch an onslaught of his own. Zidane slashed, but each attack was side stepped and blocked. Zidane threw a spinning kick to Stratos' chest throwing him back once more a few feet. Zidane concentrated his energy to conjure flames around the steel of his blades. He then thrust the blades in to the ground. A trail of flames rushed toward Stratos. Stratos grinned and created an aura of shadow energy to disburse the flames, "You are going to have to do much better than that to defeat me, Red Dragon". "I do have much more," Zidane sheathed his blades and thrust his palms outward toward Stratos releasing a strong gust of wind. Stratos quickly sheathed his blades and motioned for the earth to create a wall in front of him to block the gust. Zidane stood in awe. He thought to himself, 'Does he have the same powers as I do?' Stratos lowered the wall of earth smiling, "You are weak Red Dragon. I saved you for last thinking you were going to be a challenge. Legend tells the Red Dragon possesses the most resilience and strength of heart to defeat their foe". Zidane then cupped his hands to his side and began to conjure white lightning. He then released the immense streaks of lightning toward Stratos. Stratos countered the attack by quickly releasing streaks of dark lightning. The streaks of lightning collided and there was a toggle of power between Stratos and Zidane. The struggle of power went back and forth as reflected in the two colliding streaks of lightning. Stratos began to overtake Zidane and eventually the white lightning dissipated and Zidane was hit in the chest with the dark lightning that threw him to the ground. Zidane started to black out, but saw that Stratos had leapt to the air and was about to slash at him. Zidane rolled out of the way and kipped up to his feet. With clenched fist, Zidane conjured intense flames. He pounded the ground sending a wall of flames rushing towards Stratos. Stratos could not react in time and was engulfed by the flames. Zidane stood there breathing heavily as he watched the flames burn at the flesh of Stratos. Stratos burst from the flames and glared at Zidane. He was scarred and burned. Zidane took a few steps backwards. Stratos conjured an aura of shadow energy around his body and it began to heal the wounds making it appear as if he were not touched by the flames.

"That was a valiant effort Red Dragon, but it was not good enough," Stratos conjured shadow energy in his fist and unleashed it on to Zidane. He was sent backwards a few feet. Zidane held his chest feeling there was a burning sensation throbbing in his chest from the attack. Stratos rushed at Zidane and unleashed a flurry of punches and kicks that Zidane could not block. The attacks landed on his ribs, jaw and head. Zidane dodged one attack, drew both blades and violently slashed at Stratos. The slashes and stabs were dodged. Stratos flipped backwards drawing both blades in mid-air, then rushed at Zidane slashing at his face. There was a deep gash across Zidane cheek. Zidane stood beaten, battered, and bloody. Stratos turned to face Zidane and held out both blades. He then brought both of the hilts together to connect them. Shadow energy emitted from the hilts and coursed through the steel of the blades to the point of the sword. Stratos then launched another assault upon Zidane with the fusion of the blades. More gashes and cuts were left on Zidane as he failed to counter and block all of Stratos' attacks. Stratos gave a thunderous kick to Zidane's chest sending him in to the massive trunk of a pine causing him to drop his blades. Zidane took a few moments to get to his feet as he saw Stratos walking toward him. As Stratos was only several feet away from him, Zidane shot a gust of wind to the ground launching him to the air. In mid-air, Zidane threw a barrage of fireballs down at Stratos. The fireballs hit Stratos and all around him leaving a cloud of smoke and dust in the air. Zidane waited for the smoke to clear as he landed. Zidane then rushed to retrieve his blades that laid on the ground. As he was about to pick them up, Stratos quickly emerged from the cloud of smoke and dust kicking Zidane in to the trunk of what seemed to be the only oak tree in the forest. Stratos pinned Zidane's arms above his head and then forcefully drove a dagger through his left wrist pinning his arm to the trunk and then another dagger was driven through his right hand. Zidane let out a blood curdling yell. He was in excruciating pain. Blood trickled from his mouth, cheek and the puncture wounds from the daggers. Zidane stood there with his arms pinned to the trunk of the great oak like a bloody, lifeless ragdoll. Stratos slowly raised the point of the fused blade to Zidane's chest and slowly ran it across where his heart was.

"I can take you heart and your power right now, but it would be worth nothing. You have not realized your full potential. You seem to deny your true Dragon abilities. Are you afraid of them or do you deny them? I want to kill the Great Red Dragon not the Weak Red Worm," Stratos gave a strong backhand to the jaw of Zidane. Stratos took apart the fused blades and then sheathed them. He began to walk away and fade in to the shadows of the forest. "You stay there and think about this. Either you realize your full potential as a Dragon or I will most assuredly take your heart!" Stratos yelled back to Zidane. Stratos finally faded in to the shadows leaving Zidane pinned to the trunk of the oak tree bloodied and beaten.

THE SWORD OF AGES

ON THEIR JOURNEY TO RETRIEVE the Sword of Ages, Kulla, Maia, Rosey saw nothing but blue skies and water as far as the horizon to the north, east, south and west. The nights were cool as the sea breeze blew across the deck of the ship. During the days, the Sun's heat beat down on them. Very few clouds offered shelter from the Sun's unrelenting rays.

Several nights in to their voyage, the moon resembled a half crescent in the sky and the stars shone brightly. Several shooting stars shot across the vast darkness of the sky. All were asleep except for Draco, who stood at the helm of the ship staring off in to the East steering the ship to their destination. The Necklace of Isis Maia wore around her neck glowed brightly as she slept. She restlessly shifted from side to side, her ears rapidly twitched, and her tail was swaying violently. Her shifting in her sleep became more violent as her slumber went on. Beads of sweat formed on her forehead. Her teeth were clenched, grinding against each other.

"Zidane!" she shot up from her sleep breathing heavily and in a cold sweat. Maia's yell startled Rosey and Kulla from their sleep and shook Draco from his trance.

"Maia, what's wrong?!" Kulla crawled over to her side with concerned eyes. Maia was breathing heavily almost to the point of hyperventilating.

"Breathe, Little Kitty. You have to breathe," Rosey spoke in a soft tone to calm Maia down.

"I saw... him," Maia said in between deep gasps. The Necklace continued to glow violently.

"You saw who?!" Kulla grabbed Maia by the shoulders.

"Zidane... I saw....Zidane," Maia was still gasping for air.

"It must've been a nightmare," Draco said.

"No, no it was real. He was in a valley forest in the mountains. There was a darkness that surrounded and overtook him. He is in great pain. He is alone... in the shadows," she started to sob. She leaned on Rosey's shoulder and was embraced by Rosey to try to calm her down.

"It must have been a nightmare. It is near impossible for Zidane to be in that sort of danger," although his tone seemed dismissive, he was really attempting to put Maia at ease.

"But it was real. It was as if I was there and felt his pain," Maia implored him to believe her.

"We have to keep the faith that Lord Zidane is in good health and is safe," Maia looked up to Rosey, then Kulla and nodded. The glowing of the Necklace continued throughout the night.

Early the next morning, Draco, Rosey, and Kulla were eating their meal while Maia stood at the bow of the ship looking off to the horizon. Her slender fingers lightly caressed the Necklace. She still felt the darkness that overwhelmed her the night before.

"She is terribly troubled by last night. What if she was right? What if Lord Zidane is in dire need of help?" Rosey looked to Maia.

"We better hope that she is wrong. If she is right, then there is nothing we can do now but to accomplish our mission," Kulla sighed.

"I've noticed the charm around her neck has been glowing since last night," Draco looked up to them from his meal. All looked at Maia as she continued to be in a trance staring off toward the east.

"Kulla, what exactly can the Necklace of Isis do?" Rosey looked to him with curious eyes.

"It enhances the strength of the possessors mind," Kulla took a bite of food.

"Then is it possible the Necklace is causing her to have premonitions?" Draco asked. Kulla took a moment to think on the possibility Draco presented.

"Something is wrong," Maia called back to them.

"What is it?" Rosey rose to her feet.

"The air smells differently," Maia sniffed the air.

"How so?" Kulla took whiffs of the air as well.

"It smells like something is coming for us," she looked off to the east.

"It's a Seadragon. They rule these waters of the Atlantic. It smells fresh flesh," urgency and agitation were in Draco's voice as he quickly rose to his feet

"How do you kill one?" Rosey, as well as the others. were sharing in Draco's anxiety.

"I cannot tell you that because I don't know. The only one who was able to is now dead," Draco responded.

"That is of much help," Kulla said sarcastically.

"Look!" Maia pointed off toward starboard. All of them ran to the edge of the ship. They saw off in the distance a grouping of air bubbles on the surface of the water. The bubbles then began to slowly make their way to the ship.

"Go down below and get the harpoons!" Draco rushed to the helm and turned the rudder of the ship so that they headed away from the mass of bubbles. Kulla, Maia, and Rosey rushed down below the deck and retrieved several harpoons and crossbow-like weapons to fire them at the beast. The creature quickly closed the distance on the ship as it slithered through the waters.

"It's getting closer!" Maia urged Kulla and Rosey to hurry.

"Let us see what this beast is made of!" Draco yelled as he turned the bow of the ship back, now on a collision course with the beast. As the creature drew closer, the scaly blue dorsal fin rose from underwater and cut through the surface with great speed. Kulla and Rosey grabbed cross-bows, then loaded the harpoons and took aim. Maia took her bow and quiver of arrows and took aim as well. Draco continued the course they were taking. The head began to emerge from the water. Its head was massive and then its long, thick neck began to emerge. Its demonic yellow eyes fell upon the ship and Kulla, Maia, Rosey, and Draco. It let out a thunderous roar that sent waves toward the ship and sent it reeling. Maia, Rosey, and Kulla fired their harpoons and arrows at the beast. They struck the beast but seemed to have no affect on it. It gave another roar and sent another wave at the ship knocking everyone off of their feet. Draco was almost thrown overboard but he grabbed a hold of a strand rope. The ship tilted, almost capsizing. All four regained their footing and fired more harpoons and arrows at it, this time aiming for the head. The beast reeled it head back avoiding the harpoons and arrows. Maia was firing arrow after arrow at the beast. A few arrows struck the beast in its neck. The beast reeled back once more and then released a blast of wind from its mouth blowing everyone overboard and capsizing the ship. Rosey was the first to surface. She vanished into a cloud of shadows and then reappeared on the neck of the sea beast. She drew her kunai, then began to stab and slash at the neck of the beast. Maia and Draco were next to surface. Maia looked at Draco and then to her Necklace.

"I am going to throw you on to the beast's head!" she yelled to him.

"How?!" Draco yelled back. Maia closed her eyes and held out her palm to him. The Necklace glowed as Maia lifted Draco out of the water. With one swift motion of her hand, Maia tossed Draco toward the head of the beast. While flying through the air, Draco drew his broad sword and held it outstretched ready to slash at the sea monster. Kulla was next to surface and saw that Rosey and Draco were on top of the beast slashing and stabbing at it. Kulla then looked at Maia then to the Scepter of Osiris. Maia looked from Kulla and clasped the Necklace of Isis. They then nodded to each other.

"Draco, Rosey, Get down!" Kulla yelled to them. Draco and Rosey looked down and then dove in to the water below. The sea beast bore deep gashes in its neck and deep puncture wounds to the head but still was ready to attack. Maia and Kulla began to draw energy from the Relics. Maia drew an arrow from her quiver and began to focus the energy of the Necklace to the head of the arrow. Kulla began to conjure the energy in the Scepter and sparks of soul energy began to gather and grow around the head of it. They both emerged from the water as the energy was concentrated more intensely. They finally hovered several feet above the water.

"Arrow of Isis!" Maia released the energy charged arrow.

"Soul Spark!" Kulla released barrage of soul energy towards the beast. As the onslaught of pure energy was being released side by side, they began to merge in to one entity of energy. The beam of energy swelled and pulsed as it surged toward the sea monster. The energy cut through the throat of the beast decapitating it and cauterizing the blood vessels of the beast's neck. The body and head sunk to the depths of the ocean.

"We have defeated the Great Sea Serpent!" Draco rejoiced and laughed, throwing his hands in the air. Kulla and Maia lowered themselves back in to the water.

"Now how are we goin' to get to Stone Island? The ship has been capsized," Rosey sighed seeing the ship in its helpless state.

"It would seem our journey has ended here," Kulla's voice held his defeat. Maia then looked to the Necklace and then to everyone else, "There is a way".

"How?" Draco furrowed his eyebrows.

"Just watch," Maia closed her eyes and concentrated her energy. The Necklace began to glow vibrantly. Maia held out her palms toward the capsized ship. A pulsing aura of energy engulfed Maia's body. She emerged from the water and levitated above the surface. Bubbles slowly formed around the ship. A thin aura formed around the ship as the aura around Maia glowed more vibrantly and pulsed even more. The ship began to shift and levitate from the water. It emerged completely and hovered above the water. Maia turned the ship so that it was right side up. She then slowly set it back to the water. Kulla, Rosey, and Draco stayed afloat in the water in awe of the power that Maia demonstrated before them. After the ship was set back in the water, the aura around Maia faded and then plunged in to the water.

"Maia!" Kulla yelled as she plunged in to the water. Kulla and Rosey swam to Maia. Kulla and Rosey grabbed Maia and kept her head above water. Draco swam to the ship and clung to the ship's hull. Kulla and Rosey pulled Maia through water to the ship. Draco pulled Maia out of the water and carried her up to the ship. Kulla and Rosey pulled themselves up the side and then in to the ship. Draco had laid Maia on her back and checked her breathing, "She is still alive. She is breathing anyway".

"She must be drained from the energy surge from the Necklace in the attack on the sea monster and then turning the ship right side up," Kulla said with heavy breaths.

"What can we do for her?" Rosey looked to Kulla.

"All we can do is let her rest and keep a watchful eye on her. She may just need to rest and regain her strength," Kulla responded.

"In that case, let us continue on our quest," Draco rose to his feet and walked back to the helm of the ship to steer it back to their original heading.

Two days later, the seventh day of their sea journey, Maia awoke from her unconscious state. She groaned as her eyes fluttered open. A cold compress was placed on her brow and a blanket was placed over her body to keep her warm. Her feet were slightly propped up. She slowly sat up and pushed aside the blanket from her body and compress from her brow. It was mid-day when she awoke. Kulla and Rosey were at the bow of the ship looking for their destination.

"It appears that someone has woken up," Draco announced. Kulla and Rosey turned to see that Maia was sitting up. Rosey walked to her and knelt beside her, "How are you feeling, Little Kitty".

"I have a dreadful headache," she held her head in her hands.

"It would seem there are powers that can be conjured by the Relics that we have not discovered yet," Kulla said.

"It would appear so," Maia winced in pain with her panther ears flattening against her head.

"What did you feel when the power of the Necklace took a hold of you?" Kulla crouched by her side.

"Do you remember what Zidane felt like when the Spirit of Gilitia took over his body when we were in the pit in the Northern Mountains?" Maia looked up to Kulla with half open eyes trying to save her eyes from the Sun's bright rays.

"Yes," Kulla nodded.

"It was similar to that. I felt the energy of the Necklace surge throughout my body and take over. One moment I was in the air about to overturn the capsized ship and then the next I am waking up on the ship," she still held her head in her hands. Kulla then looked to the Scepter of Osiris and gazed upon it with fascination.

"Zidane found the Bracelet of Ra's true power. Maia felt the power of the Necklace of Isis. What secrets do you hold, Scepter of Osiris," Kulla said to the Scepter.

"Land ho!" Draco pointed beyond the bow of the ship. All looked and found they were approaching Stone Island. Kulla and Maia sniffed the air and then grimaced.

"What do you smell?" Rosey asked.

"The faint odor of Orc," Kulla wrinkled his nose in disgust of the odor.

"There are many of them," Maia grimaced.

"Sekmet's forces?" Rosey looked to Kulla.

"It would seem so," Kulla turned his head away from the scent.

"Are we in for more trouble?" Draco raised an eyebrow.

"I believe so," Rosey sighed as if the sea dragon was enough.

"Good," Draco chuckled as if looking forward to the fight. Kulla, Maia, and Rosey looked at Draco as if he were insane.

"Do you think it will be an ambush?" Maia asked.

"There is no doubt that this is an ambush," Kulla looked to the island. "Orcs are bred for war, and will have a difficult time in staying hidden. They lack in discipline," Kulla thought aloud.

"Unless they are led by one of Sekmet's Generals," Maia folded her arms in front of her chest and looked to the Island.

"This is true," Kulla nodded in agreement.

"We draw closer to land. I suggest you devise a plan quickly," Draco said. Several moments passed as they were trying to think of a plan of action.

"I have a thought," Rosey spoke up.

The ship was docked and tied off on the shore of the Island. Kulla and Maia disembarked from the ship and began to walk up the beach and then up the grassy hill. There were plenty of fallen rocks and boulders where the Orcs could hide behind. Kulla was twirling the Scepter of Osiris between his fingers and Maia was reflecting the light from the Sun off of the Necklace of Isis. They walked further and further up the grassy hill passing each fallen boulder expecting an attack. Maia looked out of the corner of her eye and saw a war hammer stick out from behind a boulder.

"They are up ahead, Kulla. They are closer to the top of the hill," Maia whispered. Kulla nodded his head and placed a hand near the hilt of his sword. Maia held her bow and drew an arrow from her quiver.

"Their body odor is stronger the closer you draw to them," Kulla whispered through clenched fangs. It was then an Orc rushed from behind a boulder and swung its massive war hammer at Maia. Maia leapt backwards and shot an arrow piercing the Orc between the eyes. Kulla avoided a slash of a heavy broad sword from an Orc. He rolled and cut out the legs from the Orc. As the Orc fell to the ground, Kulla slashed the head from the Orc's shoulders. Then, several other Orcs rushed from the behind the boulders with heavy broad swords and war hammers raised above their heads. Both Maia and Kulla leapt back and waited for the small patrol to get within twenty yards from them. They both smiled and Kulla whistled. Rosey then appeared out of a cloud of shadows, along with Draco. Both were with sword and kunai drawn. Rosey and Draco landed in the middle of the small patrol and began slashing and stabbing at the Orcs. Rosey was

attacking and vanishing in clouds of shadow, moving from Orc to Orc
stabbing them in the neck and head. Maia was drawing her arrows
as quickly as she was taking aim and releasing them in to the skulls
of the Orc soldiers. Draco was slashing and stabbing at the attacking
Orcs. His attacks and counter attacks were wild, swift, and intense.
Kulla looked upon Draco's fighting style as if he had seen it before.
Kulla regained his focus just as Kain appeared and swung his war
hammer at his head. Kulla leapt high in to the air above Kain's attack.
Kain continued his onslaught of deadly swings with his war hammer
at Kulla. Each attack was swiftly avoided by Kulla. Rosey was quick
to join Kulla in fighting against Kain. Kain swung at her too, but
missed each time. Rosey vanished in to a cloud of shadow before
the war hammer could hit her. Kulla and Rosey fought side by side
against Kain launching attacks to throw the large man off balance.
Kulla blocked an attack of Kain's allowing Rosey to launch herself off
of his shoulders and throw a forceful kick to Kain's head sending him
spinning through the air. Kain was quick to get to his feet and ready
to swing his war hammer, but the sleeve of his tunic was pinned to the
ground by several arrows. Maia drew arrow after arrow and released
them to the ground around Kain's arm. Using his brute strength,
Kain ripped the sleeve from the arrows and charged at Maia. In
the middle of his charge, Kain felt a sharp pain shoot through his
leg. He turned to find a kunai had been stabbed through his thigh.
Rosey had appeared out of a cloud of shadow and stabbed the kunai
through his leg. Kain gave a forceful backhand at Rosey sending her
in to a rock. Seeing Rosey get hit sent Kulla in to a rage. He charged
at Kain with his sword ready to slash. As Kulla was charging, Maia
drew and released several arrows at Kain, but they were blocked by
his war hammer. Kulla sidestepped an overhead smash of the war
hammer and used it to launch himself at Kain. Kulla slashed at Kain's
face leaving a scar across it. Kain grimaced in pain and held the gash
that was left. Maia took three arrows from her quiver and took aim
with all three of them. She used the power of the Necklace to charge
the heads of the arrows with pure energy.

"Tri-Shot!" she shouted releasing the arrows at Kain. Kain leapt out of the way of the attack, but was caught in the sheer force of the attack and was thrown in to the air and landed in the water. Maia saw the last of the Orcs fall to the blade of Draco, who stood over the corpses looking down upon them. His dreadlocks blew in the wind and his eyes were quiet yet held an unparalleled intensity in them. Maia looked to him with a strange familiarity, but soon dismissed it. Kulla rushed over to Rosey who sat by the rock that she was thrown in to. Kulla helped her to her feet and looked upon her with an expression of concern and worry for her.

"Is everyone alright?" Maia was breathing heavily. Everyone nodded and all sheathed their weapons and continued their ascent up the hill. Once they reached the top of the hill, they saw at the middle of the hill, thick stone columns that were stacked on top of each other. These stone columns formed an outer ring and then there was an inner ring of smaller stone columns. They walked toward the massive stone formation and gazed upon it in awe.

"Do y' know who built this wondrous sight?" Rosey asked Kulla.

"No one knows. This has been here for ages," Kulla looked up at the stone columns as they passed by.

"Why was it built?" Maia looked all around her at the stones' formations.

"Ancient rituals were once performed here," Kulla responded.

"Look there," Draco pointed ahead of them, "I see a pedestal, but there is nothing there".

"Just wait," Kulla covered his eyes and looked to the sky. In the sky, the Sun was bright and beating down upon them. Then a dark circle slowly crept closer and closer to the Sun.

"It's the Moon. The Eclipse is about to happen," Maia pointed to the sky. The Moon crept closer and closer in front of the Sun. The sky began to darken as the rays of the Sun were being blocked. Then the Moon covered the Sun's rays leaving only a halo of light around the dark mass of the Moon. The light from the halo shone down to the middle of the stone formation, onto the pedestal of stone. An explosion of light erupted from the pedestal. As the light from the halo touched it, out of the light, a sword materialized on the stone pedestal.

"The Sword of Ages," all said in unison in awe. The light from the halo glinted off of the steel blade. The grip of the sword was metallic, as well as its guard. It was unlike any other sword they had ever seen. The blade was narrow towards the hilt and then widened at the tip of the blade. As they drew closer to the pedestal and gazed upon the blade, they could see there was an inscription engraved on the steel of the blade.

"What is that inscription on the blade? Can you translate it Kulla?" Maia's ears had flattened against her head showing her caution.

"No. I cannot," Kulla examined it closer. Kulla tried to take the blade by the grip, but it burnt his hand as he drew within inches of it. He pulled his hand back and grimaced.

"Are you alright?!" Rosey took his hand and looked at the scalding the sword left.

"Yes, I am fine," he grit his teeth. "Why did it do that?" Kulla asked as Rosey gently held his hand. As if as a response to his question, energy from the wind, the earth, and the water began to gather and swirl in a maelstrom above their heads. They slowly began to meld in to one. From a burst of light, a translucent face appeared. It was the face a woman whose almond shaped eyes looked upon Maia, Kulla, Rosey, and Draco. Her full lips curled in to a soft smile that highlighted her high cheekbones.

"Who is that?" Draco's eyes never left the entity.

"I do not know." Kulla shook his head.

"Welcome Kulla the Vampire Prince, Rosey Shinobi of the Shadow, Maia, and Draco. I am Mesnara, the Guiding Spirit of Rhydin and Earth. I am also the forger of the Sword of Ages," the woman's voice echoed and resonated within the stone formation.

"Why has the blade rejected Kulla?" Maia looked from Kulla to Mesnara.

"Because, young one, only a human male may wield the power of the Sword. And only a human male who is worthy of wielding this great power can read the inscription on the blade. With this Sword, he will rule the race of humans and summon the greatest army of all times," Mesnara said. All then looked to Draco who stood behind them.

"Why is everyone looking at me?" he looked as if he wanted to retreat as he took a step away from them.

"You are the only one here who has a chance of wielding the blade. You are the only one who can summon the armies of Earth. You are the only one who can help save Rhydin," Maia pleaded with him.

"I cannot lead an army. I don't have the skills," Draco shook his head.

"Have faith in your abilities, Draco. I am sensing there is a natural leader within you, deep within your heart," Maia continued plead with him. Draco sighed and nodded. He looked to the pedestal and had his eyes fixed upon it. He slowly walked to it and stood in front of the blade. He reached out his hand slowly toward it and had it hover above the hilt. The light from the blade glinted in his dark eyes.

"Four metals from Four Nations were forged to form the Sword of Ages. This Blade signifies the Union of the World of Mankind. He who wields this Blade will be the Ruler over all," he said before he took the Sword by the hilt and held it to the sky. An intense beam of light emitted from the blade and shot into the sky illuminating the area around them. The sudden jolt of light from the Sword of Ages sent Kulla, Maia, and Rosey reeling and covering their eyes from the intense light. The light slowly dissipated and the solar eclipse was over. The sky was blue again with the Sun shining upon them. Draco was standing there breathing heavily with the blade of the Sword vibrantly glowing. The light began to course through his body and then it created an aura around his body. Draco held the Sword in front of him and smiled. The light from the Sun reflected off of the blade.

"Kneel before the pedestal Draco," Mesnara instructed. Draco knelt to one knee and planted the Sword in to the ground in front of him and bowed his head.

"You will now take the Oath of Valor. Are you ready?" Mesanara looked down to the humbled Draco.

"Yes, I am," Draco replied in a solemn tone.

"You will repeat after me," she instructed. "I, Draco, will pledge my Sword to all," Mesnara started.

"I, Draco, will pledge my Sword to all," Draco repeated.

"To protect the weak and vanquish all evil," Mesnara continued

"To protect the weak and vanquish all evil," Draco repeated.

"I will dedicate my life to all that I rule," Mesnara said.

"I will dedicate my life to all that I rule," Draco repeated.

"And I further more promise to be a fair and just King," Mesnara furthermore said.

"And I further more promise to be a fair and just King," Draco repeated.

"As God, and this small assembly, as your witnesses, I now pronounce you King Draco, Ruler of Mankind," Mesnara declared. "King Draco, rise," at her words, Draco rose to his feet and looked to Mesnara.

"I thank you for this honor, Mesnara. And I thank you Kulla, Rosey, and Maia for believing in me and giving me a second chance at another life," Draco turned to face them. His eyes began to well with tears, but he fought back them and wiped his eyes.

"We are good judges of character Draco," Kulla smiled.

"We saw your inner strength," Maia's ears perked up.

"And we also thought this would be a great opportunity to regain your spirit and start another life," Rosey added.

"Turn and face me, King Draco. To unlock the armor fitting of a King, you must utter these words. 'Sword of Ages, give me Strength'. While uttering these words, hold the Sword of Ages to the sky," Mesnara instructed. Draco looked down to the Sword and took a deep breath.

"Sword of Ages, give me Strength!" he held the Sword of Ages to the sky. The Sword glowed vibrantly and the energy began to course through his arm and then throughout his entire body. A light then emitted from him. Kulla, Maia, and Rosey shielded their eyes from the blinding light. The light slowly dissipated after a few moments. Rosey, Kulla, and Maia uncovered their eyes to find that Draco had been adorned in shimmering steel armor. His shoulders and arms were covered in armor. He wore steel greaves on his shins and a steel chest plate. A red cape was attached to his shoulders and hung down to the ground. His head was covered by a steel helmet and his face was covered by a face mask, his eyes could only be seen through a narrow slit in the face mask. On the steel chest plate was a sword in the center with the blade pointing downwards and a Dragon coiled around the sword's blade. He also carried a round, steel shield on his left arm. The shield height was from his shoulder down to his knee. On the face of the shield was the same insignia as that of his chest plate.

"Oh my," Rosey said as Draco stood before them in this steel armor.

"Hold does it feel?" Mesnara asked.

"I feel the power coursing through my body," he looked down at his hands and the rest of his armor.

"Where is his army?" Maia looked up to Mesnara.

"The beam of light that emitted from the Sword when he first touched it was a beacon that can be seen by far away countries. The leaders of the armies of Egypt, Sparta, England and Asia would have seen the beacon and gathered their armies to make their journey to this place. For this day has long been foretold that the King of Men will arise and the nations whose metals formed the Sword must watch the sky for this beacon of light for it will beckon them to come," Mesnara responded.

"How long will it take for the armies to arrive?" Kulla's anxiousness was heard in his voice.

"Seven days from now," Mesnara responded.

"Seven days?!" Rosey's eyes widened, "We do not know if the Elf Empire will be able to survive that long!".

"Still your heart and ease your mind, young Shinobi. Have faith the Elf Empire has the strength to endure the onslaught of Sekmet. I will return in seven days when the army arrives," Mesnara said.

"What are we to do in the meantime?" Maia asked.

"Have patience," Mesnara responded. Maia sighed.

"Patience is not one of Maia's strongest virtues," Maia growled at Kulla's mocking tone. Rosey shook her head at them.

"I will take my leave now. I have a message for Lord Zidane," Mesnara said as she started to fade. All looked to each other confused as to how she would know Zidane.

"What is it?" Maia stepped toward her.

"That I will see him in ten years," Mesnara disappeared in to a bright light. Draco, Kulla, Maia, and Rosey were left in the middle of Stone Island. Draco then flipped the mask of his helmet from his face. There seemed to be a new life in his eyes now. When Maia, Rosey, and Kulla first met him in the Port City tavern, they found his eyes to be cold and dull, now they seem to be full of life, energy, and a sense of purpose. He appeared to be several years younger as if the Sword had turned back the hands of time.

"What shall we do now, seein' as though we have seven days until the armies arrive?" Rosey looked to her comrades.

"We wait. There is nothing else we can do," Kulla sighed.

"There is one thing that I ask you help me to do," Draco looked to the sea.

"What is it?" Maia turned to face him.

Hours later, after offloading what food and supplies they had left, the four stood on the shores of the Island and watched as the ship Draco had built with his own hands float toward the horizon to the west. A tear rolled down Draco's cheek. Maia and Rosey noticed and both gave a warm embrace. Kulla placed a hand on Draco's shoulder.

"One life sails away while another begins," he drew the Sword of Ages from its sheath on his left hip and looked at it again as if in disbelief.

For the next seven days Rosey, Maia, Kulla, and Draco began to explore each other's limits in abilities and powers. They sparred and meditated over the span of seven days. They helped each other improve their combat abilities and focus. Kulla explored the powers of the Scepter of Osiris and Maia did the same with the Necklace of Isis. The more they explored the powers and limits of the Relics, the more they learned about them and themselves. The more they trained with the Relics, the more they became as one with them.

It was on the seventh day, while they were resting, that Kulla and Maia caught a scent in the air. Maia's ears perked up as if listening for something. Both rose to their feet and examined their surroundings. Draco and Rosey rose to their feet as well looking at Maia and Kulla.

"What is it? What do you smell?" Draco walked to them.

"Man flesh," Kulla took in another waft of the air.

"Could it be?" Rosey's heart rapidly beat within her chest with anticipation.

"I hope so," *tap tap tap* went Maia's finger against her thigh. Then, on the north side of the hill, banners became visible. The clamor of armor and shields was heard by the four. A man suited in full traditional armor of English Knights with a broad sword strapped to his hip and a steel shield on his left arm walked up the hill. The Knight stopped at the northern edge of the stone formation. On the eastern side of the hill, another set of banners was seen and a man of dark complexion with a dark beard carrying a spear in one hand, a bow in the other, and had a scimitar sheathed on one hip and a quiver of arrows was strapped to his back was seen coming up the hill. He wore scaled armor across his chest and gold greaves on his shins and forearms. The man stopped on the eastern side of the stone formation.

"Look!" Maia pointed to the south. A man wearing a dark leather cuirass protecting his torso and chrome, folding greaves on his shins appeared. He carried a round brass shield, and a spear in his left hand and a falcate sword that was traditional of Spartan warriors was strapped to his hip. The man stopped at the southern end of the stone formation.

"Oh my heavens," Rosey gasped in awe. Her eyes were wide as if not believing what she was seeing. Coming up the western side of the hill was a man suited in armor traditional of the samurai. Two katana were both strapped to his left hip. He did not wear a helmet.

"What is it Rosey?" Kulla's eyes followed where Rosey's were gazing.

"It's my teacher. Raoko Shun," Rosey's lips curled in to a wide smile. Raoko Shun stopped on the western end of the stone formation. Raoko Shun saw Rosey and with a smile on his face bowed his head slightly to her. Rosey smiled and returned the bow. Each leader of the four armies stood on the north, east, south, and west sides at the top of Stone Island. Not only did these men wear their armor and carried weapons, but also had conical horns that were strapped to their waist belt. They were all not the same length or thickness. The man suited in full armor removed his face mask and took the horn from his hip. He took a deep breath and blew into the horn. Its sound bellowed throughout Stone Island. The other three men did the same. Each horn had a distinct pitch and timbre but once all four horns were sounded, the sound from them melded in to a unison chorus. This unison chorus of the four horns bellowed, resonated and echoed throughout Stone Island and could be heard for miles in each direction. At the moment, the Sword of Ages glowed vibrantly reacting to the unison chorus of the four horns.

"What is happening?" Draco held the Sword in front of him.

"I do not know," Kulla looked on in awe of what was going on. The leaders of each army then strapped the horns to their waists and then approached the center of the stone formation and walked toward Maia, Kulla, Draco, and Rosey. Meeting at the center of the rings of the stone formations, they stood in front of Draco, placed their clenched fists over their heart and bowed.

"I, Sir Galidan of England, pledge my sword and shield to you, my King," his armor clamored with each step he took toward Draco.

"I, Ahmaar of Egypt, pledge my scimitar and my bow to you, Ruler of All," his voice was dark and resonant.

"I, Lioneus of Sparta, pledge my spear and shield to you, King of Men," his posture was tall and strong.

"And I, Raoko Shun of Asia, pledge my katana to you, Almighty King," he bowed with humility. Draco walked to the men and stood in front of them. He looked at them and observed them. Their weapons, armor, and appearances were different. It was as if they were not of the same world. Despite their differences, they all had one thing in common, they were human; they had a beating heart within their chests and a strong spirit to want to go to war for their new King. Draco took the Sword of Ages and held it out to them. He touched the flat of the blade to each of the shoulders of the men who stood in front of him.

"I dub thee, Sir Galidan, Ahmaar, Lioneus, and Raoko Shun, Generals in my army," Draco said as he sheathed the blade.

"We thank you for this esteemed honor, Majesty," they said in unison. At that moment, an explosion of light erupted above their heads. And then the face of Mesnara formed from that light, "Welcome Sir Galidan, Ahmaar, Lioneus, and Raoko Shun. Your services in the King's Army are greatly appreciated and will not go unnoticed. Your union, under one banner, will send a message to Sekmet. That message being that there is strength in man and that man is not weak against his powers".

"We thank you for this great honor," the newly dubbed General's said in unison.

"Generals, summon your armies. King Draco, Maia, Kulla, and Rosey, prepare yourselves for battle, for it will be the battle of your lives and one that will be documented for later generations to read about," Mesnara's voice echoed within the stone formations. The Generals took their horns and sounded for their armies to ascend the hill. Each of the four armies ascended the hill in response to the call of the horns. Each soldier in the army was wearing similar armor and carried similar weaponry to that of their leader. All were mounted on horses which were suited with light armor on their head and bridges of their noses and across their chests. The Generals mounted their horses and one soldier from each army brought a horse for King Draco, Kulla, Maia, and Rosey. Each mounted the horses and looked to Mesnara who hovered above them all. Then, Mesnara closed her eyes and a burst of bright emitted from her. A column of white light was opened in the middle of the stone formation.

"Go forth, and fear no evil in the valley of darkness," Mesnara faded and left the four armies.

"Men of Earth, let's ride to glory!" Draco drew the Sword of Ages and raised it to the sky and rode into the column of light with the four armies riding behind him.

A Dragon's Awakening

THERE WAS A STREAK OF dried blood trailing from the corners of his mouth, and dried blood under his eyes. His eyes were blackened and swollen. His chest plate was dented inward and his clothes were tattered and torn. Slash marks were made across his torso. His head hung low from his shoulders, limp and lifeless. His eyes dulled and became glossy. The daggers in his wrist and hand were the only things that were holding him up for the ten days he was pinned to the oak. His skin had torn from the weight of his body bearing down on the daggers. Zidane had stayed pinned to the oak tree for nearly two weeks. Without food or water, he had become delirious trying to hold on to whatever life was within his being. His vision was blurred and was seeing things that were not really there. Zidane lifted his head slightly to see a light fog gather several yards in front of him. He tried to focus in on the gathering fog, but could not. He was too weak. The fog slowly parted and became two individual clouds of fog floating above the ground. These two clouds of fog started to take on the shape of an individual. The arms, legs, and head were the first to form. Zidane could not distinguish any detail. He strained his eyes to see if what was happening in front of him actually there or a figment of his delirium. The clouds of fog began to form the details of their faces and clothing. They were both of the Elf race. They were wearing dark hooded, long coats and wore elven forged swords strapped to their waists. They stopped several feet in front of Zidane and stared at him, scowling.

"Zidane," one called to him. Zidane did not answer thinking this was being conjured by his mind.

"Zidane," the other called to him. Still Zidane did not answer. The two Elves looked at one another and then back to what they thought a pitiful sight.

"Look at you Zidane, bloodied and beaten," one's tone was of disgust.

"Do you not possess the Essence of the Red Dragon?" the other said.

"Who... who are you?" Zidane weak voice had to force the words to leave his lips.

"He does not recognize his own kin," one said to the other.

"I am King Cretus, past Ruler of the Eastern Province," he responded.

"And I am King Tidus, past Ruler of the Western Province," the other replied.

"W-why are you here?" Zidane's voice was raspy.

"We saw what the Black Dragon did to you," Cretus shook his head.

"You had no chance against his powers," Tidus sighed.

"He was too... powerful," Zidane tried to focus his vision on them.

"No! You only think that he is more powerful than you!" Tidus scolded.

"When in actuality, all five Dragons are equal to one another," Cretus folded his arms in front of his chest. "You have yet to realize your full potential like the Black Dragon, even after all of these months," Tidus's disappointment was heard in his voice.

"But... how do I... do that?" Zidane gasped for air through his dried lips.

"You are a being that was fused from two souls. Your body may be fused but you have yet to fuse your mind and abilities," Cretus responded. "That is why your memories seem disjointed and why you were easily defeated by the Black Dragon," he explained.

"If I fuse… the minds and souls of…. Giltia… and Fid… I will realize… my full…potential?" Zidane asked in between gasps of air.

"It took you several months to realize this, but yes, that is correct," Tidus let out a deep breath.

"You must be at peace with your mind, body, and soul in order to achieve this. You must attain the highest level of focus and concentration. You cannot falter. If you do, you will be killed and your powers will belong to the Black Dragon," although he was already dead, Cretus's fear of this happening showed on his face.

"I do not… believe Stratos… is evil in nature. I think… he has been… corrupted," Zidane strained to say.

"It appears that you are correct. Dragons are not malicious in nature. In fact, they tend to separate themselves from the rest of the World. However, Dragons do have weaknesses. You, the Bearer of the Red Dragon Essence are susceptible to anger, rage, and vengeance while the Black Dragon can become corrupt by greed or power," Cretus explained.

"What you must decide is if you want to find out what motivates the Black Dragon to attack you," Tidus said.

"Are you prepared to face the Black Dragon once more Zidane, Bearer of the Red Dragon Essence? Are you prepared to face the shadows in which you will be engulfed?" Cretus turned to be more ominous. Zidane lowered his head to face the ground and moments later, he slowly looked back up and found Cretus and Tidus had vanished.

"C-Cretus? T-Tidus?" Zidane called out in to the empty night. No one answered. He was alone once more. Nothing but the hush of the forest was around him. He lowered his head once more looking to the ground at his feet. "Fuse the two souls and become one. Fuse the two souls and become one," he began to chant to himself with his eyes closed.   Moments passed and Zidane was still chanting that one phrase over and over again. As Zidane was muttering to himself, a dark shadow crept upon Zidane. An evil laugh echoed throughout the forest and then Stratos emerged from the shadows.

"I see that you have not died from starvation or thirst. Your will has gone beyond my expectations," Stratos walked from behind the tree Zidane was pinned to. Zidane continued to chant that same phrase as Stratos circled the great oak. "You are starting to show the resilient spirit of the Red Dragon," he walked away drawing his blades. Zidane was still chanting and started to focus on the fire of his Essence. "But, I am a Dragon of my word. You have yet to show me your true power. Now I will take your heart and your powers," Stratos whirled around and lunged at Zidane. The Dragon mark on Zidane's left wrist and hand brightly glowed red and flames crept along the image of the Dragon. That same fire burst and an aura of fire began to spread and radiate from Zidane's body. The daggers in his wrist and hand slowly turned to ash and crumbled to the ground. Stratos stopped his attack only a few feet away from Zidane when he saw that he was being engulfed in flames. Zidane hovered a few inches above the ground bending at the waist slightly as if the muscles in his body had gone limp and his eyes were closed with his head lowered to the ground below him. The aura of fire grew and pulsed the more focused Zidane became. The puncture wounds from the daggers in his wrist and forearm were being closed and healed by the flames, the swelling around his eyes had gone down, the bruises and cuts on his face and torso faded away. The chest plate he wore turned to ash and slowly crumbled to the ground below. The eyes of Stratos widened in disbelief at this sight, but then the look of disbelief turned to an evil smile. Stratos sensed the increasing energy within Zidane as the wounds on his body fully healed and the flames from his body became more intense. Zidane outstretched his arms with palms outward. He hovered further off the ground and the flames began to ignite the oak tree behind him. With his palms outstretched, Zidane used lashes of wind to bring forth his Twin Dragon Blades to him. The blades flew from the ground to his outstretched hands. As he caught the blades by the hilts, the steel of the blades throbbed with intense energy and a spiral of flames swirled around them. Zidane slowly lowered himself to the ground below. As he touched down to the ground and raised his head, his eyes vibrantly glowed red and his dreadlocks sparked with burning embers with an aura of flame around his body. The great oak behind him was fully ignited in flames sending an immense cloud of smoke into the air above them. Though the flames were wild and intense, the rest of the forest did not ignite in those same flames, remaining untouched. Stratos took a few steps backwards as to not be burned by the wildfire that ignited the great oak. With each step Zidane took, a trail of flames followed him. His eyes continued to glow vibrantly.

"Well it appears the Red Dragon has awakened from his slumber," Stratos crouched in to a defensive position. He summoned an aura of shadows around his swords.

"The Red Dragon has awakened. It is a shame that it has taken this long for it to happen," Zidane stopped several feet in front of Stratos who remained in a defensive position.

"Now I can take your heart and your powers with you at full strength," although a fight to the death was about to ensue, Stratos maintained his dark grin.

"Why do you want my powers? Dragons were not meant to act in this manner. You seem to hunger for power when Dragons are not meant to be gluttons," Zidane lowered his blades.

"My reasoning is none of your concern, Red Dragon," he spat as his eyes flashed black.

"I believe it is, considering you are attempting to slay me," Zidane's eyes blazed even more.

"Well that is a secret that will not be revealed to you," Stratos lunged at Zidane with both of his blades. Zidane quickly blocked the attack and braced himself by setting his feet firmly into the ground. As the blades clashed, sparks flew from the steel.

"Dragons are noble creatures. They protect all those closest to them and those who are in dire need. They are not murderers," Zidane continued to hold his ground.

"That is none of your concern, Red Dragon!" he exclaimed pushing off of Zidane. Stratos once more lunged at Zidane slashing and stabbing at him. With great ease, Zidane side stepped, blocked, and countered these attacks. Stratos leapt away from a swing of Zidane's blade. As he landed, he found Zidane lunging at him once more. He swung his blade to cut at Zidane's throat, but his attack was deflected downward and the hilt of Zidane's blade struck Stratos in the jaw causing him to stumble backwards.

"It appears I have underestimated you, Red Dragon," he and Zidane began to circle each other.

"I have become stronger, Stratos. I am now what I was destined to be. I am not afraid anymore," his eyes burned a fiery red.

"Well that is good. That means I can say I have slain the Red Dragon while he was at his strongest," he lunged at him with ferocity. Zidane side stepped the first slash from one blade and blocked the second attack from the other. Zidane spun and slashed at Stratos's neck. Stratos ducked under the slash and swept the legs from under Zidane putting him on his back. As he looked up, Stratos was poised to stab at his chest. Zidane blocked the attack and kicked at Stratos' knee. Stratos stumbled backwards as Zidane kipped up to his feet. Stratos stood there and gave a grin to Zidane, "This will truly be a triumph when I take your heart".

"You need not do this. Dragons are not to act in this manner. We can leave this matter, forget about it, and part with no ill will towards each other," Zidane pleaded with him.

"No, Red Dragon! There can be only one true Lord of All Dragons!" Stratos's eyes flashed black as he bore his teeth.

"It does not have to be that way. We are evenly matched. Why can we not use our strength together to vanquish evil?" Zidane further pleaded. He saw the potential in Stratos to do good with his powers.

"No, Red Dragon! I need your powers!" Stratos roared as a wild look came about his piercing eyes.

"You need, or you want?" Zidane's retort caused the anger to swell even more within Stratos. An aura of malicious shadows enveloped his body. He clenched both blades in his hands tightly. Like wisps of fog creeping across the forest floor, the shadows crept through his body and in to his blades. Stratos took the hilts of his blades and fused them. The shadows surged from the hilts and in to the steel of the blades. The powers of the shadows became more intense. He then stood poised and ready to unleash an onslaught of attacks against Zidane.

"It would appear that you have your mind set upon killing. I have no choice but to defend myself," Zidane closed his eyes and focused his energy. Fire coursed through his arms and then through the hilts and steel of the blades. Zidane opened his eyes and then fused the two hilts together. A bright light emitted from the point of fusion. Stratos had to shade his eyes from the blinding light. The light then turned to a violent wildfire and coursed through the hilts and steel of the fused blades. Flames fumed from his eyes and the aura of his fire grew more intense. Stratos also was focusing his energy and then crouched down ready to attack. Zidane charged at Stratos with the Fusion Blade in hand ready to strike. Stratos took a few steps back and held out his palm. Shadows gathered in his palm just before unleashing a barrage of shadow orbs at the charging Zidane. Zidane swiftly dodged from side to side to avoid each exploding orb. Stratos continued his onslaught of shadow orbs, but they dissipated when they drew close to the aura of intense flames that surrounded Zidane's body. Zidane was within several feet of Stratos and he swung his Fusion Blade at Stratos' neck. Stratos blocked the attack. With the clashing of steel, a fusion of shadows and fire jumped from the Blades. They kicked one another other in the torso sending the other several feet backwards. Both created a trench in the earth as they landed and skidded across the dirt and rock. Both quickly rose to their feet and leapt to the air. In mid-air, they slashed at each other with nothing but the steel of the Blades clashing, causing more sparks to jump in to the air. The embers from the blades fell to the ground and created small pockets of what seemed to be a fusion of shadows and fire. Zidane saw this out of the corner of his eye as he was on his way back to the ground. As soon as Stratos landed on the ground, he whirled around and lunged at Zidane as he was about to land to the ground. As Stratos was about to slash at him, Zidane landed on to the ground. He flipped backwards above the slash, and over Stratos. In mid-air, over the head of Stratos, Zidane gave a kick to his back sending him forward. Stratos rose to his feet as soon as he hit the ground. He whirled around to find Zidane standing only a few feet away from him.

"You are not trying. Show me your rage!" Stratos exclaimed.

"Why use rage to defeat you when I am presently calm and in control of my emotions as I command this fight?" the fire calmly burned around Zidane. No rage or hate were within those flames. Stratos clenched his teeth and stomped the ground to quake the earth beneath Zidane's feet to knock him off balance. Zidane leapt backwards several feet. When he landed he conjured fire on one end of the Fusion Blade and a small cyclone of wind around the other blade.

"Wildfire Tornado!" Zidane spun the Blade between his hands. The fire and the wind began to fuse and form a cyclone of fire. The cyclone reached eight feet in to the air and was several feet at the base. The fire of the cyclone was intense and bright. Zidane sent the cyclone of fire rushing toward Stratos. Stratos held out his Fusion Blade to rouse a dome of shadow to protect him. The wildfire tornado overtook the shield of shadow. The tornado violently whirled about the dark shield. Several moments passed, the shadow shield began to crack and then finally shatter under the pressure of the raging winds of fire. With the shield gone, the wind lifted Stratos in to the air and spun him in all directions. The tornado of wildfire spat Stratos out sending him in to the branches of a pine. Stratos landed on his back creating a small crater under the branches of the pine tree. He was slow to get to his feet. His eyes were fixed on Zidane as he slowly approached him with Fusion Blade in hand. As Zidane was within a few feet of him, Stratos slashed at Zidane's neck. Zidane spun, narrowly avoiding the steel, and gave his own attack but stopping only a few inches of his neck. Zidane found that Stratos had the same idea and stopped his Blade a few inches short of Zidane's neck. Both glared at each other. Auras of fire and shadow emitted from their bodies and Fusion Blades. Their eyes flashed violently with energy fuming from them.

"Why did you not follow through?" Zidane asked through heavy breaths. Stratos was silent as if he was struggling with the decision. The ground then quaked throwing Zidane and Stratos off balance. Neither lowered their Blades from each other's throat and did not take their eyes off of the other.

"Are you causing the quakes, Red Dragon, just to distract me?" Stratos accused.

"No. I need not distract you," Zidane replied as another quake rumbled about the earth. The small quakes became more frequent and more intense. The trees behind Zidane bent to either side, while other pine trees were toppled over. Both Zidane and Stratos looked to each other and lowered their Blades and faced whatever was heading for them.

"What is it?" Stratos's grip on his weapon tightened.

"Something you may have conjured," Zidane retorted.

"I should take your heart at this moment Red Dragon and then fend off what evil is heading toward our way," Stratos said through his clenched teeth. Zidane furrowed his eyebrows in confusion at Stratos. From behind the trees, emerged a large figure. It was as tall as the pine trees it had torn down in its path and was as wide as a great red wood. The creature was carrying a club in each hand. It wore nothing but a loin cloth around its waist.

"It is a Cyclops," Zidane took a few steps backwards.

"Do not tell me the Great Red Dragon is afraid of a mere behemoth," Stratos mocked Zidane. Zidane bore his teeth at Stratos and gave a low dragon-like growl. He gave a grin to Zidane and, with his Fusion Blade in hand, he launched himself at the neck of the Cyclops. The Cyclops swung one club at Stratos, hitting him. He landed on his back next to Zidane.

"Do you wish to take on this behemoth by yourself and continue to fall on your back or shall we attempt to slay a common foe?" Zidane looked down to Stratos. He looked up to Zidane then to the Cyclops. Zidane held out his hand to Stratos to help him to his feet. Stratos scowled as he took Zidane's hand tightly and was helped to his feet. As Stratos got to his feet, he glared in to Zidane's eyes. His grip on Zidane's hand became tighter and more forceful. Zidane tightened his grip as well to match the strength of Stratos. Their hands and forearms began to tremble from the amount of strength each was exuding. Stratos began to give off an aura of shadows around his forearm and hand. Zidane began emitting an aura of fire around his forearm and hand. Both of the auras met at the clasped hands of the two Dragons and began to fuse together in to a dark fire. Zidane noticed on the right wrist of Stratos was a similar Bracelet to that of the Bracelet of Ra. Instead of it being gold, like Zidane's, it was silver and had an engraving on it, but Zidane could not make it out. The Cyclops gave a thunderous roar and beat his chest with clenched fists and clubs in both hands. Zidane and Stratos dropped to defensive stances with their Fusion Blades in hand. The Cyclops charged at the two ant-like creatures that stood in front of him. Zidane and Stratos looked to each other and nodded their heads. Both charged at the Cyclops with their Blades ready to strike. They both began to run from side to side, crisscrossing each other's path. The Cyclops was being thrown off balance by trying to follow two fast moving objects with only one eye to follow with. It became enraged and swung its club wildly at the ground and air. Still charging toward the Cyclops, Zidane and Stratos quickened their speed and in doing so left a trail of fire and shadow behind each of them. The Cyclops continued on his rage swinging its clubs wildly, growling and snarling. Stratos and Zidane continued their side winding charge at the creature. Stratos leapt to the air. The Cyclops saw Stratos in mid-air and swung its club at him. Stratos slashed at the club slicing it in to two. The Cyclops then saw Zidane on the ground out of the corner of its eye. It swung its other club at the ground. Zidane sidestepped the club and ran up the club and the arm of the Cyclops. Zidane brought his Blade back and swung it at the Cyclops' neck. The Cyclops avoided the slash and swatted at Zidane with its free hand sending Zidane plummeting the ground. Zidane landed a few feet away from Stratos.

"Come on, Red Dragon. Get off of your face. Are you going to allow me to take the head of this behemoth by myself?" Stratos's grin was arrogant as he looked down upon his rival Dragon. Zidane spun up to his feet and gave a glare to Stratos.

"Follow my lead," Zidane growled as his eyes flared red at Stratos. Zidane's eyes then turned to the Cyclops. Zidane undid the hilts of the Blade and sheathed them. He leapt toward the Cyclops and pointed the Bracelet of Ra at it. Stratos leapt in behind Zidane with his Blade ready to slash.

"Solar Flare!" Zidane yelled as he came within inches of the face of the Cyclops. A blinding light flashed from the Bracelet. The Cyclops reeled back in pain from the blinding light. Its eye was burning. It growled and whined. As the Cyclops was blinded, Stratos slashed at the neck of the Cyclops, taking its head from its shoulders. The head landed to the ground with a dull thud and the body soon followed, toppling over with a thunderous quake. Stratos landed to the ground and looked upon the decapitated body of the Cyclops and gave a satisfied grin.

"Now, we have a fight to finish, Red Dra-," he turned to say to Zidane, but he was not in sight. Stratos looked all around him and saw no sign of Zidane. He grew frustrated and enraged. His eyes violently flashed black. The grip on his Blade tightened as he clenched his other fist. Shadow energy fumed from him as his rage grew.

"I will hunt you down Red Dragon! You cannot run from me! I will find you! I will follow you to the ends of Earth and Rhydin! Nothing will stop me! I will become the Lord of All Dragons!" Stratos hoped that Zidane heard his foreboding vow where ever he was. His voiced carried throughout the valley of pine. Zidane was running through the forest of pine as fast as he could. He heard the voice of

Stratos yell to him as it echoed in his ears. He leapt to the branches of the pine and jumped from branch to branch and tree to tree.

He headed further west in the valley with dusk approaching. The Sun was setting over the Western Mountains. Zidane stopped on one of the branches and crouched down looking off to the sunset. He watched the Sun's rays color the sky red and orange. He closed his eyes and inhaled a deep breath as if trying to absorb the last rays of the Sun before it disappeared behind the Mountains. As he opened his eyes, the rays of the Sun glinted off of his silver eyes. Just below the setting Sun, he saw a cavern several miles away leading in to one of the mountains. He then noticed, about one hundred yards east from the cavern, a village surrounded by a stone wall with two entrances. One of the entrances faced east and another opening faced toward the cavern in the mountainside.

"I wonder if the village knows if there is anything in the mountain," he thought aloud. "Well there is only one way to find out," he leapt to the ground and sprinted off to the village.

Night fell over the valley as Zidane reached the entrance of the village where he stopped short to catch his breath. On either side of the entrance, there were two tall stone statues of dragons. It was as if the statues were the guardians of the village keeping a vigil eye for any foe. Zidane gazed in to what were the eyes of one of the stone dragons. It seemed familiar to him for some reason as if he had seen it before. His eyes then turned from the stone dragons to the stone wall. He walked to the wall and placed his hand on it. The stone was smooth. There were no rough edges or divots in the stone. The stones were not cemented together, but seemed to be fused together.

"Intense fire must have fused these stones together," Zidane continued to run his hand across the stone wall.

"Can I help you?" a woman's voice asked from behind him. Zidane turned to face a woman who was standing there with a pail of water in hand. Beside her stood an adolescent boy who was also carrying a pail of water. Zidane looked upon the two. The woman wore a dark brown garment that only had one sleeve leaving the other arm bare. She wore a necklace of small beads that were the color of mahogany. Her hair was the color of the earth beneath their feet. It was long and thick. Her sky blue eyes searched Zidane trying to figure him out, mostly to see if he was friend or foe. She had not seen anyone like him before. The young boy next to her also looked upon Zidane with curiosity, but was also on guard. Not only did he carry a pail of water, but in the other he carried a spear. His fist tightened around the shaft of the spear and his eyes narrowed and focused on Zidane. Zidane looked upon the boy and concluded that he was around the age of fifteen and that he was the son of the woman he stood next to. He had her eyes and hair. He seemed protective of her. Zidane saw the boy was wearing a jade crystal around his neck. It looked familiar to him and he clasped the ruby crystal that hung from his neck. Zidane took a few steps toward them. The boy quickly put the pail to the ground and stepped between his mother and Zidane.

"I mean you two no harm," Zidane stopped several feet in front of them.

"Who are you?" the woman calmly asked.

"My name is Zidane. I am the Elf Ruler of the Western Province," his hands were up to show no aggression toward them. "Why are you here?" the boy's voice was forceful as he gripped the spear in his hands. His mother placed her hands on his shoulders to calm him.

"I came looking for something, or someone. I am not sure," he shook his head not knowing what it was that beckoned him there, "I have been drawn here by some unknown force," Zidane's hands went back to holding the ruby crystal between his fore and middle fingers.

"You wear the ruby crystal of the Elf Rulers. That symbolizes the alliance between the Elf Empire and the Dragon Knights," the boy pointed the tip of his spear to Zidane's crystal. The boy then lowered his spear and held the crystal that hung from his neck. Zidane walked to the boy and knelt to him looking at the jade crystal that hung from the boy's neck. Both the ruby crystal and the jade crystal vibrantly glowed in reaction to each other.

"Are you a Dragon Knight?" Zidane looked from the crystal to the boy.

"I am in training," he responded.

"What is your name?" Zidane asked.

"My name is Arteus," he responded.

"That is a strong name. I trust you are learning your lessons well and are remaining focused on your training," Zidane grinned.

"Yes sir," the boy nodded. The mother smiled in approval of her son and then looked to Zidane.

"Won't you come in to the village," the woman offered. Zidane rose to his feet and nodded in acceptance of her offer. She reached down for the pail of water.

"No, allow me. Please," Zidane stopped her hand from grasping the pail handle. She nodded and allowed Zidane to reach down to grasp and pick up the pail of water. The boy took his pail of water.

As the three entered, the village reminded Zidane of the home he grew up in on Earth. It was plain. The people who inhabited the village were much like the villagers in Zidane's own village. They were plain looking folk, much like Arteus and his mother with similar clothing and demeanor. The huts were built from stone that was similar to that of the stone used to build the wall. The stones of the huts were fused together much like the wall. The huts of stone were built side by side from one end of the village to the other end. Zidane's eyes wandered from hut to person. He felt at home. This place felt warm to him as if he were back on Earth in his village. The mother and Arteus led Zidane to the hut in which they lived. The mother pushed on the wooden door and entered the stone hut followed by Arteus and then Zidane. Zidane's silver eyes wandered about the hut. It was small, but it was enough room for the two of them. He saw, on the right side of the hut, there was a metal wood burning stove which was enough to warm the hut on cool nights. Next to the stove he saw a pile of cut wood piled halfway to the ceiling. On the opposite wall were two cots set side by side. In the middle of the hut was a small wooden table that had a candle that was half burned down and a set of clay plates and wooden utensils. Arteus set his spear in the corner closest to the door of the hut and then took the pail of water from Zidane. Arteus walked over to the other side of the hut and emptied the pails in to a small well.

"Won't you take a seat?" the mother asked as she pulled a chair for Zidane to sit.

"Thank you, madam. Please excuse my lack of manners, but I did not catch your name," Zidane stated as he sat.

"No, please excuse my lack of manners. I did not introduce myself to you. My name is Afelina," an embarrassed grin graced her face.

"It is a pleasure to meet you and your son Arteus," he gave a glance to Arteus who took a seat on one of the cots.

"What has led you here, Lord Zidane?" Afelina took a seat at the small wooden table.

"A series of events has occurred throughout the past several months that have led me to this valley village. I, at first, was in pursuit of a vampire horde who ravaged and destroyed my home village back on Earth. I exacted my revenge and in doing so I found that I was a part of the Elf royal blood line here on Rhydin. As the months passed, I began to discover these slumbering abilities and powers that dwelt within me. There were so many secrets within me that with time were unlocked. I eventually became what I am meant to be," Zidane looked down to his hands and the Bracelet of Ra.

"And what is that?" Afelina gave a tilt of her head.

"I am the Bearer of the Red Dragon Essence," Zidane looked in to the dark eyes of Afelina. Arteus slowly rose from the cot to his feet. His eyes were widened in disbelief. Afelina's eyes widened as well and covered her mouth.

"It cannot be," Arteu's mouth was agape.

"This village and the Dragon Knights have been waiting for the day the Bearer of the Red Dragon Essence would come. More importantly, the Great Tufar has been awaiting your arrival," her voice grew with excitement.

"Do you mean the Red Dragon Tufar?" Zidane placed his palm on his chest and felt his beating heart.

"Mother, we must take him to the Dragon Council. They have been waiting for many years for the Bearer of the Red Dragon Essence," Arteus's urgency was heard in his voice. Afelina nodded her head and rose from the table. Arteus went to the corner and took his spear. Zidane rose to his feet and looked in to the hopeful eyes of Afelina and Arteus, "Where am I to go?".

"I will lead you in to the mountain where the Dragon Knights, Knights in training, and Dragon Council are," Arteus began to walk out of the door. Zidane nodded and then turned to Afelina. She stood at the table with her hands folded in front of her. A joyous smile came across her face. Zidane smiled also and bowed to her, "It was a pleasure to meet you, and I thank you for your hospitality".

"Likewise, Lord Zidane," she bowed as well. Arteus then led Zidane out of the stone hut. Zidane was led down the main road of the village toward the cave opening in the mountain. Zidane looked around at the villagers. He saw women of all ages but only saw younger boys and older men. This was curious to Zidane, "It seems to me the young men of the village are not present".

"When the males of the village come of age, they undergo the rite of passage to test their physical strength, endurance, and strength of heart," Arteus's pace to the cave opening was quick.

"The rite of passage to become a Dragon Knight?" Zidane's eyebrow raised.

"Yes. It is the goal of all the men of this village to become a soldier wearing the armor worthy of a Dragon Knight," Arteus said with pride.

"What is entailed in the trials?" to Zidane, it sounded more intensive than that of the training the Elf soldiers undergo.

"A young man is paired with a young drake. They are sent in to the most harsh and violent region of the mountains where Mountain Trogs and Cyclops roam freely. The only way for them to conquer the ordeal is to work together which would lead the two in creating an unbreakable bond. This Trial is so perilous that there are those who die from the elements or are killed by the creatures that dwell within the mountain forests," Arteus seemed to look forward to his Trial.

"I understand now," Zidane nodded, "I must ask, why are you not training with the other young men of the village?".

"At times during the year, a small group of trainees get a certain amount of time away from training. And we rotate. This is my group's last day," Arteus seemed to look forward to training once more.

"It does not appear that this valley has been under recent attack. Has this valley village been attacked by the forces of Sekmet?" Zidane looked to the village and saw no urgency or worry in the eyes of these villagers, unlike what he has seen in the Elf Kingdom.

"Those cursed creatures do not even make it in to the valley. We have watch towers on the north, east, south, and west corners of the valley. They alert us by lighting a torch that can be seen here in the village and a Dragon Knight watches from the mountain for any sign of trouble," Arteus pointed to where the watchtowers were.

"That is an impressive system," Zidane nodded with raised eyebrows. He searched the borders for the watch towers and saw them. They were several hundred yards from the village. "There were rumors of an Elf who crossed in to the valley, but was not thought of to be a threat. But weeks later, the great oak in the center of the valley was set on fire. Soldiers were sent to scout it and found nothing but small craters in the ground, broken tree limbs, cracked tree trunks, and dark fire," Arteus sounded perplexed when he uttered the words 'dark fire'.

"The Elf you speak of is me. I am the one who ventured in to the valley in search of whatever is summoning me. I ventured deeper and deeper in to the forest and found myself engulfed by shadows. A man who manipulated the shadows attacked me and pinned me to the great oak. A week passed, with no food or water I stayed there against the tree. I looked within myself and gathered my strength to free myself. With the burst of wildfire, I fought the man of the shadows. In the middle of our fight, we were attacked by a behemoth.

We defeated it but, shortly afterwards, I fled without the man of the shadows knowledge," Zidane looked over his shoulder as if searching for a shadow of Stratos.

"So the man of the shadows is still out there?" Arteus stopped and took a hold of his spear with both hands as if preparing for a fight.

"Yes, but you need not worry. He wants me and no one else," Zidane he placed his hands on the Arteus's shoulders to ease his nerves. Arteus nodded and smiled out of trust in Zidane. Zidane gave a grin and turned to find they had arrived at the opening in the mountain. He let out a deep breath and then looked to Arteus who gave a nod for reassurance. Zidane then looked back to the opening in the mountain and entered the cave opening.

Walking deeper and deeper in to the cave, the entering became scarce. Zidane squinted his eyes to try to see in the dark. There was a slight smell of ash and brimstone in the air. He saw the tunnel take a slight turn. Zidane saw a dim light illuminate the tunnel ahead of him. He took caution and kept his footsteps quiet. When he got to the corner of the tunnel, Zidane peered his head around to see what may be awaiting him. He saw at the end of the tunnel an immense brass door. On it was the carving of a great winged dragon breathing fire in to the sky. At the top of the door was the carving of the Eye of Ra. Zidane looked down at the Bracelet on his wrist and ran his finger across the engraving of the Eye of Ra. Then his eyes turned back to the door to find there were two soldiers on either side of the door. Their feet were together, stomachs were in, and chests were out. They stood firm as they held their posts. They had in one hand a long spear and in the other a tower shield. Both soldiers were suited in full armor. Their breast plate was adorned with the emblem of the Red Dragon with the Eye of Ra behind it. Their shoulders, arms, and forearms were covered with the metallic armor. Greaves made with the same metal protected their shins and knees. Their helmets looked like the head of a dragon which only allowed for the eyes to be seen. The eyes of the soldiers were focused and ever vigilant. Above them were the two torches in which illuminated the tunnel. Zidane looked down to the Bracelet of Ra that was fastened to his wrist and then to the soldiers who guarded the door. He inhaled a deep breath and then let it out before walking down the hall toward the guards. The soldiers saw Zidane and in one motion crouched down, placed their tower shields in from of them, and held their spear firmly above the shield.

"Halt! Friend or foe?!" one guard yelled at Zidane.

"I enter with no malicious intentions," Zidane slightly raised his hands in the air.

"What is your business here?!" the second demanded.

"This is my business," he presented the Bracelet of Ra for the guards to see. The guards relaxed lowering their shields and spears. Zidane slowly approached the guards and looked in to their eyes. They were focused and unwavering.

"What is your name?" the first guard still seemed defensive, but that was their duty.

"My name is Zidane. I am the Elf Ruler of the Western Province," Zidane spoke clearly.

"What do you have to prove that you are an Elf Ruler of Rhydin?" the second guard inquired.

"I wear the ruby crystal in which the Elf Rulers of Rhydin are given. It symbolizes the alliance between the Elf Kingdom and the Dragon Knights," he showed the crystal that hung from his neck. The light from the torches glinted off of the ruby crystal. The guards then took the crystals that hung from their neck. They wore the jade crystals of the Dragon Knights. Zidane took several more steps toward the guards. The ruby crystal began to glow vibrantly in reaction to the presence of the jade crystals. The jade crystals around the necks of the guards reacted as well.

"He speaks the truth," the second guard looked to the other. The first guard nodded to the other and then both looked at Zidane, "We must escort you to the Dragon Council, Lord Zidane". Zidane nodded in acknowledgement. The second guard turned to the brass door and pulled down on a lever that was set next to the door. The scraping of metal against rock filled the tunnels and the ears of the guards and Zidane. The strong smell of ash and brimstone flooded Zidane's nostrils as the doors opened. Zidane was taken aback by the smell. He then inhaled a deep breath and allowed the odor to fill his nose and lungs. He now became accustomed to the smell of ash and brimstone. Zidane found himself in a civilization that was built inside of the mountain. There were large huts built from stone. The stones used to build the huts were fused together much like the huts in the village. Men in similar armor as the guards walked about the civilization in the mountain. These soldiers were all that he saw. These men carried their spears and tower shields with them where ever they went. Walking further and further in to the mountain civilization, Zidane started to feel the ground under his feet rumble and shake. Zidane looked around and from behind one of the stone huts walked a dragon. It was not large in size but was as large as two of the stone huts put together. Its wings were folded against the side of its body. Small horns lined the bridge of its nose, horns protruded from its brow and from the crown of its head. Zidane also noticed a young man walking beside the dragon talking to it. The young man was suited in the armor in which the Dragon Knights wore. He carried his spear and shield in one hand and helmet in the other hand. Walking deeper and deeper in to the mountain stronghold, Zidane began to see more and more dragons dwelling. Some were lying down and others were walking with who seemed to be their Dragon Knight companion. In passing, Dragon Knights and Dragons looked upon the stranger who has entered their realm.

"I suppose you do not receive many outsiders here," Zidane's continued to marvel at the various dragons that walked about this mountain civilization.

"No, we do not," the first guard eyes continued to look forward.

"Our civilization is in seclusion so that the Knights, Dragons, and Knights in training are not distracted by the outside world," the second guard stated.

"That is understandable. Where are the Knights in training?" Zidane looked around for the young trainees.

"They train under that pavilion," the first guard pointed with his spear. Zidane looked and saw the structure. It reminded him of the dojo he trained in with Chen Shun the pavilion was at least fifty yards away, but he saw the young men going through their exercises with who seemed to be their instructor. He heard all of the orders being called out to the trainees, "Block! Side step! Thrust!". Zidane then felt gusts of wind beat down upon him. He looked down to the ground and saw clouds of dirt and ash swirl above the ground. Zidane looked up and saw numerous dragons above them. It seemed to Zidane they were training as well. They all seemed to be young except one dragon who seemed to be the elder of them. The Elder Dragon hovered growling instructions to the younger dragons. The younger dragons, at the command of the Elder, each dove toward the ground. Once they were within feet of the ground below, they pulled up and flew back up to the Elder Dragon. There was one dragon who narrowly missed hitting the ground and pulled up behind the rest of the Dragons. The Elder Dragon began to hurl massive rocks down at the younger dragons as they approached. The younger dragons dodged the rocks as they flew upward. More rocks were thrown and the Dragons responded by blowing fireballs at the rocks obliterating them. A chunk of rock was bypassed by the other Dragons but the one who fell behind was struck on its wing. The dragon spiraled downwards, but recovered quickly. Beating its wings, the young dragon raced to join the other young dragons.

"Young dragons, your exercises are over for the day. We will reconvene at dawn tomorrow. You are dismissed," the Elder Dragon growled, "Chakaar, I want to speak with you alone," the younger dragons flew to the ground below leaving Chakaar with the Elder Dragon. "You cannot falter as you have demonstrated in this exercise, young Chakaar," the Elder Dragon leaned his head down to meet Chakaar's eyes.

"Yes, I understand, Master," Chakaar lowered his head knowing he disappointed his teacher.

"Focus is essential to combat and everything else in life," the Elder Dragon's voice was that of someone who cared for their student.

"I will train harder," Chakaar looked into the yellow eyes of the Elder Dragon.

"No. Train smarter, not harder," the Elder Dragon shook his head.

"I understand, Master," Chakaar responded with a nod.

"Do not begin to doubt yourself, young one. I see that you have the potential, but you must look within yourself and tap in to that potential," the Elder Dragon's voice boomed with strength.

"Yes, Master," Chakaar nodded. The Elder Dragon nodded and lowered himself to the ground below. Chakaar started to lower himself, but looked up to the rocks on the sides of the interior. Chakaar flew up and took one of the larger stones with his tail. He looked up to the ceiling of the mountain and then to the ground below. The Elder Dragon looked back up as did the other younger Dragons, "Chakaar, what are you doing?!". Chakaar hurled the rock in to the air and then spiraled toward the ground. Within feet of the ground, Chakaar quickly pulled up from the ground flawlessly. The rock he had thrown to the air began to plummet toward him. Chakaar focused on the rock and then blew a fireball at the rock turning it to dust as the fireball obliterated it. Chakaar flew through the dust and then flew back down to the ground.

"Why did you do that?" the Elder Dragon approached Chakaar with questioning eyes.

"I had to prove to myself that I could execute with no flaw, Master," he responded standing at attention.

"And that you did. Well done, Chakaar," the Elder turned then walked away. Chakaar gave a smile and followed the Elder and the other younger dragons. Zidane smiled as the dragons walked away as their thunderous footsteps were heard.

"We must not linger here Lord Zidane," the first guard placed a hand on his shoulder.

"We must get you to the Dragon Council," the second nodded in the direction they were to go.

"I am sorry," Zidane followed the two guards. It was to the other side of this civilization that the Dragon Guards led Zidane. In front of them was a set of large brass doors similar to the ones the Zidane first entered. On each door was the same engraving as the first door. A great dragon was breathing an inferno to the sky and the Eye of Ra was at the top of the door. The difference was that these doors were larger, as if they were made for the largest of the dragons to walk through and join the rest of this Mountain Village.

Zidane stood in front of the brass doors in awe of the engravings. The first guard approached the massive door and, with a closed fist, he knocked on the door four times. The sound echoed throughout the mountain. A few moments later, one of the doors creaked open. A soldier adorned in the same armor as many of the other soldiers, carrying a spear and shield, emerged from behind the door. His eyes fell upon the two guards who flanked Zidane and then his eyes fell upon the stranger who stood in front of him. The soldier examined him from toe to head.

"Who is this stranger?" he facial expression was stern.

"I am Zidane, the Elf Ruler of the Western Province of Rhydin. I wish to have an audience with the Dragon Council," Zidane approached the soldier.

"What is your business here, Lord Zidane?" the soldier's voice lightened, but maintained its strength.

"I am the Bearer of the Red Dragon Essence. I also wield the Twin Dragon Blades and I wear the Bracelet of Ra," Zidane showed the Bracelet of Ra to the guard. The guard looked at Zidane and then at the Bracelet that was fastened to his wrist.

"The Dragon Council will decide whether you are the Bearer of the Red Dragon Essence. Follow me.," the guard turned to lead

Zidane past the doors, "You two return to your posts," he turned his head to face the escorting guards.

"Yes sir," the two guards said in unison. They turned to return to the main door.

"Follow me, Lord Zidane," Zidane followed the guard deeper in to the mountain. Zidane was led down a dimly lit corridor. Their footsteps echoed throughout the hall. The guard was silent with his eyes forward. Zidane ran his fingers against the stone on the wall. All were fused together by fire.

"How long has this civilization been in existence?" Zidane's eyes marveled at how well this mountain civilization was built. It almost rivaled the Dwarves.

"Since the times of Giltia and Tufar. It is said they both built it with their own hands so that humans and dragons can live and work together," the guard responded.

As they walked further down the corridor, Zidane found the hall led to a high archway. It was lined with gold and intricate adornments, that weaved and intertwined, were carved in to the smoothed stone. On either side of this archway were tall stone dragons whose eyes were vigilant. They were similar to the stone dragons that stood watch at the Village Gate's entrance. Zidane stood several yards in front of the archway, gazing up it.

"What are you waiting for, Lord Zidane? They are waiting for you," the guard urged for him to move forward.

"Yes. Yes. They are," Zidane said stepped forward. His eyes were still on the archway. When his eyes looked forward, there was the tallest of the Dragon Guards he had seen. His armor was heavy and thick; the shield he held was strong and durable; he tightly grasped his spear at his side. This Guard's eyes fell upon Zidane as he approached.

"Guard, who is this stranger?" the Archway Guard's tone was demanding and deep.

"I present to you Lord Zidane, the Elf Ruler of the Western Province," the guard responded.

"What is your proof that you are in fact an Elf Ruler?" the Archway Guard's vision narrowed on Zidane.

"This is my proof," Zidane stepped toward the Guard and took the ruby crystal in to his palm. The eyes of the man gazed upon the glowing crystal. The illumination of the crystal reflected in the man's eyes. His eyes then moved from the crystal back to Zidane, "What is your business here, Lord Zidane?".

"I wish to have an audience with the Dragon Council," Zidane met the eyes of the Guard.

"What is the matter that you wish to discuss?" he asked.

"I am the Bearer of the Red Dragon Essence," Zidane said confidently. The eyes of the Archway Guard widened and then regained his stone cold composure.

"The Dragon Council will decide whether you are the Bearer of the Red Dragon. You may enter these hallowed halls," the Archway Guard nodded to Zidane. His eyes then went to his fellow guard, "Guard, you are dismissed," the guard bowed and returned to his post. The Archway Guard pivoted to lead Zidane in to the Chambers of the Dragon Council. "Please follow me in to the chambers, Lord Zidane," the Archway Guard beckoned Zidane to follow. Zidane looked to him and inhaled a deep breath before entering the Chambers. Upon entering the chamber, on the other end was a dark corridor that led to darkness. Even his acute vision could not pierce the darkness within that corridor. To Zidane, it was an abyss in to the unknown. On either side of the Council Chamber, there were two long tables set. On either side of the tables sat men dressed in crimson robes with the Dragon and Eye of Ra embroidered on the front. Behind each man sat a Dragon. Each Dragon was of a different size and appearance. All of their eyes were upon Zidane as he entered the Chamber.

"Step forward," one of the Dragons said. Zidane did so in response. Taking several steps forward, Zidane found himself in the middle of the chamber and standing on top of the Eye of Ra that adorned the stone floor. He looked down to the floor and then up to the Council whose eyes were upon him. Zidane felt anxiety in the pit of his gut. He did not know what the Council was to do with him.

"Word has reached our ears you are the Elf Ruler of the Western Province. Is this true?" one of the councilman asked is a raspy tone.

"It is true, honorable Councilman. I am the Elf Ruler of the Western Province," Zidane nodded.

"Do you have proof that you are indeed an Elf Ruler?" a Dragon immediately asked.

"Yes," Zidane answered as he took the ruby crystal between his fore and middle fingers to show it to the Dragon Council. All of the members of the Council nodded their heads in approval.

"Why have you requested an audience with the Dragon Council, Lord Zidane?" one of the Councilmen. Zidane looked to the floor of the Chamber at the Eye of Ra and took a few moments to answer. Looking at the Eye of Ra it was if he slipped in to a trance.

"Lord Zidane," one of the Dragons called to him. Zidane snapped out of his trance and looked to the Council.

"I have requested an audience because I am the Bearer of the Red Dragon Essence," the Council murmured amongst each other in disbelief.

"What proof do you have that you are indeed the Bearer of the Red Dragon Essence?" a Dragon asked with skepticism in his voice.

"I wear the Bracelet of Ra, the same insignia that your soldiers and you, as the Councilmen, bear on your chests," Zidane held up his right wrist to show the Council members. Another murmur emitted from the Council.

"How did you acquire that item?" one Councilman asked.

"And furthermore, how do we know the Bracelet on your wrist is in fact the real Bracelet of Ra?" a Dragon asked. Zidane took a few moments to take several deep breaths, "Shortly after I was born, this Bracelet was given to my aunt and my father to give me when I became old enough to bear the responsibility given by the Red Dragon, Tufar". The Council members looked at each other and whispered to one another. Several moments passed as the Council members spoke amongst each other. As they finished their deliberation, one of the members looked upon Zidane.

"We have one more question, Lord Zidane?" the Councilman rose to his feet and made his way toward Zidane.

"Yes?" Zidane's eyes watched the Councilman approach.

"It has been said the Bearer of the Dragon Essence will bear the mark of the dragon. Our question is, do you bear such a mark?" the Councilman raised an eyebrow and leaned in toward Zidane. Zidane looked in to the cold dark eyes of this Councilman. Zidane stood frozen in place. 'What is this mark that they speak of?' he internally wondered. His mind froze, no thoughts passed through his head. A look of disappointment came upon the face of Zidane.

"I do not believe I bear this mark of which you speak," Zidane lowered his head.

"I see," the Councilman responded with a raised eyebrow and folded arms.

"I apologize for wasting the time of the Council," Zidane said in a hushed and defeated tone. The members of the Council rose from their seats and began to exit the chamber. At the moment, Zidane felt a slight burning sensation radiate from his left hand and wrist. Zidane then looked down and saw the dragon mark that he bore on his left wrist and hand glowing red. Zidane's eyes widened at what he saw, "Councilmen!". All of the councilmen and dragons turned their attention to Zidane. Zidane held out his palm to the show the glowing mark of the dragon. The councilmen and dragons stood in awe as they saw the fiery red dragon mark on Zidane's hand.

"That is truly the mark of the Dragon," a Councilman said in excitement. Smiles came across the faces of each of the council members, even the dragons.

"We will go inform Tufar of your arrival, Lord Zidane," one of the dragons said as the council members turned to go in to the dark corridor. He reached under his tunic when he felt another burning sensation and began to rub the spot from which the sensation radiated. Zidane raised an eyebrow as he began to run his fingers along his shoulder and his right pectoral. What he felt were scars on his body. He did not recall being burned or cut. He then looked underneath his tunic to find what these scars were from.

"Councilmen," Zidane hesitantly called to them.

"You have something further to discuss Lord Zidane?" a Dragon turned his head.

"I do," Zidane began to un-strapped the Twin Dragon Blades from his waist and set them on the floor beside him. Then he took his tunic off and dropped it to the ground. On his right pectoral there was an image burned in to his skin. The council members took a closer look to see what the image was. The scars formed the image of a dragon's head breathing flames across his chest.

"What is this?" one Councilman asked as he took a closer look at the scars. Zidane slowly turned around and found there were many more scars that wrapped around his body forming the body and wings of the dragon. The council members stood in awe of the markings on the body of Zidane.

"This is remarkable," one Councilman's voice held his amazement.

"These are the markings signifying the Lord of All Dragon's, but it is not complete," a Dragon leaned down to examine the markings on Zidane's body more closely.

"Have you gone to the parallel universes and slain the other Dragon Essence Bearers, Lord Zidane?" one of the Councilmen asked raising an eyebrow.

"No Councilman, I have not. Another Dragon has and is on Rhydin searching for me," Zidane gave a shake of his head.

"It was wise for you not to slay him, Lord Zidane. The parallel universes need balance. If the powers of the Dragons were in one Bearer of the Dragon Essence, there would be no balance," one of the Dragons as if to warn Zidane.

"Thank you Councilman for saying so," Zidane said with a bow. The Council members then huddled together away from Zidane as he put his tunic back on and strapped the Twin Dragon Blades to his waist. Several moments later, a Councilman and a Dragon approached Zidane while the others looked on.

"We, the Council, will now go talk to Tufar and he will decide whether he will see you," the Councilman said calmly, but his eyes were bright with excitement.

"In the meantime, we ask that you wait here," the Dragon said. Zidane nodded his head in acknowledgement.

"We will return with the decision of Tufar," the Councilman and the Dragon then turned to join the other Council members. They all turned to walk in to the abyss of a cavern.

Moments passed and still not one member of the Council emerged from the cavern. Zidane sat on the floor in the middle of the Eye of Ra with his legs crossed and the Twin Dragon Blades by his side. Placing his hands on his knees, he closed his eyes and slipped in to a state of meditation. A faint, fiery red aura rose from his body moments later after beginning his meditation. Soon, the fiery red aura around his body slowly formed the body, limps, wings, neck and head of an immense Dragon made entirely of his flaring aura. It flew and serpentined around Zidane's body as he slipped deeper and deeper in to his meditative state. He was focusing on the powers that were within him. The fire, the lightning, the wind, and the ability to move and shape the earth at will. As he focused on each ability, the burnt etchings on his body glowed with a calming warmth, not the agonizing, internal burning that swept throughout his body when they first came upon him. Along with the etchings on his body, the marks of the dragon on his wrist and hand glowed with a flaring brilliance. Each strand of his dreadlocks sparked and crackled with bright embers that floated in the air around him. The metallic gold of the Eye of Ra he sat on shimmered even more brightly with the fire of his aura. The shimmering gold of the Eye of Ra and the fiery red of Zidane's dragon aura swirled about the other and rose high above his head. The intensity of these intermingling colors grew the more focused Zidane became in his meditation. It appeared that he was bathing in the light of the Sun and the flames of a raging wildfire as he patiently sat and meditated.

"Lord Zidane, Tufar has decided to see you," one of the Councilmen called from the dark tunnel. The Councilman entered the chambers with his eyes widening to find Zidane surrounded by an aura of an immense, flamed dragon and the shimmering gold from the Eye of Ra mimicking the rays of the Sun. Zidane opened his eyes to reveal they were wreathed with a bright flame. The Councilman took a few steps backwards as he became overwhelmed with amazement. The aura that surrounded Zidane slowly dissipated, as did the flame in his hair and the fire in his eyes. He inhaled and then exhaled a deep breath through his nostrils. With that deep exhalation came wisps of dark smoke that quickly faded in to the air. He stood to his feet and took up his Twin Dragon Blades to strap on to his waist.

"I am ready," Zidane said with another deep breath.

"P-Please…f-follow me," the Councilman stammered still wide eyed. Zidane nodded and followed the Councilman in to the abyss of a cavern.

The smell of ash and brimstone grew more potent as the Councilman and Zidane entered the cavern. The smell hung thick in the air. Zidane coughed and wheezed before his body accepted the air in to his lungs after several inhalations. The cavern they were walking through was wide and high enough for a dragon to walk through. They traveled this cavern tunnel for several minutes when at last they reached a large circular chamber where the walls were lined with small torches that dimly lit the room. Zidane saw the Councilman and Dragons lined up next to each other along one side of the chamber. Next to them, Zidane noticed a rack of some sort but it was veiled for some reason that he could not figure out. At the center of the room was a shallow but rather wide pit with coals and ash covering the bottom. Opposite of the Councilmen and the Dragons, there was a deep, dark alcove in the chamber. Clouds of smoke billowed from this alcove.

"Lord Zidane, please stand in front of the Council and face that corner," the Councilman pointed towards the dark alcove. Zidane looked at the Councilman and nodded. He walked over to the Council and looked at each member, then turned to face the dark corner. He was only a few feet in front of the pit of ash and coal. There was still heat radiating from the coal and ash. Zidane looked down to the pit and saw there were still red coals in the pit. He then looked up from the pit of ash and coal to the dark corner of the chamber. Dark smoke continued to billow from the darkness.

"Lord Zidane," a deep, dark voice called from the dark alcove.

"Yes, it is me," Zidane responded attempting to hide that he was shaken by the thunderous voice calling to him.

"It has been a long time since I have seen you. You were but a newborn," the voice was not aggressive, but was truly powerful.

"Please forgive me but I do not recall," Zidane's fist tightened as his heart raced.

"I did not expect you to remember," the voice sounded amused by Zidane's response.

"Am I in the presence of the Great Red Dragon Tufar?" Zidane tightened his fist even more.

"I am the Dragon of whom you speak," Tufar took one step out of the shadows of the alcove causing the floor to rumble and quake under Zidane and the Council members. One foot emerged from the shadows. The foot was massive, larger than any one of the Dragons on the Council. His talons dug in to the rocky chamber floor. Tufar then took several steps out of the shadows. Every step sounded like a clap of thunder echoing throughout the enclosed chamber. Zidane saw the golden underbelly of Tufar. That gold lining ran from his underbelly up his long, thick neck to the underside of his thick, powerful jaw. The rest of Tufar's scales were a crimson red. Zidane's eyes scanned from the talons of Tufar up the broad body and long neck. His wings were folded behind him but Zidane could tell the span was immense. Then Zidane's silver eyes went to the eyes of Tufar. They were a pale yellow with pupils the color of a raging fire. His body tensed as fear and anxiety overtook him as he beheld the sight of Tufar. The presence of Tufar would truly send the devil cowering in to the farthest corner of Hades. Zidane's first impulse was to step backwards away from Tufar. Then Zidane looked deeply in to the fire wreathed eyes of Tufar and found a quiet intensity in his soul much like his own. He found no evil within Tufar. Zidane then relaxed his muscles and was at ease. Tufar was within feet of the edge of the pit of hot coals. Tufar lowered his head over the pit of coals and came within inches of Zidane's face. They were both eye to eye. Their eyes were beginning to glow, Zidane's a bright silver and Tufar's a deep red as if they were reacting to each other.

"Your eyes tell a story, young Zidane," Tufar's eyes did not waver from Zidane.

"As do yours, Tufar. Many stories that span more than a thousand years," Zidane said with a grin. Tufar grinned as well with a cloud of smoke billowing from his nostrils.

"You have a question to ask me, do you not?" Tufar asked still leaning in toward Zidane.

"Yes I do. How did I come to bear the Red Dragon Essence? Your Essence," he asked without any hesitation.

"It would be best that I start from the beginning, young one. When I was but a young dragon, I was attacked by Dragon Hunters. I was severely wounded. Giltia, a Knight of the Northern Mountain Realm, whose soul fused with the soul of Fid, came and slain the hunters. He wrapped my wounds and protected me until I was healthy to fend for myself again. I owed him my life. Years later, there was a battle. A horde of goblins raided a caravan of Knights escorting the royal family and precious treasures to its destination. Giltia was one of a few Knights along with the Royal Family who survived. I was flying overhead when I saw the attack. I flew in to save them. From then, Giltia and I made a blood pact. His blood with mine, my blood with his. From that point on, we wanted to build a civilization in which humans and Dragons could live in harmony. You know of the battle in which the forces of Rhydin and Earth fought Sekmet and his forces a millennia ago. It is the same war in which you find yourself in the middle of today. Giltia, Cretus, Tidus, and the Keshnarians led their armies against Sekmet. At the end of the war, Giltia died from the wounds he endured from the battle. Almost a millennia later, I heard of a newborn child who was suffering from a bad heart. I believe the Heavens called me to this young boy. That day, I gave this young boy a portion of my Essence. In doing so, I and this child would have a blood connection. In my blood also ran the blood of Giltia. This boy would now have his own blood as well as mine and the blood of Giltia," Tufar continued to look in to the eyes of Zidane which were still glowing silver. Zidane stood in awe from hearing the story.

"So in you giving me a part of your Essence, I acquired a portion of your life force. And this would explain why I would hear the voice of Giltia in my head because he was a part of me. Giltia directed me here to you," Zidane's voice grew with excitement. Tufar grinned and nodded his massive head then looked to the onlooking Council. He then rose up and looked down to Zidane.

"Zidane, with the powers and abilities you possess, your destiny is to become the Dragon Lord," Tufar's voice rumbled and echoed.

"The Dragon Lord?" Zidane asked with a look of confusion on his face and a raised eyebrow.

"The Dragon Lord is the leader of the Dragon Knights and this civilization. The civilization in which Giltia and I built," Zidane nodded his head at Tufar's explanation.

"If this is my destiny and these are the responsibilities of the Dragon Lord, then I accept," Zidane bowed his head to Tufar.

"You must then undergo the Trial by Fire," at Tufar's words, the muscles in Zidane's body tensed.

"If you pass this Trial, you will become the Dragon Lord," one of the Councilmen stepped forward.

"Do not worry, young Zidane. This is the test to tell that you are truly ready to take on the responsibility of being the Dragon Lord," Zidane gave a nervous smile to Tufar in an attempt to disguise his anxiety.

"We ask that you remove your tunic and boots, then lay the Twin Dragon Blades down," a Dragon from the Council instructed. Zidane obeyed the instructions of the Council with no hesitation or questions. He took off his boots and tunic and laid them down several feet from the pit of coals and ash. And then he laid the Twin Dragon Blades beside his tunic and boots.

"We now ask that you step in to the pit," Zidane looked back to the Councilman as if he were insane.

"You are requesting me to step in to this pit of hot coals and ash with no protection for my feet?" Zidane's eyebrows furrowed.

"This is a Trial by Fire, young Zidane," Zidane looked up to Tufar as he spoke, then back to the Council members who were looking on. He then looked down to the pit of red hot coal and ash. Taking a deep breath, he hesitantly took one step forward and in to the pit. The skin at the bottom of his foot sizzled as he touched the hot coals. Zidane winced in pain, but soon became numb to it. He then took another step putting his other foot in to the coals. Zidane felt the heat from the coal radiate through his feet and up his legs. His muscles were tense to the point of trembling and eyes were closed trying to show no pain. With several moments of concentration, the pain faded away and Zidane was at ease. He opened his eyes and looked to Tufar who stood with a grin.

"I am ready," Zidane took a deep breath to calm himself.

"Very well then," Tufar also took a deep breath and reeled his head back. Flames gathered in his mouth.

"W-wait, Tufar what are you doing?!" Zidane stammered with his eyes widened. Tufar released a ball of fire down in to the pit. Before Zidane could react, the ball of flames was upon him. All Zidane could do was to set his feet, duck his head down and cross his forearms in front of him to brace himself for the flames. The ball burst in the pit and erupted in a great column of flames with Zidane at the center. The flames almost reached to the top of the chamber. Zidane struggled to fight off the flames, but was only met with the flames lashing at his flesh.

"Do not fight the flames, young one! You and the flames must be one!" hearing Tufar's words, Zidane hesitantly lowered his arms and allowed for the flames to burn around him. His body soon started to accept the flames in to his body. Zidane felt the flames soak in to the pores in his skin and run through his veins. His eyes changed from their bright silver color to that of a raging wildfire as his body was accepting Tufar's fire. The fire soon began to fade in to Zidane body. The fire collected and swirled where his heart was. In a small burst of flame, the fire was totally absorbed in to his chest. Zidane was bent over at the waist with smoke rising from him. Breathing heavily he stood straight. He placed one hand over his heart. Every beat felt stronger. Zidane looked up to Tufar who had a smile on his face and then to the Dragon Council who had their heads bowed. Zidane looked down to the pit and found nothing but cool, dry ash.

"Now you will be suited with armor suitable for the Dragon Lord," Tufar declared.

"Please step this way, Lord Zidane," one of the Councilmen motioned to Zidane. Zidane turned and stepped out of the pit and walked to the rack that stood next to the Council. It was veiled with a dark covering. One of the Councilmen removed the veil revealing a suit of armor.

"This is the Wildfire Dragon Armor, young Zidane. This is the armor in which you will wear," pride was in Tufar's voice when the armor was presented to Zidane.

"The Wildfire Dragon Armor," Zidane repeated as he looked at the armor in awe.

"I am known as the Wildfire Dragon," Tufar leaned down toward Zidane with a grin on his face. Zidane looked up to Tufar and smiled also.

"What is the armor forged from?" Zidane's eyes gazed all about the armor.

"Dragon Scales. Tougher than iron or bronze and more flexible than cloth," Tufar watched as Zidane walked to the armor and ran his fingers along it. The helmet was the shape of a Dragon's head opening its jaws. Two horns jutted from the crown of the helmet and the eyes on the helmet were as red as the fire Zidane was consumed by. The helmet itself was in the likeness of Tufar.

"Whose scales are these?" Zidane looked up to Tufar.

"Mine. A Dragon sheds its scales twice in their lifetime. The second time is when the scales are taken and melted by the most intense flames of our furnaces. They are then tempered and molded in to the armor in which their Knight will wear," Tufar grinned as he explained a Dragon Knight tradition.

"So I will be wearing a part of you," Zidane concluded with a grin.

"In addition to having a part of my Essence beating in your chest," Tufar nodded. Zidane then looked again to the armor. He tapped his knuckles against the chest plate. From what Zidane could tell, it was the strongest he had ever come across. It was even stronger than the Elf Armor he was given by Aero and Paige. The shin guards, shoulder and upper arm armor were tempered from the same scales as the helmet and chest plate. Zidane then noticed a dark cape draping from the shoulder armor.

"The armor is made from your scales, but what is the cape made from?" Zidane turned to Tufar.

"Much like we Dragons shed our scales, we also shed the skin on our wings. The skin is taken and treated with a special blend of oils to strengthen the fibers," Tufar responded.

"I have never heard of this before. Scales used to make armor and skin used for a cape," Zidane's eyes were bright with amazement.

"The skin on our wings is what helps us to fly. It will not help you fly, but will help you slow your descent to the ground allowing you to glide for a short distance," Tufar said.

"That will be of great use," Zidane then noticed a conical horn with the wider end chiseled to form the image of a dragon head with its mouth open in a mighty roar. Its teeth were sharp and eyes menacing.

"And what is this?" Zidane took it from the rack and held it.

"That is the Horn of Summoning Dragon. When blown in to, any Dragon who hears it will hurry to your aid," Tufar responded.

"Most helpful," Zidane looked at the Horn again. It was then the Archway Guard jogged in to Tufar's Chamber and spoke to one of the Dragons of the Council. After his message was delivered, he left to return to his post.

"Lord Zidane. Time is short. Word has reached our ears that Sekmet's forces are gathering and are preparing to launch their final assault upon your allies. I suggest that you prepare yourself quickly," a Dragon Council member interrupted.

"That would be best," Zidane began to take the armor in haste.

"Gather the Dragon Knights. Tell them to prepare for battle," Tufar told the Council. The Council bowed and made haste to rally the Knights. Zidane then took his tunic and boots from the side of the coal pit and put them on quickly. Then he went to the armor rack and began to strap on the Wildfire Dragon Armor.

Several moments later, Zidane was adorned in the Wildfire Dragon Armor with the Twin Dragon Blades strapped to his waist. The armor gleamed from the light of the torches in the chambers. He held the helmet in one hand and looked to Tufar for approval.

"You remind me of a great Dragon Knight of the past," Tufar smiled.

"And who would that be?" Zidane asked with a grin, although he already knew the answer.

"Are you ready to face the army of darkness, young one?" Tufar asked.

"I do believe so. Just as long as you are by my side," Zidane responded

"I am with you to the very end, young one," Zidane looked up smiling at Tufar. Tufar returned the smile.

"Then let us vanquish this evil and save Rhydin," Zidane's voice was strong and confident. Tufar nodded and they both exited the chambers and made their way out to the Dragon Civilization.

Army of Darkness

ONCE ZIDANE EXITED TUFAR'S CHAMBERS and the Council Chambers, he found armored Knights brandishing spears, tower shields, and broad swords. All stood at attention with their eyes unwavering. Behind each Knight stood a dragon, who also stood at attention with their wings folded behind them and eyes with quiet intensity and focus.

"This is the Dragon Army?" Zidane looked up to Tufar who stood beside him.

"Only a quarter of the army," Tufar responded.

"Why only a quarter?" Zidane raised an eyebrow.

"Each Knight and Dragon count for ten Orc," Tufar grinned confidently.

"And if Kulla, Maia, and Rosey were successful in retrieving the Sword of Ages they would have raised the Armies of Earth," Zidane's eyes brightened at the prospect of what army they would have.

"And added with the Elf Alliance you and your allies have gathered, we will have more than enough power to overtake Sekmet," Tufar said. Zidane then looked to the army and nodded in approval. In front of the Dragon Knights and Dragons, stood a soldier who seemed to be the leader of the army. Zidane approached the Knight.

"What is your name, Soldier?" Zidane looked in to the eyes of the Knight.

"My name is Antillus. I am the Captain of the Dragon Knights," his voice was strong and confident. There was a resemblance that

Zidane could not place. Antillus's strong, brown eyes reminded him of someone, but he could not think of who it was.

"Do you have a family, Captain Antillus?" after looking at this brave man a little while longer, Zidane had a suspicion of who he resembled.

"I do," he looked to his right to a group of Knights in training. Arteus among that group.

"Arteus is your son?" Zidane's eyes followed to where Antillus was pointing.

"Yes, m' lord," Antillus looked upon his son proudly.

"Are you certain you want to lead the Knights in to battle. I would not want to take a father away from his son and wife," Zidane looked back to Antillus and saw the pride and joy on his face.

"They both understand it is my duty to serve the Dragon Knights to the best of my ability. This ideal is being instilled in to my son as well," Antillus said confidently.

"I will bring you back to your family. I promise," Zidane placed one hand on the Knight's shoulder.

"Dragon Knights and Dragons, what is our creed?" Tufar roared.

"We, the Dragon Knights of Rhydin, pledge our hearts, our souls, and our bodies to protect those who are in need and to uphold and enforce the laws of this land. To vanquish any evil that may threaten or plague this land," the Knights' voices rang out in a resounding chorus of bravery and strength. After the creed was said, Tufar reeled his head back and let out a thunderous roar that echoed throughout the mountain civilization shaking the ground and walls around them. The other Dragons followed suit and let out earth trembling roars.

"Dragon Knights, take flight!" Zidane yelled out as he put on his helmet and leapt onto the neck of Tufar. The Dragon Knights followed Zidane's example and leapt on to the backs of their Dragons. With Zidane and Tufar leading, they took flight up and out of the mountain. Below, the villagers could see the dragons and their knights take flight out of the side of the mountains toward the east to battle. Antillus looked down and saw his wife, Afelina, standing at the entrance of the village watching the Dragons and Dragon Knights fly to battle.

In the darkest region of Rhydin, the forces of Sekmet were gathering. Orcs wore heavy armor and helmets made from dense iron. They carried broad swords and thick shields. The largest of the Orcs were beating their chests and grunting preparing themselves for the battle to come. Above their heads hovered the Winged Demons who guarded the airs above the Dark Fortress. There were hundreds of these demons who let out banshee-like shrieks filling the air with their wretched, shrill cries. On the balcony overlooking this massive army, Sekmet stood with Naafar, Ivy, and Kain, who had a look of shame on his face, behind him. From underneath his dark helmet, Sekmet gave an evil smile as he looked upon his army.

"This night, we will strike the final blow to the Elf Empire! They are weak and vulnerable to our onslaught of brute force! We will annihilate the Elf Empire and their allies! Once we crush them, Rhydin shall be ours! Go forth and eradicate them!" Sekmet yelled out to them with outstretched arms. The Orcs and Winged Demons let out their war cries. The clanging of the Orc armor was thunderous and heard throughout the land of darkness. "Go now! Eradicate the insects! Take no prisoners, but bring the Red Dragon to me!" Sekmet sent them forth with a sweep of his arm. Sekmet's forces shouted and turned to march toward the Elf Kingdom.

With the Dragon Knights in the sky beside him and behind him in formation, Zidane and Tufar flew toward the Elf Empire encampments. Within a few hours the Sun would rise over the eastern horizon.

"Tufar, do you think the Elf Alliance is holding up the defenses?" Zidane's voice betrayed the burden of concern for his loved ones.

"What does your heart tell you?" Tufar asked in response.

"I believe so," he answered after taking a moment to search his heart.

"You must have faith, young one. It is the greatest weapon any creature can have," Tufar said just as Antillus and his Dragon returned from scouting ahead of the Dragon Knight Army and flew alongside Zidane and Tufar.

"Lord Zidane, we have spotted a rather large army riding out of the Woodland Realm," he pointed in to the direction with his spear.

"Did you see who they were?" Zidane turned his eyes and attempted to use his Elf vision, but it was too dark.

"We could not tell," Antillus gave a shake of his head.

"There is only one way to find out," Tufar said.

"Indeed," Zidane gave an agreeing nod.

Riding out of the Woodland Realm were the four armies from Earth led by Kulla, Maia, Rosey, and King Draco. Close behind them were the Generals of the four armies, Sir Galidan, Ahmaar, Lioneus, and Raoko Shun. The moon lit their southward bound path to join the Elven Army.

"How much further to the encampment?" King Draco's voice was raised so that he was heard over the beating hooves.

"It is not far," Rosey replied.

"We should get there by the first rise of the Sun," Kulla added as the wind around them kicked up and began to blow violently. Shadows streaked across the ground around them. Maia's ears perked up and began to look around. She then looked to the sky to see massive creatures flying above them and beginning to circle above.

"Kulla!" her eyes went from the creatures above to Kulla.

"Yes?" Kulla turned his head.

"Look!" Maia pointed to the sky. He looked up as did Draco and Rosey.

"What are those?" Rosey's eyes showed her uncertainty.

"I do not know," Draco raised his hand to signal the army to slow their pace and wait to see what these creatures were doing. All were on edge and ready to defend themselves if need be.

"They are rather large, but I cannot tell what manner of creature these are," Kulla tried to focus his vision, but the creatures' silhouettes were unfamiliar. The army, along with Draco, Kulla, Rosey, and Maia came to a complete halt and watched to see what the creatures would do. All were on guard and watchful for any type of onslaught. Several moments of watching, a figure leapt from the back of one of the flying creatures and seemed to glide through the sky above them and slowly descended to the ground. The figure landed ten yards in front of them. Neither Kulla, Maia, Draco, or Rosey could make out who the figure was for the darkness of the night concealed the identity of the stranger. The light from the moon was being shrouded by the circling creatures above. Ahmaar, Sir Galidan, Lioneus and Raoko Shun quickly dismounted and drew their weapons and charged at the figure.

"Wait!" Maia's voice stopped their charged. They looked back to Maia and then to the dark figure. Maia dismounted and took several steps toward the figure, then looked up to the creatures above them. Maia looked upon the figure darkened by the shroud. Taking a few more steps closer, she began to sniff and take in the scent of the dark figure. Maia began to make out what the figure was. It was a man wearing armor that she had never seen before. His face was hidden by the shadow.

"Who are you?" Maia tilted her head to the side.

"Maia, you do not recognize your own Love?" he said as he removed the helmet. His silver eyes glowed brightly, revealing his face from underneath the shroud of shadow.

"Zidane? Is that you?" her eyes widened and brightened. Zidane nodded his head with a grin on his face. Maia leapt in to his arms and wrapped hers around him. Zidane looked and waved to the creatures flying overhead. All spiraled to the ground. As they landed, the ground quaked. Tufar landed behind Zidane and let out a thunderous roar that shook the ground beneath the feet of the army of men. The eyes of every soldier, Draco, Kulla, Rosey, and Maia widened as they watched the Dragons along with their Dragon Knights land. All were struck with awe and amazement.

"Are those…?" Maia started to ask with a hint of fear in her voice.

"Dragons, yes," Zidane finished still holding her.

"It would seem you fulfilled your destiny Zidane," Kulla said as he dismounted.

"Thank the Heavens that you are in good health, m' lord," Rosey dismounted as well.

"It is good to see you all. I would like for all of you to meet Tufar, the Great Red Dragon," Zidane presented Tufar who grinned and blew black smoke from his nostrils.

"And we would like for you to meet Sir Gaildan, Leader of the army from England. Ahmaar, Leader of the army of Egypt. Lioneus, the Leader of the Spartan army. And I am sure you know Raoko Shun, younger brother of Chen Shun and Leader of the Dynasty Samurai of Asia," Kulla announced.

"It is an honor to meet a student of my brother's," Raoko Shun bowed. These Generals placed their clenched fist against their chests and bowed their heads. Zidane returned this gesture of respect.

"We would also like to introduce the one who wields the Sword of Ages, the King of Man, King Draco," Kulla presented the man in regal armor.

"Draco?" Zidane looked to the man who Kulla introduced as King with a surprised expression on his face. Draco dismounted from his horse and walked to Zidane. As he was a few feet from him, Draco removed his helmet revealing his face and dreadlocks. Zidane eyes widened and got weak at his knees as if he had seen a ghost.

"Zidane? What is it?" Maia asked with concern in her voice and on her face.

"He is…. my father," Zidane said with widened eyes.

"How is that possible? I thought you said your father was killed by the Vampire horde," Kulla looked from Draco to Zidane. Draco stepped closer to Zidane and looked in to his eyes, "Are you truly my son, Fid?".

"Yes, but my name is no longer Fid. That is another story for another time," Zidane drew one of the Twin Dragon Blades and showed him the Bracelet of Ra on his wrist. Draco looked at them closely.

"It is true. I gave this to you for your fourteenth birthday. The Bracelet on your wrist was given to me and your Aunt by this very Dragon, Tufar. I knew I recognized him," Draco looked from Zidane to Tufar with tears welling in his eyes. Draco and Zidane shared in a father-son embrace. Tears rolled down both of their cheeks.

"I thought you were killed in the attack," Zidane still held on to his embrace.

"I left in chase of the horde, but I lost the trail. I then returned to find the village in flames and ash. I found no survivors," Draco's voice shook as if he were reliving that night.

"I am not the only survivor. Some of us scattered in to the woods. Many came back after a few days in hiding. Myself, Aunt Addie, and Rosey here ran together and hid," Zidane stepped aside and pointed to Rosey. Draco turned to face Rosey, "You are from our village?".

"I am, m' lord. Zidane actually saved me from Brakus," she gave a grateful smile to Zidane.

"This does an old man's heart good," Draco smiled looking to them both.

"I am sorry to interrupt this reunion, but Sekmet's forces will be moving onto the Elf Army very soon. If we leave now, we will arrive at the battlefield by sunrise and aid the army," Tufar leaned his head down them.

"You are right, Tufar," Draco nodded to Tufar. "We had better make haste before it is too late," he then looked to his new allies in this war.

"Agreed," Kulla showed his fang in a confident smile.

"I never would have thought I would fight alongside my son in one of the greatest battles in the history of Earth and Rhydin," Draco smiled proudly.

"Let us make the best of it and save the Twin Planets," Zidane said as they both clasped wrists. With the Dragons and Dragon Knights behind Zidane and Maia with Kulla, and Rosey by their side and Ahmaar, Sir Gaildan, Raoko Shun, Lioneus, and the Army of Man behind Draco, they prepared to go in to the battle that will decide the fate of Rhydin and Earth.

In the encampment, at the southern border of the Woodland Realm, Aero, Paige, Melina, Craven, Chen Shun, Raziel, and Zell were sitting in the main tent devising the best plan of defense. There was a wooden table in the middle of the tent with a map of Rhydin laid out.

"We are low on man power, Aero. The most recent wave of attacks by Sekmet have decreased the size of our army significantly," Paige pointed to the map.

"Paige is correct, Aero. This coalition already loses numbers during the day because my troops cannot fight in the sunlight," Zell grimly said.

"These battles have proven difficult with the armies spread thin. Sekmet knows we are weak in numbers and sends wave after wave of Orc soldiers upon us," Melina added to Zell's sentiments.

"I know this, but what else can we do but hold off as long as we can. Zidane, Kulla, Maia, and Rosey will return with reinforcements," Aero rubbed his forehead as if trying to get rid of a headache.

"In the meantime, I suggest placing a barrier of Earth Shinobi and archers between Sekmet's force and the borders of the Elf Kingdom. That should slow down their troops," Chen Shun pointed to the locations of their camps on the map with his staff.

"It is our only option to hold off Sekmet's forces until Lord Zidane, Lord Kulla, Lady Maia, and Rosey arrive with reinforcements. The archers will greatly help against the aerial assault of those cursed winged demons," Raziel nodded in agreement with Chen Shun's plan. At that moment, a commotion was heard outside of the tent among the soldiers. The full gallop of two horses was heard and they stopped just outside of the main tent. Lieutenants Demus and Aldar rushed in to the tent breathing heavily.

"Demus, Aldar what is wrong?" Paige asked as all rose to their feet.

"Sekmet's forces are on a march here," Demus said in between deep breaths.

"How many?" Aero's eyebrows furrowed with concern.

"*All* of Sekmet's forces, Lord Aero," Aldar's voice held a grim tone. All looked to each other. Aero sat back down and placed his head in his hands. 'Is this the end?' Aero thought to himself.

"What are we to do?" Raziel asked. A sense of discouragement filled the tent. All hope seemed to have faded out of the hearts of everyone gathered.

"This is what Sekmet wants to happen!" Shun drove his staff in to the ground causing a small tremor, "He is attempting to intimidate us by sending his entire Dark Army to battle us. Crushing our spirits and lowering our morale. What happened to the high spirits of the Elf Empire? What happened to the strong minds of the Vampire Coven? What happened to the strong hearts of the Shinobi? What happened to the strong bond among the Lycan pack? Sekmet has planned for us to have all of these virtues weakened. These virtues have kept this resistance alive. These virtues have kept us fighting. These are also the virtues that brought us together as a united army. What has also helped us throughout this war is something we all have deep within our hearts and souls," Shun looked in to the eyes of everyone who stood in the tent.

"And what would that be Master Shun?" Craven's tone was low and held on to discouragement.

"Faith. Faith in ourselves and faith in each other. And faith in the forces that surround us all. That this force will empower those who stand for what is right to defeat all that have malicious intentions," Shun strongly gripped his staff.

"What do you suggest we do?" Melina asked.

"We go on with the plan we initially devised. We put the Elf soldiers with tower shields and Earth Shinobi on the front line for defense. Then we place two lines of archers behind them to keep a look out for those Winged Demons. And finally, we will have the

Lycans and remaining troops in the rear as reinforcements," Aero said as he pointed to the map.

"I certainly hope we can hold the line until Zidane and the others arrive," Paige gave a heavy sigh.

"I pray that we do as well, Sister," Aero looked to her with the same concerned eyes she had.

"We all do," Zell nodded.

"Shall we prepare for war then?" Shun looked to all those who were in the tent. All nodded and then left the tent.

"Lord Zell, I will arrange for some soldiers to guard the camp while you and the rest of your Coven sleep during the day. It is almost sunrise," Aero called to him.

"That will be much appreciated, Lord Aero," Zell looked back to Aero leaving the tent. Aero, Melina, and Paige were left in the tent.

"Do you think we have any chance of holding out?" Paige turned to Aero.

"What does your heart tell you?" Aero asked in response. Paige grinned and then left the tent. Aero inhaled a deep breath then exhaled it. Melina stayed behind and helped put on his armor. No words were spoken between the two. Her demeanor and the way she strapped on his armor was strong. Her eyes were focused on each piece of armor that she strapped on. Her inner strength showed through these subtle actions. The strength and focus she showed inspired Aero to enter in to this battle.

With the morning light beginning to rise over the horizon and the morning fog starting to fade away, the Elf Army awaited the forces of Sekmet. Two lines of Elf soldiers with tower shields were at the very front standing shoulder to shoulder and behind them were the Earth Shinobi lead by Raziel. Not far behind them were the Ranger and Elf Archers led by Lieutenant Demus and Aldar. Their quivers were full with arrows. They kept their eyes vigilant of the skies watching for the Winged Demons. At the very back of the army were the Lycans, led by Craven, along with Master Shun, Aero, Paige, and Melina on horseback in full armor. Tension and anxiety were in the hearts and the bodies of each soldier. The eyes of Paige and Aero were watchful of the far off hills for the forces of Sekmet.

"They are coming," Aero's eyes narrowed as he spotted the enemy. Off in the distance were dark clouds moving across the sky toward the Elf Army.

"I do see the shroud of darkness," Shun focused as a shroud of darkness was moving underneath the dark clouds. Lightning streaked across the dark skies and thunder was heard off in the distance.

"There is no turning back now," Paige muttered to her comrades.

"No, there is not. We need to do this. For Rhydin and for Earth," Aero looked to those who would fight by his side. Paige and Shun nodded to Aero in agreement.

"We will hold this Dark Army off for each other," Melina's eyes were unwavering.

"We do need to do this. For Zidane and the others," Paige's voice grew with intensity. The darkness crept closer and closer to the frontlines of the Elf Army.

"Prepare yourselves!" Raziel called out to the Earth Shinobi and Elf soldiers. The clamor of heavy armor, swords and shields was heard from the creeping darkness. Sekmet's army stopped their march four hundred yards away from the Elf Army. Aero could see an Orc of a larger size holding a battle axe in one hand and a broad shield in the other step out of the ranks of the army of Orcs and Winged Demons hovering above. The Orc raised its battle axe to the sky and the soldiers in Sekmet's army began to beat their chests and drive the butts of their spears in to the ground in unison. The Winged Demons above let out shrill screeches. The thunderous sound of the armor clamoring filled the ears of the soldiers of the Elf Army. Some became more anxious when they saw the sheer size of Sekmet's grand army.

"Ease your hearts! Steady your hands! Focus your minds! Do not let the scum of Rhydin bring fear in to your hearts! Together we can hold these beasts! Give them no ground, but bring upon them the wrath of the Elf Empire!" Aero cried out to the troops. The soldiers tightened their grips on their shields and weapons. They let out their war cries raising their weapons to the sky and beat on their shields, drowning out the war cries of Sekmet's army. At that moment, the Orc brought his axe down signaling for the first wave of soldiers to attack. The first wave of soldiers let out their war roars as they charged towards the Elf Army.

"Steady!" Raziel shouted to the Elf soldiers and Earth Shinobi. The Orc troops drew closer and closer, but the troops of the Elf front line stood firm, gripping their shields with the Earth Shinobi close behind. As the Orc troops drew within fifty yards of the Elf Army, arrows were shot in to the air from Sekmet's army.

"Shinobi, get under our shields!" one of the Elf soldiers shouted. The Earth Shinobi rushed and shared cover with Elf troops. Some Shinobi and Elf troops were hit by arrows wounding them or killing them. As this was happening, the Orc troops continued their charge. When the shower of arrows ceased, the Shinobi quickly rose to their feet and summoned mounds of earth and rock. The remaining Shinobi hurled the mounds of earth in to the ranks of charging Orc soldiers. These mounds crushed many Orc soldiers. The remaining Orc soldiers continued their charge trampling over the dead. The Earth Shinobi ducked behind the Elf soldiers as they formed a solid wall of Elf shields. Orc soldiers crashed upon the wall. Some broke through slashing violently and wildly. The Elf soldiers fought back slashing and stabbing at the Orcs. The Earth Shinobi used the earth to knock the Orcs off balance and to crush them. The first wave of Orcs were slain, but there were many more waiting to strike with only a few Elf troops and Shinobi on the frontlines. The Orc leader ordered for a second wave of Orc troops to charge. The second wave of Orc soldiers was larger than the first and the soldiers were even more heavily armored and armed.

"Ready yourselves!" an Elf officer shouted. The Elf soldiers and Shinobi crouched down in to defensive positions.

"Steady!" Raziel shouted as the second wave drew closer.

"Archers ready!" Demus yelled to the line of Ranger and Elf archers. The second wave drew closer and now within one hundred yards.

"Take your aim!" at Aldar's order, the archers took their aim at the charging wave of Orc soldiers who were now fifty yards away from the Elf frontlines.

"Fire!" Aldar and Demus shouted. The archers released a shower of arrows upon the Orc soldiers who fell to the arrows. The Orcs who survived the shower of arrows continued their charge toward the frontlines. These Orcs fell to the swords and mounds of earth of the Elf soldiers and Earth Shinobi who stood waiting for them.

"If this is all Sekmet has to throw at us, we will have no troubles fending him off," a confident grin grew on Aero's face. At that moment, war drums sounded off in the distance and war cries were heard coming from Sekmet's army. Aero's eyes widened, as did everyone one else's who beheld the same sight. Creatures of larger size and build began to rush through the lines of Sekmet's Army. They appeared to be larger Orcs, but they had the size of a Mountain Ogre. They were heavily armed with war hammers, spiked clubs, heavy maces, and battle axes. Their iron armor was broad and thick.

"What manner of creature are those?!" Melina's eyes widened in shock, and disgust was in her voice.

"Abominations they are," Chen Shun said with the same disgust in his voice.

"You spoke to soon Brother," Paige said dryly.

"It would seem so," Aero's eyes were still on these hybrid Abominations that continued their charge at the frontlines.

"Shinobi, quake the earth beneath their feet!" Raziel shouted. The Shinobi stepped from behind the Elf shields and stomped at the earth causing a quake knocking the Abominations off balance.

"Fire at will!" Demus shouted to the archers. A shower of arrows rained upon the stumbling Abominations. The arrows could not penetrate the heavy armor, but there were some that found weak points where the armor did not protect. The Abominations regained their balance and continued their charge and crashed through the frontlines.

"Keep firing!" Aldar shouted. The arrows still could not penetrate the thick, broad armor. The Abominations wildly swung their clubs and battle axes.

"We need to go!" Paige was the first to spur her horse toward the battle.

"Yes we do," Aero closely followed her. Paige, Aero, Melina, Chen Shun, Craven and the remaining Lycans and Elf soldiers made a charge in to the fray. As the last of the troops, led by Paige and Aero, drew closer to the battle Chen Shun raised his staff to the air. He summoned a whirlwind in front of the Abominations forcing them backwards just enough to knock them off balance.

"Hooves that quake the earth, a horn that protects its own, and a hide like armor....," Melina began to chant a summoning incantation with her head lowered and hands folded in front of her face. "Giant Black Rhinoceros, I summon thee!" a circular seal of intricate runes appeared on the ground in front of them. With a loud grunt, a large Black Rhinoceros appeared from the seal. An aura of blue light surrounded the body of the summoned creature. "Charge upon the Abominations and the Orc Army!" Melina commanded. The Black Rhinoceros pawed at the ground, grunted, and made a charge at the Sekmet's forces. Aero and Paige rode side by side behind the summoned Rhinoceros with their weapons drawn. Craven charged in to the fray shifting to his wolf form after the Rhinoceros cleared a path of a few of the Abominations and Orc soldiers. Craven leapt at the neck of one Abomination biting at it and slashing at it with his razor sharp claws. Aero and Paige continued riding side by side toward a heavily armored Abomination. They looked to each other and then held out one hand to each other. An orb of energy began to fuse between their two palms. It grew and pulsed as they rode closer to the Abomination. The Abomination raised both of its clubs to the air and was about to bring it done upon Aero and Paige. At the last moment, Paige and Aero released the orb of energy at the Abomination hitting it in the chest. Before falling, the Abomination slammed its club in to the ground throwing Aero and Paige from their horses. The Abomination fell forward, almost crushing Aero. With swords drawn Aero and Paige stood back to back fending off two Abomination. Paige slashed at both of its knees bringing it to her level and then slashed its neck. Aero leapt over the swing of an Abomination battle axe and then slashed at the neck of it bringing it down.

"Aero, I do not think we can hold out much longer," Paige's eyes shifted from side to side waiting for the next enemy to attack.

"We have to, Paige," Aero responded as both leapt at an Abomination cutting it down at the knees and then stabbing it in the head. Chen Shun rushed to their sides as did Craven.

"Where is Raziel?" Craven growled.

"Closer to the frontlines," Shun pointed as they saw Raziel, the Earth Shinobi and other Elf soldiers fend off the Orcs and Abominations.

"Lord Aero, look to Sekmet's army," Craven pointed to the shroud of darkness. All looked and saw a third, even larger wave of soldiers. Orcs and other Abominations charged toward the remaining soldiers of the Alliance. The eyes of everyone widened and all who remained grouped together. Raziel, Demus, Aldar, Craven, Shun, Paige, Melina, and Aero along with a handful of Earth Shinobi, Rangers, Elves, and Lycans stood together awaiting the onslaught that was about to crash upon them. The third wave was enough to finish off the remains of the Alliance.

"Zidane, where ever you are, we really need your help now," Aero said as all braced for the oncoming onslaught. At that moment, horns sounded off in the distance. There were four distinct tones blending together, echoing throughout the southern plains. The wave of Orcs, Abominations, and Winged Demons ceased in their charge. Their eyes were wide and jaws dropped almost in fear and hesitation. Aero turned his head as did the others to find a massive army nearly three hundred yards behind them. It seemed to Aero and Paige there were four armies that joined to form one massive army. All were from different lands. Leading the army was a Knight suited in steel armor.

Riding with the Knight suited in steel armor were Rosey, Maia, and Kulla. In the sky, above the army was a fleet of winged dragons with who seemed to be knights mounted on their backs. Leading the dragons was the largest of them. The dragon was the color of a raging wildfire. Its eyes a crimson red. The talons were large and sharp enough to rip apart a Cyclops in one slash. Mounted on the red dragon's back was a knight suited in crimson red armor. The knight wore a helmet that resembled that of the dragon he rode.

"Is that...?" Paige started to ask.

"Zidane," Aero's mouth was agape, "Yes it is. Along with the Wielder of the Sword of Ages. Commanding the Army of Men," Aero's voice grew with excitement. The Army of Men and the Dragons stopped two hundred yards from the Alliance. The dragons hovered above the Army of Men.

"They are vastly outnumbered, Father!" Zidane shouted down to Draco. Looking up, Draco nodded his head.

"We must get them out of there so that we may regroup and devise a plan of attack," Kulla shouted to his allies.

"I agree, Lioneus, Ahmaar," Draco called to them.

"Yes, my King," Ahmaar responded with Lioneus beside him.

"I want you and your armies to form a line between the Alliance and the wave of Sekmet's forces on my signal," Draco's eyes were focused and his voice was commanding.

"Understood," Lioneus said as they both motioned for their armies to follow them down the left side of the battle field.

"Raoko Shun and Sir Galidan, you and your armies will accompany myself, Maia, Kulla, and Rosey to extract the remaining troops of the Alliance," Draco turned his eyes to them.

"We are with you, King Draco," Raoko and Sir Galidan said in unison.

"Son, you and the other Dragons and Dragon Knights form a wall of fire between the wave of Sekmet's troops cutting them off from the rest of the mass army," Draco shouted up to him. "And hold off the Winged Demons from joining their comrades!" he pointed to the area of the battlefield he wanted Zidane to execute. Zidane motioned for Antillus and several other Dragons and Knights to follow him. Zidane, Antillus, and several others flew down the right side of the battlefield as Draco led the rest of the army down the middle of the battle field to extract the rest of the Alliance. As the third wave of Sekmet's Army saw Draco and the others behind him charge toward them, they turned to retreat as did the Winged Demons when they saw the Army of Dragons flying to join the battle.

"They are trying to run," Zidane said to Tufar.

"What creature born on Earth or Rhydin who can outrun a Dragon," Tufar responded with a smirk on his face. Behind Tufar and Zidane were Antillus and his Dragon and several other Dragons.

"Get ready!" Zidane shouted to Antillus and the other Dragon Knights. They began to slowly fly in to a formation resembling a "V" with Zidane and Tufar leading them.

"Tufar, unleash your inferno!" Zidane shouted. Tufar reeled his head back, gathering intense flames in his mouth as did the other Dragons. Tufar and the other Dragons unleashed a fury of flames cutting the wave of Orcs from the rest of Sekmet's grand army. The wall of flames was intense and hotter than that of a volcano. The wall of flames stood fifteen feet in the air. The Orcs turned to find the Spartans and Egyptians had dismounted their horses and stood in front of them. The Spartans formed a wall of shields with another line behind the front. All with their spears pointed at them over their shields. The Egyptians were behind the Spartans with their bows drawn and arrows aimed. The Orcs stood knowing they faced death.

"Fire!" at Ahmaar's order, the Egyptian soldiers released their arrows wounding several and killing many.

"Forward!" the Spartan soldiers moved as one wall toward the wounded soldiers when Lioneus gave the order. The Orc soldiers were caught between the wall of intense flames and the brass shields of the Spartan Army. The Spartans continued their march forward. The frontline pushed their shields in the soldiers knocking them off balance then thrust their spears in to them. The second line then came forward forming a new line of shields. They pushed the Orc soldiers backwards again knocking them off balance. The Egyptian soldiers then fired another volley of arrows at Sekmet's troops killing them. There was only a handful of the last wave left.

"Lioneus, I believe these beasts need to be sent to hell!" Ahmaar smirked.

"I full heartedly agree," Lioneus gave a wide, maniacal smile, "Spartans, let us send these beasts to the flaming pits of Hades! Forward!" the Spartans shouted in unison as they pushed forward with the Orcs trying to push back. There were too many of the Spartans for Sekmet's soldiers to overcome and then they were eventually pushed in to the wall of flames in which came from the mouths of dragons.

In the mean time, while the third wave of Sekmet's forces were being slain and the Dragons and Dragon Knights hovering above, Draco, Maia, Kulla, Rosey, Raoko Shun, and Sir Galidan along with the rest of the Army of Men extracted Aero, Paige, Melina, Craven, Chen Shun, Raziel, and the remaining Alliance army. Sir Galidan and Raoko Shun blew in to their horns to signal their rescue mission was accomplished.

"Let us meet back at the Eastern encampment!" Zidane shouted down to Draco. Draco raised his Sword in acknowledgement. Zidane and Tufar led the Dragon Knights to the encampment. Draco led the extraction unit to the encampment and Lioneus and Ahmaar led their unit to the encampment not far behind Draco.

A few hours passed since the rescue of Aero, Paige, Melina, Craven, Raziel, and Master Chen Shun along with the surviving soldiers of the unit they led. All were tending to the wounds they suffered at the hands of the army of Sekmet. Many were lost in the unrelenting waves of Sekmet's forces. Aero and the others thanked the Heavens that Zidane, Maia, Kulla, and Rosey returned with the Armies of Men and the Dragon Knights.

Zidane was sitting on a rock with his legs crossed looking toward the south, in the direction of Sekmet's stronghold. He was still suited in his armor with his helmet and Dragon Blades leaning against the rock. Maia exited one of the tents and saw Zidane in, what seemed to her, a trance. She walked to be next to him, but was cautious as not to disturb him.

"You need not be quiet. I am not in meditation," he said to her.

"A coin for your thoughts then?" she asked as she hopped on to the rock and sat next to him, leaning her head on his shoulder.

"How do I defeat Sekmet? With the power that I possess, I am not certain I can defeat Sekmet. That is the quandary I face right now," he leaned down to kiss the top of her head.

"You mean, how do *we* defeat Sekmet," Tufar said as he lowered himself to the ground next to Zidane and Maia.

"You are right, Tufar," Zidane said as Tufar laid beside them.

"So how are we going to defeat Sekmet?" Maia looked up from his shoulder.

"We need to defeat him as one unit," Aero said from behind them. Zidane, Maia, and Tufar turned their heads to find Aero, Paige, Melina, Draco, Kulla, Rosey, Chen Shun, Craven, Raziel, and the four leaders of the Army of Men were all standing behind them. Zidane and Maia smiled and rose to their feet atop the rock. Zidane took up his helmet and sheathed Dragon Blades. Tufar then rose to his feet as well looking down upon the unity of the various races of Rhydin and Earth. Elf kind, Humans, Lycans, and Vampires, all were represented under this one banner. All united to accomplish one goal, to defend the land on which they lived.

"So, do you have a plan to defeat Sekmet once and for all?" Paige crossed her arms in front of her chest, seemingly impressed with what Zidane had become.

"I believe I do. Using all of the strengths each race possesses. We need every advantage that we have to defeat Sekmet. That is why we attack at night so that Zell's and Kulla's Coven are able to join the ranks in the assault. Every step in this war we have been on the defense, we have been pushed back onto our heels, fearing when the next attack from Sekmet's horde would be. Tonight we take the fight to Sekmet's gate! Tonight we will not have to fear when the next attack will be! Tonight we will enter the Valley of the Shadows and we will fear no evil! We stand united as one Kingdom! After this night, this Kingdom of Elves, Humans, Lycans, and Vampires will be known as the Krystal Kingdom!" Zidane proclaimed as he fused the two hilts of the Twin Dragon Blades and raised it to the sky with everyone rejoicing. Zidane leapt down from the rock and on the ground in front of everyone, he began to reveal his plan of attack.

At the edge of the Southwest Region, with the Sun beginning to set over the Western Mountains, the Four Armies of Men awaited, along with the Lycan pack, the Earth Shinobi, Rangers from Earth, Demus and Aldar leading the Elf soldiers, Zell and the Vampire Coven who were all covered by cloth protecting them from the Sun's rays. Lioneus, Ahmaar, Sir Galidan, Raoko Shun, and a veiled Zell were at the front. The four Generals and Zell were mounted on horses who wore light flexible armor on their faces, chests, and lower legs while most of the other soldiers were on foot. They waited for the thick iron gates to open four hundred yards away.

"Do you suppose they know we are here?" Sir Galidan looked to his fellow Generals.

"I cannot see why not," Raoko Shun gave a shrug of his shoulders, "There is an immense army threatening to crash down their gates".

"Do you suppose we should knock?" a mischievous grin grew on Lioneus's face.

"You are mad," Ahmaar shook his head at Lioneus.

"No, I am a Spartan," Lioneus chuckled. The other Generals chuckled as well.

"All of you are mad," Zell said from under the veil. The men chuckled, but were interrupted by the shrill creaking and scraping of the iron gates of Sekmet's fortress. Lioneus, Ahmaar, Sir Galidan, Raoko Shun, and Zell along with the rest of the army drew their weapons and prepared themselves. The Sun finally set behind the Western Mountains. The Sun's rays were finally blocked allowing for Zell and the other Vampires to throw off their veils. Out of the gates, the Army of Sekmet poured out. First out were dog-like creatures that stood five feet from the ground. Their eyes glowed yellow and were lidless. Chunks of fresh were missing and at certain spots the flesh hung freely. Their teeth were so sharp that they could rip through the flesh of a full grown bear. These beasts were in chains held by fully armored Abominations. There were many of these demon hounds. To Lioneus, Ahmaar, Sir Galidan, and Raoko Shun, it seemed these hounds were sniffing at the air as if they caught the scent of something. Then they let out a spine chilling howl which was heard by the entire Allied Army.

"What is wrong, Lord Zell?" Raoko Shun turned to find Zell trembling, seemingly out of fear.

"What are those creatures?" disgust was in Ahmaar's voice.

"Those are Hellhounds," a Lycan responded as the pack made their way to the front lines.

"These Hellhounds are the natural predators of the Vampires here on Rhydin. They can smell Vampire flesh miles away. We, the Lycans, protected the Vampires against these creatures when we were the daylight protectors generations ago. There were times when these Hellhounds caught Vampires during their walks at night. Some Vampires survived, but many others fell victim to the Hellhounds," another Lycan said.

"Is this true, Lord Zell?" Sir Galidan looked to him, but Zell said nothing. He nodded his head and kept his eyes forward. His hand was trembling trying to maintain his grip on the reins of his horse. His jaw was clenched and teeth grinding.

"Do not worry, Lord Zell. We will protect you," a Lycan said to Zell. Zell turned to the Lycan and forced a grin.

"Lycans!" the Lycan shouted. At that moment, all of the Lycans shifted in to their giant wolf form and all let out howls toward the moon that would send chills even up the spine of the devil. The Hellhounds heard the howls of the Lycans and then began to ferociously bark. Behind the Hellhounds were ranks upon ranks of Orcs and Abominations. The Army of Sekmet continued to pour out of the gates wave after wave of troops. Sekmet's Army stopped two hundred yards away from the Alliance. The Hellhounds were on chains held by Abominations on the frontlines continuing to bark ferociously. The Orc troops began to drive the butts of their spears in to the ground. They were beating their fists against their chest plates. The clamor of Orc armor sounded like thunder rolling from the iron gates. The Lycans crouched down ready to make a charge for the Hellhounds of the frontlines.

"For valor!" Sir Galidan shouted as he drew his broad sword.

"For honor!" Raoko Shun shouted drawing his katana.

"For glory!" Lioneus yelled readying his spear and shield.

"For Earth!" Ahmaar shouted drawing his scimitar.

"For Rhydin!" Zell shouted drawing his sword and raising it to the air. The soldiers of the Alliance all drew their weapons letting out war cries and howls. The Hellhounds on the opposite end of the battlefield attempted to pull away from the Abominations barking and growling violently. The Orcs let out blood curdling war cries. The Abominations unchained the Hellhounds letting them charge toward the soldiers of the Alliance, followed by the rest of the troops.

"Do not stray from the plan!" Zell shouted.

"Spartans!" at Lioneus's war cry, two long lines of Spartan soldiers began to march forward with raised shields. Each soldier was shoulder to shoulder to the man next to them. The Hellhounds continued their charge as did the soldiers of Sekmet's army. The Spartans continued their slow march forward.

"Earth Shinobi!" as Zell yelled, the Earth Shinobi stepped forward from behind the first line of Spartan soldiers. They crouched down in ready positions, "Now!" with a sweep of his hand, Zell signaled the Earth Shinobi to stomp the ground rousing chunks of earth and rock. With powerful motions of their hands, the Shinobi hurled these chunks of earth and rock in to the air toward the charging troops of Sekmet.

"Incoming!" an Orc soldier pointed at the chunks of rock and earth in the sky. The chunks of earth and rock crashed to the ground, crushing Orcs and Abominations. Some Hellhounds were crushed beneath the massive mounds as well. The rest of the troops continued their charge trampling over the crushed bodies.

"Lycans, go!" Zell ordered with another sweep of his hand. The Lycan pack let out chilling howls and charged from the frontlines of the Alliance. They leapt over the two lines of Spartan soldiers and ran passed the Earth Shinobi. The Hellhounds and Lycans were now on a collision course with each other. The forces of Sekmet were not far behind the Hellhounds charging toward the wall of Spartan shields.

"Egyptians, fire!" Ahmaar ordered. The soldiers of the Egyptian army aimed to the air and then released their arrows in to the sky. The arrows rained down upon Sekmet's troops leading the charge against the Alliance. The arrows pierced the helmets and armor of the charging Orc and Abomination troops. Those troops dropped to the ground only to be trampled by the wave of troops behind them. The Lycans and Hellhounds then leapt to the air colliding with each other. Bones were snapped and blood ran as the Lycans and Hellhounds tore in to each other. The Spartans continued their slow march with the Earth Shinobi close behind them. The Lycans finished off the last of the Hellhounds, with few casualties on their side, then ducked behind the wall of Spartan shields. The Orc and Abomination soldiers soon crashed upon the Spartan shields with bone crushing force. The frontlines of the Spartan wall only budged a bit and then held its ground. The frontline pushed Sekmet's soldiers backwards then the second line stepped up and lunged their spears and swords in to them. The second line then stepped up to form the new frontline of shields. The Earth Shinobi and Lycans remained crouched behind the wall of Spartan shields. The Earth Shinobi stepped several yards away from the Spartans and Lycans. They formed a line and roused chunks of earth and rock. With strong motions of their hands, they hurled these chunks of earth and rock in to the horde of Sekmet's soldiers crushing them. One of the Earth Shinobi saw in the sky an arrow with the arrowhead on fire. He then saw a swarm of dark Winged Demons fly in to the sky from behind the fortress walls.

"Watch the skies!" the Shinobi shouted. Each of the Winged Demons were carrying huge boulders as they flew toward the Spartan frontlines.

"Egyptian archers, target those Winged Demons!" Ahmaar pointed to the dark skies. The Egyptian archers then turned their sights upon the flying Demons. They aimed and released a barrage of arrows at the Demons. A number of the Demons were brought down by the arrows, but the others quickly dodged the arrows and drew closer to the front lines of the Spartans. The Shinobi kicked up chunks of earth and rock and then hurled them upwards at the Demons. The Demons easily dodged the huge chunks of earth and rock. The Demons dropped the boulders down upon the Spartans. The front line of the Spartan wall was broken and the soldiers of Sekmet broke through. The Spartans tried to reform the lines, but to no avail. The Spartans, Lycans, and Earth Shinobi were soon fighting off the horde of Sekmet's soldiers.

"Sir Gaildan and Raoko Shun! Take your men and sweep down the left and right flanks!" Sir Galidan and Raoko Shun nodded at Zell's order. Raoko Shun led the Dynasty Samurai down the left flanks and Sir Galidan led the Knights down the right flanks. The Spartans, Lycans and Shinobi were beginning to become surrounded on three sides by the horde of Sekmet's soldiers. The Winged Demons were swooping down, clawing at, lifting and dropping the Spartans, Lycans, and Shinobi. The Samurai and Knights swept through and gave aid to them. The battle field was now in carnage. The clashing of swords against shields resonated, the earth trembled when Abominations fell to the ground, and the shrill shrieks of the Winged Demons were heard. "I believe it is time," Zell turned to Ahmaar.

"I agree," Ahmaar nodded his head. Ahmaar signaled to the Egyptian archer next to him. The archer released a flaming arrow to the sky. Raoko Shun, Sir Galidan, and Lioneus saw the flaming arrow high in the sky. They all took their horns and blew in to them. The sound of four harmonious tones sounded and resonated throughout the dark valley. Then behind the Alliance Army, Tufar with Zidane and Maia on his back emerged from their hiding places as did the other Dragon's and Dragon Knights. Aero, Paige, Kulla, Rosey, Draco, Melina, Chen Shun, Raziel, and Craven were partnered with Dragon Knights sitting on the backs of their respective Dragons. Zidane raised the Dragon Blade to the sky signaling the charge. Tufar and the other Dragons took to the sky. The horde of Winged Demons spotted the Dragons and Dragon Knights flying toward them about to launch an offensive assault. The Winged Demons stopped their attack on the Alliance troops on the ground and turned their attention to the incoming Dragons and Dragon Knights. As the Dragon Knight Army drew closer to the center of the fray, they began to fly in a V-shaped formation with Tufar in the front. Zidane fused the hilts of the Dragon Blades and held it in an attack ready position on Tufar's back. Maia readied her bow and arrows, aiming at oncoming Demons.

"Send them to Hades, Tufar!" Tufar grinned at Zidane's war cry and let out a thunderous roar that shook the ground under the troops of both the Alliance and Sekmet. Tufar gathered intense flames in his mouth and held it. The Winged Demons drew closer and closer to the legion of Dragons, shrieking at the top of their lungs, smelling the blood of their potential prey. Maia drew an arrow from her quiver and took aim at the center of the horde. The Necklace of Isis glowed vibrantly as she began to channel the energy toward the head of the arrow.

"Tufar, unleash your Inferno!" Zidane's voice echoed in the winds. Tufar unleashed the building flames in to a massive inferno toward the horde of winged demons.

"Arrow of Isis!" Maia unleashed the energy charged arrow at the same instance Tufar unleashed the inferno from his mouth. The intense flames from Tufar's mouth and the energy charged arrow began to spiral and meld together. This energy surged toward the Winged Demons. The Winged Demons shrieked as they saw this entity of fire and energy surge at them. The ones leading the charging tried to turn back for fear of being engulfed by its fury. The surge of fire and pure energy streaked through the horde turning all those it touched in to a cloud of ash and dust. Those Demons who escaped the furious attack soon attacked the Dragons and Dragon Knights. Several demons attacked Antillus, Melina, and his Dragon. They soon began to plummet toward the ground below.

"Melina!" Aero looked down to watch Melina hang on to the back of Antillus's Dragon. While she was falling, Aero could see an aura surround her body. A seal opened in the air and from that seal of intricate runes flew a Harpy. Its wings spanned eight feet. Its talons could shred the flesh of a bear. The Harpy saw that her Summoner was in danger and clawed at the Winged Demons to save and protect Melina.

"Antillus!" Zidane shouted. Maia looked down to the plummeting Melina, Antillus, and his Dragon as the demons clung to and tore in to his wings. Master Shun was on the Dragon next to Zidane and Maia. Seeing Melina, Antillus, and his Dragon fall to the ground in the middle of Sekmet's army, Shun leapt from his Dragon to the ground to aid Melina, Antillus, and his Dragon.

"Master Shun, no!" Zidane reached out his hand as if attempting to catch him.

"Let them go, young one. They will be fine," Tufar turned his eyes to him. Zidane and Maia looked back to find Master Shun and Antillus back to back fending off Orc troops. When Melina had both of her feet under her, she quickly summoned her Minotaur to her side. The Minotaur aided Shun and Antillus with disposing of the Orcs and Abominations that surrounded them while her Harpy attacked the Winged Demons that drew too close to them. The Dragon's wing was obviously wounded and was somewhat limp. The Dragon was shooting balls of flame in to charging hordes of Orc and Abomination troops sending them high in to the air. Antillus used his shield to bash in to the charging Orcs. He slashed at the knees of the Abominations who were attacking his Dragon. Chen Shun summoned gusts of wind to throw Abominations in to Orc troops. Shun thrust his staff in to the ground causing the earth to ripple and quake under the feet of charging Abominations. He scorched the skin of other Orc troops with lashes of fire. He disappeared in to clouds of shadow to avoid the attacks of Abominations. Melina's Minotaur gored Abominations in the weak points in their armor with its horns and crushed Orc soldiers with its war hammer.

Tufar, with Zidane and Maia on his back, along with other Dragons and Dragon Knights partnered with Aero, Paige, Kulla, Rosey, Draco, Raziel, and Craven flew passed the fortress wall. Passing the front wall, they faced flying rocks hurled by catapults and a barrage of arrows. The Dragons avoided these obstacles with great ease showing their agility through the air. They breathed balls of flames at the ranks of archers below and with one blast of fire they destroyed the catapults.

"Zidane, there is the courtyard. We should drop there!" Aero pointed to it.

"Are you ready, Maia?" Zidane looked over his shoulder to her.

"I think so," her voice was low and trembled showing her nervous. After strapping her bow to her back she inhaled a deep breath and *tap tap tap tap* went her fingers against the side of her thigh.

"You will be fine. Just focus," despite the chaos ensuing below and all around, Zidane's voice was calm.

"Now is the time, young one," Tufar growled. Zidane nodded his head and sheathed the Twin Blades preparing for the leap to the grounds of the courtyard. Aero, Paige, Draco, Kulla, Rosey, Craven, and Raziel all prepared themselves as well. Zidane was the first to take the great leap downwards. With the aid of his cape, Zidane glided through the air toward the courtyard grounds. Everyone else followed suit and leapt. Maia was the last to leap and immediately summoned the power of the Necklace. She lowered herself along with everyone else gently to the ground. Seeing them land safely in the court yard, Tufar led the Dragons and Dragon Knights back to the battle. Once everyone had touched down in the courtyard of stone and brick, Zidane at once looked for the main entrance in to the fortress.

"Zidane, there," Paige pointed to an immense iron door. They all quickly made their way across the courtyard toward this iron door. Zidane tried to push it open, but it did not budge.

"It will not move," Zidane's feet were firmly planted as he used all of his leg strength to push open the doors. All joined Zidane in attempting to make the giant iron door budge, but to no avail.

"How are we to get in if the door won't move?" Rosey looked for a window or a balcony.

"There does not seem to be any windows Maia can lift us to," Paige also looked around for another way in.

"Allow me to try something," Kulla stepped forward. Everyone stepped backwards several paces allowing Kulla to have some space. Kulla held the Scepter of Osiris out away from him. He lowered his head and closed his eyes concentrating and drawing power from the Scepter. The head of the Scepter glowed brightly as its power gathered and throbbed throughout. Kulla opened his eyes. They glowed white with energy seeping from them, "Scepter of Osiris, bring forth the spirit of he who possessed the strength of twenty men". A growing aura of light began to surround Kulla. The light bent and warped all around him to form an immense man. It was the Spirit of the man of who Kulla summoned. The size of the Spirit grew in size and towered over all of them. The man was broadly built with massive muscles. This Spirit stood behind Kulla. Kulla's eyes glowed a pure white and were fixed upon the iron door. Kulla walked to the door with the spirit matching every movement. Kulla looked to his fist as did the Spirit. Kulla drew his hand back and threw a punch at the thick iron door. The Spirit's massive fist crashed in to the iron door causing an immense hole in the iron door that was large enough for a small dragon to walk through. Once the hole was made, the Spirit faded and Kulla fell to one knee seemingly fatigued.

"Are you alright?" Rosey rushed to his side. Kulla nodded and slowly rose to his feet with Rosey's help. One by one they entered the fortress through the opening. They found themselves in a dark hallway. The floor was made from stone. On either side of the hallway were tall stone columns. All drew their weapons and quickly made their way down the hall. All were on alert, feeling there may be an ambush awaiting them. With Zidane leading them, they came to what seemed to be a large foyer. There were suits of dark demonic armor lining the left and right walls. There were also two other openings that led to darker hallways. On the opposite side of the room, they saw a wooden door with two stone gargoyles on either side of it. Zidane rushed to the wooden door. Several feet from the door, his ears twitched.

"Zidane, look out!" Maia yelled out to him. Zidane looked to his right and saw several arrows flying at his head. He spun out of the way. The arrows narrowly missed him by only a few inches. Orc soldiers poured in to the room with weapons drawn and arrows aimed at the group.

"Maia, place a shield around everyone!" Raziel shouted. Maia used the power of the Necklace and placed a shield of energy around everyone in the group. Raziel stomped on the floor creating a quake knocking the Orc troops off balance. Once the quake was over, Maia lowered the shield and Zidane knocked the door down. All rushed through the door with Raziel last. Raziel felt a piercing pain in his leg. He fell forward and looked to his leg. He found an arrow had pierced his leg. He yelled as he pulled the arrow out of his leg. He struggled to his feet and took a deep defensive stance facing the Orc troops.

"Raziel!" Zidane tried to turn back for him.

"No, Lord Zidane! You must go and fight Sekmet. It is the only hope Rhydin has," Raziel looked over his shoulder. He looked back to the Orc troops and found a sword cutting the air toward his neck. He closed his eyes bracing himself. A moment later, he found the Orc had fallen at his feet. Raziel looked up to find Rosey had emerged from a cloud of shadow with kunai in hand.

"Shadow Shinobi," Raziel grinned.

"Earth Shinobi," Rosey responded with a grin. Both then looked to find several Orcs charging toward them. They took defensive stances and readied themselves for the onslaught. They then heard a haunting howl from behind them. Then Craven, in his beast form, leapt over them and ripped in to the Orc troops.

"Raziel, Rosey, Craven!" Zidane shouted still attempting to go back for them, but Aero and Kulla were holding him back.

"Do not worry about us, m' lord. We will be fine," Rosey called back to him.

"It has been an honor to serve with you, Lord Zidane," Raziel shouted still bleeding from his wound.

"It was an honor for me to fight alongside you, Zidane," Craven growled. Zidane then shrugged Aero and Kulla from him and led the rest of his comrades down the second hallway. Kulla looked back to Rosey. Rosey looked back to him and winked. She mouthed to him 'You will see me again'. Kulla then turned down the hallway. Rosey, Raziel, and Craven then charged toward the group of armed Orcs.

The sound of swords clashing and blood curdling screams were heard down the hall by Zidane, Maia, Kulla, Aero, Paige, and Draco. They ran as fast as they could down the dark halls of this massive fortress. Their footsteps echoed throughout the stone halls as they made their way through the maze of corridors. They soon found themselves in another room. The ceiling was high and the room was wide. Several stone columns lined the room. There were many dark corners making Zidane, Aero, Maia, Paige, Kulla, and Draco were cautious. They looked for any signs of another ambush. Maia then sniffed the air as did Kulla. Zidane was ahead of the group.

"Zidane wait!" Maia called to him.

"What is it?" Zidane turned to face them.

"I smell man flesh," Kulla sniffed once more.

"Perhaps it is me," Draco looked to him.

"No, we know your scent. We smell a foreign scent," Maia shook her head. At that moment, small blades cut the air toward Zidane. Maia pushed him out of the way and stopped the blades with the power of the Necklace. Maia looked at the blades and then her eyes narrowed on to them, "I know these blades". She then lowered the blades to the floor. Out of the corner of her eye she saw a figure leap toward her with a weapon drawn and about to strike. Maia leapt backwards to the group.

"Ivy," Maia scowled with clenched teeth. Ivy stood in front of them with an evil grin. From the dark corners of the room Naafar and Kain emerged with twin sickles and war hammer in hand. They stood between them and the door.

"Naafar," Kulla tightly gripped the Scepter while he reached for his sword. Kulla sensed something odd from Naafar. With the power of the Scepter of Osiris, he was able to read the souls of those around him. What struck him to be odd was that he sensed no soul within Naafar where in previous encounters he did.

"And Kain," Aero's eyes glowed and clenched his fists. Ivy, Kain, and Naafar all wore evil grins on their faces.

"You are going to have to go through us to get to Lord Sekmet," Ivy cracked her bladed whip.

"And that is no easy feat," Naafar scraped the blades of his sickles together creating sparks.

"Do you not remember the broken ribs I gave to you, Aero," Kain gave an evil chuckle. Aero clenched his teeth and his eyes glowed more brightly.

"Paige, Zidane, Draco go," Aero said through his clenched teeth. Zidane, Draco, and Paige looked from the group who were focused on their enemies in front of them and then to the door behind the Generals of Sekmet. Zidane looked to Paige and Draco then charged toward the Generals of Sekmet, as did Draco and Paige. Ivy, Kain, and Naafar were about to attack them but Zidane, followed by Draco and Paige, leapt over them in a single bound. Once he landed behind the Generals, Zidane looked back and made eye contact with Maia. Maia mouthed to him 'I love you' and then blew a kiss to him. Draco and Paige grabbed Zidane and led him through the door. Ivy, Naafar, and Kain turned to chase them, but a shower of energy charged arrows struck and exploded in front of them. They turned to find Maia had released those arrows and was shaking her head at them.

"It is rude to turn your back on your guests, is it not?" an evil smirk bearing his fangs was on Kulla's face.

"This will prove interesting," Naafar glared at Kulla with glowing blood red eyes.

"Revenge will be mine," Aero said with energy gathering in his hand.

"I will crush you!" Kain spat.

"It appears the Little Kitty has grown some fangs," Ivy's eyes narrowed on to Maia.

"This *Little Kitty* is going to sink her claws in to you and rip you apart!" Maia shouted as she shifted in to her panther form and charged at her. Kulla and Aero followed behind Maia charging toward Naafar and Kain.

Continuing down the maze of hallways, Zidane, Paige, and Draco ran in search of Sekmet's chambers. The halls were still dark and there were no windows in any of the hallways they ran through. Darkness was throughout this fortress as was a noticeable chill in the air. At the end of the maze of hallways, Zidane, Paige, and Draco arrived at a large empty room. All that was there was a ten foot stone statue of a demonic behemoth with rows of horns on the crown of its head. Its left arm was significantly more muscular and larger than the right arm. Instead of a hand, it was a claw that was on its left arm and one massive horn grew from its left shoulder. It held a massive battle axe in its right hand. This ten foot statue was built next to a massive bronze door.

"That seems to be Sekmet's chambers," Zidane pointed the Dragon Blade at it. They walked further in to the room but were weary of an ambush. Once they reached the center of the room, the floor quaked slightly.

"What was that?" Draco clenched the Sword of Ages firmly as he looked for the origin of the tremor.

"I have no idea," Paige ahook her head. The floor quaked once more. They then found the ten foot statue had taken two steps closer to them.

"No," Zidane groaned.

"It is no wonder Sekmet has this behemoth guarding his door," Paige firmly clenched both her short swords. The behemoth took a few more steps toward them and raised its battle axe. Zidane, Draco, and Paige took several steps back ready to dodge the attack. The massive axe was brought down upon them. Draco, Zidane, and Paige leapt out of the way as the axe crashed on to the floor cracking it.

"Zidane, you must go through those doors and go on to Sekmet. Paige and I can handle this stone goliath," Draco raised his sword at the behemoth.

"But Father...," Zidane started to say.

"Zidane you have to go. Your father and I will be fine. Besides I will be watching out for him," Paige grinned. She gathered energy in her palm and hurled it at the stone beast. The stone creature reeled backwards.

"Go now, Son!" Draco shouted. Zidane hesitated then ran toward the door behind the huge stone behemoth. The beast grabbed at Zidane, but he flipped over the hand and crashed through the door. Draco and Paige looked at each other and nodded. They both then lunged at the behemoth with weapons readied to attack.

Zidane found himself in the dark chambers of Sekmet. One end of the chamber was lined with suits of demonic armor. The opposite wall was lined with the heads of various dragons. There was a thick aura of darkness and evil within. Zidane had never felt such a malice before. Not even from the Vampire Brakus. At the center of this chamber was a throne carved from marble. Zidane was on edge as he ventured further in to the chamber. His breathing became heavy and took more frequent breaths. He was cautious as to not allow Sekmet to attack him from behind. His hand was tense around the hilts of the Dragon Blade. A small window was on the opposite side of the chamber letting in a small amount of light from the Moon. Next to the window was a tall, dark figure. It stood nearly eight feet. It wore dark armor with massive wrist gauntlets and three, one foot long claws on each fist. It stood with its back towards Zidane. A demonic sword leaned against the wall next to it.

"It would appear the heart of the Red Dragon is much stronger than I had initially anticipated," the armored figure said in a cold dark voice.

"Sekmet," Zidane clenched his fists and teeth.

"Indeed. I am Lord Sekmet, the Dark Ruler of this Region of Rhydin and soon to be the Ruler of all Rhydin and Earth once I have carved out your heart and your powers," Sekmet did not bother to lay eyes on Zidane

"I will not give you the opportunity," Zidane crept closer to Sekmet.

"You have no choice in the matter. You will not see the strike coming," Sekmet said coldly with his back still facing Zidane.

"You greatly underestimate me, Sekmet. It is you who will be defeated and your reign of darkness will end this night. The people of Rhydin will no longer have a reason to fear. It is not the Dragon that will be slain this night, but the Dragon Hunter," Zidane crouched in to a fighting stance.

"We shall see, Red Dragon," Sekmet took his demonic blade and in the blink of an eye, Sekmet whipped around and charged at Zidane with a slash at his neck. Zidane blocked the attack with the Dragon Blade.

"Very good, Red Dragon. This fight may prove interesting," Sekmet said with an evil grin under his helmet.

"Did you honestly think I would make it easy for you," Zidane said with a sarcastic tone. Zidane pushed aside Sekmet's blade and threw an attack of his own toward his knee. Sekmet leapt over the attack and in mid-air lifted his knee in to Zidane's jaw sending him backwards. Zidane's vision momentarily blurred. He shook it off in time to see Sekmet bring his demonic blade above his head, ready to bring it down upon Zidane's head. Zidane avoided the attack by rolling out of the way and then spinning up to his feet.

"It would appear that I have misjudged you as well, Sekmet," Zidane's stance was low.

"How so, Red Dragon?" he and Zidane began to circle around each other.

"I overestimated you. That hit you delivered did not hurt," Zidane said with a grin. Sekmet's eyes glowed violently red; he clenched his demonic blade tighter and swung violently at Zidane. Zidane dodged and blocked each attack. With one hand, Sekmet swung his blade. Zidane blocked this attack, but was not quick enough to block the knee to the ribs. Zidane doubled over then Sekmet swung the point of his elbow to Zidane's jaw sending him spinning backwards. The air was driven from Zidane's lungs causing him gasp for air. Sekmet threw a backhand at Zidane, slashing at his chest plate with those one foot long claws. Zidane was sent spinning backwards again landing on his back. Sekmet leapt to the air with the demonic blade over his head preparing to come down upon Zidane. Zidane rolled out of the way, once more narrowly dodging Sekmet's violent attack. As Zidane rose to his feet, he saw a massive crack in the stone floor from the demonic blade. Zidane's eyes widened at the demonstration of power shown by Sekmet. Sekmet stood several yards away from Zidane. His eyes glowed brightly red, his fist was clenched tightly around the demonic blade that began to glow with a dark energy. This dark energy slowly crept up Sekmet's arm and eventually the rest of his body. Zidane began to hesitate and question himself whether he was strong enough to defeat Sekmet.

"I smell your fear, Red Dragon. Your fear sustains me. My power grows with your swelling fear of me," Sekmet hissed. Zidane began to circle around the chamber as did Sekmet. Zidane quickly detached the hilts and sheathed the Twin Dragon Blades.

"I fear you not, Sekmet," Zidane crouched down in an attack stance then motioned for Sekmet to attack him.

"You are a fool!" Sekmet shouted and began his charge. Zidane waited until Sekmet was within a few feet away in front of him.

"Tri-Form!" Zidane shouted as he split in to three separate but identical entities just before Sekmet slashed at him. Sekmet looked up to find three versions of Zidane had surrounded him, all crouched down in a stance, preparing to attack.

"You are only delaying the inevitable!" Sekmet exclaimed looking at each version of Zidane. They then began to run in a circle around Sekmet. Becoming more and more infuriated, Sekmet violently swung his demonic blade at the three versions of Zidane. The Zidanes dodged each attack Sekmet threw at them. The three versions of Zidane quickened their speed and started to run as fast as they could. Sekmet could not keep up with the speed being demonstrated by the three entities of Zidane. In their palms closest to Sekmet, the Zidanes gathered balls of flames. They all released these intense flames at Sekmet. They hit Sekmet leaving scorch marks on his dark armor. The Zidanes did not relent in their fire attack. Fireball after fireball was thrown at Sekmet leaving scorch mark after scorch mark on his armor. A cloud of dark smoke hovered around Sekmet. The Zidanes ceased their onslaught and stood next to each other to see whether Sekmet survived their attack or not. Several moments passed and the smoke began to clear from around Sekmet. All were crouched in to a guarded stance. With great speed, Sekmet emerged from the smoke and swung his demonic blade destroying one of the energy copies of Zidane. Two remained. One fake version of Zidane and the other one was the actual Zidane.

"White Lightning!" both Zidanes shouted as they both leapt to the air unleashing streaks of white lightning from their fingertips. Sekmet placed a shroud of darkness in front of him to absorb the streaks of lighting. The Zidane made of pure energy landed on the ground first and stomped on the ground to create the floor quake under the feet of Sekmet. Sekmet was knocked off balance and then the real Zidane took the opportunity to create a whirlwind and send it toward Sekmet. Sekmet was sent backwards a few feet, but he set his feet firmly to the floor.

"It will take more than a mere gust of wind to faze me, puny Dragon!" Sekmet shouted as he crashed his massive fist to the stone floor. The floor under the feet of both Zidanes quaked and both stumbled and struggled to keep their footing. Sekmet rushed at them and slashed at one of them with his demonic blade. The version of Zidane in which Sekmet had attacked was the one made of energy destroying it leaving only the real Zidane. Zidane flipped out of the way of another one of Sekmet's attacks. In mid-air, Zidane drew both Twin Blades. Landing on his feet, Zidane immediately charged at Sekmet with both Blades. Slashing and stabbing, Zidane unleashed an onslaught upon Sekmet with great ferocity and quickness. Sekmet blocked each of Zidane's attacks with great ease. Sekmet then found an opening in Zidane's attacks and gave a kick to his sternum throwing Zidane backwards. Sekmet then swung his demonic blade at Zidane. Zidane ducked then leapt away from each attack. Zidane leapt in to the air and fused the hilts of the Dragon Blades. Once he landed on his feet, Zidane summoned an aura of flames on one blade and lightning on the other.

"Firestorm!" Zidane spun the Dragon Blade fusing the fire and lightning together to become one. He unleashed this fusion of flames and lighting at Sekmet. Sekmet was consumed by this onslaught. Zidane ceased his attack and found a trench was left in the floor from this powerful attack. A cloud of smoke was left around Sekmet and Zidane waited for the smoke to clear. Zidane was on guard since Sekmet survived his previous attacks. The smoke settled, then cleared. Zidane's eyes widened when he found Sekmet standing there breathing heavily and eyes violently glowing red. Scorch marks covered his armor.

"You are a fool to think that you could have defeated me with that. Now I will show you what true power is!" Sekmet exclaimed as he gathered dark energy in to his palm. Zidane readied himself. Sekmet then unleashed a barrage of dark orbs toward Zidane.

"Flare up!" Zidane summoned an aura of flames around the blades. Zidane began to deflect many of the dark orbs aside. An orb was thrown at Zidane's feet while he was distracted by the others. Zidane was tripped up and fell victim to the onslaught of dark orbs. He was hit with dark orb after dark orb. A larger orb was sent at Zidane hitting him and sending him in to the suits of armor lining the wall. Sekmet charged at Zidane grabbing him and then throwing him in to the marble throne. Zidane crashed through it causing him to drop his Dragon Blade. As Zidane was slowly attempting to get to his feet, Sekmet charged at him and kicked him in the ribs, sending him in to the wall. A large dark orb was unleashed upon Zidane as soon as he hit the wall. Zidane crossed his forearms in front of his face to try to block the attack, but it was too powerful and Zidane fell victim to it. Zidane's eyes slowly began to blur and then black out. He awoke a moment later to find Sekmet slowly walking toward him, almost standing over him. Zidane tried to get to his feet, but Sekmet grabbed him by the neck and held him in the air. Zidane looked in to the cold, red eyes of Sekmet.

"This is where you die Dragon!" Sekmet exclaimed triumphantly. Sekmet then threw Zidane face first to the stone floor. He raised his demonic blade over his head to give the final strike to the helpless and vulnerable Zidane. Sekmet brought the sword down toward Zidane's neck.

"I have failed," Zidane said to himself, but inches away from decapitation, the sound of steel meeting steel sounded throughout the chamber. Zidane felt a dark presence in the chamber and it was not emitting from Sekmet. It was a familiar darkness, but one he had not felt in a while.

"I am not about to let you throw you life away. Especially when it is not me you are throwing your life away to," a dark voice resonated. Zidane slowly looked up to find Sekmet struggling with another dark figure. Zidane's vision was so blurred that he could not make out who was standing between him and Sekmet, but he vaguely recognized the voice.

"S-Stratos?" Zidane called out. Stratos stomped on the ground causing it to quake and knock Sekmet off balance. Taking this opportunity, Stratos conjured an orb of shadow and released it in to Sekmet's chest plate sending him backwards.

"No one is going to kill you but me," Stratos hoisted Zidane to his feet. Zidane began to regain his strength and composure.

"Why are you helping me?" Zidane furrowed his eyebrows in confusion.

"As I said, no one is going to kill you but me. I am going to have your power and if that means killing anyone who wants your power, then so be it," Stratos responded through clenched teeth.

"If it be that way, then shall we slay a common foe?" Stratos nodded at Zidane's proposal.

"You cannot fight without your Dragon Blade though," Stratos's voice was cold. Zidane looked around and saw it lying on the floor next to the throne made of marble. He held out his hand and conjured a vortex of wind, summoning it to him. He felt his strength renewed as he held his weapon.

"Who is this infidel, Red Dragon?!" Sekmet pointed the tip of his demonic blade at Stratos.

"You face the Black Dragon!" Stratos growled with wisps of smoke pouring from his nostrils. Both Zidane and Stratos dropped in to defensive stances.

"How is this possible?! The Red Dragon and the Black Dragon here?!" Sekmet's eyes glowed brighter.

"That is correct Sekmet. Now you have both of us to contend with. Unless you want to surrender now and leave Earth and Rhydin peacefully," Zidane said with a small smirk on his face.

"I will never surrender to the likes of you!" Sekmet shouted angrily.

"So be it. We gave you the opportunity to leave peacefully and with your life," Zidane responded. Sekmet let out a thunderous yell. An aura of darkness throbbed around his body. His eyes glowed more violently. It seemed to Stratos and Zidane that he grew in height and mass.

"What have you gotten us in to, Red Dragon?" an air of hesitation in Stratos's voice.

"Do not tell me the Great Black Dragon is afraid," Zidane mocked.

"I did not have to come and rescue you," Stratos retorted.

"I *am* grateful Stratos," Zidane said. Sekmet focused dark energy to his demonic blade and then unleashed a wave surging toward Stratos and Zidane. Stratos stepped forward and stomped on the ground rousing a chunk of stone to block the surging wall of dark energy. Zidane then took apart his Dragon Blade and sheathed the Twin Blades. An intense aura of fire grew around Zidane. His eyes flared red and his dreadlocks sparked with bright embers from underneath his helmet. The flames around his fist started to form the head of a Dragon. "Wildfire Dragon Fist!" he shouted as he used the wall of stone to vault himself in to the air. His fiery eyes were fixed on to Sekmet's chest plate when he threw his fist at him. Zidane's fist roared through the air as he threw his Dragon Fist at Sekmet. The dragon head exploded upon impact with Sekmet's chest plate. The force of Zidane's Dragon Fist threw Sekmet backwards in to the opposite wall. A cloud of black smoke hovered and filled the air of the opposite end of the chambers. Once the smoke cleared, Zidane and Stratos found Sekmet against the opposite wall with stone fallen from the wall around him and a dark scorch mark on his armor. Sekmet was doubled over and breathing heavily. He could barely grip the hilt of his sword. Zidane and Stratos cautiously approached. As Stratos and Zidane drew within several yards of Sekmet, his eyes glowed red and his grip tightened. Sekmet rushed at Zidane and Stratos slashing and stabbing his demonic blade at them violently. Zidane and Stratos spun and flipped away from Sekmet's swift and violent attacks. Sekmet then gathered dark energy in his hand and unleashed a barrage of dark orbs at them. Stratos and Zidane narrowly dodged each orb and explosion. In mid-air, Zidane drew both Twin Blades.

As he landed on his feet, Zidane swung both Blades to deflect an orb back at Sekmet. The orb hit Sekmet in the shoulder throwing him off balance. Stratos took the opportunity and charged at Sekmet. Several yards away, Stratos leapt to the wall and launched himself toward Sekmet with his Dragon Blade in hand. Stratos slashed at the same shoulder the dark orb hit cutting in to the armor. Dark energy began to seep from the gash in the armor. The blow from Stratos caused Sekmet to spin. In mid-spin, Sekmet found Zidane flipping over him. Sekmet swung his blade at Zidane, but was not quick enough to harm him. Stratos waited for Zidane with the Dragon Blade in a position that he can land on it. Zidane landed on Stratos's Dragon Blade and immediately launched himself at Sekmet with his own Dragon Blade in hand. Zidane slashed at Sekmet's chest plate. His weapon easily cut through Sekmet's armor. More of Sekmet's dark energy seeped from the new wound. Stratos then charged at Sekmet and slashed at his legs bringing Sekmet to his knees. Zidane and Stratos stood side by side with Dragon Blades in hand facing a weakened Sekmet. Both sheathed their Dragon Blades. Zidane began to gather flames in his left hand and Stratos began to gather shadow energy in his right hand. As the energies of the flames and shadows grew and throbbed, they began to fuse together as one. Zidane noticed this fusion of flame and shadows. It was the same fusion he noticed in the mountain valley where he last fought Stratos. Stratos noticed this fusion as well. They both began to feel stronger. They looked to each and nodded. Both crouched down and cupped their hands together. Zidane continued to conjure flames and Stratos continued to conjure shadow energy. The shadow energy and the flames began to swirl and fuse together. Zidane's eyes glowed red with an aura of flames seeping from them. Stratos' eyes glowed black and seeped shadow energy. Sekmet struggled to get to his feet but the wounds inflicted by Zidane and Stratos greatly weakened him. Dark energy continued to pour from the slash marks in his shoulder and chest plate. The fusion of flames and shadow energy grew and throbbed in the hands of Stratos and Zidane.

"Dark Fire!" Zidane and Stratos cried as they unleashed the fusion of flame and shadow at the weakened Sekmet. The eyes of Sekmet widened as he saw this dark fire surge toward him. In desperation Sekmet, with one hand, raised his demonic blade to deflect the dark fire. The energy from the dark fire fury caused the demonic blade to crack along the steel of the blade. With time the blade shattered leaving Sekmet vulnerable. With the other hand he quickly conjured dark energy and unleashed it, countering the dark fire. The dark fire of Zidane and Stratos was now in a toggle for dominance with the dark energy from Sekmet's hand. Neither power was overtaking the other, but was going back and forth.

"Do not give up Red Dragon! I will not allow it!" Stratos grit his teeth.

"Neither will I let you give up!" Zidane set him feet firmly. Zidane and Stratos began to push their strength and overtake Sekmet. Seeing the dark fire beginning to overtake him, Sekmet stomped his foot to the floor causing a quake under the feet of Zidane and Stratos. Stratos was thrown backwards and landed hard on to the stone floor. He was unable to continue the fusion of fire and shadows leaving only Zidane to fend off the dark energy of Sekmet. The dark energy quickly overpowered the flames and pushed toward Zidane. Zidane's strength waned and could not keep up the inferno. Zidane dropped to one knee and looked up to find the dark energy surging towards him. Zidane crossed his forearms in front of him and braced for a tremendous impact. Zidane heard the explosion, but felt nothing. He looked up to find Stratos had stepped in front of the blast sacrificing his body, but he seemed unscathed. The Bracelet on Stratos' wrist was glowing. Zidane wondered if that Bracelet helped Stratos endure the blast of dark energy. When the smoke cleared, Stratos found Sekmet charging at him at full speed with his fists glowing with dark energy. With a clash of dark energy, Sekmet collided with Stratos. Sekmet and Stratos were now in a toggle for dominance. Their hands were interlocked and dark energy throbbing from both.

"Zidane!" a voice cried from the entrance to the chambers. Zidane turned to find Maia along with Aero, Paige, Kulla, Draco, Rosey, Craven, and Raziel. All rushed to Zidane's side.

"Who is that fightin' Sekmet?" Rosey looked to the being that looked like Zidane.

"His name is Stratos. He is the Bearer of the Black Dragon Essence," all looked at Zidane with confusion.

"But how is that possible?" Kulla looked back and forth between Stratos and Zidane.

"There is no time to explain, Sekmet is losing his dark power and we need to destroy him now," Zidane urged.

"What should we do then?" Aero looked from Zidane to Stratos.

"I need my father, Maia, and Kulla to stay with me. The rest of you are to get out of here," Zidane looked to them all.

"What do you plan to do?" Paige asked.

"Use the combined powers of the Relics," Zidane was unsure of that would even work.

"Are you sure that'll work?" Rosey asked.

"For Rhydin and Earth's sake, pray that it does," Zidane let out a deep breath. They nodded and left the chambers.

"Good luck, Brother," Aero said before leaving. Draco, Zidane, Maia, and Kulla were left in the chambers.

"Whatever you are planning on doing Red Dragon, I suggest you execute your plan NOW!" Stratos shouted at him through clenched teeth.

"Father, step in front of us and kneel down holding the Sword of Ages out and pointing upwards from you. Kulla stand to my right and Maia to my left. Ready your Relics," Zidane's eyes were growing with a fiery intensity. Draco knelt with the Sword of Ages outstretched and the point of the Sword up toward the ceiling. Maia, Zidane, and Kulla readied their Relics. Stratos' strength began to wane. The Bracelet on his wrist glowed brightly and little by little his strength grew pushing Sekmet backwards on to his heels.

"Summon the powers of the Relics!" Zidane cried.

"I summon the power of Osiris!" Kulla shouted pointing the Scepter at the Sword of Ages. A bright light emitted from the Scepter and rushed toward the Sword. The Sword of Ages absorbed the energy from the Scepter.

"I summon the power of Isis!" Maia cried as she focused a beam of light from the Necklace at the Sword of Ages. The Sword absorbed that energy as well continuing to accept the power from the Scepter of Osiris.

"I summon the power of Ra!" Zidane cried pointing the Bracelet at the Sword of Ages and releasing pure energy from it. The Sword of Ages absorbed the energy from the Bracelet of Ra and retaining the energies from the Scepter of Osiris and the Necklace of Isis. The Sword of Ages began to throb with the energies being emitted from the other Relics. Stratos looked back to see what the three were conjuring. He then looked back to Sekmet and held on for a little while longer. Sekmet saw what Zidane and the others were conjuring, but could not escape Stratos' grip.

"You sacrifice yourself for them?!" Sekmet exclaimed.

"Not for them. I have my own reasons," Stratos replied through his teeth.

"You will die for nothing. My soul will be resurrected!" Sekmet attempted to push back against Stratos's strength.

"No, it will not. Your dark soul will go straight to hell!" Stratos shouted as his eyes glowed with shadow energy.

"I will see you there for an eternity of damnation!" Sekmet shouted.

"You go first you bastard!" Stratos shouted back with his eyes flashing violently. The light from the Relics emitted a bright light illuminating the whole chamber.

"Sword of Ages, be my Strength!" Draco shouted as he unleashed the tremendous power of the Relics upon Sekmet. The walls shook and cracked as the wave of power surged. The floors quaked under their feet. This power from the Ancient Relics shook the foundation of the dark fortress. The suits of demonic armor that lined the wall were obliterated in the wake of this power. The heads of various Dragons that were kept as trophies disintegrated from the might of the pure energy from the Relics. This surge of power left a trench several feet in to the stone floor. The surge of energy made contact with Sekmet and Stratos. An evil laugh was heard from the deafening explosion. This explosion was seen from the battlefield as Aero, Paige, Rosey, Craven, and Raziel were exiting the iron gate.

"Oh my," Rosey said in amazement as a dark cloud of smoke emitted from the explosion.

"I pray that Zidane and the others escaped with their lives," concern was in Paige's voice as she looked upon the billowing smoke.

"We all do," Aero said just before the ground shook from the aftershock of the explosion. Several moments later, Tufar along with other Dragons and Dragon Knights flew toward the fortress to search the rubble. The Orcs soldiers already began to retreat and scatter away from the Allied Army in different directions. Some were in large groups and others were in smaller groups.

After what seemed to be an eternity, Tufar and the other Dragons and Dragon Knights returned. The Allied Army gathered around Aero, Paige, Rosey, Craven and Raziel waiting for Tufar's return, hopefully with Zidane, Maia, Kulla and Draco in good health. Tufar landed on the ground with two other Dragons on either side of him. On their backs were Zidane, Maia, Kulla, and Draco. Aero, Paige, and the others assisted in bringing them down to the ground. They were laid side by side. Their eyes were closed. Black soot covered their faces and armor. Their bodies were limp.

"Are they…?" Rosey asked as she knelt beside Kulla with tears welling in her eyes.

"I pray they are not," Paige shook her head.

"Have faith," Tufar looked down upon the four that lay before him. Moments passed and neither of them as so much flinched or showed any sign that they were alive. Rosey held Kulla's head in her lap. Kulla's hand was still gripped around the Scepter of Osiris and Draco hand a firm grip on the hilt of the Sword of Ages. Tears rolled down Rosey's cheeks and then fell upon Kulla's forehead. The Scepter of Osiris began to glow. Rosey's eyes widened when she noticed this, "Lord Aero!" she called to him with excitement in her voice. Soon after, the Necklace of Isis, the Bracelet of Ra, and the Sword of Ages glowed brightly and throbbed with energy. That energy began to slowly creep throughout their bodies. A bright aura formed around their bodies that throbbed and pulsed. This energy emitting from the Relics lifted their bodies in to the air. Their arms were outstretched to their sides. Throughout this, their eyes were still closed and their bodies still limp. The Allied Army watched in amazement and hope. The auras of energy around their bodies slowly began to be absorbed through their clothes and armor and then soon through their skin. In a final flash of bright light, Zidane was the first to open his eyes. They seemed to glow with new life. Maia, Kulla, and Draco opened their eyes shortly after. Their eyes also seemed to have new life in them. After they awakened and absorbed the new energy from the Relics, Zidane, Maia, Kulla, and Draco slowly descended back to the ground.

"Zidane are you alright?" Aero stepped toward him.

"Yes. I am fine," he nodded.

"And the rest of you?" Paige looked to them.

"The rest of us are well and unscathed," Kulla breathed a sigh of relief.

"It is done then?" Rosey asked walking up next to Kulla and held on to his arm.

"It is," Maia took Zidane's arm in to hers.

"Sekmet is finished then," a triumphant grin grew on Craven's face.

"Yes. And will not be returning from the land of the dead," Zidane grin with relief on his face.

"Three cheers for the Trinity and the King of Men!" Aldar raised his fist to the sky.

"Huzzah! Huzzah! Huzzah!" all cried with their fists and weapons raised to the sky. Zidane, with Maia on his arm, and Kulla next to Rosey and Draco joined in the rejoicing of the destruction of Sekmet and his reign of terror. Zidane looked around and a look of concern slowly crept upon his face, "Where are Master Shun and Antillus?". They all stopped and looked around.

"And Melina!" Aero called out.

"I am here," Shun called out as he emerged from the crowd of soldiers.

"As am I," Melina emerged from the crowd and was met by Aero.

"And Captain Antillus?" Zidane's eyes searched the crowd.

"I am here as well, Lord Zidane. You kept your promise," Antillus also emerged from the crowd of soldiers. Antillus had a sling wrapped about him to keep his left arm from moving. His dragon was among the others behind the Army. Zidane breathed a sigh of relief. Maia then turned Zidane to face her and held him.

"I have been waiting months for this day," she said as she rose to the tips of her toes and gave a passionate kiss to Zidane. Zidane returned the embrace and kiss. He then held her close to his heart wrapping his arms around her firmly. She found comfort in his arms and purred lightly.

"Zidane, you still owe me," Maia looked up to him with a bright smile.

"I do," he reached in to his belt and pulling out a golden chain with a ruby crystal dangling from it. Maia's eyes were fixed upon the crystal that reflected the Moon's light. Zidane then knelt down to one knee. His silver eyes met with Maia's amber eyes.

"Maia, we have been through many trials. Many obstacles were in our path. You were by my side every step of the way down this path. I do not believe I could have survived these past several months without you. There will be more obstacles down this path. Will you face these obstacles with me, as my wife?" Zidane's soft, tender voice was none like Maia has ever heard from Zidane. It had a calming and soothing effect upon her heart. His hand was outstretched to her with the ruby crystal in hand.

"Yes! Yes I will marry you!" Maia squealed with excitement. Tears of joy welled in her eyes. Zidane rose to his feet. He looked in to her eyes and fastened the ruby crystal around her neck. Once it was on, Maia looked down to it and held it between her forefinger and thumb. She then looked back to Zidane who was gazing at her with a bright smile on his face. She rose to the tips of her toes once more and gave a tender kiss to his lips. Rosey then looked at Kulla out of the corner of her eye with a smile on her face. She then turned Kulla's head to face her and gave a deep kiss. Kulla was surprised by this, but then relaxed and then returned the kiss.

"Finally," Chen Shun said with a shake of his head and a sigh. Raoko stood beside his brother and gave a hearty laugh.

Months passed since the destruction of Sekmet's empire. The Orcs, Abominations, and Winged Demons who served under the rule of Sekmet and his Generals were now scattered throughout the regions of Rhydin and Earth, hiding from the hands of the new alliance now known as the Krystal Kingdom. The Krystal Kingdom was the alliance of the Elf Kingdom under the rule of Aero, Paige, Melina, Zidane, and Maia; the Vampire realm was under the rule of Kulla and Zell; all of the Shinobi throughout the regions of Rhydin. The hands of this alliance even reached to Earth with King Draco, the father of Zidane. The nations of Sparta, Asia, England, and Egypt answered to King Draco's call. The Rangers who answered Paige's call became King Draco's special guard. King Draco rigorously trained them all. Much like the alliance between the Elf Kingdom and the Dragon Knights, the nations in the Krystal Kingdom wore crystals around their necks as well. Those who lived in the Elf Kingdom continued to wear the ruby crystals and the Dragon Knights continued to bear the jade crystals. The Vampire realm now wore crystals that were as blue as the midnight sky. The Shinobi throughout the regions wore crystals the color of the setting Sun. The humans throughout Rhydin and those who answered the call of King Draco wore the crystals the color of blooming orchids. These crystals signified the allegiance each race and each nation vowed to one another. To answer the call for aid if one needed so. These crystals were also a sign of peace throughout Rhydin and Earth.

The day came when Zidane and Maia were to be wed. It was a truly beautiful day. No clouds were in sight and the Sun was shining brightly with a pleasant warmth. A gentle breeze blew about that refreshed those who were sitting in the congregation. Those representing the Earth and Shadow Shinobi were in attendance. Elves from the Eastern Province, Woodland Realm, and Western Province were in attendance as well. Those who came from Zell's Coven wore black, hooded cloaks to protect themselves from the Sun while sitting in the open. There was not one empty seat to view this ceremony. The ceremony was held in the Courtyard of the Western Palace. Lilacs adorned both sides of the makeshift aisle. The alter stood in front of the main door to the Palace. A red velvet covering, trimmed in gold embroidery was draped over the alter. Sitting on top of the alter was a wooden cross with a Dove perched at the top. At the foot of the cross was an opened book with tattered pages.

Zell, who wore a black hooded robe, presided over the ceremony. He wore the hood of the robe over his head and gloves on his hands to shield his skin from the Sun's harsh rays. Zidane, Aero, and Kulla stood to his left. Zidane stood proudly, but anxiously, with his hands folded behind his back. For the ceremony, Zidane wore a white tunic, and slacks along with a matching long jacket that had intricate, crimson embroidery on the back. Kulla and Aero wore similar attire, but were much simpler than Zidane's.

Trumpets heralded the entrance of the bridesmaids. Melina, Paige, and Rosey were the Bridesmaids in this ceremony. Paige was the first to make her way down the aisle. Paige's dirty blonde hair was worn long and hung to the middle of her back. This was the first time Zidane had seen his sister's hair down. It was always in a ponytail or in a tight bun. When Paige was midway down the aisle, Rosey made her appearance. Kulla's heart jumped in his chest when he saw her. Her red hair was braided all the way down to the middle of her back. Her emerald eyes were vibrant against the shimmering of her dress.

When Rosey was midway down the aisle, it was Melina's turn to walk down the aisle. Her raven hair was in a similar style as Paige's. All of the Bridesmaids wore a sleeveless dress that was form fitting in the upper body and then bloomed out from the waist down. The portion of the dress below the waist was layered and stopped just above the ankle.

Now that the Bridesmaids had made their entrance, it was now time for the Bride to make her appearance. This anticipation made Zidane a bit more anxious. His fingers became busy even though his folded his hands behind his back.

"It is only too late when you say, 'I do'," Aero jokingly whispered to Zidane. Zidane gave a chuckle that relaxed his anxiousness.

"It was too late when I laid eyes on her," Zidane whispered back.

"I know the feeling," Aero said as he looked to Melina who stood on the other side of the alter. Both exchanged a loving smile and looked in to each other's eyes, getting lost in each other.

The final trumpet fanfare sounded, heralding the entrance of the Bride. Zidane took in a deep breath and Aero patted Zidane on the shoulder. The congregation stood when Maia stood at the head of the aisle. Zidane could see the beaming smile she wore from underneath the white veil. Her dress too was sleeveless and hugged her body down to her hips where the dress bloomed outward. Shimmering, white crystals embroidered the train that trailed behind her walk. Zidane could not take his eyes from the radiant beauty that was making her way down the aisle to meet him at the altar. Their eyes locked and hands were tenderly held when she arrived.

"You are a true work of Heaven," Zidane said to her in a hushed tone. She blushed at these words and her smile became wider. This is when Zell called for the ceremony to commence.

During the time of the reconstruction of Rhydin, Zidane spent many days on the balcony outside of his bed chambers staring off in to the setting Sun. It was as if he were pondering the deepest of questions. Maia would stand in the doorway and watch him for hours upon hours contemplating what thoughts raced through the mind of her beloved.   On the day the Sun was brightest, as it set behind the Western Mountains, Maia walked up behind Zidane and wrapped her arms around his waist. Zidane turned to face her and looked deep in to her glowing amber eyes as the light from the setting Sun gleamed in her eyes.

"What is on your mind?" he asked her in the calmest of voices.

"Something wonderful has happened, my husband," she responded with bright eyes and the happiest of smiles Zidane had ever seen on her.

"And what is that?" she took a few moments to answer. She took his hand in to hers and placed it on her stomach.

"I am pregnant," her smile grew with this revelation. Zidane smiled the brightest smile Maia had ever seen from him. He hoisted her in to the air by her waist. That evening the Sun shone brightest as it was setting.

Writing Chronicles of Rhydin: Legend of the Red Dragon was quite a journey for me. There were times where I questioned whether I was going to finish this, let alone publish it. This was my first attempt at writing a novel. Writing term papers in college is quite different from writing something of fiction and not based on facts, figures, or history. It was challenging, yet fun. I am so grateful for the opportunity to have this novel published. I am also thankful to those individuals who helped me along the way with this project.

I want to say thank you to my family, the Gooding family, for all of your unconditional love and support. For the inspiration for the characters and plot, I want to thank Carol, Joey Woody, Wesley Mayers, and Elizabeth Treichler. I also want to thank Tiffany Fields for not only your support, but your suggestions and corrections you came across while reading the manuscript.

Thank you all for reading. Hopefully there will be more to come....

Printed in the United States
By Bookmasters